The Collected Supernatural and Weird Fiction of Mary Elizabeth Braddon Volume 4

The Collected Supernatural and Weird Fiction of Mary Elizabeth Braddon Volume 4

Including Three Novelettes "His Secret",
"Herself" and "The Ghost's Name", and
Fifteen Short Stories
of the Strange and Unusual

Mary Elizabeth Braddon

LEONAUR

The Collected
Supernatural and Weird
Fiction of
Mary Elizabeth Braddon
Volume 4
Including Three Novelettes "His Secret",
"Herself" and "The Ghost's Name", and
Fifteen Short Stories
of the Strange and Unusual
by Mary Elizabeth Braddon

FIRST EDITION

Leonaur is an imprint
of Oakpast Ltd

ISBN: 978-0-85706-056-3 (hardcover)
ISBN: 978-0-85706-055-6 (softcover)

http://www.leonaur.com

Publisher's Notes

In the interests of authenticity, the spellings, grammar and place names
used have been retained from the original editions.

The opinions of the authors represent a view of events in which she
was a participant related from her own perspective,
as such the text is relevant as an historical document.

The views expressed in this book are not necessarily
those of the publisher.

Contents

My Wife's Promise

It was my fate at an early period of my life to abandon myself to the perilous delights of a career which of all other's exercises the most potent fascination over the mind of him who pursues it. As a youth I joined a band of brave adventurers in an Arctic expedition, and from the hour in which I first saw the deep cold blue of the northern sea, and felt the subtle influence of the rarefied polar air, I was for all common purposes and objects of life a lost man.

The expedition was unfortunate, though its leader was a wise and scientific navigator—his subordinates picked men. The result was bitter disappointment and more bitter loss—loss of valuable lives as well as of considerable funds. I came back from my cruise in the *Weatherwise*' to the western world, rejoiced beyond measure at the idea of being once more at home, and determined never again to face the horrors of that perilous region which had lost me so many dear companions.

I, Richard Dunrayne, was the elder son of a wealthy house, my father, a man of some influence in the political world, and there were few positions which need have been impossible for me had I aspired to the ordinary career affected by British youth. I had been indulged in my early passion for the sea, in my later rage for Arctic exploration; and it was hoped that, having satisfied these boyish fancies, I should now settle down to a pursuit more consonant with the views and wishes of my people.

My mother wept over her restored treasure, and confessed how terrible had been her fears during my absence; my father congratulated me upon having ridden my hobby, and alighted therefrom without a broken neck; and my family anxiously awaited my choice of a profession.

Such a choice I found impossible. If I had bartered myself body and soul, by the most explicit formula, to some demon of the icebergs, or incarnate spirit of the frozen sea, I could not have been more completely bound than I was. From the Christmas hearth round which dear friends were gathered, from my low seat at my mother's knee, from worldly wealth and worldly pleasure, the genius of the polar ocean beckoned me away, and all the blessings of my life, all the natural affections of my heart, were too weak to hold me.

In my dreams, again and again, with maddening repetition, I trod the old paths, and saw, ghastly white against the intense purple of that northern sky, the walls of ice that had blocked our passage. It seemed to me that if I could but find myself again in that dread solitude, success would be a certainty. It seemed to me as if we had held the magic clue to that awful labyrinth between our fingers, and had, in very folly, suffered it to escape us. 'A new expedition, aided by the knowledge of the past, *must* succeed,' I said to myself; and when I could no longer fight against the prepossession that held me, I consulted the survivors of our unfortunate voyage, and found in their opinions the actual echo of my own convictions.

We met many times, and our meetings resulted in the organization of a new expedition. Money was poured into our little treasury like water, so poor a dress did it seem to us compared with the jewel we went to seek. Our preparations had begun before I dared tell those who loved me that I had pledged myself to a second expedition. But at last, one bright spring evening, I went home and announced my decision.

I look back now and wonder at my own heartlessness, and yet I was not indifferent to their grief. The cry that my mother gave when she knew the truth rings in my ears as I write this. No; I was not indifferent. I was possessed. My second voyage resulted in little actual success, but was to me one prolonged scene of enjoyment. I was a skilled seaman and navigator, no indifferent sportsman, and having acquired some slight reputation during the previous voyage, now ranked high among the junior officers on board the *Ptarmigan*.

We wintered at Repulse Bay, with a short stock of fuel, and a shorter supply of provisions; but we managed with a minimum of the former luxury, and supplied all deficiency of the latter by the aid of our guns. Never was a merrier banquet eaten than our Christmas dinner of reindeer steaks and currant dumplings, though the thermometer had sunk 79° below freezing-point, and our jerseys and trousers sparkled with hoar-frost.

The brief summer of that northern latitude brought us some small triumphs. We spent a second winter in snow houses, which resembled gigantic beehives, and were the snuggest possible habitations, and in the second summer turned our course homeward, in excellent health and spirits, but my gladness was to be sorely dashed on landing in England.

I returned to find my mother's grave bright with familiar autumnal flowers in a suburban cemetery, and to know that the tender arms which had clung about me in the hour of parting would never encircle me again. The blow was a severe one, and for some time to come I thought with aversion of that strange northern world which had cost me, and which was yet to cost me, so much.

Time passed, and I remained in England, at twenty-five years of age a broken man. With the men I met I had no point of sympathy. Their pursuits bored me, their paltry ambitions disgusted me. The pleasures of civilized life had not the faintest charm for me. A polar bear would have been as much at home as I was in a West-end ball-room, and would have been as interested in the conversation of a genteel dinner-table.

Away from my old comrades of the *Weatherwise* and the *Ptarmigan*, I had not a friend for whom I really cared; and as the civilized world grew day by day more distasteful to me, the old longing revived—the old dreams haunted my sleep. In my father's handsome drawing-rooms I yearned for the rough stone cabin of Repulse Bay, or the snow-hives of Cape Crozier. Another expedition was afloat, and letters from my old messmates announced anticipated triumphs, and warned me of the remorse which I should suffer when the hardy victors returned to reproach the idler who preferred to live at home at ease, while old friends were drifting among the ice-floes, and bearding the grisly tyrant of the north.

I let them go without me, at what sacrifice was only known to myself. My father's health had been declining from the hour of my mother's death, and I was determined not to leave him. This duty at least I would not abnegate. This last sad privilege of attending a father's death-bed I would not barter to the all-exacting demon of the frozen seas. For three empty, patient years I remained at home. My hands reverently closed the eyes that had never looked upon me but with affection, and I alone watched the last quiet sleep.

This being done, I was free once more, and the old infatuation held me close as ever. My father's death left me wealthy, and to my mind wealth had but one use. All the old yearnings were intensified by tenfold, for the saddest reason. The *Ptarmigan* had never been heard of since the hour she left Baffin's Bay, and the fate of those familiar comrades with whom I had lived in the closest communion for two happy years was a dark enigma, only to be solved by patient labour. The expedition had not been of sufficient importance to attract much attention from the scientific world; there had been too much of a volunteer and amateur character in the business; but when the fact of the *Ptarmigan's* disappearance became known, a meeting of the Royal Society gave all due consideration to the case, and promised help to a party of investigation.

My ample fortune enabled me to contribute largely to the expenses of the new voyage, while volunteers and voluntary contributions poured in from every quarter. I had difficulty in selecting officers and crew from so large a number of hardy adventurers; but I was prudent enough to engage the crew of a battered old whaler for the staple of my men. "We were away in all six years, wintering sometimes in South America—once in New York, and getting our supplies as best we might. We made some discoveries, which the Royal Society received with civil approval; but of those we went to seek we found no trace; and I began to think that the fate of my old friends was a mystery never to be solved below the stars.

I came back to England at thirty-four years of age, a hardy wanderer, with a long brown beard that seemed lightly powdered with the northern snow, and with the strength of a sea-lion. For the best years of my life I had lived in snow-hives and stone-cabins, or slept at night amidst the wilderness of ice, in a boat which my stalwart shoulders had helped to carry during the day. Heavens! what a rough, unlicked cub, what a grim sea-monster I must have been; and yet Isabel Lawson loved me! Yes, I came back to England to find a fairer enchantress than the spirit of the frozen deep, and to barter my liberty to a new mistress. One of my sisters had married during my absence, and it was at her country house I took up my abode. The young sister of her husband, Captain Lawson, was here on a visit, and thus I met my fate.

I will not attempt to describe her; the innocent face, so lovely to my eyes, was perhaps less perfect than I thought it; but if perfection wears another shape, it is one that has no charm for me. Isabel was my junior by sixteen years, and for a considerable period of our acquaintance regarded me as a newly-acquired elder brother, whose age gave something to a paternal character to the relationship. For a long time I looked upon her as a beautiful picture, an incarnate presentment of all that is tender and divine in womanhood, and as far away from me as the stars which I pointed out to her in our summer evening rambles by the seashore near our country home.

How I grew to love her I will not ask myself. She was a creature whom to know was to love. How she grew to love me is a mystery I have often tried to solve; and when I have asked her, with fear and wondering, why I was so blessed, she told me it was because I was brave and frank and true, and worthy of a woman's love. God help my darling, the glamour of the frozen north was upon me, and the mere story of the wondrous world I knew had magic enough to win me the heart of this angel. She was never tired of hearing me describe that wild region I loved so well. Again and again I told her the histories of my several voyages, and the record seemed always to have a new charm for her.

'I think I know every channel in Davis's Strait and Baffin's Bay,' she said to me a day or two before our wedding; 'and the icebound coast, from Repulse Bay to Cape Crozier, and the ice-packs over which you carried your boats, and the shoals of seals and clouds of ducks, and the colony of white whales, and the dear little snow-houses in which you lived so snugly. Don't you think we ought to spend our honeymoon at Cape Crozier, Richard?'

'My precious one, God forbid that I should ever see you in that wild place.'

'Be sure, Richard, if you went there, I should follow you.'

And she kept her word.

Dreamlike, and oh, how mournful, seems the bright scene of my bridal day, as I recall it tonight beside a lonely hearth in the house of a stranger. My Isabel looked like a spirit in her white gown and veil; and I, to whom the memories of the North were ever present, could well-nigh have fancied she was clad in a snow-cloud. I asked her if she were content to have given her young beauty to a battered veteran like me; and she told me yes, a thousand times more than content—inexpressibly happy.

'But you will never leave me, Richard?' she said, looking up at me with divine love in her deep-blue eyes; and I promised again, as I had promised many times before, that the North should never draw me away from my beloved.

'You shall be my pole-star, dearest, and I will forget that earth has any wilder region than the woods and hills around our happy home.'

My darling loved the country, and I loved all that was dear to her: so I bought a small estate in North Devon—a grange and park in the heart of such a landscape as can only be found in that western shire. I was rich, and it was my pride and delight to make our home as beautiful as money and care could make it. The restoration of the house, which was as old as the Tudors, and the improvement of the park, employed me for more than a year,—a happy year of home joys with as sweet a wife as Heaven ever gave to man since Adam saw Eve smiling on him among the flowers of Paradise,—and during the whole of that time I had scarcely thought of the North.

With the beginning of our second year of happy union, I had even less inclination to think of my old life; for God had blessed us with a son, pure and blooming and beautiful as the region in which he was born. Upon this period of my life I dare not linger. For nearly two years we held our treasure; and if anything could have drawn us nearer to each other than our love had made us long ago, it would have been our affection for this child. He was taken from us. *The Lord gave, and the Lord taketh away; blessed be the name of the Lord.* We repeated the holy sentences of resignation; but it was not resignation, it was despair that subdued the violence of our grief.

I laid my darling in his grave under the midsummer sky, while a sky-lark was singing high up in the heaven, where I tried to picture him, among the band of such child-angels; and I knew that life could never again be to me what it had been. People told me I should perhaps have other children as dear as this. 'If God would give this one back to me, He could not blot from my memory his suffering and his death,' I answered impiously.

For some time my sorrow was a kind of stupor—a dull dead heaviness of the soul, from which nothing could raise me. Isabel's grief was no less intense, no less bitter; but it was more natural and more unselfish. She grew alarmed by my state of mind, and entreated me to try change of scene.

'Let us go to London, Richard,' she said; 'I shall be glad to leave this place, beautiful and dear as it is.'

Her pale face warned me that she had sad need of change; and for her sake, rather than my own, I took her to London, where we hired a furnished house in a western square.

Being in town, and an idle man, with no London tastes and no friends, it is scarcely strange that I should attend the meetings of the Royal Society. The fate of Franklin was yet unknown, and the debates upon this subject were at fever-heat. A new expedition was just being fitted out by the Government, and there could be no better opportunity for a volunteer band, which might follow in the track of the Government vessel.

In the rooms of the Society I encountered an old comrade who had served with me in my first voyage on board the *Weatherwise*, and he exerted his utmost powers of persuasion to induce me to join himself and others in a northward cruise, to search for Franklin and for our lost companions of the *Ptarmigan*. I was known to be an old hand, well provided with the sinews of war, adventurous and patient, hardened by many a polar winter; and my friend and his party wanted me for their leader. The proposal flattered me more than I can describe, and caused me the first thrill of pleasure I had known since my son's death. But I remembered my promise.

'No, Martyn,' I answered; 'the thing is impossible. I am a married man, and have given my word to the dearest wife in Christendom that I will never go out yonder again.'

Frank Martyn took no pains to conceal his disappointment at my decision, nor his contempt for my motives.

It was my habit to tell my wife everything; and I told her of the debates of the Royal Society, and of this meeting with an old comrade.

'But you will keep your promise, Richard?' she asked, with a sudden look of fear.

'Until the end of life, my darling, unless you should release me from it'

'Oh, Richard, that is not likely; I am not capable of such a sacrifice.'

I went again and again to the Royal Society: and I dined at a club, with my friend Martyn, who made me known to his friends, those eager volunteers who panted for the icy winds of the Arctic zone, and languished to tread the frozen labyrinth of polar seas. I listened to them, I talked with them, and the demon of the North resumed his hold upon me. My wife saw that some new influence was at work, that my home life was no longer all in all to me.

One day, after much anxious questioning, she beguiled me of my secret. The old yearning was upon me. I told her how every impulse of my mind—every longing of my heart urged me to join the new enterprise; and how, for her dear sake, I was determined to forego the certainty of pleasure, and the chances of distinction. She thanked me with a sigh.

'I stand between you and the purpose of your life, Richard,' she said; 'how selfish I must seem to you!'

'No, darling, only tender and womanly.'

Upon my persistent refusal to command the expedition, my friend Martyn was unanimously elected captain. A wealthy brewer of an adventurous turn provided the larger part of the funds, to which I gladly contributed my quota.

'I know Dunrayne will go with us,' said Frank Martyn. 'He'll turn up at the last moment, and beg leave to join. But remember, Dick,' he added, turning to me, 'if it is the last moment you'll be welcome, and I shall be proud to resign the command to a fellow who knows the Arctic zone as well as a Cockney knows the Strand.

The preparations for the voyage lasted longer than had been anticipated. Months went by, and I still lingered in town, though I knew that Isabel would have preferred to return to Devonshire. I could not tear myself away while the *Forlorn Hope*, the vessel chartered by the brewer, was still in dock. I saw the adventurers almost daily, assisted in their preparations, pored over the chart with them, and travelled over every inch of the old ground with a pencil for their edification.

It was within a week of the departure, and the fever and excitement of preparation was stronger upon me than on any one of the intending voyagers, when my wife came to me suddenly one morning, and threw herself, sobbing, into my arms.

'My dear Isabel, what is this?' I asked in alarm.

'O Richard, you must go,' she sobbed; 'I cannot hold you from your destiny. My selfish fears are killing you. I can see it in your face. You must go to that wild, awful world, where Heaven has guided you in safety before, and will guard and guide you again. Yes, darling, I release you from your promise. Is God less powerful to protect you yonder than here. He made that world of eternal ice and snow; and where He is there is safety. No, Richard; I will not despair. I will not stand between you and fame. I heard you talking in your sleep last night, as you have talked many nights, of that distant solitude: and I know that your heart is there. Shall I keep my husband prisoner when his heart has fled from me? No, Richard, you shall go.'

She kissed me, and fell fainting at my feet. I was blinded by my own selfish folly, and did not perceive how much of her fortitude was the courage of despair. I thought only of her generosity, and my release. It was not too late for me to accept the command of the *Forlorn Hope*. I thanked my wife with a hundred kisses as her sweet eyes opened upon me once more.

'My darling, I shall never forget this,' I cried; 'and it shall be the last journey, the very last. I swear it, by all that is most sacred to me. There is no danger, believe me, none, for a man who has learned prudence as I have done—in the school of hardship.'

There was only a week for leave-taking.

'I can bear it better so,' said my wife: 'such a blow cannot be too sudden.'

'But, my darling, it is no more than any other absence; and, remember, it is to be the last time.'

'No, Richard, do not tell me that. I think I know you better than you know yourself. A man cannot serve two masters. Your master is there. He beckons you away from me.'

'But for the last time, Isabel.'

'Well, yes,' she answered, with a profound sigh, 'I think that when you and I say goodbye next week, we shall part for the last time.'

The sadness of her tone seemed natural to the occasion; nor

did I remark the melancholy significance of her words, though they often recurred to my mind in the time to come.

'I will make you a flag, Richard,' she said to me next day. 'If you should discover any new spot of land out yonder, you will like to raise the British standard there, and I should like to think that my hands are to be associated with your triumph.'

She set to work upon the fabrication of a Union Jack. I remembered a melancholy incident in the life of Sir John Franklin, and I hardly cared to see her thus employed; but I could not sadden her with the story, and she worked on, with a happier air than I could have believed possible to her. Alas! I little knew that this gaiety was but an heroic assumption sustained to save me pain.

My darling insisted upon examining my charts, and made me show her every step of our projected journey—the point where we hoped to winter—the land which we intended to explore on sledges—the spots where we should erect cairns to mark our progress. She dwelt on every detail of the journey with an interest intense as my own.

'I think I know that distant world as well as you, Richard,' she said to me on the last day of all. 'In my dreams I shall follow you—yes, I know that I shall dream of you every night, and that my dreams will be true. There must be some magnetic chain between two beings so closely united as we are, and I am sure that sleep will show you to me as you are—safe or in danger, triumphant or despondent. And in my waking dreams, too, dear, I shall be on your track. My life will be a double one—the dull, commonplace existence at home, where my body must needs be, and the mystic life yonder, where my spirit will follow you. And, dear husband,' she continued, clinging to me and looking up with a new light in her eyes, 'if I should die before you return—'

'Isabel!'

'Of course that is not likely, you know; but if I should be taken from you, dearest, you will know it directly. Yes, dear, at the death-hour my spirit will fly to you for the last fond parting look upon earth, as surely as I hope it will await you in heaven!'

I tried to chide her for her old-world Scottish superstition; but this speech of hers, and the looks that accompanied it, shook me more than I cared to confess to myself; and if it had been possible to recede with honour, I think I should have resigned the command of the *Forlorn Hope* and stayed with my wife. O God, that I had done so, at any cost of honour, at any sacrifice of friendship!

But my fate drew me northward, and I went. We started in July, and reached the point that we had chosen for our winter harbour at the end of August. Here we walled our vessel round with snow, and roofed her over; and in this grim solitude prepared to await the opening seas of summer. To me the winter seemed unutterably long and dreary. I was no longer the careless bachelor who found amusement in the rough sports of the sailors, and delight in an occasional raid upon the reindeer of the ice-bound coast. I had indeed tried to serve two masters; and the memory of her I had left behind was ever with me, a reproachful shadow. If, now, I could have recalled the past, and found myself once more by that hearth beside which I had languished for the old life of adventure, how gladly would I have made the exchange!

The long, inactive winter that was so dreary to me seemed pleasant enough to my companions. We had plenty of stores, and all were hopeful as to the exploits of the coming summer. We should find the crew of the *Ptarmigan*, perhaps, hardy dwellers in some inaccessible region, patiently awaiting succour and release. With such hopeful dreams my comrades beguiled the wasted days; but I had lost my old power of dreaming, and a sense of duty alone sustained my spirits. My friend Frank told me that I was a changed man—cold and stern as the veriest martinet.

'But all the better man for your post,' he added; 'the sailors love you as much as they fear you, for they know that they would find you as steadfast as a rock in the hour of peril.'

The summer came, the massive ice-packs were loosened with sounds as of thunder, and drifted away before a southern breeze.

But our freedom brought us nothing save disappointment. No traces of our friends of the *Ptarmigan* gladdened our eyes: no discovery rewarded our patience. Scurvy had cost us four of our best men, and the crew was short-handed. Before the summer was ended we had more deaths, and when the next winter began, Martyn and I faced it drearily, with the prospect of scant stores and scanter fuel, and with a sickly and disheartened crew. We had reason to thank God that the poor fellows were faithful to us under conditions so hopeless.

Before the coldest season set in, we left our vessel in tolerably safe harbour, and started on a land expedition, still bent on our search for traces of the missing *Ptarmigan*. We had a couple of sledges and a pack of Esquimaux dogs, faithful, hardy creatures, who thrived on the roughest fare, and were invaluable to us in this toilsome journey. No words can paint the desolation of this wild region—no mind can imagine that horror of perpetual snow, illimitable as eternal.

Martyn and I worked hard to keep up the flagging spirits of our men. One poor fellow had lost his foot from a frostbite, and but for our surgeon's clever amputation of the disabled member, must have surely perished. He was of coarse no small drag upon us in this time of trial, but his own patient endurance taught us fortitude. We had hoped to fall in with a tribe of Esquimaux, but saw none after those from whom we bought our dogs.

So we toiled on, appalled by the grim change in each other's forms and faces, as short rations and fatigue did their work. The dead winter found us again reduced in number.

We built ourselves a roomy snow-house, with a cabin for the dogs; and here my friend Frank Martyn lay sick with three other invalids throughout our hopeless Christmas. My own health held out wonderfully. My spirits rose with the extremity of trial, and I faced the darkening future boldly, beguiling myself with dream-pictures of my return home, and my wife's glad face when she looked up from her lonely hearth and saw me standing on the threshold of the door.

It was Christmas-day. We had dined on *pemmican*—a peculiar

kind of preserved meat—biscuit, and rice. Spirit we had none, save a little carefully stored in case of urgent need. After our scant repast the able men went out in a body in search of sport for their guns, but with little hope of finding anything. The invalids slept, and I sat by the fire of dried moss which served to light our hut, with the aid of a glimmer of cold, dull daylight that came to us through a window of transparent ice in the roof.

I was thinking of England and my wife—what else did I ever think of now?—when one of the men rushed suddenly into the hut, and fell on the snow-bank that served for a bench. He was white to the lips, and shivering as no man shivers from cold alone.

'Good God, Hanley, what is the matter?' I cried, alarmed by the man's terror.

'I went away from the others. Captain,' he began, in rapid, gasping accents, 'thinking I saw the traces of a bear upon the snow; and I had parted from them about half-an-hour when I saw——'

His voice died away suddenly, and he sat before me, with lips that moved but made no sound.

'What? For pity's sake speak out, man.'

'A woman!!'

'Yes; and of an Esquimaux tribe, no doubt. Why didn't you hail her, and bring her back to us? Why, you must be mad, Hanley. You know how we have been wishing to fall in with some of those people, and you see one, and let her slip through your fingers, and come back scared, as if you'd seen a ghost.'

'That's it, your honour,' the man answered hoarsely. 'What I saw was a ghost.'

'Nonsense, man!'

'But I say yes, Captain, and will stand by my word. She was before me, moving slowly over the snow; you could scarce call it walking, 'twas such a smooth gliding motion.

She was dressed in white—no common dress—but one that turns the heart cold only to think of. While I stood, too scared to move hand or foot, she turned and beckoned to me, and I saw her face as plain as I see yours at this moment, a sweet face, with blue eyes, and long fair hair falling loosely round it.'

I was on my feet in a moment, and rushing towards the door.

Great God of Heaven!' I cried, 'my wife!'

The conviction that possessed me was supreme. From the moment in which the sailor described the figure he had seen, there was no shadow of doubt in my mind. It was Isabel, and she only. The wife who had promised that her spirit should follow me step by step upon my desolate journey was near me now. For one moment only I considered the possibility or impossibility of her presence, and pondered whether some northern-bound vessel might have brought her to an Esquimaux station near at hand that we knew not of; for one instant only, and then I was hurrying across the snow in the direction to which the sailor pointed as he stood at the door of our hut.

The brief winter day was closing in, and there was only a long line of faint yellow light in the west. Eastwards the moon was rising, pale and cold like that region of eternal snow. I had left our hut some two hundred yards behind me, when I saw a white-robed figure moving towards the low western light; a figure at once so dear, so familiar, and yet in that place so awful, that an icy shiver shook me from head to heel as I looked upon it.

The figure turned and beckoned. The sweet face looked at me, awfully distinct in that clear cold light. I followed, and it drew me on, far across a patch of snowy waste that I had left unexplored, or had no memory of traversing until now. I tried to overtake the familiar form, but though its strange gliding movement seemed slow, it eluded my pursuit, follow swiftly as I might. In this manner we crossed the wide bleak waste, and as the last glimmer of the western light died out, and the moon shone brighter on the frozen plain, we came to a spot where the snow lay in mounds—seven separate mounds ranged in the form of a cross beneath that wild northern sky.

A glance told me that civilized hands had done this work.

The Christian emblem told me more. But though I saw the snow-mounds at my feet, my eyes seemed never to leave the face of my wife—God, how pale in the moonlight!

She pointed with extended finger to one of the mounds, and I saw that it was headed by a rough wooden board, almost buried in snow. To snatch a knife from my belt, and throw myself on my knees, and begin to scrape the coating of mingled ice and snow from this board, was the work of a few moments. Though it was of her I thought only, yet it was as if an irresistible force compelled me to stop, and to obey the command of that pointing hand. When I looked up I was alone beneath the wintry sky. My wife was gone. I knew then what I had felt from the first—that it was her shadow I had followed over that wintry waste, and that on earth she and I would never look upon each other again.

She had kept her promise as truly as I had broken mine. The gentle spirit had followed me to that desolate world in the very moment it was liberated from its earthly prison.

It was late that night when Hanley and his messmates found me lying senseless on the snow-mound, with the open knife beside my stiffening hand.

They brought me back to life somehow, and by the light of the lanterns they carried, we examined the board at the head of the mound. An inscription roughly cut upon it told us we had found the lost crew of the *Ptarmigan*.

'Here lies the body of Morris Haynes, commander of the *Ptarmigan*, who died in this unknown region, Jan. 30th, 1829, aged 35.'

The other mounds also had headboards bearing inscriptions, which we dug out from the snow on the following day, and carefully transcribed. After this we found a cairn containing empty provision-tins, in one of which was a book that had evidently been used for a journal; but rust and snow had done their work, and of this journal nothing was decipherable but the name of the writer, Morris Haynes.

These investigations were not made by me. The new year

found me laid low with rheumatic fever, and Frank Martyn had to take his turn as sick-nurse beside the snow-bank where I lay. Our provisions held out better than we had expected, thanks to the game our men shot, and the patience with which they endured privation. The spring came, and with it release. We contrived to make our way to Baffin's Bay,—a consummation I scarcely thought possible in my dreary reveries of mid-winter,— and a Greenland whaler brought us safely home, I went straight to my brother-in-law's house at the West end of London, he was at home, and came without delay to the library where I had been ushered, and where I sat awaiting him with a gloomy face.

Yes; as I expected: he was in mourning: and behind him came my sister, with a pale face, on which there was no smile of greeting.

Lawson held out both his hands to me.

'Richard,' he began in a faltering voice, 'God knows I never thought it possible I could be otherwise than glad of your coming home—but—'

'That will do,' I said; 'you need tell me no more. My wife is dead.'

He bent his head solemnly.

'She died on the twenty-fifth of last December, at four o'clock in the afternoon.'

'You have been told, then,' cried my sister; 'you have seen someone?'

'Yes,' I answered, 'I have seen *her!*'

Eveline's Visitant

It was at a masked ball at the Palais Royal that my fatal quarrel with my first cousin André de Brissac began. The quarrel was about a woman. The women who followed the footsteps of Philip of Orleans were the causes of many such disputes; and there was scarcely one fair head in all that glittering throng which, to a man versed in social histories and mysteries, might not have seemed bedabbled with blood.

I shall not record the name of her for love of whom André de Brissac and I crossed one of the bridges, in the dim August dawn on our way to the waste ground beyond the church of Saint-Germain des Prés.

There were many beautiful vipers in those days, and she was one of them. I can feel the chill breath of that August morning blowing in my face, as I sit in my dismal chamber at my *château* of Puy Verdun tonight, alone in the stillness, writing the strange story of my life. I can see the white mist rising from the river, the grim outline of the Châtelet, and the square towers of Notre Dame black against the pale-grey sky.

Even more vividly can I recall André's fair young face, as he stood opposite to me with his two friends—scoundrels both, and alike eager for that unnatural fray. We were a strange group to be seen in a summer sunrise, all of us fresh from the heat and clamour of the Regent's saloons—André in a quaint hunting-dress copied from a family portrait at Puy Verdun, I costumed as one of Law's Mississippi Indians; the other men in like garish frippery, adorned with broideries and jewels that looked wan in the pale light of dawn.

Our quarrel had been a fierce one—a quarrel which could have but one result, and that the direst. I had struck him; and the welt raised by my open hand was crimson upon his fair woman-ish face as he stood opposite to me. The eastern sun shone on the face presently, and dyed the cruel mark with a deeper red; but the sting of my own wrongs was fresh, and I had not yet learned to despise myself for that brutal outrage.

To André de Brissac such an insult was most terrible. He was the favourite of Fortune, the favourite of women; and I was nothing,—a rough soldier who had done my country good service, but in the *boudoir* of a Parabère a mannerless boor.

We fought, and I wounded him mortally. Life had been very sweet for him; and I think that a frenzy of despair took posses-sion of him when he felt the life-blood ebbing away. He beck-oned me to him as he lay on the ground. I went, and knelt at his side.

"Forgive me, André!" I murmured.

He took no more heed of my words than if that piteous en-treaty had been the idle ripple of the river near at hand.

"Listen to me, Hector de Brissac," he said. "I am not one who believes that a man has done with earth because his eyes glaze and his jaw stiffens. They will bury me in the old vault at Puy Verdun; and you will be master of the *château*. Ah, I know how lightly they take things in these days, and how Dubois will laugh when he hears that Ca has been killed in a duel. They will bury me, and sing masses for my soul; but you and I have not finished our affair yet, my cousin.

"I will be with you when you least look to see me,—I, with this ugly scar upon the face that women have praised and loved. I will come to you when your life seems brightest. I will come between you and all that you hold fairest and dearest. My ghost-ly hand shall drop a poison in your cup of joy. My shadowy form shall shut the sunlight from your life. Men with such iron will as mine can do what they please, Hector de Brissac. It is my will to haunt you when I am dead."

All this in short broken sentences he whispered into my ear. I had need to bend my ear close to his dying lips; but the iron will of André de Brissac was strong enough to do battle with Death, and I believe he said all he wished to say before his head fell back upon the velvet cloak they had spread beneath him, never to be lifted again.

As he lay there, you would have fancied him a fragile stripling, too fair and frail for the struggle called life; but there are those who remember the brief manhood of André de Brissac, and who can bear witness to the terrible force of that proud nature.

I stood looking down at the young face with that foul mark upon it, and God knows I was sorry for what I had done.

Of those blasphemous threats which he had whispered in my ear I took no heed. I was a soldier, and a believer. There was nothing absolutely dreadful to me in the thought that I had killed this man. I had killed many men on the battlefield; and this one had done me cruel wrong.

My friends would have had me cross the frontier to escape the consequences of my act; but I was ready to face those consequences, and I remained in France. I kept aloof from the court, and received a hint that I had best confine myself to my own province. Many masses were chanted in the little chapel of Puy Verdun, for the soul of my dead cousin, and his coffin filled a niche in the vault of our ancestors.

His death had made me a rich man; and the thought that it was so made my newly-acquired wealth very hateful to me. I lived a lonely existence in the old *château*, where I rarely held converse with any but the servants of the household, all of whom had served my cousin, and none of whom liked me.

It was a hard and bitter life. It galled me, when I rode through the village, to see the peasant-children shrink away from me. I have seen old women cross themselves stealthily as I passed them by. Strange reports had gone forth about me; and there were those who whispered that I had given my soul to the Evil One as the price of my cousin's heritage. From my boyhood I had been dark of visage and stern of manner; and hence, perhaps, no woman's love had ever been mine.

I remembered my mother's face in all its changes of expression; but I can remember no look of affection that ever shone on me. That other woman, beneath whose feet I laid my heart, was pleased to accept my homage, but she never loved me; and the end was treachery.

I had grown hateful to myself, and had well-nigh begun to hate my fellow-creatures, when a feverish desire seized upon me, and I pined to be back in the press and throng of the busy world once again. I went back to Paris, where I kept myself aloof from the court, and where an angel took compassion upon me.

She was the daughter of an old comrade, a man whose merits had been neglected, whose achievements had been ignored, and who sulked in his shabby lodging like a rat in a hole, while all Paris went mad with the Scotch Financier, and gentlemen and lacqueys were trampling one another to death in the Rue Quincampoix. The only child of this little cross-grained old captain of dragoons was an incarnate sunbeam, whose mortal name was Eveline Duchalet.

She loved me. The richest blessings of our lives are often those which cost us least. I wasted the best years of my youth in the worship of a wicked woman, who jilted and cheated me at last.

I gave this meek angel but a few courteous words—a little fraternal tenderness—and lo, she loved me. The life which had been so dark and desolate grew bright beneath her influence; and I went back to Puy Verdun with a fair young bride for my companion.

Ah, how sweet a change there was in my life and in my home! The village children no longer shrank appalled as the dark horseman rode by, the village crones no longer crossed themselves; for a woman rode by his side—a woman whose charities had won the love of all those ignorant creatures, and whose companionship had transformed the gloomy lord of the *chateau* into a loving husband and a gentle master. The old retainers forgot the untimely fate of my cousin, and served me with cordial willingness, for love of their young mistress.

There are no words which can tell the pure and perfect happiness of that time. I felt like a traveller who had traversed the frozen seas of an arctic region, remote from human love or human companionship, to find himself on a sudden in the bosom of a verdant valley, in the sweet atmosphere of home. The change seemed too bright to be real; and I strove in vain to put away from my mind the vague suspicion that my new life was but some fantastic dream.

So brief were those halcyon hours, that, looking back on them now, it is scarcely strange if I am still half inclined to fancy the first days of my married life could have been no more than a dream.

Neither in my days of gloom nor in my days of happiness had I been troubled by the recollection of André's blasphemous oath.

The words which with his last breath he had whispered in my ear were vain and meaningless to me. He had vented his rage in those idle threats, as he might have vented it in idle execrations.

That he will haunt the footsteps of his enemy after death is the one revenge which a dying man can promise himself; and if men had power thus to avenge themselves, the earth would be peopled with phantoms.

I had lived for three years at Puy Verdun; sitting alone in the solemn midnight by the hearth where he had sat, pacing the corridors that had echoed his footfall; and in all that time my fancy had never so played me false as to shape the shadow of the dead. Is it strange, then, if I had forgotten Andre's horrible promise? There was no portrait of my cousin at Puy Verdun.

It was the age of *boudoir* art, and a miniature set in the lid of a gold *bonbonnière*, or hidden artfully in a massive bracelet, was more fashionable than a clumsy life-size image, fit only to hang on the gloomy walls of a provincial *château* rarely visited by its owner. My cousin's fair face had adorned more than one *bonbonnière*, and had been concealed in more than one bracelet; but it was not among the faces that looked down from the panelled walls of Puy Verdun.

In the library I found a picture which awoke painful associations. It was the portrait of a De Brissac, who had flourished in the time of Francis the First; and it was from this picture that my cousin Andre had copied the quaint hunting-dress he wore at the Regent's ball. The library was a room in which I spent a good deal of my life; and I ordered a curtain to be hung before this picture.

We had been married three months, when Eveline one day asked, "Who is the lord of the *château* nearest to this?"

I looked with her in astonishment.

"My dearest," I answered, "do you not know that there is no other *château* within forty miles of Puy Verdun?"

"Indeed!" she said; "that is strange."

I asked her why the fact seemed strange to her; and after much entreaty I obtained from her the reason of her surprise.

In her walks about the park and woods during the last month, she had met a man who, by his dress and bearing, was obviously of noble rank. She had imagined that he occupied some *château* near at hand, and that his estate adjoined ours. I was at a loss to imagine who this stranger could be; for my estate of Puy Verdun lay in the heart of a desolate region, and unless when some traveller's coach went lumbering and jingling through the village, one had little more chance of encountering a gentleman than of meeting a demigod.

"Have you seen this man often, Eveline?" I asked.

She answered, in a tone which had a touch of sadness, "I see him every day."

"Where, dearest?"

"Sometimes in the park, sometimes in the wood. You know the little cascade, Hector, where there is some old neglected rock-work that forms a kind of cavern. I have taken a fancy to that spot, and have spent many mornings there reading. Of late I have seen the stranger there every morning."

"He has never dared to address you?"

"Never. I have looked up from my book, and have seen him

standing at a little distance, watching me silently. I have continued reading; and when I have raised my eyes again I have found him gone. He must approach and depart with a stealthy tread, for I never hear his footfall.

Sometimes I have almost wished that he would speak to me. It is so terrible to see him standing silently there."

"He is some insolent peasant who seeks to frighten you."

My wife shook her head.

"He is no peasant," she answered. "It is not by his dress alone I judge, for that is strange to me.

He has an air of nobility which it is impossible to mistake."

"Is he young or old?"

"He is young and handsome."

I was much disturbed by the idea of this stranger's intrusion on my wife's solitude; and I went straight to the village to inquire if any stranger had been seen there. I could hear of no one. I questioned the servants closely, but without result. Then I determined to accompany my wife in her walks, and to judge for myself of the rank of the stranger.

For a week I devoted all my mornings to rustic rambles with Eveline in the park and woods; and in all that week we saw no one but an occasional peasant in sabots, or one of our own house-hold returning from a neighbouring farm.

I was a man of studious habits, and those summer rambles disturbed the even current of my life. My wife perceived this, and entreated me to trouble myself no further.

"I will spend my mornings in the *pleasaunce*, Hector," she said; "the stranger cannot intrude upon me there."

"I begin to think the stranger is only a phantasm of your own romantic brain," I replied, smiling at the earnest face lifted to mine. "A *châtelaine* who is always reading romances may well meet handsome cavaliers in the woodlands. I daresay I have Mdlle. Scuderi to thank for this noble stranger, and that he is only the great Cyrus in modern costume."

"Ah, that is the point which mystifies me, Hector," she said. "The stranger's costume is not modern. He looks as an old picture might look if it could descend from its frame."

Her words pained me, for they reminded me of that hidden picture in the library, and the quaint hunting costume of orange and purple, which André de Brissac wore at the Regent's ball.

After this my wife confined her walks to the *pleasaunce*; and for many weeks I heard no more of the nameless stranger. I dismissed all thought of him from my mind, for a graver and heavier care had come upon me. My wife's health began to droop. The change in her was so gradual as to be almost imperceptible to those who watched her day by day. It was only when she put on a rich gala dress which she had not worn for months that I saw how wasted the form must be on which the embroidered bodice hung so loosely, and how wan and dim were the eyes which had once been brilliant as the jewels she wore in her hair.

I sent a messenger to Paris to summon one of the court physicians; but I knew that many days must needs elapse before he could arrive at Puy Verdun.

In the interval I watched my wife with unutterable fear.

It was not her health only that had declined. The change was more painful to behold than any physical alteration. The bright and sunny spirit had vanished, and in the place of my joyous young bride I beheld a woman weighed down by rooted melancholy. In vain I sought to fathom the cause of my darling's sadness. She assured me that she had no reason for sorrow or discontent, and that if she seemed sad without a motive, I must forgive her sadness, and consider it as a misfortune rather than a fault.

I told her that the court physician would speedily find some cure for her despondency, which must needs arise from physical causes, since she had no real ground for sorrow. But although she said nothing, I could see she had no hope or belief in the healing powers of medicine.

One day, when I wished to beguile her from that pensive silence in which she was wont to sit an hour at a time, I told her, laughing, that she appeared to have forgotten her mysterious cavalier of the wood, and it seemed also as if he had forgotten her.

To my wonderment, her pale face became of a sudden crimson; and from crimson changed to pale again in a breath.

"You have never seen him since you deserted your woodland grotto?" I said.

She turned to me with a heart-rending look.

"Hector," she cried," I see him every day; and it is that which is killing me."

She burst into a passion of tears when she had said this. I took her in my arms as if she had been a frightened child, and tried to comfort her.

"My darling, this is madness," I said. "You know that no stranger can come to you in the *pleasaunce*. The moat is ten feet wide and always full of water, and the gates are kept locked day and night by old Massou. The *châtelaine* of a mediaeval fortress need fear no intruder in her antique garden."

My wife shook her head sadly.

"I see him every day," she said.

On this I believed that my wife was mad. I shrank from questioning her more closely concerning her mysterious visitant. It would be ill, I thought, to give a form and substance to the shadow that tormented her by too close inquiry about its look and manner, its coming and going.

I took care to assure myself that no stranger to the household could by any possibility penetrate to the *pleasaunce*. Having done this, I was fain to await the coming of the physician.

He came at last. I revealed to him the conviction which was my misery. I told him that I believed my wife to be mad. He saw her—spent an hour alone with her, and then came to me. To my unspeakable relief he assured me of her sanity.

"It is just possible that she may be affected by one delusion," he said; "but she is so reasonable upon all other points, that I can scarcely bring myself to believe her the subject of a monomania.

I am rather inclined to think that she really sees the person of whom she speaks. She described him to me with a perfect minuteness. The descriptions of scenes or individuals given by patients afflicted with monomania are always more or less disjointed; but your wife spoke to me as clearly and calmly as I am now speaking to you. Are you sure there is no one who can approach her in that garden where she walks?"

"I am quite sure."

"Is there any kinsman of your steward, or hanger-on of your household,—a young man with a fair womanish face, very pale and rendered remarkable by a crimson scar, which looks like the mark of a blow?"

"My God!" I cried, as the light broke in upon me all at once. "And the dress—the strange old-fashioned dress?"

"The man wears a hunting costume of purple and orange," answered the doctor.

I knew then that André de Brissac had kept his word, and that in the hour when my life was brightest his shadow had come between me and happiness.

I showed my wife the picture in the library, for I would fain assure myself that there was some error in my fancy about my cousin. She shook like a leaf when she beheld it, and clung to me convulsively.

"This is witchcraft, Hector," she said. "The dress in that picture is the dress of the man I see in the *pleasaunce*; but the face is not his."

Then she described to me the face of the stranger; and it was my cousin's face line for line—André de Brissac, whom she had never seen in the flesh. Most vividly of all did she describe the cruel mark upon his face, the trace of a fierce blow from an open hand.

After this I carried my wife away from Puy Verdun. We wandered far—through the southern provinces, and into the very heart of Switzerland. I thought to distance the ghastly phantom, and I fondly hoped that change of scene would bring peace to my wife.

It was not so. Go where we would, the ghost of Andre de Brissac followed us. To my eyes that fatal shadow never revealed itself. That would have been too poor a vengeance. It was my wife's innocent heart which Andre made the instrument of his revenge. The unholy presence destroyed her life. My constant companionship could not shield her from the horrible intruder. In vain did I watch her; in vain did I strive to comfort her.

"He will not let me be at peace," she said; "he comes between us, Hector. He is standing between us now. I can see his face with the red mark upon it plainer that I see yours."

One fair moonlight night, when we were together in a mountain village in the Tyrol, my wife cast herself at my feet, and told me she was the worst and vilest of women. "I have confessed all to my director," she said; "from the first I have not hidden my sin from Heaven. But I feel that death is near me; and before I die I would fain reveal my sin to you."

"What sin, my sweet one?"

"When first the stranger came to me in the forest, his presence bewildered and distressed me, and I shrank from him as from something strange and terrible. He came again and again; by and by I found myself thinking of him, and watching for his coming. His image haunted me perpetually; I strove in vain to shut his face out of my mind. Then followed an interval in which I did not see him; and, to my shame and anguish, I found that life seemed dreary and desolate without him.

"After that came the time in which he haunted the *pleasaunce*; and—O, Hector, kill me if you will, for I deserve no mercy at your hands!—I grew in those days to count the hours that must elapse before his coming, to take no pleasure save in the sight of that pale face with the red brand upon it. He plucked all old familiar joys out of my heart, and left in it but one weird unholy pleasure—the delight of his presence. For a year I have lived but to see him. And now curse me, Hector; for this is my sin.

"Whether it comes of the baseness of my own heart, or is the work of witchcraft, I know not; but I know that I have striven against this wickedness in vain."

I took my wife to my breast, and forgave her. In sooth, what had I to forgive? Was the fatality that overshadowed us any work of hers?

On the next night she died, with her hand in mine; and at the very last she told me, sobbing and affrighted, that he was by her side.

Good Lady Ducayne

Bella Rolleston had made up her mind that her only chance of earning her bread and helping her mother to an occasional crust was by going out into the great unknown world as companion to a lady. She was willing to go to any lady rich enough to pay her a salary and so eccentric as to wish for a hired companion. Five shillings told off reluctantly from one of those sovereigns which were so rare with the mother and daughter, and which melted away so quickly, five solid shillings, had been handed to a smartly-dressed lady in an office in Harbeck Street, W., in the hope that this very Superior Person would find a situation and a salary for Miss Rolleston.

The Superior Person glanced at the two half-crowns as they lay on the table where Bella's hand had placed them, to make sure they were neither of them forms, before she wrote a description of Bella's qualifications and requirements in a formidable-looking ledger.

'Age?' she asked curtly.

'Eighteen, last July.'

'Any accomplishments?'

'No; I am not at all accomplished. If I were I should want to be a governess—a companion seems the lowest stage.'

'We have some highly accomplished ladies on our books as companions, or chaperon companions.'

'Oh, I know!' babbled Bella, loquacious in her youthful candour. 'But that is quite a different thing. Mother hasn't been able to afford a piano since I was twelve years old, so I'm afraid I've forgotten how to play. And I have had to help mother with her needlework, so there hasn't been much time to study.'

'Please don't waste time upon explaining what you can't do, but kindly tell me anything you can do,' said the Superior Person, crushingly, with her pen poised between delicate fingers waiting to write. 'Can you read aloud for two or three hours at a stretch? Are you active and handy, an early riser, a good walker, sweet tempered, and obliging?'

'I can say yes to all those questions except about the sweetness. I think I have a pretty good temper, and I should be anxious to oblige anybody who paid for my services. I should want them to feel that I was really earning my salary.'

'The kind of ladies who come to me would not care for a talkative companion,' said the Person, severely, having finished writing in her book. 'My connection lies chiefly among the aristocracy, and in that class considerable deference is expected.'

'Oh, of course,' said Bella; 'but it's quite different when I'm talking to you. I want to tell you all about myself once and for ever.'

'I am glad it is to be only once!' said the Person, with the edges of her lips.

The Person was of uncertain age, tightly laced in a black silk gown. She had a powdery complexion and a handsome clump of somebody else's hair on the top of her head. It may be that Bella's girlish freshness and vivacity had an irritating effect upon nerves weakened by an eight hours day in that over-heated second floor in Harbeck Street. To Bella the official apartment, with its Brussels carpet, velvet curtains and velvet chairs, and French clock, ticking loud on the marble chimneypiece, suggested the luxury of a palace, as compared with another second floor in Walworth where Mrs Rolleston and her daughter had managed to exist for the last six years.

'Do you think you have anything on your books that would suit me?' faltered Bella, after a pause.

'Oh, dear, no; I have nothing in view at present,' answered

the Person, who had swept Bella's half-crowns into a drawer, absentmindedly, with the tips of her fingers. 'You see, you are so very unformed—so much too young to be companion to a lady of position. It is a pity you have not enough education for a nursery governess; that would be more in your line.'

'And do you think it will be very long before you can get me a situation?' asked Bella, doubtfully.

'I really cannot say. Have you any particular reason for being so impatient—not a love affair, I hope?'

'A love affair!' cried Bella, with flaming cheeks. 'What utter nonsense. I want a situation because mother is poor, and I hate being a burden to her. I want a salary that I can share with her.'

'There won't be much margin for sharing in the salary you are likely to get at your age—and with your—very—unformed manners,' said the Person, who found Bella's peony cheeks, bright eyes, and unbridled vivacity more and more oppressive.

'Perhaps if you'd be kind enough to give me back the fee I could take it to an agency where the connection isn't quite so aristocratic,' said Bella, who—as she told her mother in her recital of the interview—was determined not to be sat upon.

'You will find no agency that can do more for you than mine,' replied the Person, whose harpy fingers never relinquished coin. 'You will have to wait for your opportunity. Yours is an exceptional case: but I will bear you in mind, and if anything suitable offers I will write to you. I cannot say more than that.'

The half-contemptuous bend of the stately head, weighted with borrowed hair, indicated the end of the interview. Bella went back to Walworth—tramped sturdily every inch of the way in the September afternoon—and 'took off' the Superior Person for the amusement of her mother and the landlady, who lingered in the shabby little sitting—room after bringing in the tea-tray, to applaud Miss Rolleston's 'taking off'.

'Dear, dear, what a mimic she is!' said the landlady. 'You ought to have let her go on the stage, mum. She might have made her fortune as a hactress.'

Bella waited and hoped, and listened for the postman's knocks which brought such store of letters for the parlours and the first floor, and so few for that humble second floor, where mother and daughter sat sewing with hand and with wheel and treadle, for the greater part of the day.

Mrs Rolleston was a lady by birth and education; but it had been her bad fortune to marry a scoundrel; for the last half-dozen years she had been that worst of widows, a wife whose husband had deserted her. Happily, she was courageous, industrious, and a clever needle-woman; and she had been able just to earn a living for herself and her only child, by making mantles and cloaks for a West-end house.

It was not a luxurious living. Cheap lodgings in a shabby street off the Walworth Road, scanty dinners, homely food, well-worn raiment, had been the portion of mother and daughter; but they loved each other so dearly, and Nature had made them both so light-hearted, that they had contrived somehow to be happy..

But now this idea of going out into the world as companion to some fine lady had rooted itself into Bella's mind, and although she idolized her mother, and although the parting of mother and daughter must needs tear two loving hearts into shreds, the girl longed for enterprise and change and excitement, as the pages of old longed to be knights, and to start for the Holy Land to break a lance with the infidel.

She grew tired of racing downstairs every time the postman knocked, only to be told 'nothing for you, miss,' by the smudgy-faced drudge who picked up the letters from the passage floor.

'Nothing for you, miss,' grinned the lodging-house drudge, till at last Bella took heart of grace and walked up to Harbeck Street, and asked the Superior Person how it was that no situation had been found for her.

'You are too young,' said the Person, 'and you want a salary.'

'Of course I do,' answered Bella; 'don't other people want salaries?'

'Young ladies of your age generally want a comfortable

home.

'I don't,' snapped Bella; 'I want to help mother.'

'You can call again this day week,' said the Person; 'or, if I hear of anything in the meantime, I will write to you.'

No letter came from the Person, and in exactly a week Bella put on her neatest hat, the one that had been seldomest caught in the rain, and trudged off to Harbeck Street.

It was a dull October afternoon, and there was a greyness in the air which might turn to fog before night. The Walworth Road shops gleamed brightly through that grey atmosphere, and though to a young lady reared in Mayfair or Belgravia such shop-windows would have been unworthy of a glance, they were a snare and temptation for Bella. There were so many things that she longed for, and would never be able to buy.

Harbeck Street is apt to be empty at this dead season of the year, a long, long street, an endless perspective of eminently re-spectable houses. The Person's office was at the further end, and Bella looked down that long, grey vista almost despairingly, more tired than usual with the trudge from Walworth. As she looked, a carriage passed her, an old-fashioned, yellow chariot, on cee springs, drawn by a pair of high grey horses, with the stateliest of coachmen driving them, and a tall footman sitting by his side.

'It looks like the fairy god-mother's coach,' thought Bella. 'I shouldn't wonder if it began by being a pumpkin.'

It was a surprise when she reached the Person's door to find the yellow chariot standing before it, and the tall footman waiting near the doorstep. She was almost afraid to go in and meet the owner of that splendid carriage. She had caught only a glimpse of its occupant as the chariot rolled by, a plumed bon-net, a patch of ermine.

The Person's smart page ushered her upstairs and knocked at the official door. 'Miss Rolleston,' he announced, apologetically, while Bella waited outside.

'Show her in,' said the Person, quickly; and then Bella heard her murmuring something in a low voice to her client.

Bella went in fresh, blooming, a living image of youth and

hope, and before she looked at the Person her gaze was riveted by the owner of the chariot.

Never had she seen anyone as old as the old lady sitting by the Person's fire: a little old figure, wrapped from chin to feet in an ermine mantle; a withered, old face under a plumed bonnet—a face so wasted by age that it seemed only a pair of eyes and a peaked chin. The nose was peaked, too, but between the sharply pointed chin and the great, shining eyes, the small, aquiline nose was hardly visible. 'This is Miss Rolleston, Lady Ducayne.'

Claw-like fingers, flashing with jewels, lifted a double eyeglass to Lady Ducayne's shining black eyes, and through the glasses Bella saw those unnaturally bright eyes magnified to a gigantic size, and glaring at her awfully.

'Miss Torpinter has told me all about you,' said the old voice that belonged to the eyes. 'Have you good health? Are you strong and active, able to eat well, sleep well, walk well, able to enjoy all that there is good in life?'

'I have never known what it is to be ill, or idle,' answered Bella.

'Then I think you will do for me.'

'Of course, in the event of references being perfectly satisfactory,' put in the Person.

'I don't want references. The young woman looks frank and innocent. I'll take her on trust.'

'So like you, dear Lady Ducayne,' murmured Miss Torpinter.

'I want a strong young woman whose health will give me no trouble.'

'You have been so unfortunate in that respect,' cooed the Person, whose voice and manner were subdued to a melting sweetness by the old woman's presence.

'Yes, I've been rather unlucky,' grunted Lady Ducayne.

'But I am sure Miss Rolleston will not disappoint you, though certainly after your unpleasant experience with Miss Tomson, who looked the picture of health—and Miss Blandy, who said she had never seen a doctor since she was vaccinated—'

'Lies, no doubt,' muttered Lady Ducayne, and then turning

to Bella, she asked, curtly, 'You don't mind spending the winter in Italy, I suppose?'

In Italy! The very word was magical. Bella's fair young face flushed crimson.

'It has been the dream of my life to see Italy,' she gasped.

From Walworth to Italy! How far, how impossible such a journey had seemed to that romantic dreamer.

'Well, your dream will be realized. Get yourself ready to leave Charing Cross by the *train deluxe* this day week at eleven. Be sure you are at the station a quarter before the hour. My people will look after you and your luggage.'

Lady Ducayne rose from her chair, assisted by her crutch-stick, and Miss Torpinter escorted her to the door.

'And with regard to salary?' questioned the Person on the way.

'Salary, oh, the same as usual—and if the young woman wants a quarter's pay in advance you can write to me for a cheque,' Lady Ducayne answered, carelessly.

Miss Torpinter went all the way downstairs with her client, and waited to see her seated in the yellow chariot. When she came upstairs again she was slightly out of breath, and she had resumed that superior manner which Bella had found so crushing.

'You may think yourself uncommonly lucky, Miss Rolleston,' she said. 'I have dozens of young ladies on my books whom I might have recommended for this situation—but I remembered having told you to call this afternoon—and I thought I would give you a chance.

Old Lady Ducayne is one of the best people on my books. She gives her companion a hundred a year, and pays all travelling expenses. You will live in the lap of luxury.'

'A hundred a year! How too lovely! Shall I have to dress very grandly? Does Lady Ducayne keep much company?'

'At her age! No, she lives in seclusion—in her own apart-ments—her French maid, her footman, her medical attendant, her courier.'

'Why did those other companions leave her?' asked Bella.

'Their health broke down!'

'Poor things, and so they had to leave?'

'Yes, they had to leave. I suppose you would like a quarter's salary in advance?'

'Oh, yes, please. I shall have things to buy.'

'Very well, I will write for Lady Ducayne's cheque, and I will send you the balance—after deducting my commission for the year.'

'To be sure, I had forgotten the commission.'

'You don't suppose I keep this office for pleasure.'

'Of course not,' murmured Bella, remembering the five shillings entrance fee; but nobody could expect a hundred a year and a winter in Italy for five shillings.

CHAPTER 3

'From Miss Rolleston, at Cap Ferrino, to Mrs Rolleston, in Beresford Street, Walworth.

'How I wish you could see this place, dearest; the blue sky, the olive woods, the orange and lemon orchards between the cliffs and the sea—sheltering in the hollow of the great hills—and with summer waves dancing up to the narrow ridge of pebbles and weeds which is the Italian idea of a beach! Oh, how I wish you could see it all, mother dear, and bask in this sunshine, that makes it so difficult to believe the date at the head of this paper. November!

'The air is like an English June—the sun is so hot that I can't walk a few yards without an umbrella. And to think of you at Walworth while I am here! I could cry at the thought that perhaps you will never see this lovely coast, this wonderful sea, these summer flowers that bloom in winter. There is a hedge of pink geraniums under my window, mother—a thick, rank hedge, as if the flowers grew wild—and there are Dijon roses climbing over arches and palisades all along the terrace—a rose garden full of bloom in November! Just picture it all! You could never imagine the luxury of this hotel.

'It is nearly new, and has been built and decorated regardless of expense. Our rooms are upholstered in pale blue satin, which shows up Lady Ducayne's parchment complexion; but as she sits all day in a corner of the balcony basking in the sun, except when she is in her carriage, and all the evening in her armchair close to the fire, and never sees anyone but her own people, her complexion matters very little.

'She has the handsomest suite of rooms in the hotel. My bedroom is inside hers, the sweetest room—all blue satin and white lace—white enamelled furniture, looking-glasses on every wall, till I know my pert little profile as I never knew it before. The room was really meant for Lady Ducayne's dressing-room, but she ordered one of the blue satin couches to be arranged as a bed for me—the prettiest little bed, which I can wheel near the window on sunny mornings, as it is on castors and easily moved about. I feel as if Lady Ducayne were a funny old grandmother, who had suddenly appeared in my life, very, very rich, and very, very kind.

'She is not at all exacting. I read aloud to her a good deal, and she dozes and nods while I read.

'Sometimes I hear her moaning in her sleep—as if she had troublesome dreams. When she is tired of my reading she orders Francine, her maid, to read a French novel to her, and I hear her chuckle and groan now and then, as if she were more interested in those books than in Dickens or Scott. My French is not good enough to follow Francine, who reads very quickly. I have a great deal of liberty, for Lady Ducayne often tells me to run away and amuse myself; I roam about the hills for hours.

'Everything is so lovely. I lose myself in olive woods, always climbing up and up towards the pine woods above—and above the pines there are the snow mountains that just show their white peaks above the dark hills. Oh, you poor dear, how can I ever make you understand what this place is like—you, whose poor, tired eyes have only the opposite side of Beresford Street? Sometimes I go no farther than the terrace in front of the hotel, which is a favourite lounging-place with everybody.

'The gardens lie below, and the tennis courts where I sometimes play with a very nice girl, the only person in the hotel with whom I have made friends. She is a year older than I, and has come to Cap Ferrino with her brother, a doctor—or a medical student, who is going to be a doctor. He passed his M.B. exam at Edinburgh just before they left home, Lotta told me. He came to Italy entirely on his sister's account. She had a troublesome chest attack last summer and was ordered to winter abroad.

'They are orphans, quite alone in the world, and so fond of each other. It is very nice for me to have such a friend as Lotta. She is so thoroughly respectable. I can't help using that word, for some of the girls in this hotel go on in a way that I know you would shudder at. Lotta was brought up by an aunt, deep down in the country, and knows hardly anything about life. Her brother won't allow her to read a novel, French or English, that he has not read and approved.

'"He treats me like a child," she told me, "but I don't mind, for it's nice to know somebody loves me, and cares about what I do, and even about my thoughts."

'Perhaps this is what makes some girls so eager to marry—the want of someone strong and brave and honest and true to care for them and order them about. I want no one, mother darling, for I have you, and you are all the world to me. No husband could ever come between us two. If I ever were to marry he would have only the second place in my heart. But I don't suppose I ever shall marry, or even know what it is like to have an offer of marriage. No young man can afford to marry a penniless girl nowadays. Life is too expensive.

45

'Mr Stafford, Lotta's brother, is very clever, and very kind. He thinks it is rather hard for me to have to live with such an old woman as Lady Ducayne, but then he does not know how poor we are—you and I—and what a wonderful life this seems to me in this lovely place. I feel a selfish wretch for enjoying all my luxuries, while you, who want them so much more than I, have none of them—hardly know what they are like—do you, dearest?—for my scamp of a father began to go to the dogs soon after you were married, and since then life has been all trouble and care and struggle for you.'

This letter was written when Bella had been less than a month at Cap Ferrino, before the novelty had worn off the landscape, and before the pleasure of luxurious surroundings had begun to cloy. She wrote to her mother every week, such long letters as girls who have lived in closest companionship with a mother alone can write; letters that are like a diary of heart and mind. She wrote gaily always; but when the new year began Mrs Rolleston thought she detected a note of melancholy under all those lively details about the place and the people.

'My poor girl is getting homesick,' she thought. 'Her heart is in Beresford Street.'

It might be that she missed her new friend and companion, Lotta Stafford, who had gone with her brother for a little tour to Genoa and Spezzia, and as far as Pisa. They were to return before February; but in the meantime Bella might naturally feel very solitary among all those strangers, whose manners and doings she described so well.

The mother's instinct had been true. Bella was not so happy as she had been in that first flush of wonder and delight which followed the change from Walworth to the Riviera. Somehow, she knew not how, lassitude had crept upon her. She no longer loved to climb the hills, no longer flourished her orange stick in sheer gladness of heart as her light feet skipped over the rough ground and the coarse grass on the mountain side. The odour of rosemary and thyme, the fresh breath of the sea, no longer filled her with rapture. She thought of Beresford Street and her mother's face with a sick longing. They were so far—so far away! And then she thought of Lady Ducayne, sitting by the heaped-up olive logs in the over-heated salon—thought of that wizened-nut-cracker profile, and those gleaming eyes, with an invincible horror.

Visitors at the hotel had told her that the air of Cap Ferrino was relaxing—better suited to age than to youth, to sickness than to health. No doubt it was so. She was not so well as she had been at Walworth; but she told herself that she was suffering only from the pain of separation from the dear companion of her girlhood, the mother who had been nurse, sister, friend, flatterer, all things in this world to her. She had shed many tears over that parting, had spent many a melancholy hour on the marble terrace with yearning eyes looking westward, and with her heart's desire a thousand miles away.

She was sitting in her favourite spot, an angle at the eastern end of the terrace, a quiet little nook sheltered by orange trees, when she heard a couple of Riviera *habitués* talking in the garden below. They were sitting on a bench against the terrace wall.

She had no idea of listening to their talk, till the sound of Lady Ducayne's name attracted her, and then she listened without any thought of wrong-doing. They were talking no secrets-just casually discussing an hotel acquaintance.

They were two elderly people whom Bella only knew by sight. An English clergyman who had wintered abroad for half his lifetime; a stout, comfortable, well-to-do spinster, whose chronic bronchitis obliged her to migrate annually.

'I have met her about Italy for the last ten years,' said the lady; 'but have never found out her real age.

'I put her down at a hundred—not a year less,' replied the parson. 'Her reminiscences all go back to the Regency. She was evidently then in her zenith; and I have heard her say things that showed she was in Parisian society when the First Empire was at its best—before Josephine was divorced.'

'She doesn't talk much now.'

'No; there's not much life left in her. She is wise in keeping herself secluded. I only wonder that wicked old quack, her Italian doctor, didn't finish her off years ago.'

'I should think it must be the other way, and that he keeps her alive.'

'My dear Miss Manders, do you think foreign quackery ever kept anybody alive?'

'Well, there she is—and she never goes anywhere without him. He certainly has an unpleasant countenance.'

'Unpleasant,' echoed the parson, 'I don't believe the foul fiend himself can beat him in ugliness. I pity that poor young woman who has to live between old Lady Ducayne and Dr Parravicini.'

'But the old lady is very good to her companions.'

'No doubt. She is very free with her cash; the servants call her good Lady Ducayne. She is a withered old female Croesus, and knows she'll never be able to get through her money, and doesn't relish the idea of other people enjoying it when she's in her coffin. People who live to be as old as she is become slavishly attached to life. I daresay she's generous to those poor girls—but she can't make them happy. They die in her service.'

'Don't say they, Mr Carton; I know that one poor girl died at Mentone last spring.'

'Yes, and another poor girl died in Rome three years ago. I was there at the time. Good Lady Ducayne left her there in an English family. The girl had every comfort. The old woman was very liberal to her—but she died. I tell you, Miss Manders, it is not good for any young woman to live with two such horrors as Lady Ducayne and Parravicini..They talked of other things-but Bella hardly heard them. She sat motionless, and a cold wind seemed to come down upon her from the mountains and to creep up to her from the sea, till she shivered as she sat there in the sunshine, in the shelter of the orange trees in the midst of all that beauty and brightness.

Yes, they were uncanny, certainly, the pair of them—she so like an aristocratic witch in her withered old age; he of no particular age, with a face that was more like a waxen mask than any human countenance Bella had ever seen. What did it matter? Old age is venerable, and worthy of all reverence; and Lady Ducayne had been very kind to her. Dr Parravicini was a harmless, inoffensive student, who seldom looked up from the book he was reading. He had his private sitting-room, where he made experiments in chemistry and natural science-perhaps in alchemy.

What could it matter to Bella? He had always been polite to her, in his far-off way. She could not be more happily placed than she was—in this palatial hotel, with this rich old lady.

No doubt she missed the young English girl who had been so friendly, and it might be that she missed the girl's brother, for Mr Stafford had talked to her a good deal—had interested himself in the books she was reading, and her manner of amusing herself when she was not on duty.

You must come to our little salon when you are "off," as the hospital nurses call it, and we can have some music. No doubt you play and sing?' upon which Bella had to own with a blush of shame that she had forgotten how to play the piano ages ago.

Mother and I used to sing duets sometimes between the lights, without accompaniment,' she said, and the tears came into her eyes as she thought of the humble room, the half-hour's respite from work, the sewing-machine standing where a piano ought to have been, and her mother's plaintive voice, so sweet, so true, so dear.

Sometimes she found herself wondering whether she would ever see that beloved mother again. Strange forebodings came into her mind. She was angry with herself for giving way to melancholy thoughts.

One day she questioned Lady Ducayne's French maid about those two companions who had died within three years.

'They were poor, feeble creatures,' Francine told her. 'They looked fresh and bright enough when they came to Miladi; but they ate too much and they were lazy. They died of luxury and idleness. Miladi was too kind to them. They had nothing to do; and so they took to fancying things; fancying the air didn't suit them, that they couldn't sleep.'

'I sleep well enough, but I have had a strange dream several times since I have been in Italy.'

'Ah, you had better not begin to think about dreams, or you will be like those other girls. They were dreamers—and they dreamt themselves into the cemetery.'

The dream troubled her a little, not because it was a ghastly or frightening dream, but on account of sensations which she had never felt before in sleep—a whirring of wheels that went round in her brain, a great noise like a whirlwind, but rhythmical like the ticking of a gigantic clock: and then in the midst of this uproar as of winds and waves she seemed to sink into a gulf of unconsciousness, out of sleep into far deeper sleep—total extinction. And then, after that blank interval, there had come the sound of voices, and then again the whirr of wheels, louder and louder—and again the blank—and then she knew no more till morning, when she awoke, feeling languid and oppressed.

She told Dr Parravicini of her dream one day, on the only occasion when she wanted his professional advice. She had suffered rather severely from the mosquitoes before Christmas—and had been almost frightened at finding a wound upon her arm which she could only attribute to the venomous sting of one of these torturers. Parravicini put on his glasses, and scrutinized the angry mark on the round, white arm, as Bella stood before him and Lady Ducayne with her sleeve rolled up above her elbow.

'Yes, that's rather more than a joke,' he said, 'he has caught you on the top of a vein. What a vampire! But there's no harm done, *signorina*, nothing that a little dressing of mine won't heal.

You must always show me any bite of this nature. It might be dangerous if neglected. These creatures feed on poison and disseminate it.'

'And to think that such tiny creatures can bite like this,' said Bella; 'my arm looks as if it had been cut by a knife.'

'If I were to show you a mosquito's sting under my microscope you wouldn't be surprised at that,' replied Parravicini.

Bella had to put up with the mosquito bites, even when they

came on the top of a vein, and produced that ugly wound. The wound recurred now and then at longish intervals, and Bella found Dr Parravicini's dressing a speedy cure. If he were the quack his enemies called him, he had at least a light hand and a delicate touch in performing this small operation.

'Bella Rolleston to Mrs Rolleston—April 14th.

'Ever Dearest,—Behold the cheque for my second quarter's salary—five and twenty pounds.

'There is no one to pinch off a whole tenner for a year's commission as there was last time, so it is all for you, mother, dear. I have plenty of pocket-money in hand from the cash I brought away with me, when you insisted on my keeping more than I wanted. It isn't possible to spend money here—except on occasional tips to servants, or *sous* to beggars and children—unless one had lots to spend, for everything one would like to buy—tortoise-shell, coral, lace is so ridiculously dear that only a millionaire ought to look at it. Italy is a dream of beauty: but for shopping, give me Newington Causeway.

'You ask me so earnestly if I am quite well that I fear my letters must have been very dull lately. Yes, dear, I am well—but I am not quite so strong as I was when I used to trudge to the West-end to buy half a pound of tea—just for a constitutional walk—or to Dulwich to look at the pictures. Italy is relaxing; and I feel what the people here call "slack".

'But I fancy I can see your dear face looking worried as you read this. Indeed, and indeed, I am not ill. I am only a little tired of this lovely scene—as I suppose one might get tired of looking at one of Turner's pictures if it hung on a wall that was always opposite one. I think of you every hour in every day—think of you and our homely little room—our dear little shabby parlour, with the armchairs from the wreck of your old home, and Dick singing in his cage over the sewing-machine. Dear, shrill, maddening Dick, who, we flattered ourselves, was so passionately fond of us. Do tell me in your next that he is well.

'My friend Lotta and her brother never came back after all. They went from Pisa to Rome.

Happy mortals! And they are to be on the Italian lakes in May; which lake was not decided when Lotta last wrote to me. She has been a charming correspondent, and has confided all her little flirtations to me. We are all to go to Bellaggio next week—by Genoa and Milan. Isn't that lovely? Lady Ducayne travels by the easiest stages—except when she is bottled up in the train *de luxe*. We shall stop two days at Genoa and one at Milan. What a bore I shall be to you with my talk about Italy when I come home.

'Love and love-and ever more love from your adoring, Bella.'

Chapter 4

Herbert Stafford and his sister had often talked of the pretty English girl with her fresh complexion, which made such a pleasant touch of rosy colour among all those sallow faces at the Grand Hotel. The young doctor thought of her with a compassionate tenderness—her utter loneliness in that great hotel where there were so many people, her bondage to that old, old woman, where everybody else was free to think of nothing but enjoying life. It was a hard fate; and the poor child was evidently devoted to her mother, and felt the pain of separation-only two of them, and very poor, and all the world to each other,' he thought.

Lotta told him one morning that they were to meet again at Bellaggio. 'The old thing and her court are to be there before we are,' she said. 'I shall be charmed to have Bella again. She is so bright and gay—in spite of an occasional touch of homesickness. I never took to a girl on a short acquaintance as I did to her.'

'I like her best when she is homesick,' said Herbert; 'for then I am sure she has a heart.'

'What have you to do with hearts, except for dissection? Don't forget that Bella is an absolute pauper. She told me in confidence that her mother makes mantles for a West-end shop. You can hardly have a lower depth than that.'

'I shouldn't think any less of her if her mother made match-boxes.'

'Not in the abstract—of course not. Match-boxes are honest labour. But you couldn't marry a girl whose mother makes mantles.'

'We haven't come to the consideration of that question yet,' answered Herbert, who liked to provoke his sister.

In two years' hospital practice he had seen too much of the grim realities of life to retain any prejudices about rank. Cancer, phthisis, gangrene, leave a man with little respect for the outward differences which vary the husk of humanity. The kernel is always the same—fearfully and wonderfully made—a subject for pity and terror.

Mr Stafford and his sister arrived at Bellaggio in a fair May evening. The sun was going down as the steamer approached the pier; and all that glory of purple bloom which curtains every wall at this season of the year flushed and deepened in the glowing light. A group of ladies were standing on the pier watching the arrivals, and among them Herbert saw a pale face that startled him out of his wonted composure.

'There she is,' murmured Lotta, at his elbow, 'but how dreadfully changed. She looks a wreck.'

They were shaking hands with her a few minutes later, and a flush had lighted up her poor pinched face in the pleasure of meeting.

'I thought you might come this evening,' she said. 'We have been here a week.'

She did not add that she had been there every evening to watch the boat in, and a good many times during the day. The Grand Bretagne was close by, and it had been easy for her to creep to the pier when the boat bell rang. She felt a joy in meeting these people again; a sense of being with friends; a confidence which Lady Ducayne's goodness had never inspired in her.

'Oh, you poor darling, how awfully ill you must have been,' exclaimed Lotta, as the two girls embraced.

Bella tried to answer, but her voice was choked with tears.

'What has been the matter, dear? That horrid influenza, I suppose?'

'No, no, I have not been ill—I have only felt a little weaker than I used to be. I don't think the air of Cap Ferrino quite agreed with me.'

'It must have disagreed with you abominably. I never saw such a change in anyone. Do let Herbert doctor you. He is fully qualified, you know. He prescribed for ever so many influenza patients at the Londres. They were glad to get advice from an English doctor in a friendly way.'

'I am sure he must be very clever!' faltered Bella, 'but there is really nothing the matter. I am not ill, and if I were ill, Lady Ducayne's physician—'

'That dreadful man with the yellow face? I would as soon one of the Borgias prescribed for me. I hope you haven't been taking any of his medicines.'

'No, dear, I have taken nothing. I have never complained of being ill.'

This was said while they were all three walking to the hotel. The Staffords' rooms had been secured in advance, pretty ground-floor rooms, opening into the garden. Lady Ducayne's statelier apartments were on the floor above.

'I believe these rooms are just under ours,' said Bella.

'Then it will be all the easier for you to run down to us,' replied Lotta, which was not really the case, as the grand staircase was in the centre of the hotel.

'Oh, I shall find it easy enough,' said Bella. 'I'm afraid you'll have too much of my society.

Lady Ducayne sleeps away half the day in this warm weather, so I have a good deal of idle time; and I get awfully moped thinking of mother and home.'

Her voice broke upon the last word. She could not have thought of that poor lodging which went by the name of home more tenderly had it been the most beautiful that art and wealth ever created. She moped and pined in this lovely garden, with the sunlit lake and the romantic hills spreading out their beauty before her.

She was homesick and she had dreams: or, rather, an occasional recurrence of that one bad dream with all its strange sensations—it was more like a hallucination than dreaming—the whirring of wheels; the sinking into an abyss; the struggling back to consciousness. She had the dream shortly before she left Cap Ferrino, but not since she had come to Bellaggio, and she began to hope the air in this lake district suited her better, and that those strange sensations would never return.

Mr Stafford wrote a prescription and had it made up at the chemist's near the hotel. It was a powerful tonic, and after two bottles, and a row or two on the lake, and some rambling over the hills and in the meadows where the spring flowers made earth seem paradise, Bella's spirits and looks improved as if by magic.

'It is a wonderful tonic,' she said, but perhaps in her heart of hearts she knew that the doctor's kind voice and the friendly hand that helped her in and out of the boat, and the watchful care that went with her by land and lake, had something to do with her cure.

'I hope you don't forget that her mother makes mantles,' Lotta said, warningly.

'Or match-boxes: it is just the same thing, so far as I am concerned.'

'You mean that in no circumstances could you think of marrying her?'

'I mean that if ever I love a woman well enough to think of marrying her, riches or rank will count for nothing with me. But I fear—I fear your poor friend may not live to be any man's wife.'

'Do you think her so very ill?'

He sighed, and left the question unanswered.

One day, while they were gathering wild hyacinths in an upland meadow, Bella told Mr Stafford about her bad dream.

'It is curious only because it is hardly like a dream,' she said. 'I daresay you could find some commonsense reason for it. The position of my head on my pillow, or the atmosphere, or something.'

And then she described her sensations; how in the midst of sleep there came a sudden sense of suffocation; and then those whirring wheels, so loud, so terrible; and then a blank, and then a coming back to waking consciousness.

'Have you ever had chloroform given you—by a dentist, for instance?'

'Never—Dr Parravicini asked me that question one day.

'Lately?'

'No, long ago, when we were in the train *de luxe*.'

'Has Dr Parravicini prescribed for you since you began to feel weak and ill?'

'Oh, he has given me a tonic from time to time, but I hate medicine, and took very little of the stuff. And then I am not ill, only weaker than I used to be. I was ridiculously strong and well when I lived at Walworth, and used to take long walks every day. Mother made me take those tramps to Dulwich or Norwood, for fear I should suffer from too much sewing-machine; sometimes—but very seldom—she went with me. She was generally toiling at home while I was enjoying fresh air and exercise. And she was very careful about our food—that, however plain it was, it should be always nourishing and ample. I owe at to her care that I grew up such a great, strong creature.'

'You don't look great or strong now, you poor dear,' said Lotta.

'I'm afraid Italy doesn't agree with me.'

'Perhaps it is not Italy, but being cooped up with Lady Ducayne that has made you ill.'

'But I am never cooped up. Lady Ducayne is absurdly kind, and lets me roam about or sit in the balcony all day if I like. I have read more novels since I have been with her than in all the rest of my life.'

'Then she is very different from the average old lady, who is usually a slave-driver,' said Stafford. 'I wonder why she carries a companion about with her if she has so little need of society.'

'Oh, I am only part of her state. She is inordinately rich—and the salary she gives me doesn't count. *Apropos* of Dr Parravicini, I know he is a clever doctor, for he cures my horrid mosquito bites.'

'A little ammonia would do that, in the early stage of the mischief. But there are no mosquitoes to trouble you now.'

'Oh, yes, there are, I had a bite just before we left Cap Ferrino.

She pushed up her loose lawn sleeve, and exhibited a scar, which he scrutinized intently, with a surprised and puzzled look.

'This is no mosquito bite,' he said.

'Oh, yes it is—unless there are snakes or adders at Cap Ferrino.'

'It is not a bite at all. You are trifling with me. Miss Rolleston—you have allowed that wretched Italian quack to bleed you. They killed the greatest man in modern Europe that way, remember. How very foolish of you.'

'I was never bled in my life, Mr Stafford.'

'Nonsense! Let me look at your other arm. Are there any more mosquito bites?'

'Yes; Dr Parravicini says I have a bad skin for healing, and that the poison acts more virulently with me than with most people.'

Stafford examined both her arms in the broad sunlight, scars new and old.

'You have been very badly bitten, Miss Rolleston,' he said, 'and if ever I find the mosquito I shall make him smart. But, now tell me, my dear girl, on your word of honour, tell me as you would tell a friend who is sincerely anxious for your health and happiness—as you would tell your mother if she were here to question you—have you no knowledge of any cause for these scars except mosquito bites—no suspicion even?'

'No, indeed! No, upon my honour! I have never seen a mosquito biting my arm. One never does see the horrid little fiends. But I have heard them trumpeting under the curtains, and I know that I have often had one of the pestilent wretches buzzing about me.

Later in the day Bella and her friends were sitting at tea in the garden, while Lady Ducayne took her afternoon drive with her doctor.

'How long do you mean to stop with Lady Ducayne, Miss Rolleston?' Herbert Stafford asked, after a thoughtful silence, breaking suddenly upon the trivial talk of the two girls.

'As long as she will go on paying me twenty-five pounds a quarter.'

'Even if you feel your health breaking down in her service?'

'It is not the service that has injured my health. You can see that I have really nothing to do—to read aloud for an hour or so once or twice a week; to write a letter once in a way to a London tradesman. I shall never have such an easy time with anybody else. And nobody else would give me a hundred a year.'

'Then you mean to go on till you break down; to die at your post?'

'Like the other two companions? No! If ever I feel seriously ill—really ill—I shall put myself in a train and go back to Walworth without stopping.'

'What about the other two companions?'

'They both died. It was very unlucky for Lady Ducayne. That's why she engaged me; she chose me because I was ruddy and robust. She must feel rather disgusted at my having grown white and weak. By-the-bye, when I told her about the good your tonic had done me, she said she would like to see you and have a little talk with you about her own case.

'And I should like to see Lady Ducayne. When did she say this?'

'The day before yesterday.'

'Will you ask her if she will see me this evening?'

'With pleasure I wonder what you will think of her? She

looks rather terrible to a stranger; but Dr Parravicini says she was once a famous beauty.'

It was nearly ten o'clock when Mr Stafford was summoned by message from Lady Ducayne, whose courier came to conduct him to her ladyship's salon. Bella was reading aloud when the visitor was admitted; and he noticed the languor in the low, sweet tones, the evident effort.

'Shut up the book,' said the querulous old voice. 'You are beginning to drawl like Miss Blandy.'

Stafford saw a small, bent figure crouching over the piled-up olive logs; a shrunken old figure in a gorgeous garment of black and crimson brocade, a skinny throat emerging from a mass of old Venetian lace, clasped with diamonds that flashed like fireflies as the trembling old head turned towards him.

The eyes that looked at him out of the face were almost as bright as the diamonds—the only living feature in that narrow parchment mask. He had seen terrible faces in the hospital-faces on which disease had set dreadful marks—but he had never seen a face that impressed him so painfully as this withered countenance, with its indescribable horror of death outlived, a face that should have been hidden under a coffin-lid years and years ago.

The Italian physician was standing on the other side of the fireplace, smoking a cigarette, and looking down at the little old woman brooding over the hearth as if he were proud of her.

'Good evening, Mr Stafford; you can go to your room, Bella, and write your everlasting letter to your mother at Walworth,' said Lady Ducayne. 'I believe she writes a page about every wild flower she discovers in the woods and meadows. I don't know what else she can find to write about,' she added, as Bella quietly withdrew to the pretty little bedroom opening out of Lady Ducayne's spacious apartment. Here, as at Cap Ferrino, she slept in a room adjoining the old lady's.

'You are a medical man, I understand, Mr Stafford.'

'I am a qualified practitioner, but I have not begun to practise.'

'You have begun upon my companion, she tells me.'

'I have prescribed for her, certainly, and I am happy to find my prescription has done her good; but I look upon that improvement as temporary. Her case will require more drastic treatment.

'Never mind her case. There is nothing the matter with the girl—absolutely nothing—except girlish nonsense; too much liberty and not enough work.'

'I understand that two of your ladyship's previous companions died of the same disease,' said Stafford, looking first at Lady Ducayne, who gave her tremulous old head an impatient jerk, and then at Parravicini, whose yellow complexion had paled a little under Stafford's scrutiny.

'Don't bother me about my companions, sir,' said Lady Ducayne. 'I sent for you to consult you about myself—not about a parcel of anaemic girls. You are young, and medicine is a progressive science, the newspapers tell me. Where have you studied?'

'In Edinburgh—and in Paris.'

'Two good schools. And you know all the new-fangled theories, the modem discoveries—that remind one of the mediaeval witchcraft, of Albertus Magnus, and George Ripley; you have studied hypnotism—electricity?'

'And the transfusion of blood,' said Stafford, very slowly, looking at Parravicini.

'Have you made any discovery that teaches you to prolong human life—any elixir—any mode of treatment? I want my life prolonged, young man. That man there has been my physician for thirty years. He does all he can to keep me alive—after his lights. He studies all the new theories of all the scientists—but he is old; he gets older every day—his brain-power is going—he is bigoted—prejudiced—can't receive new ideas—can't grapple with new systems. He will let me die if I am not on my guard against him.'

'You are of an unbelievable ingratitude, Ecclenza,' said Parravicini.

'Oh, you needn't complain. I have paid you thousands to keep me alive. Every year of my life has swollen your hoards; you know there is nothing to come to you when I am gone. My whole fortune is left to endow a home for indigent women of quality who have reached their ninetieth year. Come, Mr Stafford, I am a rich woman. Give me a few years more in the sunshine, a few years more above ground, and I will give you the price of a fashionable London practice—I will set you up at the West-end.'

'How old are you, Lady Ducayne?'

'I was born the day Louis XVI was guillotined.'

'Then I think you have had your share of the sunshine and the pleasures of the earth, and that you should spend your few remaining days in repenting your sins and trying to make atonement for the young lives that have been sacrificed to your love of life.'

'What do you mean by that, sir?'

'Oh, Lady Ducayne, need I put your wickedness and your physician's still greater wickedness in plain words? The poor girl who is now in your employment has been reduced from robust health to a condition of absolute danger by Dr Parravicini's experimental surgery; and I have no doubt those other two young women who broke down in your service were treated by him in the same manner. I could take upon myself to demonstrate—by most convincing evidence, to a jury of medical men—that Dr Parravicini has been bleeding Miss Rolleston, after putting her under chloroform, at intervals, ever since she has been in your service.

'The deterioration in the girl's health speaks for itself; the lancet marks upon the girl's arms are unmistakable; and her description of a series of sensations, which she calls a dream, points unmistakably to the administration of chloroform while she was sleeping. A practice so nefarious, so murderous, must, if exposed, result in a sentence only less severe than the punishment of murder.'

'I laugh,' said Parravicini, with an airy motion of his skinny fingers; 'I laugh at once at your theories and at your threats. I, Parravicini Leopold, have no fear that the law can question anything I have done.'

'Take the girl away, and let me hear no more of her,' cried Lady Ducayne, in the thin, old voice, which so poorly matched the energy and fire of the wicked old brain that guided its utterances. 'Let her go back to her mother—I want no more girls to die in my service. There are girls enough and to spare in the world, God knows.'

'If you ever engage another companion—or take another English girl into your service, Lady Ducayne, I will make all England ring with the story of your wickedness.'

'I want no more girls. I don't believe in his experiments. They have been full of danger for me as well as for the girl—an air bubble, and I should be gone. I'll have no more of his dangerous quackery. I'll find some new man—a better man than you, sir, a discoverer like Pasteur, or Virchow, a genius—to keep me alive. Take your girl away, young man. Marry her if you like.

I'll write her a cheque for a thousand pounds, and let her go and live on beef and beer, and get strong and plump again. I'll have no more such experiments. Do you hear, Parravicini?' she screamed, vindictively, the yellow, wrinkled face distorted with fury, the eyes glaring at him.

The Staffords carried Bella Rolleston off to Varese next day, she very loath to leave Lady Ducayne, whose liberal salary afforded such help for the dear mother. Herbert Stafford insisted, however, treating Bella as coolly as if he had been the family physician, and she had been given over wholly to his care.

'Do you suppose your mother would let you stop here to die?' he asked. 'If Mrs Rolleston knew how ill you are, she would come post haste to fetch you.'

'I shall never be well again till I get back to Walworth,' answered Bella, who was low-spirited and inclined to tears this morning, a reaction after her good spirits of yesterday.

'We'll try a week or two at Varese first,' said Stafford. 'When you can walk half-way up Monte Generoso without palpitation of the heart, you shall go back to Walworth.'

'Poor mother, how glad she will be to see me, and how sorry that I've lost such a good place.'

This conversation took place on the boat when they were leaving Bellaggio. Lotta had gone to her friend's room at seven o'clock that morning, long before Lady Ducayne's withered eyelids had opened to the daylight, before even Francine, the French maid, was astir, and had helped to pack a Gladstone bag with essentials, and hustled Bella downstairs and out of doors before she could make any strenuous resistance.

'It's all right.' Lotta assured her. 'Herbert had a good talk with Lady Ducayne last night and it was settled for you to leave this morning. She doesn't like invalids, you see.'

'No,' sighed Bella, 'she doesn't like invalids. It was very un-lucky that I should break down, just like Miss Tomson and Miss Blandy.'

'At any rate, you are not dead, like them,' answered Lotta, 'and my brother says you are not going to die.'

It seemed rather a dreadful thing to be dismissed in that off-hand way, without a word of farewell from her employer.

'I wonder what Miss Torpinter will say when I go to her for another situation,' Bella speculated, ruefully, while she and her friends were breakfasting on board the steamer.

'Perhaps you may never want another situation,' said Stafford.

'You mean that I may never be well enough to be useful to anybody?'

'No, I don't mean anything of the kind.'

It was after dinner at Varese, when Bella had been induced to take a whole glass of Chianti, and quite sparkled after that unac-customed stimulant, that Mr Stafford produced a letter from his pocket.

'I forgot to give you Lady Ducayne's letter of *adieu*" he said.

'What, did she write to me? I am so glad—I hated to leave her in such a cool way; for after all she was very kind to me, and if I didn't like her it was only because she was too dreadfully old.'

She tore open the envelope. The letter was short and to the point:

'Goodbye, child. Go and marry your doctor. I enclose a farewell gift for your trousseau.—Adeline Ducayne.'

'A hundred pounds, a whole year's salary—no—why, it's for a—A cheque for a thousand!' cried Bella. 'What a generous old soul! She really is the dearest old thing.'

'She just missed being very dear to you, Bella,' said Stafford.

He had dropped into the use of her Christian name while they were on board the boat. It seemed natural now that she was to be in his charge till they all three went back to England.

'I shall take upon myself the privileges of an elder brother till we land at Dover,' he said; 'after that—well, it must be as you please.'

The question of their future relations must have been satisfactorily settled before they crossed the Channel, for Bella's next letter to her mother communicated three startling facts.

First, that the enclosed cheque for £1,000 was to be invested in debenture stock in Mrs Rolleston's name, and was to be her very own, income and principal, for the rest of her life.

Next, that Bella was going home to Walworth immediately.

And last, that she was going to be married to Mr Herbert Stafford in the following autumn.

'And I am sure you will adore him, mother, as much as I do,' wrote Bella. 'It is all good Lady Ducayne's doing. I never could have married if I had not secured that little nest-egg for you.

Herbert says we shall be able to add to it as the years go by, and that wherever we live there shall be always a room in our house for you. The word "mother-in-law" has no terrors for him.'

His Secret

Time out of mind, since the very beginning of things, as it seemed to the parishioners of Boscobel, the Abbey had belonged to a Trevannion, It was not possible to conceive any other association with those old grey walls, those wide gardens and lawns, and flower-beds, melting almost imperceptibly into fair water-meadows, a fertile table-land sheltered by a range of green hills. Boscobel is a little town in a valley, where sweet pastoral Devon borders her wilder sister Cornwall—a quiet little town, nestling in a hollow between moorland and hill, rich in well-watered pastures, and in an ideal trout-stream, and set in the heart of a fine hunting country.

It was a shock to Boscobel when the last of the Trevannions died, leaving only a daughter behind him to inherit the Abbey estate. That the young lady was one of the handsomest women in the neighbourhood offered no consolation, since it was all the more likely that she would marry, and bring a stranger to rule over the estate, and dictate to the tenants, and make things generally unpleasant. The Squire's will stipulated that any such husband was to assume the name and arms of Trevannion: but this, in the opinion of the parish, would be an idle falsification, a poor and shallow pretence. The only Trevannions Boscobel could honour and revere were Trevannions raised on the soil. There was a general leaning to the idea that Miss Trevannion would throw herself away, albeit she was considered a young lady of good parts as well as of fine person. And this foreboding was supposed to be fully realized when it was known that she had engaged herself to Captain Wyatt, who had not an acre of land in the county, and who must therefore necessarily be unworthy of credit.

He was an officer, who had come down to Boscobel to hunt; and his only friend in the neighbourhood was Squire Faversham, of the Copse, a young man who enjoyed the reputation of leading a wild life in London, when he was neither hunting nor shooting in Devonshire. The fact of his friendship with Faversham was taken as all-sufficient evidence that Captain Wyatt was wild, and that whatever means he had possessed at the beginning of his career had been gambled or horse-raced away before now.

Whether this dismal view of the case were true or false, Isabel Trevannion married this stranger to the soil, only six weeks after she met him for the first time at a ball in the old Town Hall; not the splendid Gothic edifice of the existing Boscobel, but the Town Hall of a hundred years ago, when George the Third was king, and when a Devonshire heiress with an estate worth three thousand a year was a much more central and important feature in the world where she lived than she would be nowadays.

Boscobel was so far correct in its theorizing: the Captain was decidedly out-at-elbows. He was a younger son in a good old Shropshire family, in which means were not abundant; and whatever small patrimony had been his at the outset, had dwindled and vanished in the course of a somewhat distinguished military career. He had fought in the East Indies under Clive and Mann, and his handsome features still bore the bronze of an Indian sun. But although Geoffrey Wyatt was about as poorly off as a man could be, his marriage with Isabel Trevannion was not the less a love match.

He had fallen in love with her on that first night at the Town Hall, having ample opportunity to admire the fair frank face, to sun himself in the radiance of blue eyes, during the leisurely progress of country dance and cotillon. He had time while they promenaded the rooms to discover that the girl's mind was as bright as her eyes, and that she was disposed to think well of him. His friend, Squire Faversham, congratulated him on his conquest, as they drove home to Copse Hill in a rumbling old chariot.

'It would have been the making of me, if she'd ever been as civil to me,' said Faversham, with a pang of envy. 'I paid her a good deal of attention last winter, but it was no use. I'm not good-looking enough, I suppose; and then you see these young women like the idea of a soldier—an Indian hero, who may be a lord some day, like Bob Clive.'

The two young men went a few days afterwards to call on the heiress. The Favershams and Trevannions had always been friendly, and the Squire had the right of approach.

Isabel received them with smiles and blushes and happy looks, which were not meant for Faversham. That hare-brained young gentleman knew only too well that it was not for him the blue eyes sparkled and danced so beautifully, while dimples came and went in the fair cheeks. But he was a good-natured youth, and did not want to spoil sport. He asked Isabel to let his friend see the Abbey, which was fall of beauty and interest from an archaeological point of view, and she rose gaily to accompany them through the rooms.

'Servants are so stupid,' she said, 'they can never explain things properly. I had better take Mr. Faversham's friend round myself, had I not, Auntie?'

This question was addressed to the dearest old lady in the world, who pretended to take care of Isabel, but whose guardianship was very mildly exercised; insomuch as she spent her existence knitting, or reading the British Essayists, in one particular armchair, which stood by the fire in winter and in a sunny window in summer, and never troubled herself about anything, so long as her niece was well and happy. The question was therefore merely a matter of form. The old lady smiled and nodded; the young one went off with the two gentlemen. The house took a long time to see. It was so rich in relics and memories; the remains of old monastic days, the portraits of dead and gone ancestors; curious little cabinet pictures collected in the Low Countries, mosaics and marbles bought by dilettante Trevannions in their Italian travels. Miss Trevannion and her guests lingered in the corridors, where there were most inviting velvet-cushioned window-seats. They loitered over the old china, Isabel explaining and exhibiting the family treasures with a pardonable pride. She had seen so little of this world, outside Boscobel Abbey, that she might be forgiven if she fancied the old house just the one most interesting thing in the universe. Her father had been born in it, her mother had lived and died in it, and she had loved them both so well, that the mere sense of its association with them made the gray old mansion sacred. She was pleased by Captain Wyatt's warm admiration of the place.

'You ought to see the gardens in summer,' she said, as they stood in one of the windows looking out at blossom-less lawns.

When summer came Geoffrey Wyatt was master at Boscobel Abbey, and signed himself Wyatt Trevannion. His wife idolized him, and he doted upon her; yet, like many doting lovers, they sometimes quarrelled. That even and placid affection which the poet calls thrice blessed was not theirs. They were both hot-tempered; the heiress had always been, in the language of admiring friends, high-spirited; and her high spirit showed itself occasionally, even to an idolized husband.

She was jealous, suspicious of his attentions to other women; and it was Geoffrey's habit to be attentive to every pretty woman. She was jealous of his pleasures—hated him to be away from her; and she could not quite forget that he owed her everything, that he had been penniless Geoffrey Wyatt of nowhere in particular before her love made him Wyatt Trevannion, master of the dearest old house in the world, and the first gentleman in Boscobel. It never occurred to her rustic innocence that Boscobel was a very small dominion in which to be Prince Consort.

Aunt Tabitha, the dear little old lady in black brocade and gold-rimmed spectacles, did her best to keep peace between the married lovers, so long as she sat beside their hearth; but the first winter of their domestic life saw the evanishment of that gentle figure, and then there was no one to murmur tender little conciliatory speeches when the two quarrelled. Happily their quarrels, though not unfrequent, were brief, and generally ended with one of those tender reconciliations which are said to be the renewal of love.

Several winters and summers had come and gone since Geoffrey looked out at the Abbey gardens for the first time, and it could not be said that Isabel was otherwise than happy in her married life. There were no children, but this fact was taken to heart much more deeply by the inhabitants of Boscobel in general than by Isabel herself. She loved her husband too entirely and profoundly to have any sense of loss in the absence of other ties. So long as she had him she had everything; her chief trouble was that she had not always him.

He was an ardent sportsman, and from September to April his days were devoted to hunting and shooting. He was fond of racing, and in the summer was often away at distant race meetings. He had a modest racing stud of his own, and had won cups in a small way. Isabel had never grudged him the money which he wasted on this expensive amusement; but she resented his frequent absence from home, and this was their chief ground of quarrel.

It was a delicious morning in July, and Geoffrey had returned the night before from one of those odious race-meetings, and there was no hunting or shooting possible—not even otter-hunting. Isabel and her husband strolled in the lovely old gardens; all flowers and sunlight, and velvet lawn and glancing shadows of birds; she with her hands clasped round his arm, he looking down with tender admiration at the beautiful face, the soft chestnut hair falling in loose curls upon the white neck.

'Upon my soul you grow handsomer every day, Belle!' he exclaimed.

'If you really think so it must be because you see me so seldom,' she said, pleased at his praise, yet with an undertone of resentment. 'I possess that charm of novelty which other men's wives can hardly have.'

'I protest now, Bella, I was only away a fortnight this last bout; a fortnight from here to York and back again, allowing three days for the races. If you knew at what a rate I travelled, every bone in my body shaken within an inch of dislocation in their confounded post-chaises.'

'I wish it might cure you of ever wanting to go away again, love,' she said, ' and then I would be grateful to York races all the days of my life.'

'You ought to be very grateful as it is for the cup I won for you with Meer Jaffier. I don't think you've so much as looked at it since I put it in the glass case in the hall.'

'Those cups in the hall will get the house robbed some of these days,' answered Isabel petulantly. 'Vulgar, ugly things! I hate the sight of them, for they remind me how much of my married life I have had to spend alone.'

'You know you might sometimes go with me, if you pleased,' remonstrated Geoffrey.

'Yes, and have my bones shaken in your post-chaises, and mix with the horrible coarse creatures you meet at such places, and see sights and hear language which would make me despise myself for the rest of my life. Why cannot you stay at home, where we are so happy?'

'Yes, love, thank God we are very happy. Let us make the most of our happiness while it lasts; one can never tell how long the sun may shine. Is not this summer morning lovely—and that sunny stretch of grass—and the river beyond it—and the lights and shadows dancing on the hill? I have been reminded of my own good fortune today by a long letter from an unhappy beggar who was my brother officer and my equal in everything, before I won your love. Don't you think such a comparison as that should make me grateful to Providence ? What am I better than Jasper Dane that I should be so blest by Fate?'

'Jasper Dane. Is that your friend's name? Tell me all about him,' Isabel answered gently, touched by her husband's talk of his happiness.

What could she wish for in life more than to make him happy! She knew that she had sometimes wounded him, had been cruel and bitter of speech, out of overweening love which ran into jealousy.

'He is one of the cleverest fellows I ever knew,' said Geoffrey; 'not showy or brilliant, but a man of unbounded common sense and solidity. We were together in India. He fought like a devil at Buxar, and yet he is one of those slender, pale-faced men who would seem more in his place in a library. He rose from the ranks—a small tradesman's son, who ran away from home on account of a stepmother's severity; and some of our fellows slighted him on that score. But thank God I had none of their petty prejudices.

'Dane was the cleverest officer in the regiment, and about the best behaved, and he and I were close friends. And now he has left the army, broken in health, he tells me, and he wants civilian's employment of some kind, and fancies I can help him. Yet, Heaven knows how I could do so, unless'—here he hesitated a little, as if his thoughts were straying far ahead of his speech—'unless you would like me to carry out an idea which has come into my head while I have been talking to you.'

'I should like you to do anything that is kind and friendly to an old friend, answered Isabel. 'But what is this idea of yours?'

'I've been thinking what a capital fellow Jasper would be to manage your property for me—a kind of steward and accountant; a factotum to look after everything and keep everybody else in check. We've a bailiff for the home-farm, but the bailiff wants supervision; and we've an agent to collect the rents, and draw up leases, and so on; but we want a general custodian; one all-pervading mind; a man who could have no interest outside our interests. I have often felt the want of such a fellow—a man who would have the pluck to pull me up when I was spending too much money—who wouldn't be afraid to tell me I was a fool!'

'I don't think you'd like that, Geoffrey, even from Mr. Dane.'

'Oh yes, I should. Dane is one of those plain-sailing, hard-headed fellows, from whom one can stand a great deal. He used to talk to me very freely in days gone by.'

'Perhaps,' answered Isabel; 'but then you were not my husband.'

'To be sore, that makes a difference, doesn't it? But I think I could bear Dane's lecturing even now, knowing it was all for my own good. He was adjutant of our regiment—a wonderful hand at accounts; a thoroughly commercial mind, inherited from the tradesman father, no doubt. And you would not find him a disagreeable fellow about the house. He is very quiet and gentlemanlike, and has refined tastes.'

'In spite of the tradesman father?'

'Oh, blood will tell of course. I daresay you would see a difference between him and a man of family.'

'Like Faversham, for instance, who made me an offer in a letter which might have been written by my cowboy—and then was surprised that I refused to marry him. Will it please you to have this Mr. Dane here, Geoffrey?'

'I really think it will be a relief to my mind,' answered her husband. 'I have felt myself getting into a financial muddle lately, and I believe that we both are cheated and imposed upon to a large extent. Yon are so generous, and I am so careless. A cool, clear-headed fellow like Dane would be a treasure to us.'

'And you will not let him interfere with our domestic life? You will not let him deprive me of your society?'

'My dearest, what are you thinking of? I want the man for his usefulness—not for his company.'

This assurance satisfied Mrs. Trevannion, and her husband wrote to his old friend by that evening's mail, offering him rooms at the Abbey, with a modest salary. 'As the movement is one of economy you must not expect me to be lavish!' he wrote. 'I daresay with your talents you might do something better, but place-hunting is hard work. You say you are out of health. Our mild climate, pure air, and quiet life ought to go a long way towards curing you; and perhaps you may like to be domiciled with an old friend who has not forgotten old times.'

Dane wrote by return of poet, gratefully accepting the offer; and a week afterwards he came to the Abbey, arriving in the late twilight of a lovely day.

Geoffrey and his wife were sitting on the terrace in front of the drawing-room windows, with their field and household favourites—a brace of Irish setters, a Blenheim spaniel, and a greyhound or two grouped about them. In a home where there are no children, dogs are apt to come conspicuously into the foreground.

The butler brought Mr. Dane to the terrace, and the two men greeted each other heartily; Geoffrey receiving his friend with loud-voiced genial welcome, Jasper Dane quietly cordial

'If you knew How cheering it is to be so welcomed in such a home as this after ten years of Indian exile, you would have some idea of what I must feel for your husband, Mrs. Trevannion,' said Mr. Dane, when Geoffrey had presented him to the mistress of the Abbey.

She murmured some vague civility, and looked at him, not unkindly but critically, a little doubtful as to her wisdom in having allowed a new element to be introduced into her domestic life. 'I hope he will keep his place,' she thought.

The man looked every inch a gentleman, in spite of his obscure origin. He was tall and slim, pale, delicate-featured, with dreamy gray eyes, and the whitest hands Mrs. Trevannion had ever seen in a man. Indian suns which had baked Geoffrey's complexion to a warrior-like bronze, had only given a faint yellow tinge, like the hue of old ivory, to Jasper's pale countenance. He had never affected out-of-door pursuits, preferring books and seclusion.

'He looks as if he would keep his place,' mused Mrs. Trevannion, whose chief thought about the stranger was an ardent hope that she and her husband might see as little as possible of him.

'If he absorbs Geoffrey I shall hate him,' she said to herself.

The first effect of Mr. Dane's arrival was to give Mrs. Trevannion more of her husband's society than she had enjoyed before his coming. His scrutiny of the financial position revealed a state of things which demanded an immediate narrowing of Captain Wyatt-Trevannion's expenses. He had been spending his wife's money with the recklessness of a man who, having had hitherto to deal with hundreds, believed thousands inexhaustible. With crave straightforwardness, Jasper Dane showed his friend that he had been imposing on his wife's generosity, taking an unworthy advantage of her unquestioning love. If he were to continue his present course, he would end by encumbering the Trevannion estate by making his wife a beggar. The first thing to be done was to give up the racing stud.

'It's such a small one,' said Geoffrey, pathetically.

'It is big enough to spoil two thousand a year,' answered Dane. 'And then there are your bets.'

'A gentleman ought to back his own horses. It shows good faith,' said Geoffrey. 'But the stud shall be sold, and I'll bet no more. You are right, Dane. Bell has been too generous to me. I am bound to consider her welfare above everything. But a country gentleman's life without a racing stable is deucedly humdrum.'

'Humdrum, with such a wife as yours,' exclaimed Dane, with a faint glow on his sallow cheeks. 'You ought to be happy with her in a desert island.'

'I'm going to sell the racers, so you needn't sermonize,' retorted Geoffrey; and the horses were sold at Exeter shortly afterwards, Mr. Dane having held his friend to his resolution, meanwhile, with a firmness of hand remarkable in a dependent. Indeed, there were many things in which Mr. Dane soon showed himself master; Geoffrey's self-indulgent nature lending itself easily to leading-strings.

There was ample room for an independent existence in the spacious old Abbey. Mr. Dane had his own suite of rooms at the end of a southward-fronting wing, rooms which opened on the picture-gallery, where the effigies of departed Trevannions scowled or simpered under a top-light. He had sent to London for two large chests of books, the companions of his Indian exile, and with these, which were special in character, and the somewhat common-place library of the Abbey he had plenty of material for thought and study. He seemed fond of solitude— only came to the drawing-room when he was particularly invited, and gave Mrs. Trevannion no ground for complaining that he did not keep his place.

She was very grateful to him for the sale of the race-horses, and was too impulsive to refrain from letting him know her gratitude.

'Do you know I had an impression that we were being ruined,' she said; 'but I could not tell Geoffrey so. It would have seemed ungenerous.'

'You are a wonderful woman,' said Mr. Dane, looking at her gravely. 'A wonderful wife, and Geoffrey ought to be the happiest fellow in creation.'

'Well, I hope he is moderately happy. I only live to please him. Why do we not see more of you, Mr. Dane?' she went on in a little gush of kindliness, forgetting how anxious she had been to keep him out of the sanctuary of domestic life.

Happily Jasper Dane was too modest or too fond of solitude to take undue advantage of her kindness— but on those rare evenings which he spent with them, his society proved so agreeable to both husband and wife, that before he had been a year at the Abbey, his presence became a natural element in their lives, and, he was seldom out of their company. They had both a high opinion of his capacity, and an unlimited belief in his faithfulness, and they appealed to his superior wisdom and experience continually. He was a link between Geoffrey and his happy-go-lucky youth—that youth which a man is apt faintly to regret amidst the calmer blessings of mature life.

He was companionable to the wife in many things in which her husband could not be her companion. She had studied French and Italian literature, and he was the first person whom she had ever met able to talk to her of Corneille and Racine, Danto and Tasso. She was fond of music, and here was the very first listener who seemed thoroughly to understand and appreciate Bach. She had a taste for art, which went beyond painting on velvet, and the beautification of fire-screens, and Mr. Dane was able to assist her with his superior technical skill and knowledge.

He taught her chess, and they played many a long thoughtful game together beside the winter fire, while Geoffrey sprawled in his armchair, and slept the sleep of the tired sportsman, his only consciousness of existence a dim sense of ineffable content, mixed with the sputter and sparkle of the wide wood fire.

By the time Jasper Dane had been three years at the Abbey, Mr. and Mrs. Trevannion had come to regard him as a necessary part of their existence. It would be impossible for either to get on without him. They both owed him so much, that each would have been ashamed to confess the extent of the debt, and could only cancel it by silent gratitude. For it was not only that he had set their house in order, and introduced golden rules of thrift and method into a disorderly household, but he had brought the element of domestic peace into their lives.

The horse-racing being put aside, Geoffrey's absences from home rarely went beyond a long day's hunting or shooting; and when he was away, Mr. Dane's company went far to enliven the monotony of the tranquil hours. It was not that he intruded upon the wife's solitude; but he was in his rooms—or in the gardens—somewhere on the premises, to be appealed to if he were wanted. He was always ready to be consulted about small details—a dinner, or a hunting breakfast, an archery meeting, or any entertainment which the lady of the Abbey considered it her duty to provide for her neighbours. He took a genuine interest in these things, which always bored Geoffrey. Altogether life was harmonized into smoothness by his presence; and yet he was one of the most unobtrusive of men.

Geoffrey behaved wondrously well about the racing stable. He sighed in secret over its surrender; but he never told his wife how much the sacrifice cost him, or how sorely he missed the excitement of the turf, the intercourse with the outer world, with men of keener wit than his familiar friends of the hunt. Dane was always reminding him, in a friendly way, that he owed everything to his wife and had no right to squander her money—so when the old master of the staghounds died, and the neighbourhood wanted Captain Wyatt Trevannion to take the hounds, Geoffrey resolutely refused that honour, congenial as the office would have been to him. He told himself that Dane had spoken the truth. He had no right to waste his wife's money.

'I'm afraid if I go on in this way I shall dwindle into a stay-at-home husband, tied to my wife's apron-strings,' he thought; 'but it is something to know that Belle is happier than she used to be.'

Belle was, indeed, completely happy in these days. She hung about her husband as tenderly as she had done in the first year of her married life; and there were now few flashes of jealousy, or little gusts of bitter speech. Geoffrey was getting older. He did not admire pretty women so much as of old—was content to sun himself in that one beautiful face which he had a legal right to worship. Perhaps the placid monotony of prosperous idleness was slowly sapping his energies.

He had lost much of his old fire and impetuosity; but he was better tempered than when his wits were kept on the rack by the hazards of horse-racing, and he was more devoted to his wife than ever. The worthy inhabitants of Boscobel began to forgive him for his audacity in marrying Miss Trevannion, and readily acknowledged that he made a very good husband, and was a pleasant, hospitable kind of man to have at the Abbey, a very fair substitute for the extinct male line of the Trevannions.

There was only one cloud upon Isabel Trevannion's happiness at this period of her life, and that arose from a suspicion which she tried to dismiss from her thoughts as a foolish fancy, perhaps even an unworthy inspiration of feminine vanity.

'I hope I am not that kind of women,' she had said to herself more than once; 'a woman who believes that no man can escape falling in love with her.'

Yet, reason with herself as she might, the vague uncomfortable suspicion would flit across her mind now and again, that her husband's devoted friend and faithful steward cared for her more than was well for his peace. He had never by word or look offended her modesty. She was not a woman to live an hour under the same roof with a man who could so offend. He had been her faithful servant, her frequent companion for three placid, monotonous years: and he had never failed in the most profound respect that man can pay to woman.

Custom had not lessened his reverence for her. Had she been a queen she could not have received a more unvarying homage. Yet, by some subtle power of expression, by something so undefinable and mysterious that it seemed a kind of magnetism, he had revealed a feeling which she needs must pity, even while she tried to shut her mind against the fact of its existence.

She did pity him. There were traces of pain sometimes in that pale spiritual face which touched her heart with divine compassion. There was a mute fidelity of affection which she could neither mistake nor resent. Was she not indebted to Jasper Dane for the happiness which had made her domestic life perfect? His thoughtful wisdom, his outspoken fidelity, had given her back her husband.

As that vague suspicion of hers grew into something very near akin to certainty, Isabel contrived to spend less of her life in Mr. Dane's society. Music, art, literature, had made a meeting point for their sympathies. The lady seemed all at once to have grown weary of her books, her easel, her harpsichord. She had a sudden passion for the out-of-door life of which her husband was so fond. She rode with him, accompanied him on his trout fishing expeditions in the woody combes, following each lovely wind and reach of the romantic river.

'I hope I don't plague you with my company, Geoffrey,' she said. 'It makes me very happy to be with you.'

'Plague me, love! Do you suppose I am not glad of such a companion? You used to be such a stay-at-home, with your nose always in a book, like Dane, or studying tweedle-dum and tweedle-dee on that harpsichord of yours.'

'Do you think the change is for the better, dearest?' she asked with that vein of *coquetry* which is in the grain of a woman's love.

'I should be a curmudgeon if I did not,' he answered, laying down his rod, in order to throw his arm round the matron's slim waist, and to administer a sounding kiss on the blushing cheek. 'I shall mount you on the best hunter that was ever backed, and you shall follow the stag-hounds with me next winter.'

'I should like it of all things, Geoffrey; but don't you think it would set people talking?'

There were very few hunting ladies in those days.

'Let them talk! They shall say how handsome my wife looks when she's flushed with a quick run.'

All through the decline of summer and the slow decay of autumn, Geoffrey Trevannion and his wife were close companions; the lady spending very little of her life apart from her husband, and Jasper Dane thrown back upon a severely business-like existence. He had a great deal to do in his character of land steward, rode far and wide upon the steady old brown hack which Trevannion had allotted to him, and spent all his leisure in the seclusion of his own rooms.

'I believe Dane is writing a book,' said Geoffrey, laughing heartily at what he considered a prodigious joke; 'I see his light burning every night when we go to bed. I wonder whether it is a tragedy, or a treatise on metaphysics. He looks capable of either. I used to accuse him of writing verses when we were in India.'

One day in the beginning of November, Geoffrey and his friend went for a long ride together. The master of the Abbey was required to inspect some farm buildings which wanted important repairs; an improvement so costly that Mr. Dane refused to order it upon his own responsibility. The farm was between eleven and twelve miles from the Abbey, and the two gentlemen were away a long time upon their errand, and came back looking fagged by their ride.

'What is the matter, Geoffrey?' Mrs. Trevannion asked anxiously, as her husband stretched himself in his arm-chair before the drawing-room fire, while he waited for the dinner bell; 'I never saw you look so pale.'

'It was a chilly, wearisome ride, and Dane plagued my soul

out with his talk about business. I am sorry to tell you that he is going to leave us.'

She gave a little start, and the colour faded from her cheek, as if with the apprehension of evil. The fear which startled her was vague and far off, but it was fear.

'I am sorry for your sake,' she said quietly. 'I'm afraid you will miss him.'

'Yes, I shall have to take to business habits, to manage the property myself. I never could trust a stranger as I have trusted Dane. I knew he was incorruptible—rectitude itself in money matters. He is a man of few wants and no extravagances. Yes, he is a loss—but he must go. It is best so.'

'He is not happy with us?'

'Evidently not since he wishes to go.'

'It was his wish to leave us?'

'Yes, his and mine too. He gave me reasons which I could not gainsay. I have no right to consider my own interest before everything; useful as he has been to me I must school myself to do without him. I am afraid your estate will have a bad manager, Belle, but I shall do my best. I think, perhaps, if you were to help me a little—you have a clearer head than I have, and you know something of Dane's system—'

'Yes, he has told me a good deal,' answered Isabel eagerly. 'Why should we not manage our estate? When is Mr. Dane to go?'

'Early next week. He is going to put everything in order—to explain all his papers—and to give me all the help he can for carrying on everything upon his own plan. He has been very useful to us. We were getting poor before he came. We have been getting rich since he took our affairs in hand.'

'And I have been ever so much happier, Geoffrey,' answered Isabel, with her hand on her husband's shoulder.

She was secretly rejoiced at Dane's decision, now that the first faint thrill of fear was over. It was as if a tremendous weight had been lifted off her mind. Of late she had dreaded every meeting with the pale, earnest-eyed steward. The chief study of her life had been to avoid him without seeming to do so.

Mr. Dane did not appear that evening; he dined in his own room, and worked late after dinner. Four o'clock was the aristocratic dinner-hour in those days, and winter evenings were long. Isabel opened her harpsichord for the first time for some months, and began a light, airy Gigue of Handel's. Jasper Dane heard the gay bright music from his room above, and his face flushed angrily at the sound. It seemed to him like a little gush of joy at his announced departure. As if her heart were rejoicing in a sense of recovered freedom.

'No doubt I have been an incubus. She has seen and understood,' he said to himself.

On the next day and the next Mr. Dane was hard at work, arranging papers and going over accounts, setting his house in order before leaving it. Geoffrey spent some hours of each day in his friend's room, receiving his instructions, learning how he had managed household expenses, repairs, out-of-door servants, stable, and garden. Nothing had been too insignificant for his stewardship. Rectitude and plain-dealing were shown in every detail of his management.

The third day was Sunday, Jasper Dane's last day at Boscobel Abbey. He was to leave by the London coach, at seven o'clock next morning.

Boscobel, never remarkable for stir or haste in its streets, a place indeed which always seemed half asleep, save when mildly revived by market-day, wore its Sabbath solemnity with a difference. There were more people in the streets; people in Sunday clothes, going to or coming from the old Gothic church; boys in sleek broad-cloth, without the least idea of what to do with their Sabbath leisure, and yawningly longing for dinner or supper time. Bells clashed out at intervals upon the dim autumn stillness, with unnecessary vehemence; perhaps in remonstrance with the dissenters, who preferred chapel, even without bells.

Unless a man had a full mind, or a love of nature deep enough to find enchantment in the calm beauty of woodland, hill, and river, Sunday at Boscobel was passing dreary. Geoffrey Trevannion was apt to feel the Sabbath hours hang heavily, even in the company of a beloved wife. He went to church once at least, as in duty bound, and he, Isabel, and Mr. Dane made a triangle of worshippers in the large square pew, where the green baize cushions had been slowly fading for the last half century, to a dull gray.

The three knelt together this day for the last time, and it seemed as if the thought that it was so made them paler and graver than usual. They dined together after church, and spent the evening together in the spacious panelled drawing-room, with its lofty open fireplace and glorious pile of logs, burning out the dampness and chillness of those creeping November mists which wrapped all the outside world in a dim veil.

Mrs. Trevannion had been brought up in habits of simple piety, and to her Sunday evening was not as other evenings. She liked to read some religious book aloud to her husband—a sermon of Jeremy Taylor's, a chapter of Law's *Serious Call* to which Geoffrey listened with sleepy submissiveness. Then, by way of reward, she would play Handel's sacred airs, with tender, delicate touch, on her harpsichord.

This was the first Sunday evening which Dane had spent in the drawing-room for a long time. He listened to the sermon with his earnest eyes fixed on the reader in gravest contemplation, as if he were hearing something more than the sermon— as if he were listening to the Book of Fate. He hung over the harpsichord like a man entranced.

'When shall I ever hear such melody again?' he said, with a half-cynical air; 'not unless I get to Heaven, I suppose.'

'You are going to London,' said Isabel, 'where you will have the Oratorios and the King's Theatre.'

'It will not be such music as this. Besides, I am not going to stay in London. I shall volunteer to join the army in America.'

Neither Mr. Trevannion nor his wife questioned the wisdom of such an act. Geoffrey sat staring idly at the fire. Isabel touched the keys of her harpsichord silently, deep in thought.

Presently the Abbey clock chimed the half-hour after nine,

and the servants came filing in to family prayer. It was Isabel's duty to read the prayers as well as the sermon. She read them tonight in a firm, clear voice, and there was a fervour in her tone as of one relieved from trouble. The short Psalm which she read after prayers was one of thanksgiving.

'She has a heart of stone!' Jasper Dane said to himself. 'If it were flesh and blood it would bleed for me.'

When these devotions were finished, he came over to her, and held out his hand.

'Goodnight and goodbye, Mrs. Trevannion; I shall have left before you come down to breakfast.'

'Goodnight and goodbye,' she answered, looking straight before her, and letting her cold white fingers lie in his hand for an instant.

'Marble!—a mere piece of human marble!' he said to himself, as he turned away from her.

'I suppose I shall see you, Geoffrey?'

'Yes, I shall be astir before seven.'

And then all the house went to bed, and there was darkness throughout the Abbey, save for a night-lamp burning dimly in Mrs. Trevannion's bedchamber, a large tapestried room looking towards the Abbey church and the green hills behind.

The Abbey lay wrapped in its veil of river and meadow fog, and even that small light was hidden.

PART 2

There was horror in Boscobel, each as had not been known within the memory of living man, when the alarm-bell of the Abbey rung shrill in the early gray of the November morning, and men were told that Squire Trevannion had been found stabbed through the heart at the foot of his own staircase. The Abbey, guarded as few houses are guarded, by barred shutters and massive bolts, had been broken into by thieves; a pane of glass had been smashed in a narrow window in the hall, a piece cut out of the heavy shutter inside, and the bar removed. It was so narrow a window that the person entering by it must have been of slim figure—a mere slip of a boy, the constable conjectured; but a boy old enough and skilful enough to unlock and unbar the great house door without alarming the household, and to admit his confederates.

The glass cupboard in the hall had been emptied of its racing cups and jewelled-hilted swords. It was with one of these dainty court rapiers that Geoffrey Trevannion had been stabbed to death. The slim triangular blade was snapped short, near the hilt, and the chased silver hilt was missing. The thieves had begun their attack upon the plate-room. That was clear enough from the traces of their chisels on the iron-lined door; but before they could get the door open—it was in a passage behind the nail—they had been interrupted in their work by Geoffrey Trevannion, who had heard footsteps below, and had come downstairs to investigate.

One of the ruffians had been watching in the hall, while the others attacked the plate-room, and this man had stabbed Geoffrey before he could give the alarm to his household.

Mrs. Trevannion had not heard her husband leave the room, but waking a little before daybreak, she had taken alarm at his absence, and bad rung her bell, and roused the household; and the servant, going to open the hall shutters, found a window open, and his master lying at the foot of the stairs in a pool of blood.

Of course a great deal of this history rested on conjecture-on the constable's acumen in putting links together, and making them into a chain. There was the violated window; there were the marks on the strong-room door: there was the empty cupboard, which had held not only the racing-caps, but half-a-dozen tankards, from Cromwell to Queen Anne, which would now be worth their weight in gold. There was the broken sword. There were traces of muddy boots on the black and white marble pavement of the hall, and there were confused marks of footsteps on the gravel outside, as if two or three men and passed in and out of the hall door. It was all plain enough m the constable's mind; he had never known a clearer story.

'We'll have the Hue-and-cry out before tonight!' he said. 'Madam will offer a reward, I suppose?' he inquired of Mr. Dane, who stood grave and self-possessed amidst the frightened servants.

He had been interrupted in his final preparations for his journey by Mrs. Trevannion's bell, and had been one of the first to come down to the hall when the horrified footman gave the alarm.

'She will do all that is right. I believe she would give half her fortune to discover the murderer. Poor lady, it is dreadful to think of her grief. She worshipped her husband.'

'Yes, we all know that,' answered the constable, who was an old inhabitant. 'He was a fine English gentleman, a thorough sportsman, and everybody in Boscobel respected him. Folks didn't take to him just at first you see. It took time. He was a stranger, and hadn't no property of his own; and we didn't none of us think him good enough for Miss Trevannion; but he turned out the right stamp. He was true metal, kep' a good table, and a good stable, and spent his money in the town. That's what *I* call a gentleman! It's a great loss!'

The constable sighed, and thought it was time for him to get something in the way of refreshment. Mr. Dane was too preoccupied to think of such details, but the housekeeper would no doubt attend to the necessities of the hour; even though her master's corpse had just been carried up yonder staircase to the noble old tapestried bedchamber, where Solomon and the Queen of Sheba had looked down on his placid slumbers, and were now to see him lying stark under the linen sheet. While Jasper Dane stood in the open doorway, lost in thought, Mr. Truepenny, the constable, quietly retired to the servants' hall, feeling assured that Mrs. Baker, the housekeeper, would know what was right to be done in a liberal household, even under the present distressing circumstances.

Isabel Trevannion lay on a sofa In her dressing-room, next the tapestried chamber, shut in with her mighty grief—such a sorrow, it seemed to her, as no other woman had ever been called upon to bear. Her husband foully murdered in the full flush and vigour of manhood, slumbering peacefully by her side a few hours ago, now sleeping in death's icy sleep upon the same marriage-bed. Sudden death must always be awful, but could any death be so awful as this—so pitiful—so unnecessary—not the work of Providence, but the wickedness of men; ignorant, brutal men, greedy only for gain; having no grudge against their victim; no injury to avenge; only the professional criminal's reckless indifference to human life or human misery.

'I would have given them all my fortune; would have gone out of this house penniless, if they would but have spared him.'

Her grief had to be borne, and borne alone, and in darkness. She would see no one— not even the faithful Abigail who had once been her nurse, and who idolized her—not even Jasper Dane, who sent from time to time to ascertain her commands as the desolate days went by, under gray clouds, or shrouded in their dim autumnal mists, and the dreary ceremonials attending such a death had to be gone through—the inquest—the inquiry before the magistrates— the funeral.

All had to be attended to; and Jasper Dane was on the spot, cool, collected, a thorough man of business, ready to answer every question. Of his sincere sorrow for his mend's untimely fate no one could doubt. It was obvious in his every look and word, but he made no parade of his feelings. He had postponed his journey to London for a short time only, and had transferred himself and his belongings to the Duke's Head, the chief inn at Boscobel, a quiets reputable hostelry.

'I shall stay here as long as I can be of use to Mrs. Trevannion,' he told the Vicar; 'but I mean to fight the Provincials.'

There was a strong feeling—a thorough-going Tory feeling, the King and Lord North for ever—about the American war at Boscobel, and the Vicar was quite ready to sympathize with Mr. Dane in his desire to take up arms again for King George. Everybody in the town knew that he had fought the blacks, under Clive, and had won some distinction in an outlandish, far-away world. He had contrived to make himself respected in the place. There had been no meanness in his administration of his friend's affairs, careful as it had been. He had so carried himself in his somewhat delicate position as to win every man's good word. And now it seemed only natural that the thirst for military glory should revive in him, and that he should want to cross the Atlantic.

He attended Geoffrey Trevannion's funeral, he waited till all inquiries as to his friend's death had terminated. The "Hue-and-Cry" had availed nothing—the police of that day had been able to find no trace of the murderer, or of the missing property. It seemed as if the burglary at Boscobel Abbey were doomed to swell the record of undiscovered crimes. Racing-cups and tankards had been melted down, no doubt. The thieves had gone their ways on the evil road to crime, indifferent as to the honest man's blood that they had shed and the loving woman's heart that they had broken.

Before he left the little west-country town, Jasper Dane begged for an interview with Mrs. Trevannion; but she refused to see him, albeit Sarah Dodd, her faithful waiting-woman, pleaded for him earnestly.

'He looks so pale and unhappy, madam,' she said, 'and I think it would be a comfort to you to talk about poor master to one that loved him as Mr. Dane did.'

'Nothing can give me any comfort—no one. Not even God, who sees and knows my misery!' answered Isabel, and in her white rigid face Sarah saw no sign of relenting.

'It seems hard for him to go away without bidding you goodbye,'—she said, persistently, not so much because she cared for Mr. Dane's feelings, as that she thought it would be good to rouse her mistress out of this dull stupor of grief—'after being like one of the family for nearly four years, and he going to America, too, to be shot, I daresay, like so many of our brave soldiers.'

But Isabel Trevannion never lifted her eyes from that spot upon the carpet where their dull gaze rested. For her it seemed as if the world had held only one man, and he was dead. What to her was the war in America—spies hanged on either side—garrisons massacred—victories—defeats. It was of no more account to her than a war in the planet Mars. Her husband, her first and only love, was murdered. She sat staring at the carpet, and thinking of the county ball where she first met Geoffrey Wyatt, where they had been partners in three country dances, and were deep in love with each other before the night was done.

Sarah Dodd went downstairs to Mr. Dane with a point-blank refusal. 'It ain't no use, she won't see no one.' she said; throwing in superfluous negatives for the sake of emphasis.

'Did she send me no message—no kindly word?' asked Jasper, lingering on the threshold of the now cheerless house.

'Lord, no, sir; she sits all day like a statter—she hasn't a word for any of us.'

Mr. Dane gave Sarah a guinea, and turned his back upon the Abbey. His trunks and portmanteaux were at the 'Duke's Head' ready for the coach. He was gone before breakfast-time next morning; and before the week was ended Boscobel was beginning to forget him.

It was a surprise for the town when his name appeared during the following year in the newspapers, and when, as the next year, and the next went by, the grave, quiet gentleman who had done a steward's work at Boscobel Abbey, was praised for the display of distinguished valour during the changing fortunes of that terrible war which now challenged the attention of Europe.

It was two years and a half since the burglary at Boscobel Abbey, and the struggle on the other side of the Atlantic was still caging fiercely, when Isabel Trevannion sat on the terrace in front of the drawing-room windows, with her dogs grouped round her in the clear evening light, very much as she had been seated years ago, when Jasper Dane came to the Abbey—except that the husband, who sat beside her then, could never be her companion again on this side of Eternity.

His dog fawned at her knee, Duke, his favourite pointer, which she loved better than all her favourites—for the dead man's sake. But human companion she had none. She sat alone, her fair face shaded and chastened by a look of settled sorrow.

The Church and Abbey clocks were striking the half-hour after eight, the light was mellowing behind the broad boughs of the cedars on the lawn, twilight shadows were creeping up amidst the foliage of the shrubbery, and the colours of the flowers took a deeper glow as the sunset-hues brightened in the low western sky. Mrs. Trevannion closed the volume on her lap, and sat in a reverie, looking dreamily towards the sinking sun. She had never left the Abbey since her husband's death.

Many women would have fled from the house, as from an accursed place, would have put the ocean between them and the scene of such terrible memories; but Isabel hugged her grief and brooded upon it. She turned a deaf ear to the pleading of those friends who tried to tempt her to their houses. 'I like to be near him,' she answered quietly. 'If his tomb were big enough, I would like to live in it. I stay as near him as I can.' Her eyes wandered towards the churchyard, which adjoined the Abbey gardens. She could see her husband's tomb from her favourite seat on the terrace. The Abbey and the Abbey church had originally been one institution.

Little by little Mrs. Trevannion's friends had reconciled themselves to her seclusion, and had come to regard the Abbey as the tomb of the living. They called on her occasionally, but such visits were far from festive. The pale, beautiful woman, in deepest sables, exercised a depressing influence on her guests. It was, perhaps, kinder to leave her alone.

Tonight her thoughts wandered to Jasper Dane, as they had often done lately, in consequence of the mention of his name in the American news. It was on just such an evening—a sweet, peaceful summer evening—that he had first come to the Abbey. The only difference was that her cup then brimmed over with joy, as it now overflowed with sorrow. While this thought was in her mind, she looked up and saw Jasper Dane coming slowly along the gravel-walk; the white, wan ghost of his former self.

Had she loved him, or had she been superstitious, she might have taken that shrunken figure for a very ghost. As it was she had no such thought. She saw the change, and, in a world from which all she loved had perished, it seemed to her only natural that another should be so changed. He was worn to a shadow, and his empty coat sleeve was fastened to his breast. His right arm had been amputated.

She rose and gave him her hand, forgetful of everything in the past, save that he had been her husband's friend.

'I am going a little further west—to the Cornish moors,' he said, 'and I could not pass so near Boscobel without asking to see you.'

'I am sorry to see you looking so ill,' she answered, as they sat down on each side of the table, which held a tea- tray and a pile of books.

The Blenheim spaniel, which had always been a favourite of Mr. Dane's, received him with evident recognition; but Geoffrey's pointer slunk away, and did wonderful things with his spine, in the endeavour to creep under Mrs. Trevannion's armchair, from which shelter he shot baleful glances at the visitor from topaz-coloured eyes.

'I have been a little unlucky,' Jasper answered carelessly. 'I got my arm shot off in our last skirmish, and I had fever pretty badly afterwards—symptomatic fever, I think the doctors called it. They stowed me on board ship as soon they could. There are no more cats wanted yonder than can catch mice, and my mice-catching days seemed to be over.'

'That was very of ungrateful of them, after you had fought so bravely,' answered Isabel gently. 'Did you like being over there?'

'Very much. It has been a glorious time; though there have been hideous mistakes on our part. The fighting has tested the metal of our fellows, and they have given the true ring. I wish I could have held on to the end. You have been—fairly well—I hope, since I left?'

' Oh, yes, I am well enough,' she answered, with a little bitter laugh. 'I have what the doctors call a wonderful constitution. I believe if you were to cut my head off I should go on living;' and then she fixed her eyes upon him earnestly, and said, 'The murderer has not been found yet.'

'No. I know. I have watched the English papers. I fear he will never be found.'

'Oh, yes, he will!' Mrs. Trevannion answered confidently. 'God would not let such a crime as that remain forever unavenged.'

'The criminal will be punished in the next world, no doubt.'

'And in this,' she answered doggedly. 'I am sure of it. What had my husband done that he should die such a death—he who was so kind, so generous, who had never injured a living creature, who had not an enemy? Is such a life to be taken, and shall there be no redress in this world as well as in the next? I should cease to believe in the all-seeing eye of Heaven, if God's judgment failed to overtake such a crime. It may be slow, but it will come. God tries our faith. For a little while the wicked seem to rejoice in their iniquity: but judgment will come.'

'If this idea is a consolation to you.' Jasper began gently, as though he were talking to a child, whose delusions he did not care to dispel.

'It is. It is my only consolation.'

After this he tried to withdraw her mind from this agonizing theme by talking to her about the neighbourhood, her tenantry, the changes that had taken place in his absence. He stayed with her for an hour; first on the terrace, then, as it grew darker, in the candle-lit drawing-room; and when he left her to go back to the Duke's Head, where he was to stay that night, she felt just a little cheered by his visit. A friend had come back to her out of the past—her husband's friend.

Mr. Dane stayed all the next day at Boscobel. He called on the Vicar, and that gentleman, who had always liked him, welcomed him cordially, and was delighted to hear all about his American experiences. The war was the absorbing topic of the day, and here was a man who could tell more about it than all the newspapers put together. Mr. Ponsford, the Vicar, would not hear of Jasper Dane's going to the Cornish moors. Not yet awhile, at any rate. He must stay at the Vicarage, and fish in Boscobel river—nothing better than a little quiet angling for a man out of health.

'You will feel plenty of air from the hills,' said Mr. Ponsford; 'the Cornish moors would be too bleak for you.'

An invitation so heartily given could hardly be refused.

'I shall be delighted to stay,' said Jasper. 'Your society will put me in good spirits, and I am very fond of Boscobel.'

So Jasper stayed, and fished as well as he could with his single arm, and recovered his health rapidly in that sweet, pure air, the salt breath of the distant sea sweeping over moorland and valley. The river went through the Abbey grounds, and, loitering there with rod and line on the drowsy summer afternoons, Mr. Dane had frequent opportunities for conversation with Mrs. Trevannion.

She never went beyond her own gardens, except to go to church, but she spent a great part of her life in those shady old grounds, with her books, her sketching-board, and her dogs. She took no pains to avoid Jasper Dane now. The past, as regarded his feelings for her, was to her mind a dead past. She liked to talk to him because he had been Geoffrey's friend; he could tell her of her husband's youth; that adventurous time in India, when they had both served under Clive. So long as he spoke of Geoffrey she was interested; but Dane saw that his own adventures, all the toil and glory of this late war, had not a spark of interest for her.

Mr. Dane stayed more than a month at the Vicarage, and the benefit he had derived from the Boscobel climate was so great that he determined upon spending the winter in the neighbourhood. He found a decent lodging in a pastoral village about three miles from the town, a mere cluster of cottages on the slope of a heather-clad hill; and here he lived for the next year, walking or riding into Boscobel daily, and resuming the management of Mrs. Trevannion's estate.

Just a year after his return the end came, which almost everybody except Geoffrey's widow had foreseen. Mrs. Trevannion consented to marry Mr. Dane, and they were united by Jasper's good friend, the Vicar, in the same church which had seen Geoffrey's coffin under its velvet pall, borne by the best gentlemen in the neighbourhood.

She did not profess any love for him, but she was grateful for his devotion; she liked him because he had liked her husband, and she furnished one more example of the way in which any woman may be won if her lover will only persevere in his courtship.

Except by Mr. Ponsford; and by a few of the trades-people, the marriage did not find favour in the sight of Boscobel. The town had objected in the first instance to Geoffrey Wyatt, as an alien adventurer; but once having adopted him, the town objected still more strongly to a second husband, in the person of Jasper Dane. It was affirmed that Mrs. Trevannion would live to repent her folly.

Life went on very smoothly at the Abbey, in spite of adverse opinion in the town. If Mrs. Dane—the good old name had been renounced at last—were not happy, she was at least contented. She had in her second husband a man, who could sympathize with her every taste, join in all her favourite pursuits—a man who was in all things her companion and guide. He was highly accomplished, and had an ardent appreciation of all that is most beautiful in life. There could not be a more refined home, or a better matched couple.

The few friends who visited at the Abbey were compelled to acknowledge this.

'Mr. Dane is undoubtedly a gentleman,' they said; 'a man of no family, but one of Nature's gentlemen, and he is thoroughly devoted to his wife.'

'He ought to be!' growled a bachelor, who would have liked to win such a woman. 'Mrs. Trevannion—I can't school my tongue to give her the fellow's name—is one of the handsomest women in Devonshire, and the Abbey estate is one of the best in the county.'

The outer world might believe him mercenary, but those who knew him intimately could see that the desire of worldly gain had little influenced Jasper Dane in his wooing. His habits were as simple as when he had been only Geoffrey's steward. He made little use of his wife's wealth, except to dispense it largely in charity. It was he who, in her name, established and endowed the hospital just outside Boscobel.

Wherever there was sickness or want, help came from the Abbey. Mrs. Trevannion had always been liberal to those who appealed to her, but not actively and inquiringly beneficent, like her second husband. She co-operated gladly in all his good works. Schools, cottages, church, all profited by her liberality.

'Why should we hoard our money ?' said Jasper. 'We have no one to inherit it after us.'

This speech was spoken within two years of their marriage; but before the third year was out a child was born at the Abbey, and Isabel Trevannion, transfigured by the bliss of maternity, sat on the sunlit terrace with her infant son in her arms; but even in her delight in this new tie, her thoughts went back to her first husband.

'It seems hard that he never had a son!' she said to herself; and looking up at Jasper's grave face, she felt chilled by an image that kindled no warmth of womanly affection in her heart. He was her friend and companion; she respected and trusted him; but she had never loved him.

Jasper's delight in the birth of the boy was as intense as the mother's. He worshipped the child; and, as years went on, Trevannion— for the good old name was revived again in the boy, who was christened Trevannion, and was to take the name of Trevannion after Dane, when he came of age, thus becoming Trevannion Dane Trevannion—became the ruler of the Abbey. Father and mother concurred in spoiling him; old servants bowed down to him; his will was law. He was not a bad fellow, but impetuous and self-willed, sorely needing a control which was never exercised.

Neither his father nor his mother could bear to deny him anything—to oppose any whim of his, however foolish. As he grew from childhood to boyhood he had all a country-bred boy's tastes, fishing, shooting, riding, birds'-nesting, otter-hunting; no inclination towards study, which was a disappointment to the father; no love of art, which was a source of regret for the mother. He was beautiful, exceedingly; but as the young of the animal creation are beautiful, by reason of his activity and vigour, his lissome limbs, his sleekness and brilliant colour.

He was ten years old when his father fell ill of a lingering, wasting malady, which made him forsake his study—the familiar desk at which he had carried on all his steward's business—and confined him to his room. He had never slept in King Solomon's room—the tapestried bedchamber, where his friend's murdered corpse had been laid. He occupied a panelled bedroom looking into the garden and adjoining his study. King Solomon's room had been shut up ever since the murder. The housekeeper went in from time to time, the room was aired and cleaned, but the door was kept locked.

Lying on that which he felt to be his death-bed, Jasper Dane's sole delight was in the company of his wife and boy. She was with him almost always; waiting upon him, reading to him, comforting him; but the boy came fluttering in and out, like a bird or a butterfly—a bright, restless creature, tickle and untameable.

'It is so dull here,' he complained once, when his father coaxed him to remain. 'You look so grave, and mamma too. There is no fun; nothing for me to do. I want to ride my pony over the hills.'

'True, my boy, it is very dull for you, dull for mamma too. Go and have your scamper over the hills, but come and see me afterwards. It does me good to see you.'

'Oh, yes. I'll come, and tell you all about Robin Goodfellow,' answered the boy, kissing his hand as he ran off. The Robin in question was his pony.

It was the end of November, that dismal month in which Geoffrey Trevannion had met his fate. Jasper had been an invalid since the early summer. The doctors gave little hope of his recovery. It was a kind of atrophy. The mind was bright and clear enough, except in the night sometimes, when his wits wandered a little with low fever—but the body was slowly withering.

'That fever in America,' said the doctor, shaking his head, 'the hardships he suffered during the war.'

Those were painful nights of watching for Isabel, when her husband's mind was far astray, and he rambled horribly in his talk, now fancying himself in Bengal, now at Lexington, at Bunker's Hill, at Charleston, now muttering to himself vaguely, in a disconnected way, strange fragments of speech, accusing himself of monstrous wickedness, 'steeped to the lips in guilt,—a soul drowned in the blackest depths of sin.' It was all mere fever, the natural consequence of extreme debility and light-headedness. He was clear and calm enough in the day, when he was able to sit up in his bed, supported by a pile of pillows, and to take the stimulants that sustained the feeble flame of life.

Christmas was drawing near. The boys and girls at the Vicarage were preparing some kind of medieval mummery, some dressing up and fooling, and Trevannion was to have his share in it. He was full of delight in the sport, delicious to him in its novelty.

'I am to be St. George and the dragon— no, Arthur is to be the dragon, with a red coat all over scales—gilt paper scales, mamma—Rhoda is making them. And I am to have a helmet and feathers. Please find me some feathers. And we want a lot of grand clothes, for Justice, and Britannia, and Queen Elizabeth, and Old Father Christmas. Rhoda says you must have all kinds of grand things put away in chests and wardrobes, and that you can lend them to us.'

Mrs. Dane was not unwilling to be useful in the matter, but she was very anxious about her husband, whose faint hold upon life seemed growing weaker daily, and she put off compliance with her boy's reiterated request. Now to be put off about anything which he has set his heart upon is just what a spoilt child cannot endure. Trevannion made up his mind to hunt the chests and closets on his own account. The things would all be his own property by and-by, the servants had told him so.

He set out upon a voyage of discovery, ransacked closets, turned over the contents of coffers, dragged into the light of day a good many fine gowns and mantuas of a long-forgotten fashion. There was one closet which he explored last of all, the roomy receptacle in his father's study. It was locked, but there is no creature so determined as a child who has always had his own way. Among the numerous gifts which his parents had lavished upon him was a super-excellent box of carpenter's tools. With the help of these instruments Master Trevannion Dane contrived to shoot back the lock of the door, a clumsy old lock at best, ponderous but futile.

The investigation of that one closet occupied an afternoon. There were stacks of old books and papers in the foreground, so piled as to wall in the back of the closet. All these had to be taken down before Trevannion came to anything interesting. Behind the books, however, he found an old trunk, a capacious old trunk, that was damp to the touch and smelt of sea-water. This box, like the closet, was locked, but Trevannion and his chisel prevailed, and after tremendous efforts he raised the lid; on the top of the trunk there were old clothes, coats, and overcoats neatly folded; and under these the boy found a dozen or more tarnished silver cups and tankards, some of them gilded inside, three or four jewelled swords, and a silver hilt, broken short off.

The brief winter day was fading by the time he made this discovery. Here was treasure-trove. He felt himself a benefactor to his family, and rushed off to his mother, panting and triumphant.

She was just lighting a candle at a table by the fireplace in her husband's bedchamber, while Jasper lay dozing behind the heavy damask curtains, when her son ran in and took hold of her gown.

'Come, mamma, come!' he said: 'I have found such lovely things in papa's closet. Silver jugs, so big'—opening his arms to express grandeur of size—'and swords. I may have one for St. George, may I not? St. George must have a sword. Rhoda made me a cardboard one— but I'd rather have one of these.'

'Silver cups?' she repeated curiously. 'You are dreaming.'

'Come and see—come and see,' he cried; 'aren't you glad I

found them? I may have one for my very own, mayn't?'

She took up the candle and went with him—feeling as if she were moving in some horrible dream.

He led her to the closet, and showed her the open trunk—an old sea-chest that had been to India and , back—she remembered its being brought to the Abbey for Jasper Dane, after he had established himself there.

She stood with the candle in her hand looking down at her dead husband's racing-cups—the old tankards—the jewelled swords—all the contents of the glass cupboard in the hall. And there amongst them lay the rapier hilt, in chased silver—splashed with blood—a stain which time had blackened.

'Trevannion,' she said solemnly, with her hand on the boy's shoulder, 'you must never speak of these things. No one must know.'

'But why not?'

'Never mind why,' she answered, almost fiercely. 'You must obey me.'

'But mayn't I have one of those silver things?'

'Not till I am dead and gone. You may have them all then.'

'I don't want them then. I don't want you to be dead. I want one of the swords, and one of the silver mugs, now.'

'Trevannion, you must obey me. You must not say a word about these things. Do you understand?'

'Yes, mamma,' he faltered, awed by the authority of her tone, which was new to him.

'And now go to Sarah, and do not come to me any more tonight. Your father is very ill.'

She dismissed him with a hurried kiss, and went back to the sick-room, where she sat looking into the fire.

She understood it all now. The supposed burglary was a sham—an artfully contrived pretence. He had done it—he who was lying there—who had been her husband for thirteen years— to whom she had given duty and respect, whom her acts had honoured and her lips had praised. He, the father of her boy.

He was dying. She knew that the sands were running out in

the glass of life. There could be no redress.

'I never loved him,' she said to herself; 'thank God, I never loved him.'

She softly drew back the heavy curtain and looked down at the sick man meditatively—white to the lips, but with a fierce light in her dark-blue eyes. He was sleeping, but only by fits and snatches, and she wanted him to slumber soundly. She had a plan to carry out.

She looked among the bottles on a table by the bed, and selected one which contained a sedative; a dose of which was to be given him at night, if he were too restless.

'This will do it,' perhaps, she thought, and she poured out a double dose.

When next he stirred and turned upon his pillow, she put the glass to his lips, and, accustomed to be given medicine and restoratives, he swallowed the mixture submissively, she looking down at him with those terrible eyes.

An hour later, when he was sleeping profoundly, she had him carried to the tapestried room, where her first husband's corpse had been laid. He was lifted from his own bed on a mattress, and laid on that fatal couch, she telling the servants who did it that the change to the larger room was necessary to give him more air.

A fire had been lighted at her bidding, and the room had been always kept aired. There was no absolute cruelty in the change; but the servants wondered a good deal at the proceeding. It seemed hazardous, to say the least of it.

'You may depend the doctor ordered it, or my lady wouldn't have had it done,' said Sarah, who would have thrust her right arm into a furnace at her lady's bidding.

Mrs. Trevannion sat by the fire in King Solomon's chamber all night, hardly withdrawing her eyes from the sleeper on the old four-post bed, with its twisted and elaborately carved pillars and cornice, its gloomy draperies, and faded crimson plumes. Jasper slept till close upon daybreak—the cold, cheerless winter dawn, the uncanny light in which Geoffrey Trevannion's murder had been discovered. It was at this very hour the sick man's mind was always clearest. He woke and saw his wife standing at the bottom of the bed, leaning against one of the carved pillars, looking down at him.

'What a terrible long night it has been,' he said. 'I have had dreadful dreams.'

'Jasper Dane, she said, 'I have some news for you. The murderer has been found!'

'What?'

'Do you remember when you came back from America—do you remember that summer evening on the terrace—when *his* dog shrunk away from you? I told you that Geoffrey's murderer would be discovered. I was sure of it. Providence would not have it otherwise. I was right, you see.'

He lay looking at her, feebly wiping the dampness from his brow, waiting to know the worst.

'The murderer is found, and you are he,' she said; 'the falsest friend—the vilest hypocrite, the cruellest villain who ever crawled this earth.'

'No,' he answered faintly; 'I was neither false friend, nor hypocrite. My one sin was loving you. I fought against my passion—yes, I fought a good fight. I made up my mind to go—anywhere out of reach of you—to fling away my life for your sake. When I told Geoffrey that I must go he suspected me—that day we took the long ride together—I knew it more by his manner than by what he said. He was too willing that I should leave the Abbey. My face or my speech had betrayed me. No wonder, when my very soul was steeped in love for you.

'To the last I meant to deal honourably with my friend—yes, to the very last—till that last night when sleepless in my misery, I crept downstairs, and walked about the hall, and opened the window to let in the cold morning air—and, pacing up and down in this distracted state, took a rapier from the wall, and had half a mind to kill myself. when I turned and saw Geoffrey at the foot of the stairs, and the devil took possession of me that instant and prompted me to stab him. One swift, unerring thrust plunged my soul forever in the pit of hell.

'My next thought was how to profit by my crime—to keep my name clear and to win you. For this I planned things so that it should seem that the house had been robbed. I had just time enough to do what was needful before your bell rang and alarmed the house—just time enough to get back to my room after the ringing of your bell. I wish to Heaven I had been killed in America. And yet—I have been your husband—life has had its sweetness.'

'I wish I had found you out soon enough to have you hanged,' she said mercilessly. 'You are dying. You will cheat the gallows and me. Do you see where you are?' she asked, plucking back the nearest window-curtain, and letting in a flood of morning light. 'You are in his room. This is the bed on which your victim lay. Die upon it, and hope for God's mercy if you can.'

These were the last words she spoke to him. She left him to her servants, who watched him and ministered to him faithfully to the end.

He died that night, and his wife followed him to the grave within a few weeks. She hardly spoke or looked up after his death. It was a touching instance of death from a broken heart.

'You see she cared for her second husband ever so much better than she did for her first,' said everyone in Boscobel.

Trevannion Dane Trevannion grew up a fine specimen of dauntless, muscular humanity, won for himself considerable renown as a dashing soldier in the Peninsular war, and lived to be the father of many Trevannions.

Dorothy's Rival

I am more and more convinced that none escape being evil spoken of but those who deserve not to escape it.—Charles Wesley.

In the days when the thunder of Whitfield's voice had but newly resounded above the crowd at Moorfields, Mr. William Bolton, a simple country parson of the Established Church, lived very happily with his only daughter, Dorothy, on the outskirts of Hammersley.

The parsonage was a comfortable red-brick house, very square and very uninteresting from a picturesque point of view. It stood a little way back from the high coach road to London, with an orchard on one side, and on the other a common cottage garden, with two long flower-beds and a broad gravel-path, and vegetables growing in the middle distance, and espaliers in the background. All the roads were London roads in those days; and people lived and died on the London road without ever seeing the metropolis, which figured, glorious and radiant, in their daydreams: an enchanted city—not actually paved with gold, but altogether marvellous and beautiful.

To Dorothy Bolton the square red house, the orchard, and the garden were very pleasant and dear. What, indeed could be more beautiful than the parlour, with its two prim bookcases, the needlework pictures of a shepherd and shepherdess smirking from their oval frames; the little room in which her father composed his sermons, with much aid from grim-looking black-leather-bound books, labelled Barrow and Tillotson; the infallible eight-day clock in the hall, which groaned and rattled in such an awful manner before the striking of an hour, and above the dial of which there was something scientific in the way of a sun and moon that was never quite in working order.

All these things to the eyes of Miss Dorothy were beautiful; nor did she pine for any brighter or gayer existence than that which she enjoyed, or languish for any respite from the many duties of her simple life. She had no higher aspiration than to sit in the parlour wearing out her bright young eyes in the fine stitching of her father's shirts, to help her mother at bread-making, or to trudge into Hammersley on a fine morning by the parson's side, to share in his round of visits among the poor folks, or to read that delightful story of *Sir Charles Grandison* aloud to her father and mother in the long winter evenings.

These things were at once her duties and her pleasures. In this peaceful home she had grown from childhood to womanhood, and was so innocent and childlike still, that she thought it was her gipsy-hat and scarlet ribbon that made such a picture of brightness and beauty in the little mirror that reflected her fair young face every Sunday morning while the bells were ringing for church. Yes, Miss Dorothy Bolton—or Mrs. Dorothy, as people were more apt to call a damsel in those days—had grown from a sunburnt, hoydenish girl into a very lovely young woman, without any consciousness of the transformation.

The parson and his wife saw that their only child was now, indeed, a comely young person; but these good people would have cut their tongues out rather than they would have confessed as much to the damsel herself.

'Handsome is who handsome does,' said Dorothy's mother; and the girl felt as if her good looks were in some manner dependent on the neatness of her stitching and the lightness of her last batch of bread.

By-and-by, however, there came to Hammersley Parsonage someone who, although by no means prone to dilate upon Dorothy's personal attractions, permitted the young lady to discover her power to charm. This newcomer was a certain Matthew Wall, a young clergyman, who came to share the burden of the vicar's duty, and who had so far proved himself a very worthy and efficient member of the Church.

Indeed, in sober truth, efficiency and energy were much

needed for the cure of souls in Hammersley. The town was large and crowded, the population was rough and disorderly; and an awakening voice was needed to arouse a people who had long been dead to the spirit and careless as to the letter of the faith.

William Bolton, the vicar, had a simple mind and a kindly nature; but something more than these are required for the salvation of such a town as Hammersley; and this something more seemed to have been given to the poor benighted creatures in the person of Matthew Wall.

The vicar preached a very orthodox sermon of the soporific school, and had a heart and hand ever open to the appeal of the poor; but, as his means were small and his judgment very fallible, he effected, with the best intentions, very little real good. He was getting old; and he liked his after-dinner pipe in the orchard in summer, and by the chimney-corner in winter. He liked to take his nap in the long winter evenings, while Dorothy read *The Life and Surprising Adventures of Robinson Crusoe*, or *Religious Courtship*, or an odd number of the *Rambler*. He visited his poor from time to time, and he was not unwelcome to them even when he came empty-handed; but it seemed as if his visits did very little good. Hammersley was, in truth, too big a place for this simple pastor, and the people of Hammersley too rugged a race for his mild rule.

Matthew Wall was a very different kind of pastor. Fatigue and discouragement were alike unknown to him. He had the energy of a Whitfield or a Wesley; and, in that day, Whitfields and Wesleys were needed in the Established Church as well as out of it.

William Bolton invited his curate to dinner on Sundays; a dinner served directly after morning service—plain and substantial, after the old English fashion. But Mr. Wall would eat very little between the services; he did better justice to the nine o'clock supper. The vicar, who exhibited a hearty appetite both at dinner and supper, called Matthew a poor trencherman. It is possible that Matthew's chief delight at the parsonage was not to be found in his trencher. He sat by Dorothy at supper, and seemed to derive much satisfaction from her society. He found her sweet-tempered and modest as Pamela, pious as Dorcas; and before he had been six months at Hammersley he made a formal demand for her hand.

The vicar hummed and hawed, and consulted his wife.

'Sure 'twould be but a poor match for the wench,' he said. 'Matt Wall has but his cure of seventy pounds a year, and a few hundreds to come from his father by-and-by. The rogue has good parts, I daresay, and has done good service amongst Hammersley folks with his fiery talk and hunting them out in their dens; which is pushing a parson's trade farther than I should care to push it. I doubt but he's touched with the Wesley and Whitfield madness; and we shall have him deserting the Church some day, as the two Wesleys did—to the shame of family and friends.'

Happily for Matthew Wall, the vicar, after consulting his wife, thought fit to say a few words to his daughter.

The girl reddened and cast down her eyes, and when hard pushed by her father's questions, confessed with tears that she loved Matthew very dearly, and would go to her grave unmarried sooner than she would give her hand to any but him. The vicar was no Squire Western. He expressed his astonishment by a long whistle, and reproved his daughter for a sly puss; after which feeble protest he consented to receive Matthew Wall as his future son-in-law.

But there was to be no marriage for three good years to come. Matthew was but five-and-twenty, Dorothy just turned eighteen. The young people pledged themselves very readily. They met on Sundays, walked to and fro together between the parsonage and the church, dined and supped together; and whenever Matthew's business happened to bring him near the garden-gate on week-days, he would step in to say a few words to his Dorothy.

The three years passed very pleasantly. Matthew Wall had become a power in Hammersley before his period of probation was ended. There was some who called him wild and fanatic,—for to be earnest in those lukewarm days seemed a kind of fanaticism; but since, in many instances, the drunken became sober, and the reprobate became decent beneath his sway, folks were fain to admire his earnestness. The bishop of the diocese complimented the young man on the change he had brought about in Hammersley.

'I'm pleased you should show these Methodist folk that 'tis possible to do good without forsaking the Church we have sworn to hold by, sir, and that 'tis as easy to bring the stray sheep back to the true fold as to lure them into a strange one,' said the bishop, at a grand ceremonial dinner of which he deigned to partake on a certain occasion.

Parson Bolton was gratified that his curate and future son-in-law should win this meed of praise from the Episcopal lips.

'But there's more of the Methody about our Matt than I quite relish, for all that, my wench,' he said to his wife in the confidence of connubial discourse.

It is not given to mortal man—least of all to a religious reformer—to please everyone. There were people in Hammersley who did not like Matthew Wall. His long, earnest, even fervid, discourses displeased a few. He had refused invitations to tea and supper-parties,—solemn and yet boisterous festivities given by the richer tradesfolk of Hammersley—and had thus offended many. There were Wallites and anti-Wallites in Hammersley; and the anti-Wallites were strong. Amongst them the most notable people were a certain Mr. Jorboys, grocer and cheesemonger, his wife and daughters.

The Misses Jorboys—Sally and Letty—were accounted beauties. They wore hats and muffs and gowns which their father brought from London when he went thither for colonial produce; and they took it ill of Mr. Wall that he had been so prompt to devote himself to the parson's dowdy daughter, who had never known what it was to powder her hair, or sail along the High Street prim and stately in pannier-hoops.

It was nigh upon Christmas, and there was to be much joviality at the parsonage, for this must be Dorothy's last Christmas at home. A neat little house in Hammersley had been hired by the curate, and comfortably furnished out of funds provided by his father, with certain additions in the way of a dragon-china tea-service, a brass-handled bureau, and liberal store of home-spun linen, provided by Mrs. Bolton, who with her own hands prepared the nest for these young turtle-doves.

'I could have wished my Dorothy had fancied Squire Hever of Hever Farm, who was like to die for her last winter,' the parson's wife said to her gossips; 'but she's been like one bewitched since Matthew courted her. "Sure, would you have me break my faith with a saint, dear madam?' she cried, when I told her how young Hever would have made a lady of her, with her own coach and a black footboy. And I do think the simpleton's right in that,' Mrs. Bolton would add with an air of conviction. ' I've seen young men more mannerly in turning a compliment, and softer spoken; but if there ever was a saint on earth since St. Paul, I think Matthew Wall is one.'

Of late the lady's gossips had been somewhat slow to respond to this observation; and she was not a little vexed on one occasion by the conduct of her particular friend Mrs. Jorboys, who went so far as to shake her head and groan audibly at this point in the conversation.

'I hope you have nothing to say against my daughter's sweetheart, ma'am?' the parson's wife observed with some acidity.

'Oh no, ma'am,' Mrs. Jorboys replied with a sigh more dismal than the last; 'I have nothing to *say* against him.'

There was an unpleasant emphasis on the word say that went nigh to freeze Mrs. Bolton's marrow.

'I don't quite take your meaning, ma'am,' she said stiffly. 'Matthew Wall may not be a rich husband for our Dorothy, but he don't need to be groaned over as if he was a beggar.'

'You wasn't talking of beggars, as I know of, ma'am,' Mrs. Jarboys answered with acrimony. 'You was talking of saints.'

'And what then, ma'am?'

'I have my thoughts, ma'am, I should be vastly sorry to hurt your feelings, Mrs. Bolton, but my thoughts are not my own making, and I can't help it if they are of a nature to lead to what you was so civil as to call groaning;' and hereupon Mrs. Jorboys sighed again, while Miss Letty and Miss Sally sighed in chorus. This occurred at a Hammersley tea-party, from which Dorothy chanced to be absent.

The parson's wife went home perplexed and miserable. The next batch of bread was heavy, and by no fault of Dorothy's, though her simple head was a little distraught by thinking of the great change so near at hand. It was the chief bread-maker whose mind was most troubled, whose hand was most uncertain. Those groanings and head-shakings of Mrs. Jorboys haunted the good soul by day and night, and Dorothy could but wonder what made her mother so thoughtful.

'I fear there's something troubles you, ma'am,' the girl said, after the respectful manner of those days.

'Nay, my dear, I have no trouble but the thought of losing thee,' answered the mother; 'and if it's for thy good, I'm content we should part.'

'But it's not parting, dear madam; 'tis but living in separate houses. Do you think there's a week will pass without my paying my duty to you? And I'll come to help with the bread-making, if you'll suffer me.'

This was on Christmas-eve. There was to be fine fun at the parsonage that evening, ending with the compounding of a beverage, made of eggs and spices and ale, that had been so compounded at the same hour on every Christmas-eve since the vicar had kept house. The beverage was always compounded in the parlour, and partaken of with all solemnity out of a great silver tankard that was said to have belonged to Oliver Cromwell. Dorothy vowed that it was but a battered old thing, and she had seen finer, spick-and-span new, at a silversmith's in the High Street.

The curate was to drink tea at the parsonage, and assist, not only in the compounding of the beverage, but in the composition of that much more sacred mixture, the Christmas pudding. To these simple diversions Dorothy looked forward with extreme pleasure. She thought of her betrothed with unmeasured tenderness, with reverence and devotion, amounting almost to fanaticism. She believed in him as a being almost too saintly for earth.

Mrs. Bolton had ample occupation for her hands on this eve of the great Christian festival; but her mind was not free to devote itself to her labours. The image of Mrs. Jorboys pursued her through ail her duties.

'I'm very like to want more raisins and spices for the puddings between this and the New Year,' she said to herself; ' I'll walk to Hammersley this afternoon, and have it out with Mrs. Jorboys.'

Having once resolved on this course, the matron was more at ease. She set out on her expedition directly after dinner, leaving the vicar smoking his pipe by the chimney-corner, and Dorothy busy with her plain sewing. The girl had offered to accompany her mother, but the offer had been refused. The dame departed in very good spirits, promising to return by teatime. Dorothy sat sewing while her father smoked and dozed, and dozed and smoked; and at five o'clock in came the curate, tired with a day's hard work, but cheered by his Dorothy's welcome, and well pleased to find himself seated by her side.

'I've come all the way from Liscott Common,' he said, as he seated himself in the old-fashioned arm-chair which Dorothy had set ready to receive him; 'and it's a long trudge.'

It was five o'clock, and Dorothy had brewed the tea, which was an infusion to be partaken of with a certain ceremony in those days as an expensive luxury implying refined taste and much gentility on the part of the consumer. Parson Bolton took no tea—but the curate liked all that Dorothy liked.

The pretty little china teacups— fragile things, without handles, like a child's toy cups and saucers—and the quaint little teapot were set out on the polished mahogany board, but there were no signs of Mrs. Bolton's return. So the lovers sat talking together in undertones while the father dozed, for one brief happy hour; and then, after the usually preliminary groaning, the infallible eight-day clock struck six.

'I should be quite frightened about mother,' said Dorothy, 'if

I didn't know that Jorboys' man is to come home behind her with the parcels.'

She had scarcely spoken when the door was opened, and shut again with a slamming noise, and Mrs. Bolton stalked into the room.

The matron's cheeks were crimson, and the matron's eyes flashed fire. Never before had Dorothy seen such a look in her mother's face.

'You're late home, madam,' she said, trembling, she scarce knew why, unless it were because of the strange look in her mother's face.

'Thanks be to God that I'm not too late,' the parson's wife answered solemnly.

The unfamiliar tone of her voice startled her husband from his comfortable doze, and he looked up alarmed, crying, 'What, what?' like his revered sovereign King George in after-days.

'Sit down, and drink thy tea, mistress,' said the good-natured parson, as his wife stood tugging at the string of her cloak, hindered by Dorothy, who made believe to assist with trembling fingers.

'Never, while that bad man is under this roof,' answered the dame, pointing to Matthew Wall, who had risen to receive her.

'Bad man!' cried the parson; 'art thou dreaming, wife? There's no one here but Matthew Wall, thy son-in-law that is to be.'

'My son-in-law that never shall be; I would see my daughter in her winding-sheet first.'

'Why, what maggot has bitten thee, wife?'

'May I ask the meaning of this strange talk, madam?' asked the curate, with that awful calmness peculiar to a proud man who feels himself outraged.

'Thou mayst ask, and shalt be told too, as plain as I can speak before this simple tender soul that loves thee,' answered the matron. 'I wonder thou art not ashamed to come to an honest man's house and steal his daughter's heart—you, that play saint on Sundays, and sinner on Mondays, and hypocrite all the week round.'

'Mother!' cried the girl—indignation, astonishment, anguish, reproach, all expressed in that piteous cry.

'I must ask for the second time what you are pleased to mean, madam?' said Matthew Wall with unshaken calmness.

'I'll answer that question with another, sir,' returned the matron. 'Will you be so good as to tell me here—before my husband and daughter—whether you know Liscott Common?'

There was nothing very awful in the question itself, but Mrs. Bolton's tone made it awful, and it went like a pistol-shot through Dorothy's heart, as she remembered how her lover had talked of his walk from Liscott Common that very afternoon.

'Yes, Mrs. Bolton, I know Liscott Common.'

'So, sir, you don't deny your wickedness?' cried the dame; 'but perhaps you will deny your knowledge of Jane Gurd's cottage, on the other side of the common, where you've been seen to go twice, three times, four times a week for this last six months; and where you've been known to stay two hours at a spell, times and often—you, that complain of wanting leisure for good works! You could find leisure for bad works, and to spare, I reckon. What, you start and change colour at last, my fine master! I doubt you did not think Hammersley folks were sharp enough to find out your doings.'

'I did not think Hammersley folks were so wicked as to impute evil to a man who, when most unworthy, is at least urgent in his duty.'

'Upon my word, sir,' exclaimed the infuriate matron, pushing aside the trembling girl, who would fain have restrained her wrath, ' you carry matters with a bold front; and I must needs speak plainer than I care to speak before this simple child here, who was too quick to love and trust you against her parents' will, that had higher hopes for her. Nay, dry thy tears, Dolly; I'll see thee mistress of Hever Grange, belike, instead of drudge and draggletail for love of that dirt yonder.'

And the matron pointed at Matthew Wall with a trembling finger—at Matthew, whose calmness was not yet shaken.

'Will it please you to speak quietly and civilly, madam?' he said. 'You ask me if I know Liscott Common, and I answer yes; if I know Jane Gurd's cottage, and I answer yes again. I came straight from there to this house an hour ago.'

You came from there to my child? ' shrieked Mrs. Bolton; ' then, indeed, you are a shameless villain!'

'Come, come; dame,' expostulated the parson; 'civil words, civil words,'

'''Tis easy talking for you. William; but am I to pick and choose my words, when my heart is like to burst for grief and shame? That wretch yonder, that was to be married to our Dorothy a fortnight come Saturday—him that pretends to be a saint— must needs have his fancy, like a London rake-hell. He keeps a fine madam hid away in Jane Gurd's cottage, and there's scarce a day passes that he does not waste a couple hours in paying his duty to the lady; and he comes straight from that woman to my daughter; and you ask me to keep my patience, William Bolton!'

'I'll not believe it!' cried Dorothy suddenly, flinging herself away from her mother, and standing bolt upright, looking at the dame with flaming eyes. 'I'll not believe it, mother, if all the people in Hammersley were to swear it on their Bibles.'

'There is no need for so much warmth, Dorothy,' the curate said gently. 'I do not fear thou wilt believe ill of thy chosen husband. And you, madam, will soon be sorry for having done me so much wrong. Pray, who was it told you this pretty story?'

'I heard it from Mrs. Jorboys; but 'tis the common talk of Hammersley.'

'I am sorry Hammersley should choose such vile discourse.'

'Can you deny this story? '

'I will not trouble myself to deny it.'

'Oh, indeed, Mr. Brazenface! You won't deny, then, that there is a young woman living in Jane Gurd's cottage, and that you took her there?'

'That is quite true.'

'And is it true that you have paid for the vermin's board and lodging?'

'Vermin is a very hard word, Mrs. Bolton, and the girl at Jane Gurd's cottage deserves no such bad name. I have paid for her meat and drink hitherto; Jane is kind enough to give her shelter without recompense.'

'And you took her there?'

'Yes, I took her there.'

'You are a bad man, Matthew Wall.'

'I thought you were too good a woman to be so ready to think ill. or to listen to gossip that is as idle as it is wicked,' answered the curate with the gentle gravity that had distinguished his manner throughout this interview.

'If there is no harm in your doings, why have you kept them secret?' asked the dame with no less anger, but with a certain admixture of uncertainty.

'I can but answer you with Shylock, it has been "my humour." There are things a man does not care to talk about. I have had my fancy about that poor wench at the cottage on Liscott Common. The fancy might have proved a foolish one, and I might have been laughed at for my pains.'

'And this is all you have to say?'

'Yes; I will say no more tonight. If you want to know more, Mrs. Bolton, or if you would know more, Dorothy dear, you have but to walk to Liscott Common with me after service tomorrow, and you may find out more of poor Betty than you can learn of Hammersley gossip.'

'Betty!' exclaimed the matron, 'Betty what, pray, sir?'

'She has no other name,' replied Matthew; 'she had one when I first met with her; but I have done my best to rid her of it. And now I will wish you good-night, madam, and a heart less prone to give heed to slander. Sure I know 'tis a kind one.'

He took Dorothy's hand as he passed her, and pressed it tenderly to his lips.

'Thou art too pure to doubt me, dear creature,' he murmured. 'I will show thy kinsfolk tomorrow that thy purity is wiser than their experience.'

In the next moment he was gone. The parson's wife sent

Dorothy to bed—for in the days of Pamela and Clarissa it was within the scope of maternal authority to send a daughter of twenty-one years of age to bed— and immediately sat down and began to cry. She had her cry out, and then consented to answer her bewildered husband's inquiries. She told him how her suspicions had been aroused by certain hints and head-shakings on the part of Mrs. Jorboys; and how she had gone that afternoon to Hammersley determined to have it out with that lady; and how Mrs. Jorboys had told her with due solemnity that Matthew Wall's wickedness was the common talk of Hammersley, since he was known to have a mistress, some low common rubbish picked out of Hammersley gutter, hidden away in Jane Curd's cottage; and how his frequent visits to Mrs. Curd's abode had in the first place aroused suspicion, after which he had been watched by good and zealous Christians anxious for the repute of their holy Church.

'But how do these spies and watchers know that the girl is Matthew's mistress?' asked the parson.

'What else should she be, William?' exclaimed the dame, with an awful shake of the head.

There was no compounding of spiced drink on this Christmas-eve. The parson and his wife sat by the fire, sad, angry, bewildered, altogether ill at ease. Dorothy lay awake very unhappy. It was not that she suspected her lover of any wrong-doing. That was impossible. She wept over the breach between those two whom she loved so dearly, and fell asleep at last in the midst of a prayer that all might he made right again tomorrow.

The Misses Jorboys and their mother nodded and smirked at Dorothy as they passed her pew in their Christmas finery before morning service. They marvelled to see the girl's peaceful face, after the revelation at which they had assisted on the previous afternoon. It was the curate's turn to preach, and he chose for his Christmas discourse a very familiar text about the charity that thinketh no evil. Matthew Wall was a powerful preacher at all times; but today he seemed as one inspired, and the hearts of Mrs. Jorboys and her daughters quailed beneath their ribbonbedizened stomachers as they heard him.

'It was but the common talk I repeated,' thought the grocer's dame; 'and 'twas for the good of yonder silly child I spoke so plain to her mother.'

The parsonage dinner had been put off till half-past two o'clock, much to the parson's discontent, in order that there might be time for the visit to Liscott Common.

'It goes against me to go near the place where the creature lives,' said Mrs. Bolton, when the matter was discussed; 'but it's best to hear the truth from Jane Gurd.'

Mrs. Gurd was the widow of a Hammersley tradesman who had died in extreme poverty. She lived partly by her own labour, partly on charity, and was supposed to be a decent sort of person.

The day was clear and bright. Mr. Wall and the vicar met Mrs. Bolton and her daughter at the gates of the churchyard; Matthew offered his arm to Dorothy, and the mother did not interfere to prevent the girl taking it. In sober truth the dame was somewhat shaken by the young man's firmness, and she had been not a little melted by that eloquent discourse on the charity that thinketh no evil.

The walk was not unpleasant to Dorothy, in spite of the cloud that darkened her horizon. Matthew Wall, with a rare delicacy, avoided all allusion to the business of the last evening. He talked of his parish work, in which Dorothy was deeply interested. The parson and his wife trudged after the young people, both silent.

'He could never take us to that house if he was the wicked wretch Mrs. Jorboys would have me think him,' the dame thought with some sense of remorse. Her confidence in her informant was beginning to falter. She had always liked Matthew, even when most ill-pleased that her daughter should make so poor a match.

They came to the humble little cottage. Matthew lifted the latch and entered, followed by his three companions. Jane Gurd was nodding in a roomy old chair by the chimney-corner; a girl was sitting by a window staring out at the common. Such a girl!

If this was Matthew Wall's fancy, it was a passing strange caprice. The girl was the ugliest specimen of womankind on which Mrs. Bolton had ever looked. There was indeed something more than common ugliness in the dull vacant face, the heavy lower jaw, the low narrow forehead, scant sandy hair, and thick-set lumpish figure. The girl escaped by very little from being a monster.

'I have brought the vicar and his lady to see Betty, Mrs. Gurd,' said the curate, as the widow stood up and curtsied to the quality.

The girl neither rose nor turned her head at the entrance of strangers. A figure of stone could not have been more still than this clumsy peasant girl.

'You have not taught the creature manners, Matthew Wall,' said the outraged matron, 'or she'd be quicker to show her reverence for her betters.'

The curate smiled, and turned with a gentle compassionate look to the monster by the window.

'Bless your dear heart, ma'am,' cried the widow Gurd, 'Betty knows no more of your honour's coming in at that door than the Emperor of Chaney.'

'What!' cried the dame; 'can't the creature see us?'

'Lord, no, ma'am; she's stone blind.'

'But she can hear us, at any rate?'

'Not she, ma'am; the postes isn't deafer.'

'But—but she can speak, I suppose?'

'Your words, ma'am, as Mr. Wall has taught her in this last six weeks. The Lord knows how he found the patience and the cleverness to do it.'

'Blind, deaf, and dumb!' cried the vicar's wife, aghast. 'Oh, Matthew Wall, can you forgive me?'

'With all my heart, dear madam. It was but a foolish mistake of the Hammersley folk;' and the curate held out his honest hand to the woman who had wronged him. 'Yes, poor Betty yonder is blind and deaf and dumb. I found her in one of the back slums of the town, worse treated than a dog; for the sorriest cur has some ragamuffin that will stand by him; and Betty had no friend. She was beaten, starved, kept in a hole like a rat—a horror to look at, a horror to think of. I told those she belonged to that it was a sinful piece of work, and they only laughed at me. I told them it was against the law; but the law is a slow business, and they snapped their fingers at my talk of constables and justices of the peace.

'What could I do to help the poor wretch? They called her Idiot Betty, and said she wasn't worth the bite and sup they gave her. I asked if I was free to take her away. They said yes, and welcome too. So I brought her to Dame Gurd. The good soul was willing to take the charge of her and give her a comfortable shelter for nothing, and her bit of victuals costs but a few shillings a week. She was a little strange and difficult to manage at first, from never having known kindness since her wretched cradle: but she soon got to understand that we meant well by her, and between us we have taught her a good deal.'

'Between us!' cried the widow; ''twas all your doing, first and last, Muster Wall.'

'No one need call her Idiot Betty, now,' continued the curate; 'she has learnt to make baskets and rush mats, and can ask by signs for what she wants.'

As he said this, the curate went softly towards the place where the girl sat, with the winter light shining on her dull sightless face. As he came close behind her chair the face changed all at once, and when he laid his hand gently upon her head, it was the face of a creature with a soul. The dull common clay—the mindless lump of ill-used humanity—brightened into life beneath that pitying hand. Here was a new Pygmalion who might well be proud of his work.

'I have been teaching her to talk,' said Matthew, 'and I have hopes that she will do something in that way by-and-by. She can say four words—God, bread, mother (meaning the kind hearted widow there), and parson (meaning me).'

He put his hand upon the girl's clumsy fingers. She understood the sign, and obeyed it. Her mouth opened like a box, and a sound came out of it—a loud, harsh, snapping, disagreeable sound, which was meant for the word 'parson.' It was more startling than pleasant, but to Matthew Wall it was sweeter than music.

'You'd never guess the trouble he had to bring her to that, your honours,' said Mrs. Gurd, proud of this successful performance.

Mrs. Bolton took a seven-shilling piece from her capacious pocket, and bestowed it upon the widow.

'She shall want for nothing while I am alive,' cried the mollified matron; and then she turned to Matthew and kissed him. It was an audible smack that resounded in the cottage chamber.

'God bless you, Matthew Wall!' she said; 'I'd rather see my Dolly the wife of so good a man than riding in the squire's chariot.'

My Unlucky Friend

Among my fellow-passengers on the overland route from Calcutta there were many of a more lively temperament and social turn than Mr. John Angus Marlow, civil engineer; yet it was curiously to that gentleman I chiefly attached myself during my homeward voyage, some years ago. He was forty years of age, grave—nay, indeed, almost stern of speech and manner, a man whom very few feminine critics would have called handsome, but in whose dark, thoughtful face, deep-set gray eyes, and strongly-marked black eyebrows there was a stamp of intellectual power which no physiognomist could fail to recognize.

His professional position was high, and he was commonly reputed a rich man. He was a bachelor, and was now returning to his native country as an invalid, having overtaxed both mind and body in the cause of a late arduous undertaking in railway construction. I too, a lieutenant in her Majesty's service, was returning home on sick leave, but with very little claim to pity on the score of ill-health, and with most cheerful anticipations of a pleasant holiday among familiar scenes and old friends.

I had met Marlow in society before leaving Calcutta, and, the ice being thus broken between us, our acquaintance quickly ripened into something more than the ordinary companionship of fellow-travellers. He was my senior by fifteen years, and evidently in weak health; so I was pleased to be of use to him in any small matters whereby I might spare him some of the fatigue of the journey, and to defer on all occasions to his humour. I found him very variable in mood, at times silent and thoughtful to an extreme degree, at other times full of pleasant conversation. He had read much and thought much, had a warm appreciation of art, and a refined taste in all matters, but was not a man likely to shine in general society. He grew singularly depressed in manner as we drew nearer the end of our passage; and while we walked the deck of the steamer together one moonlight night, smoking our cigars in meditative silence, I ventured to make some remark on the subject.

'Gloomy do you think me?' he asked; 'and I dare say you are right. I ought to be glad to see England again, no doubt, but I cannot summon up any sense of pleasure in the anticipation. I have been so long away from—well, I suppose one must call one's birthplace home—that I have lost all interest in the place and its belongings. Those whom I loved are dead. This voyage is altogether a concession to my doctors. I was happy in the pursuit of my profession, and I like India.'

'You must find life rather dismal up the country,' said I, 'as a. bachelor.'

'Yes,' he answered, with a faint sigh, 'it is lonely enough; but a man who works as hard as I have done has little time to feel the loneliness of his life.'

'You should marry, and take a wife back to India with you,' I ventured to suggest.

He gave a short laugh as he threw away the end of his cigar.

'I finished with that kind of thing when I was twenty,' he said. 'I had my dream, and it came to a bad ending. I am not a man to be fooled twice.'

It was late in October when we landed at Southampton. I was engaged to spend the next month in Scotland with a brother officer, but my Christmas was to be passed at my father's house in Warwickshire; and before parting with John Marlow, I extorted from him a promise that he would run down to us for a week at that festive season. He made the promise somewhat unwillingly, though not ungraciously.

'It is very good of you to care for such a dull old fellow as I am, Frank,' he said; and with this we parted.

When my month's sport in Scotland was ended, I hastened home in high spirits and rude health. I found my three sisters—Clara, Georgy, and Jessy—waiting for me at the railway station; three tall blooming damsels, whom I had left some years before in pinafores, short skirts, and scarlet stockings. They were eager to tell me all the home news, and almost bewildered me by their chatter as we drove from the station to the lodge gates.

'We have a new governess, Frank,' said Clara, when they had informed me of all the births, deaths, and marriages, and engagements to many among our friends and neighbours; 'poor old Miss Colby's health gave way at last, and she has taken a dear little cottage in Lord Leigh's model village. So papa insisted on getting someone else to finish us in music and languages, and so on. Miss Lawson, our new governess, is only twenty, just two years older than I, but she is very accomplished, and so pretty. I hope you won't fall in love with her, Frank.'

This I protested was a most improbable contingency; but I was not the less curious to see the lady in question.

'You will have plenty of her society,' said Georgy; 'she is always with us. Papa likes her amazingly.'

As my father had been ten years a widower, I suggested that this liking on his part might be dangerous; but the three girls indignantly repudiated the idea, and I was content to defer to their judgement.

When we assembled in the drawing-room before dinner, I found Miss Lawson talking to Georgy in one of the windows, and I had some few minutes' leisure in which to observe her before my sister beckoned me across the room in order to present me to the stranger. She was a tall aristocratic-looking girl, with a perfect profile, dark-brown hair, hazel eyes, and a singularly pale complexion; a girl whom no one could fail to observe and admire, but about whose beauty there might nevertheless be some difference of opinion. When I had been talking to her for some minutes her expression struck me as not altogether agreeable. Her lips were too thin for my notion of feminine beauty, and her chin was too prominent. Her eyes were perfect in colour, but I thought them somewhat wanting in depth and softness. Not long, however, did I remain critical upon the subject of Miss Lawson's beauty. There was a charm about her voice and manner not easily to be resisted by a man of my age; and when I retired to my room that night I had no feeling but unqualified admiration for my sisters' governess.

I told them next day of the invitation I had given Mr. Marlow, and his acceptance thereof.

'I wish he might take a fancy to you, Clara,' I said, laughing. 'It would be a capital match. John Marlow is one of the best fellows I ever met, and a rich man into the bargain.'

'And forty years of age, as you admitted just now,' exclaimed Clara, indignantly. 'I am not so desperately in want of offers, Mr. Frank, nor so mercenary as to care for your friend's money.'

Miss Lawson looked up from a water-coloured sketch which she was finishing for Georgy.

'Mr. John Marlow,' she repeated; 'my mother once knew a gentleman of that name. Do you know if he comes from Hadleigh Court, Lincolnshire?'

'Yes, Miss Lawson. He owns a place of that name, I believe. Have you ever seen him?'

'Oh dear no! He went to India before I was born. I have heard my mother speak of him. That is all I know of the gentleman.'

Christmas came, and with it several visitors; amongst them John Marlow. He had improved in health; but his quiet manners seemed more than usually quiet when compared with the somewhat boisterous gaiety of our country friends, whose high spirits had never been subdued by hard work or Oriental sunshine. My sisters voted him the dullest of bachelors, and declared that his society was absolutely depressing.

'There must be some melancholy secret connected with the poor man's early life,' said Clara; 'and I believe Margaret Lawson knows all about it. You should have seen his face when I introduced him to her, Frank. He started as if he had seen a ghost, but said nothing, and seemed quite glad to get away from her after a few formal sentences about the weather, and so on.'

This was on the morning after my friend's arrival. I watched his movements in the drawing-room that evening, and saw that he studiously avoided Miss Lawson's society, devoting himself chiefly to my sister Clara, who seemed on this occasion to find him by no means dull or disagreeable.

We smoked our cigars together that night on a terrace outside the drawing-room windows, when the rest of our party had retired; and while we were doing so John Marlow astonished me by saying,—

'Should you be very angry, Frank, if I brought my visit to an abrupt close, and left you tomorrow morning by an early train?'

'I should be very sorry,' I replied. 'But what on earth should induce you to run away from us like that?'

'A kind of panic, Frank. You will laugh at me for my folly. I told you I had had my dream, and that it came to a bad end. I never thought to be reminded of that bitter ending as I have been since I came into this house. It's no use trying to keep my secret from you, Frank. Your sister's governess, Miss Lawson, is the daughter and the living image of the only woman I ever loved, the woman who jilted me under circumstances of peculiar heartlessness. I was her junior by a couple of years, and worshipped her with a slavish passion.

'She made me a foil to another man, and threw me off remorselessly when she had brought him to her feet. She was a girl of good birth and position, but without money. Captain Lawson, the man she married, was well off, but a dissipated scoundrel, who would have run through a much larger fortune than that which he had inherited from his father's commercial successes. He died early, and left his widow and child dependent on his family, who were not the sort of people to do much for them. She—Florence Lawson, his widow—did not long survive him. The news of her death reached me in India fifteen years ago. I never thought to look upon the face of her daughter.'

'And you would run away from here on this account?'

'Yes, Frank; I am very weak upon this subject. It seems to me as if there was a kind of fatality in my meeting Florence Lawson's daughter. I have laboured so hard to forget that woman, and the harm she inflicted on me. I thought the very memory of my wrongs was blotted from my mind; but the sight of that girl brought the old pain back with all its sharpness. I can't trust myself in her society, Frank. Let me be wise, and leave her.'

I was astonished by this almost childish weakness in such a man as John Marlow, and used my utmost eloquence to argue him out of his folly. My reasoning prevailed at last, and he consented to remain with us.

We spent the next day in an excursion to Warwick Castle. Miss Lawson was with us; and while we were exploring the fine old rooms, I saw her more than once engaged in conversation with Mr. Marlow; nor did he take any pains to avoid her in the drawing-room that evening.

Several days passed, and John Marlow said no more about leaving us. He was so undemonstrative in his manners as to attract little notice from strangers; but I, who really liked him, watched him closely, and I saw that his attention was given almost exclusively to Margaret Lawson. It seemed to me that he was drawn to her always against his will. He approached her in a kind of half-reluctant manner; but, once by her side, he never quitted her till the evening was ended. She, for her part, appeared to take much interest in his society, and was always ready to sing or play at his request. Of course this did not escape the quick observation of my sisters, and one morning when I dropped into the schoolroom during Miss Lawson's absence, the subject was discussed among them.

'I dare say she would marry him for the sake of a position,' said Clara. 'She has no prospect except matrimony, and I know she hates a life of dependence on her rich relations, purse-proud, disagreeable people, according to her account of them.'

'I hope she would marry him for his own sake,' I answered; 'I should be sorry for John Marlow if it were otherwise, for I believe him to be a man of very deep feelings.'

'Then he had better steer clear of Margaret Lawson,' said my sister. 'Whatever heart she has to give is bestowed elsewhere. She left her last situation on account of a love affair with the only son of the house, a Mr. Horace Rawdon. His father. Sir Michael Rawdon, was furious against the young man, and sent him abroad on account of the affair. Margaret told me the story with her own lips, and showed me Mr. Rawdon's portrait He and all his family are as poor as church mice, she told me, but they had great expectations in the matrimonial way for the young man. He might have married his cousin, the only child of a rich manufacturer, who has a splendid place near Rawdon Park, and who very much wished for an alliance between the two families.'

The first time I found myself alone with him after this conversation I told John Marlow what I had heard from my sister, determined that he should not suffer a second time from a misplaced affection, if any effort of mine could prevent the sacrifice. The effect of my words was much more severe than I had anticipated, and I saw that the grave iron-gray bachelor had been hard hit.

'I must know how far this affair has gone,' he said abruptly. 'I will ask Margaret for an explanation.'

'Will that be fair to my sisters?' I asked. 'Miss Lawson may very justly consider them guilty of a breach of confidence, and she will assuredly think me an arrant snob for talking of her affairs. I should not have broached the subject if you had not expressed a kind of dread of this girl's influence over your mind.'

'Yes,' he replied, 'I did fear her influence, heaven knows whether wisely or foolishly. I will take care not to commit you or your sisters. But I must know the truth from Margaret's own lips. I have the right of a future husband to question her. The die is cast, Frank. She has promised to be my wife. It is rather rapid work, no doubt; but Miss Lawson's dependent position justified my acting promptly, and no lapse of time could make me love her better than I do. I have urged her to consent to an early marriage, and I hope to marry her from her uncle's house in London before the beginning of Lent. You must not think me a fool for this sudden passion, Frank. This girl brought the memory of my youth back to me, and it is in her power to atone for all the pain her mother inflicted upon me.'

I tried to congratulate him, but it was now my turn to be weakly superstitious, and to perceive a kind of fatality in this affair. The truth of the matter was, that I could not bring myself to believe in Miss Lawson. There was a light in those brilliant hazel eyes that was not the radiance of a candid soul. I watched her closely after this conversation with John Marlow; and although her manner to him was all that it should have been, I was secretly convinced that she had no real love for her affianced husband.

Whatever explanation arose between the lovers appeared satisfactory to my friend. He told me afterwards that Margaret had behaved with perfect candour. It was true that young Rawdon had made her an offer, but she had never in any manner encouraged his attentions or returned his affection. The affair had reached his father's ears through one of his sisters. Miss Lawson's pupils, and had resulted in his banishment from home; but the heart and mind of the governess had, according to her own account, been utterly unaffected.

My sisters were speedily informed of Miss Lawson's engagement, and were too good-natured to feel anything but pleasure on hearing the news; although, in their eyes, the age of the bridegroom entirely destroyed the romance of the courtship. Clara could not banish the recollection of Horace Rawdon, the absent traveller, who had gone on a trading expedition to the coast of Africa, hoping to enrich himself by that means.

'Margaret ought to have waited for his return,' said my sister. 'I know she was very much in love with him when she first came here, let her say what she will'

In the second week in January Mr. Marlow left us to return to London in order to make all necessary arrangements for his marriage; but before bidding me goodbye at the station he invited me to join him in town at my earliest convenience. He had lodgings in the neighbourhood of Piccadilly, and ample accommodation for a visitor. Miss Lawson was to leave us a fortnight afterwards to return to her relations, who were eager to receive her now that she was about to make an advantageous marriage. Her uncle, Mr. Samuel Lawson, was a stockbroker, occupying a large, gaudily furnished house at Bayswater.

During the week following Marlow's departure I amused myself by watching Miss Lawson, in the interests of my friend. Every other morning's post brought her a letter from her lover, and several registered packets of jewellery gratified her during the course of the week; nor were Mr. Marlow's gifts by any means trifling in value. I fancied, however, that she received these tributes very much as a matter of course; and on more than one occasion when she talked to me of my friend it seemed to me that she was more intent on obtaining information as to his position and resources in India than she was interested in my praises of his character and talents.

It was on my last morning at home that the post-bag brought Miss Lawson a foreign letter, the aspect of which caused her evident agitation. She did not open this epistle at the breakfast-table, and I thought that she looked at me somewhat anxiously as she slipped it into her pocket. She knew that I was going to spend the next week with her lover, and perhaps imagined that I should mention this letter.

I found John Marlow in excellent spirits. He was to be married early in March. He had sketched out his honeymoon tour on the Continent, and had taken a pretty furnished house at the West End to receive his young wife and him on their return to London in May.

'I shall give her all the pleasures and gaieties that a woman of her age has a right to enjoy,' he said. 'She shall have no occasion to regret having married a man twenty years her senior.'

'Tell me one thing, Marlow,' I said, seriously. 'You mean this to be a love-match, don't you? You wouldn't marry Margaret Lawson if you believed her influenced by your position and fortune, would you, old fellow?'

'I would not, Frank.'

'So help you heaven?'

'So help me heaven!' he answered as earnestly. 'I believe she loves me, Frank. If I did not think that, I would sooner cut my throat than marry her.'

'There are some men who think love comes after marriage,' I said presently.

'I am not one of those. I have received Margaret Lawson's assurance that she loves me; and I believe her from my soul. Have you anything to say against her, Frank?'

'Oh, nothing,' I replied hastily, rather alarmed by that somewhat tigerish ferocity with which a man over head and ears in love is accustomed to hear the impeachment of his betrothed. I remembered that foreign letter, and the sudden flush which had overspread Miss Lawson's face as she received it, but I dared not mention the subject to my friend. It seemed so mean a thing to persist in doubting the lady, and the letter might be from anyone in the world except that absent traveller, Horace Rawdon.

I did, however, doubt this lady's truth almost in spite of myself and listened to my friend's anticipations of happiness with secret misgiving. My visit to him was prolonged much beyond the week I had intended to devote to it. I dined at Bayswater with the Lawson family—a showy, ceremonial banquet; and I spent a good deal of my time with John Marlow and his affianced at picture galleries, theatres, and other places of entertainment.

I had occasion to cross the park one morning in the direction of Bayswater, on my way to call upon some friends in Hyde Park Gardens; and in one of the lonelier walks I was surprised to meet Miss Lawson. She was quite alone, and seemed, as I thought, not a little embarrassed by meeting me. I knew that she had refused to attend a morning concert with Mr. Marlow that day, on the plea of particular business in the way of shopping, and was therefore disposed to wonder at finding her strolling idly here. She said something about an atrocious headache, which had obliged her to put off all business, and dismissed me, as I thought, rather impatiently.

My friends were not at home; and I recrossed the park within half an hour by another and longer route, taking the furthermost border of the Serpentine. Here, having no special occupation for the afternoon, I lingered to smoke a cigar, stretched at full length upon a bench by the side of the water. The day was mild for the season of the year, but the gardens were almost deserted at this time. I was roused from my reverie by a man's voice close at hand, saying loudly,—

'If you throw me over, Margaret, you will be as false and heartless a woman as ever breathed the breath of life. You know that I trusted implicitly in your promise to marry me whenever I came home to claim you, and you know that I have broken with my family for ever in order to be true to you. I might have done well abroad had I been content to wait for success; but I could not endure life away from you, and I availed myself of the first opportunity that arose for my return. I have accepted a clerkship in a merchant's office, with a salary that will just enable us to live. It is no brilliant prospect to offer you, Margaret; but it is better than the dependence of your position as a governess, and it is a life to be shared with a man you have professed to love.'

The answer to this speech escaped me. The speaker was walking slowly beside a lady on the other side of the noble horse-chestnut beneath which I was seated, completely screened by the massive trunk from these two promenaders. They walked a little way, and then returned. This time the lady was speaking, and I recognized the clear musical tones of Miss Lawson's voice.

'You know that I have always been true to you, Horace,' she said; 'but it was not the less foolish of you to come home. I was shocked by your imprudence when I received your letter from Marseilles. Such a step will be sure to aggravate your father, and all your friends.'

'I thought you would be glad of my return Margaret.'

'Of course I am glad to see you; but I am sorry that your prospects should be sacrificed to such foolish impatience. We are both young enough to wait for a few years.'

Not a word of her engagement to John Marlow. They passed the tree again, returned, and then parted within a few paces of my seat.

'May I call upon you at your uncle's?'

'No, Horace; I dare not receive you there. I will write to you in a few days. I have run the risk of all kinds of annoyance in consenting to meet you today. My uncle and aunt are straitlaced and severe to a degree. Goodbye.'

'A brief meeting and a cold parting, Margaret. When shall I see you again?'

'Indeed I don't know. I will write to you.'

He kissed her, and let her go, very reluctantly, as it seemed to me in my place of concealment. I rose as Miss Lawson hurried away, and contrived to meet the gentleman face to face. He was walking slowly along, swinging his cane to and fro, with a very moody countenance. He was a fine young fellow, with a handsome face bronzed by foreign suns.

I went back to my friend's lodgings sorely puzzled as to my line of conduct. It was evident that Margaret Lawson had deceived Marlow as to her relations with Horace Rawdon; but it did not appear to me that she meant to jilt the elder man. I had little doubt that the letter she was to write her old love would' contain the intelligence of her approaching marriage with John Marlow. She had shrunk in a cowardly manner from telling young Rawdon a truth which she would not fear to communicate in a letter. It was his anger, not his pain she dreaded.

'She is just what I thought her,' I said to myself,—'selfish and cold-hearted to the last degree. I should dearly love to see her left in the lurch by both her suitors.'

On reflection, I decided that it was best to tell John Marlow the whole truth. He was likely enough to detest me for my interference; but I was willing to suffer his dislike rather than that he should walk blindfold into a matrimonial snare for lack of fair warning. I found him reading his Indian letters, which the overland mail had just brought him.

'Another bank gone,' he said, 'the Calcutta Imperial.'

'Does that affect you?' I asked, anxiously.

'Personally to the extent of a few hundreds only, but I have many friends who will suffer.'

It struck me that this failure might be turned to some account as a trial of Miss Lawson's truth; but I said nothing about this to Marlow. I only told him, in the simplest manner, what I had heard that afternoon in Kensington Gardens.

John Marlow was deeply moved, but he said very little, and I saw how painfully weak-minded he was upon the subject. We were both to dine at Bayswater on the next evening, and I felt sure that he would take occasion to question his betrothed. He did not wait for the evening, however, but went early the following morning to call on Miss Lawson.

She was out with her aunt and cousins; and he came home looking ill, tired, and depressed. When the evening came he was too ill to dine out; and I went myself to carry his excuses and my own, about an hour before the dinner-hour.

Mr. Lawson was out; and on requesting to see his niece, I was ushered into the library, where the young lady came to me. I told her of Mr. Marlow's illness, and she received the news with evident uneasiness.

'It is very sudden, is it not?' she asked, looking at me in a searching manner.

'Yes, it is sudden. He seems to be suffering from a kind of low fever.'

'My uncle tells me there has been a great bank failure in Calcutta. I hope that does not affect Mr. Marlow?'

'Not to any great extent, I believe,' I replied with assumed hesitation, for I saw the young lady had already taken fright.

'But to some extent it does,' she answered quickly. 'Do you think it is anxiety that has made him ill?'

'He certainly does seem troubled in his mind; but his anxiety may not arise from business matters.'

'From what else could it arise?'

'You would be more likely to know that than I; for I am sure he has no secrets from you.'

'I hope not; I have a right to share his troubles.'

'I am glad to hear you say that,' I replied; 'I should be sorry for him if he were to win only a fair-weather wife.'

Miss Lawson charged me with all manner of affectionate messages for her betrothed, and I departed. My friend's illness lasted for some days, and even after his recovery the fever left him worn and pale.

'Frank,' he said to me on the first morning that we breakfasted together in the sitting-room, 'I am going to offer Miss Lawson her freedom, and I want you to be a witness of our interview. I have thought the subject out during my illness, and I trust I have come to the right way of thinking. I shall make no allusion to the meeting in the gardens, as I do not want to compromise you.'

I accompanied him to Mr. Lawson's house, and was present throughout a scene which touched me deeply. My friend spoke with a noble simplicity, offering to release his betrothed, and imploring her to withdraw from her engagement unless she could give him her whole heart.

'I am twenty years your senior, Madge,' he said, 'and have nothing but my truth to commend me to you. Let us understand each other before it is too late. Nothing but misery could come to either of us from a loveless union.'

She looked at him with a curiously searching look, and hesitated a little before replying.

'You must have some hidden reason for this formal offer, John,' she said.

'It is not a formal offer; I have no reason but my desire to be secure in the possession of your heart.'

'Have you any cause to doubt me?'

'I cannot answer that question very precisely. There is such a thing as instinctive doubt. I know and feel my own demerits. Our engagement was a hasty one, and I want to give you a fair opportunity for withdrawal before it is too late. I entreat you to be true to me, Margaret—to me and to yourself. But I do not want to hurry you; take time for reflection; let me see you again tomorrow at this time.'

Mr. Lawson came into the room as we were taking leave, and

his niece had an opportunity for speaking to me alone while Mr. Marlow was talking to him.

'Your friend is looking very ill,' she said, anxiously; 'I fear this bank business must be a serious affair.'

'Yes,' I replied, with equal gravity; 'it means ruin—for the losers.'

She had no time to question me further, and I felt assured that her mystification was complete. She attributed her lover's offer entirely to a change in his circumstances, which he was not candid enough to explain.

He had not long to wait for his answer; it came by that evening's post. She had thought earnestly upon the subject, and was convinced that his offer to release her implied a doubt that was incompatible with perfect affection. It was best, therefore, that the offer should be accepted, and that both should hold themselves free. This reply came upon John Marlow like a thunderclap. In spite of her duplicity with regard to her old engagement, he had to the last believed in Margaret Lawson's love for himself.

'You are right, Frank,' he said; 'I have only exposed myself to a second disappointment. I shall go back to India next month, and leave the ground dear for Horace Rawdon.'

'Whom she will jilt just as she has jilted you,' I replied. 'She will never consent to marry a clerk in a merchant's office; unless, indeed, the prospect of his future baronetcy should tempt her.'

The issue proved my guess correct. Miss Lawson married a merchant-prince whom she had met at her uncle's house, and whose budding attentions, taken in conjunction with the bank failure, had tempted her to the breaking of her engagement. This gentleman failed within six months of his marriage, and fled from his creditors, leaving his wife to exist as best she might on her earnings as a daily governess. This means of subsistence has, however, been augmented of late by an annuity of a hundred pounds settled on her by an anonymous benefactor, whose name I know to be John Angus Marlow. My friend returned to India, where he is now an eminently prosperous man, but a confirmed bachelor, happy in the pursuit of his profession, and with no thought beyond it.

Prince Ramji Rowdedow

I cannot say that Slimeford-on-the-Slushy is a likely town in which to make a great theatrical benefit. I cannot say that Slimeford is a good town for theatricals in any way or shape, or that the inhabitants of Slimeford patronize either the Thespian art, or any other art, or any science, amusement, or pursuit of any kind whatsoever, with much enthusiasm. I cannot say that Slimeford is a fine town or a pretty town; unless, indeed, your idea of architectural beauty is confined to one interminable street of undeviatingly ugly houses, intersected by an infinite number of smaller streets, if possible more ugly than the chief thoroughfare, and surrounded on all sides by a rising neighbourhood; a rising neighbourhood dotted with hideous manufactories, which start up, like grimy demons, with outstretched wings of brick and mortar, to shut out the country.

And, reader, what on the surface of God's earth, as man has marred it, is more frightful than a rising neighbourhood? A row of newly-finished houses, a row of unfinished *ditto*, an exhausted brickfield, and a patch of waste land—ring the changes on these as you will, and get beauty out of them if you can; and only so much beauty can you get out of a rising neighbourhood.

I cannot say that the Slushy is a beautiful river, or that the muddy banks thereof are pleasant walking, or that any mortal, not an inhabitant of Slimeford, ever expressed admiration for its dirty waters, on which dismal black barges lie at anchor here and there, and into which various dye-works and other factories discharge their viscid and rainbow-hued liquids.

One peculiarity of Slimeford is that its working classes are always on strike at the very period when a dramatic company enters the town. You are greeted with the intelligence that the weavers are out, and not likely to be in for a couple of months; and that the dyers are resolved to have an additional three half-pence an hour, or fold their arms and perish. You should have come last year; you would have done wonders last year. But unfortunately you are not in the habit of going to places last year.

Now I had the honour to be, for three seasons, first low comedian of the Theatre Royal, Slimeford; and for the first two seasons I had the honour to take benefits, whereat my labours to please were rewarded by a limited circle of from three to seven in the boxes, a dreary sprinkling in the pit, and a row-and-a-half or so in the gallery. Now, if you deduct £7 for the expenses of the house, as computed by the manager, thirty shillings for printing, an odd pound or so for properties—not a little money spent in the pursuit of that diplomatic process called benefit- making—you won't get much of a surplus out of £4 10s., two-thirds, of which surplus, if there were one, would go to the lessee. Therefore my benefits, during the first two seasons, had the disappointing result of plunging me deeply and hopelessly into debt.

The third season was drawing to a close, and Slimeford was, if possible, in a state of greater stagnation than usual. The weavers had made a most obstinate strike of it, and the only thing stirring was a penny subscription to keep the contumacious dyers from starvation. I looked around as I stood pensively on the banks of the Slushy, and meditated on my chances of filling the crazy old Theatre Royal on Wednesday, the 19th instant, which night had been set apart for the benefit of me, Mr. John Miffs.

Now I had, in the course of my professional career, beheld one marvel in theatrical statistics—or shall I say play-going human nature?—*i,e.* that however poor the inhabitants of a town, however high the price of the quartern loaf, however great the demand for blue ruin, with its attendant ills of starvation and crime; however you may have been assured again and again that

136

the people cannot come to the theatre, because they have actually not the money to pay for admission, let Mr. Sims Reeves or Mr. Sothern, Mr. Charles Mathews, Mr. Irving, or Mr. Buckstone—let, I say, any of these aforesaid artists, or many others I could mention, put out an announcement, in capitals three feet high, of their intention to appear at the Theatre Royal Anywhere, and, lo! That theatre is immediately filled. Now, I don't know whether it was an inspiration or not, but at the very moment when Venus rose pale in an opal evening sky, her beautiful face feebly mirrored in the grimy waters of the Slushy, I suddenly exclaimed, 'A star!' Yes, I would have a star to play for my benefit, and thus fill the theatre.

But then, what star? I had not the pleasure of Mr. Buckstone's acquaintance, and if I had, was it likely that distinguished comedian would withdraw himself from the part in which he was at that time delighting his friends in the Haymarket, for my pleasure and profit? I didn't know Mr. Sothern, but I knew enough of that gentleman to think it scarcely probable he would choose the Theatre Royal, Slimeford, wherein to commence his great tour of the provinces.

I didn't know the talking fish; I hadn't so much as a pig-faced lady amongst my acquaintances. What star? Ah, Venus, shining with serene radiance above the smoke-cloud that envelopes Slimeford, could you only help me with a suggestion! If the Shah of Persia had been in England, he might have obliged me by taking a private box and exhibiting himself in state apparel to Slimeford.

And if the Shah of Persia, why not an Indian prince? Yes, above all things an Indian prince! A most brilliant idea! I registered a vow, as I stood on that bridge in the twilight. I would have an Indian prince to play for my benefit.

I am not of a lymphatic temperament. I believe, indeed, that I come rather under the head of the sanguine nervous, but I leave that question in physiology to the decision of the intelligent reader, when I inform him that the next morning every patch of paling, every blank wall, every house in Chancery, every stray shutter of every shop to let, was pasted with a staring red-and-blue announcement of the first and only appearance of His Royal Highness Prince Ramji Rowdedow, from the kingdom of Goojeebadanistan, that vast territory between the Ganges and the Himalayas, for the benefit of Mr. John Miffs; while in the principal windows of the town were exhibited lithographed full-length portraits of an imposing individual of the *mulatto* race, in a gorgeous costume of the character usually worn by that interesting Moor who is familiar to all students of the Shakespearian drama.

Depressed as was the aspect of trade in Slimeford, my notion took. There was from the first issuing of the bills considerable excitement in the town on the subject of the Indian prince. The very printer who set up the bills offered to do the job at a lower rate, on condition of being one of the favoured few who were to form a little deputation to meet the prince at the railway station. Of course there were many inquiries as to why the royal personage had left his native land; and his popularity rose tremendously, especially among the fairer portion of the community, when I explained that he had been deposed from the royal *musnud* by a benighted people, on account of the advancement and enlightenment of his opinions, especially with reference to polygamy and widow-burning.

He was announced to appear in the character of Obi; and the fact of a native prince from the distant land of Bramah and Juggernaut coming down to Slimeford to enact that hero of romance, did not appear to the intelligent townsmen at all a strange occurrence. A foreign prince, a talking fish, or Mr. Charles Mathews—what are any such institutions intended for, but to minister to the amusement, gratify the admiring gaze, and stimulate the organ of wonder of the inhabitants of Slimeford? For these good people, I think, had a very limited belief in the actual existence of any world beyond the rising neighbourhood which bounded their own town.

Wednesday the 19th instant arrived, and the whole theatre-going populace was on the *qui vive*; while the question as to how and when His Highness from the principality of Goojee-badanistan would enter the town was freely discussed. Be it understood, these good people were quite assured that the prince was coming all the way from the shores of the Ganges for their amusement. Had they thought for a moment that his exiled highness might be a lodger in Marylebone, or a ratepayer of St. Pancras, the whole zest of the thing would have been gone.

Even at the theatre, amongst my companion votaries of Thespis, there was not a little curiosity; and I was compelled, with that beautiful candour which distinguishes me, to admit to one or two of my intimates that my friend Rowdedow was not in sober earnest actually the scion of a royal race, being in point of fact the private secretary of a rich indigo planter, who had accompanied his employer to England, and who had been dismissed from that service on account of a suspected leaning towards the worship of the goddess Kali, the tutelary divinity of the Thugs, or stranglers, sometimes called Noosers.

The damask cheek of my friend Percy Deloraine, *jeune premier*, blanched somewhat at this revelation; and he expressed a strong aversion from acting in the same piece with his highness; but on my assuring him that, if treated with a cold and distant respect, Ramji was the best fellow breathing, he consented to oblige me.

The prince, I informed my manager and brother actors, would not arrive until an hour or two before the commencement of the performance, as important business—no less, in fact, than an interview with the chief of the English Government concerning his restoration to that vast territory which extends from the western arm of the Ganges to the distant source of the Oxus, as I added, somewhat recklessly, with a view to local colouring—would detain him in London. I therefore read his part at rehearsal, arranged his entrances and exits, and went through all his stage business.

I also planned the construction and adornment of a temporary dressing-room, to be erected by the property-man for my royal friend's convenience, and made all arrangements necessary for the honourable reception of the royal personage. As I left the theatre, after that morning's rehearsal, a crowd of dirty little boys and one respectable maid-servant with a baby and a perambulator, did me the honour to accompany me in a little impromptu procession to my residence. Whether they imagined I might keep, the prince in my pocket, or in a sealed bottle, like the genie in the *Arabian Nights*, I know not; but they evidently thought their best chance of beholding the Oriental potentate lay in not losing sight of me.

Now, this persistent attention on the part of the public, honourable as it was to all concerned, was also somewhat embarrassing to me, as I had a good deal of work to accomplish (of a kind that must remain a secret to the British public) before His Royal Highness Ramji Rowdedow could possibly blaze, like the sun in his Oriental splendour, before the dazzled eyes of Slimeford. For this, I had need of a friend—a friend on whom I could rely—in whose hand I could lay my own, and say, 'Here is the soul incapable of treachery; here is the tongue never known to betray;' or in the more vigorous language of Seven Dials, 'This 'ere's the cove wot never rounded on his pal.'

Such a friend I could boast in the person of Mr. Richard Wittington, eccentric comedian; and to him I went. What passed between us I do not intend to reveal, but our parting agreement was to the following effect: Wittington pledged himself to superintend the reception of his highness. For this purpose he was to hire the largest and most splendid open vehicle to be procured from the King's Arms livery-yard, and a pair of white horses; with which equipage he was to proceed, at a quarter-past five o'clock, to the railway station.

He was also to hire an inferior vehicle, in which a portion of the band belonging to the theatre—namely, clarionet, cornet, and big drum—should be seated, to give effect to the procession with such soul-stirring melodies as 'See, the conquering Hero,' 'Rule, Britannia,' the March from 'Bluebeard,' &c. This my friend Wittington was to do unaided, while I departed to a distant village, some ten miles up the line, to arrange a small matter of business which it was impossible for me to postpone.

The hour came, the procession started in the following order from the King's Arms:—fly-and-pair, yellow body, pink-striped chintz lining, chocolate wheels, Mr. Richard Wittington seated *solus* in the vehicle, looking, strange to say, rather depressed than elated at the prospect of receiving his serene highness; nextly, the second-best fly, green body, red wheels, and leopard-skin chintz lining, a showy, impressive equipage, in which were seated the clarionet, comet, flute, and big drum attached to the theatre, the big drum nearly filling the interior of the vehicle, and somewhat obscuring the distinguished musicians seated therein.

This imposing procession of two carnages was followed by an immense crowd, composed of half the population of Slimeford. Of course the worthy citizens, being out of work, had nothing better to do than to pay their respects to the royal foreigner, and to show him, in the deliberate and piercing stare of the well-bred Englishman, the distinguishing mark of British hospitality.

Arrived at the station, which, with that regard to public convenience which generally characterizes the station of a provincial town, was about a mile from the high street, Mr. Wittington alone descended from his vehicle, and entered the gates of the building. He expressed a request to his friends and the public that they would not accompany him any farther, as their appearance in too abrupt a manner might disconcert the modest disposition of the great Ramji.

This mild request, however, did not prevent Mr. Bulkins of the King's Arms, renowned for possessing great sporting acumen, and being always able to name the outsider that will not win the Derby or the Leger; Mrs. Potash the washer-woman; her daughter. Miss Potash (in her best bonnet of scarlet velvet and pearl beads, a cheerful and summery headgear); Miss Hooxanise, the dressmaker's apprentice; three nursemaids, sixteen babies, and several other enterprising individuals, from penetrating to the very door of the second-class carriage, from which, with the unaffected humility that distinguishes those who are born in the purple, descended the illustrious Rowdedow.

Now, most of the inhabitants of Slimeford were well acquainted with the private life and domestic afflictions of Othello the noble Moor; and it occurred to all present that the prince bore a very strong resemblance to that individual as he would appear after exchanging his costly robes for a badly-fitting dress-coat from the emporium of Messrs. Moses and Sons. The noble physiognomy of the prince, it is marvellous to add, recalled to several among the play-going population of Slimeford a face they had seen somewhere before, though the recollection was so vague as to make very little impression on those not over impressionable citizens.

His complexion of a brownish black, was relieved by a crimson glow which illumined his cheeks and threw out the whites of his eyes with Oriental brilliancy. His long sleek hair, of rather a bluish black (in the sun it looked a thought rusty), was worn with the ends rolled under, after the manner of gentlemen of the equestrian profession. He wore a large beard and moustache, which imparted something of ferocity to his otherwise mild (sooth to say, somewhat timorous) expression of countenance. He wore a magnificent fez cap, surmounted by a rich (though rather tarnished) gold tassel, and decorated with two or three large brooches (somewhat in the style of those which issue from the hands of the theatrical ornament-makers of Birmingham and Bow street), but which, no doubt, were the royal jewels of his imperial race; he also displayed on the ample breast of his dress-coat, which was a little white about the seams, various stars and crosses, besides that noble quadruped, the elephant, usually worn by his youthful highness, Hamlet the Dane.

A superb crescent of Bristol paste, mounted on red cloth, shimmered in the dim obscurity of his waistcoat, and, seen from a distance, impressed the young mind with the idea of the diamonds of Golconda. His costume was completed by a pair of white duck trousers, patent-leather alberts, a bamboo cane, and an eye-glass, it being only becoming in royalty to be short-sighted. Nothing could exceed the *empressement* with which Mr. Wittington greeted the prince; he conversed with him apart in a foreign language with characteristic gesticulation which was eminently gratifying to the lookers on; he preceded him to the carriage, hat in hand, walking backwards, yes, actually walking backwards; a feat by which he cruelly punished the corns of the aggrieved populace who pressed dose behind him. He also handed the exiled potentate into the pink-striped fly, and seated himself respectfully opposite, with his back to the horses.

Then arose such a shout as, perhaps, since the days when the Reform Bill was passed, had never been heard in Slimeford: a shout of friendly welcome for the dark scion of a princely race, who sat bowing, smiling, and displaying a set of faultlessly white teeth to the admiring citizens.

The band began, at a wink from my friend Wittington, to play 'See, the conquering Hero,' &c., which, as within no one's knowledge had the royal person ever been in battle, was of course highly appropriate. The two flies set off at a foot pace, the delighted populace on either side. They were charmed with the prince's bow; they were enraptured with the prince's smile; and 'Oh, look at his teeth!' yes, an audible murmur was heard amongst the throng, 'Look at his teeth!'

At which, strange to say, the prince abruptly closed his mouth, and declined to exhibit his dental appendages any more. The prince was evidently of a sensitive and retiring disposition. But, above all things, that which delighted the populace was the evident and demonstrative admiration evinced by his serene highness for the town and public buildings of Slimeford, He expressed, in vehement pantomime, his opinion that Slimeford in architectural beauty surpassed the proud towers of Delhi, the city of palaces; that the river Slushy in natural beauty might dispute the palm with his native Ganges, or the classic Indus dear to his childhood.

When Mr. Wittington pointed out to him the church of St. Bulgrumblery, the chapel-of-ease, the fish market, the Baptist chapel, the post-office, and that aesthetic range of buildings known as the shambles, devoted to the sale of butcher's meat, the prince's shrugs, nods, and gesticulations evinced such admiration as the inhabitants of the town had never beheld before, even in a new candidate for the representation of the borough. The procession was, in short, intensely successful; and my new star, the illustrious Ramji, was honoured with such an ovation as I think neither Spanish dancers, talking fish, nor Mr. Charles Mathews would ever have received in Slimeford.

But in spite of the cheers, of the heartiness of that welcome which the true-born Englishman always extends to every foreigner, there was something in the prince's manner, a shiver in the prince's manly form, a chatter about the prince's teeth, and, at the same time, a paleness of complexion, verging on the ghastly, visible in my friend Mr. Wittington, difficult to account for.

Can you, sagacious reader, solve me this little enigma? Of course you can. I thought so. You know that it was because the great Ramji Rowdedow, illustrious heir to the principality of Goojeebadanistan, that vast territory between the Ganges and the Himalayas, was neither more nor less distinguished an individual than John Miffs, comedian—I, John Miffs, with the adornment of a burnt cork, a pennyworth of Armenian bole, a halfpennyworth of vermilion, a great deal of *crêpe* hair, and an Othello wig,—I, John Miffs, who had gone that morning ten miles down the line, and, at the house of a friendly innkeeper in the village of Bigglethorpe, had arrayed myself in the costly attire of the Indian potentate.

I leave it to the imagination, then, of the amiable reader whether I was not a little alarmed lest that intelligent public, which loves to be gulled, but hates to find out that it has been gulled, should by any means discover the cheat that I was putting upon it. Thus when, during my triumphal progress from the station to the theatre, the populace admired my teeth —I have a fine set of teeth, I confess—I shut my mouth, in mortal fear lest young Joe Mulkins, Mr. Forcep the dentist's assistant, who was hanging on to the door of my chariot, should see that double tooth near the front which he had stopped three days before, and which still glittered in all the first radiance of the gold filling.

Who can describe the horror of that moment, when a gentle

and refreshing shower descended from the afternoon sky, and I dreaded to behold my complexion trickling down in brown drops upon my shirt-front, and when my friend Dick's nervous attempts to shut up that mysterious vehicle, the fly, were greeted with the anger of a ferocious crowd?

'Oh, hang it! let us see un; we've come all the way to see un; don't go for to shoot up t'coach!' cried that unappeasable populace.

But the heavens were kind to the descendant of a royal race, and I shone out again in that beauty whose only blemish was its liability to come off.

'Put out your hand,' whispered Wittington; 'it looks very natural.'

I placed that member, adorned with a property diamond ring, carelessly on the carriage door, and lo! the admiring crowd exclaimed as with one voice, 'Look at his 'and!' Indeed, one old man, a determined sightseer, who had never quitted the wheels of our vehicle, laid hold with reverence upon my dexter paw, perhaps to discover whether that portion of an Indian prince's anatomy was like the flesh and blood of everyday life.

The royal *cortège* reached the doors of the theatre, still followed by the delighted crowd. The prince alighted from the stately vehicle, and then gracefully ascended, on the tips of his patent leather alberts, the green baize-covered plank which the property man, enthusiastic in the cause of exiled greatness, had placed to form an impromptu bridge leading from the kerbstone to the stage-door, so that his highnesses gracious feet should not be defiled by the puddles of Slimeford.

At the stage door the Oriental countenance of his serenity broke anew into a radiant smile, and he made a series of grateful bows to the crowd; which were responded to by three hearty cheers and ever so many little ones in. These culminated in a deafening shout as he disappeared within the building; while Mr. Richard Wittington closed the door firmly on the persevering populace, which immediately proceeded to the pit and gallery doors, there to await, armed with sterling coin of the realm, the commencement of the performance, and the first appearance on the boards of Slimeford of a prince of the blood royal.

Within the theatre, Rowdedow was greeted with bows and smiles from the ladies and gentlemen of the company, who had dressed early for their respective parts in the drama of "Obi," and assembled in the green-room for the sole purpose of staring at him. There was a little attempt at conversation.

The prince was asked his opinion of England, English manners and customs, &c., but the shrugs of his graceful shoulders, and elevations of his strongly defined eyebrows, with which he responded, evinced such an utter ignorance of the English language as rendered discourse impossible; indeed, when Mr. Spavins, a gentleman who had been in India, actually addressed his royal highness in Hindostanee, he still continued the shrug of non-comprehension, whereat that gentleman was cruelly laughed at by his compeers for having attempted a language he could not speak. 'That's your Hindostanee, is it? You see, His Excellency doesn't understand a syllable.' As indeed His Excellency did not.

The property man preceded Ramji with two composite candles to the before-mentioned temporary dressing-room, and a young man who ran errands for the company requested to know, both by talking at the highest pitch of his voice (strange that foreigners do not understand our language better when we shout it as through a ship's trumpet!) and by expressive pantomime, whether he could be of any assistance in the toilet of the star. His aid was declined; and the illustrious Ramji begged, still in pantomime, to be left alone.

About this time the manager asked with considerable surprise what had become of Miffs? and the cry of 'Where's Miffs?' was echoed through the theatre. My friend Dick Wittington explained that as I did not play in my first piece, I had taken the opportunity of running down to some friends to sell some tickets; 'or very likely,' continued my friend, 'he may be next door' (next door was a tavern much affected by the Thespian corps). Richard indeed ran into the bar and asked if anybody had seen

Miffs.

No, nobody had seen Miffs. Miffs was not to be found. He did not even make his appearance when, the last bar of the overture being played, the curtain rose to a delighted audience, and in due course the Royal Obi appeared upon the boards. The prince enacted the part entirely in pantomime, applauded to the echo, and great was the wonderment of Slimeford that a denizen of a distant land, the wanderer from another hemisphere, should be so well up in every little bit of Victoria business and claptrap, familiar to them from the performance of the great Hicks.

The curtain fell, the theatre rang with loud cries of 'Rowdedow!' the prince appeared, his hand upon his breast, his head bent, his jaws working vigorously, as if employed in chewing betel-nut, or repeating to himself inward paeans of thanksgiving. This done, he made a general bow to the company, and in spite of numerous requests that he would take wine, brandy, ale, that he would stay to supper, that he would meet a party at the 'Shakespeare' (aforesaid tavern next door), that he would stop and play for the manager's benefit, and so on, and so forth—he insisted on departing immediately, in company with my friend Mr. Wittington.

So unassuming was his disposition, so reserved his nature, that he contrived to elude the crowd waiting at the stage door to behold him emerge. So secret were his movements in the subtlety of his oriental nature, that it was never known how he got to the railway station. Nay, the clerks and porters swore to the fact that no Indian whatsoever, or indeed any individual of a coloured race, left the station either that night or subsequently; and it was never known to any one in Slimeford how this royal and interesting amateur reached India, or the Ganges, or the Himalayas, or whatever his destination might be; whether his interview with the Secretary of State for India was successful; whether he ever regained the throne of his forefathers, or any fact whatsoever connected with the illustrious Ramji Rowdedow.

A quarter of an hour after his departure, however, I, Mr. John Miffs, made my appearance, ready to play in the last piece, with a black rim round my left eye which my kind friends insinuated I had got in a fight on the previous evening. I can only say, in conclusion, that this was the best benefit I ever had in Slimeford, realizing the handsome sum of twenty-seven pounds fourteen shillings and four-pence; but that, taking into account the risk I ran of being torn piecemeal by infuriated weavers and dyers had my disguise been penetrated, the money was dearly earned.

Sir Hanbury's Request

CHAPTER 1
IN THE HEXAM LIBRARY

The great northern metropolis, Loomborough, is one of the wealthiest provincial cities in the United Kingdom. Its public buildings are palatial. Its law courts, town-hall, exchange, club-houses, warehouses, emporiums, boast an architectural magnificence which puts all other provincial cities to the blush. Its cathedral appears to have been neglected, and allowed to run to seed, as it were, for the last three hundred years; but that is a detail. Municipal authorities cannot do everything; and the dinginess of the cathedral brings out the freshness and sharpness of that grand example of the Perpendicular English order near at hand, the Law Courts.

Throughout the city there is an all-pervading air of wealth. One can see at a glance that a million of money can be as easily raised in Loomborough as a few paltry thousands elsewhere. You have only to convince Loomborough that the million is required for the maintenance of her glory, and there it is, in ready money, waiting for the architect's certificate.

Time was when Loomborough was a quiet country town, ringed in with green fields and humble rustic villages, a clear blue river winding through it, and the sweet summer air unpolluted by smoke. But within the last century Loomborough has swollen into a brick-and-mortar octopus, and with each of its hungry suckers has absorbed a village; till the names of those outlying hamlets alone are left, and now serve to distinguish some of the busiest, richest, dirtiest, smokiest, and most crowded districts of the vast city.

Of Loomborough as it was a hundred and thirty years ago —in the days of the famous Forty-five, for instance—it is difficult now-a-days to find a trace, save in some curious old print, exhibited, with proud humility, by a Loomborough printseller. Yet there is just one little bit of the great city which has an old-world look even to-day, and suggests to one's fancy the quiet provincial town of the past; there is just one building which no sacrilegious hand has improved away from its original quaint beauty; a building which belongs to the age of Elizabeth, and is as unlike any modem edifice of the Tudor or Gothic school as it is possible for one thing to be unlike another.

This is Sir Hanbury Hexam's Library, a rich collection of black-letter books left to the city of Loomborough by a wealthy citizen of the Elizabethan age—with funds for the maintenance of the same, and power to add to their number—in accordance with certain rules made and provided, and a building to contain the same, and to be used as a public reading-room, open every day, except Sunday, free of charge, to the inhabitants of Loomborough. Sir Hanbury also established a college for the youth of the city, and endowed it with an estate amply sufficient for its maintenance.

There, in a wide yard under the shadow of the dingy old cathedral, stand the two buildings: the school, tall and square, and looking of later date than the library; the library, the quaintest, most curious old place that a student need wish to enter—a long low building, with all manner of narrow passages and queer little winding stairs; time-blackened oak panelling that might pass for ebony; ceilings that a man of middle height may touch with his hand; narrow recessed chambers, like loose boxes, where the books are stored in a severe gloom, appropriate rather to meditation than study—for it is but a dusky light that creeps in through the one narrow window which illumines each several recess.

These small divisions are fenced off by carved oak doors, as delicately pierced as the tabernacle work above the stalls in a cathedral, which doors are kept religiously locked. Here, in their particular den, you may find the old Chroniclers, the Fathers of the Church, Homer and his translators, Rabelais in his various and numerous editions. Bacon,—all the mighty spirits of departed learning, each, like a hermit, in his particular cave or cell.

One of the labyrinthine passages leads to the public reading-room, where the student-world of Loomborough is to be seen on a winter's day, represented by three grim-looking men—two gaunt and elderly; one young, but singular of aspect, with elf-locks streaming over his greasy coat-collar. Taking the editions of Homer we have looked at upstairs at a rough guess we may safely say there are ten for each of the three students.

One of the grim elders has surrounded himself with stacks of brown leather-covered tomes, as if he were anxious to get a good pennyworth out of Sir Hanbury's bequest. The other has drawn his ancient armchair close to the cavernous hearth, where a might sea-coal fire roars red and glorious in a vast iron grate. The young man muses over an open folio in a nook apart—a deep recess in which there is an old painted window, overhanging the stony yard, and colouring the gray December light

The room has evidently been unaltered since Sir Hanbury devised it to his fellow-citizens. The low ceiling—the black and polished panelling—a clumsy oak table here and there—a carved oak cabinet of ponderous design—a buffet in the same style—a curious eight-day dock—all carry the evidence of their age upon them. Sir Hanbury Hexam himself, an old man with a severe visage, pointed beard, and black velvet skull-cap, surveys the students from his portrait over the high oak mantelpiece, and seems to glower upon them in the ruddy firelight.

There is no pleasanter contrast imaginable than to pass from the brisk, busy, prosperous, money-getting modern city, seething and bubbling like a commercial witches' caldron a few yards away, to this silent dusky retreat, where one might fancy the lord of Verulam musing over the uses of deduction and hypothesis, or meditating the more practical question of how to preserve dead poultry by stuffing fowls with snow.

Into this sombre apartment on a certain December afternoon, about ten years ago, came a young man who seemed to have but little in common with the grim student at the table, or the gaunt idler hugging the fire—a young man with a bright handsome face, and a tall straight figure, clad in garments which had a certain un-English look, and were by no means too new. The dark blue overcoat looked as if it had been worn to the verge of shabbiness, and the carefully brushed hat betokened that care which a man gives to his wardrobe who knows not when and how he may be able to replenish it. The three students glanced at the stranger as if they inwardly resented his intrusion. The stranger surveyed them critically, as if they had been three peripatetic folios dingily bound, like the books on the shelves in the long narrow chambers on the upper story, from which he had just descended, followed by one of the officials carrying half a dozen volumes.

The official deposited his load on one of the disengaged tables and departed. The stranger walked round the room, looked through the painted window—across which the snowflakes were drifting, whitening the stony yard beyond—contemplated Sir Hanbury's portrait, and warmed his hands at the ruddy blaze—the fire-worshipper pushing his chair back half an inch or so to make way for him, with a discontented look.

'Delicious old place!' said the strange, turning to the fire-worshipper with a pleasant smile; 'charming retreat for the studious! Do you come here often, sir?'

'Every day, except Sundays, in winter,' growled the fire-worshipper.

'And our friend with the pile of books?' asked the stranger, with a backward glance at the table in a corner, where the second grim elder sat behind a rampart of dingy volumes.

'Every day, Sundays excepted, all the year round,' answered

the fire-worshipper, gloomily. 'He's writing a book about the end of the world, with a critical analysis of all the prophets, from Daniel down to Dr. Gumming. Nobody will ever give him any money for it; nobody will ever thank him or think any better of him for having written it; no printer, unless he's a madman, will ever be found to print a page of it. But he seems to enjoy writing it,' added the fire-worshipper, with a jerk of his head in the direction of the student. 'He's been at it forty years.'

'And he?' asked the stranger, with a look towards the youthful muser, who was gently dozing over his open folio.

'Oh, he's a local poet. He comes here to read the classics. He sleeps a good deal, I observe, but I dare say his ideas come to him that way. He contributes short poems to the newspapers *gratis*, and lives on his friends.'

The stranger sighed, and strolled away from the fire. He seated himself at the table where the librarian had placed his books, opened one of them, a Horace, and tried to read.

Unhappily there are conditions of the mind in which philosophic poetry loses its soothing power. This young man had his own troubles to think about, very real, very near—staring him in the face, jogging him by the elbow. Fate took the shape of the inexorable policeman, always urging him to move on. For him there was no tarrying at street corners, no shelter for him beneath the dark arches of life.

Presently he took a roll of paper from his pocket—the establishment found pen and ink—and began to write, stooping over the page, his pen dashing along with fiery speed, writing as a man writes who pours his heart out upon paper. It was a letter evidently, but what a letter!—six sheets of Bath post covered with that black bold calligraphy. When he had signed his name at the bottom of the last page he looked at the scattered sheets dubiously, as if debating whether he should read their contents.

'No,' he muttered to himself. 'If I read them I should change my mind and tear them up.'

He folded the sheets hastily, thrust the clumsy budget into a big official-looking envelope, and addressed it to—

Miss Hexam,
Hexam Park,
Near Loomborough.

It had been almost too dark for him to write the address in the dusky corner where he sat, but glancing towards the painted window, he saw that the deep recess which it lighted was vacant. The local poet had gone home to tea. The grim elders had departed. The room was empty.

'So much the better,' muttered the young man; 'I shall have a quiet half-hour before the place closes.'

He had a vague idea that the Hexam Library closed at six o'clock all the year round, and he had not troubled himself to verify that impression.

He went to the recess, took his Horace to the window, and began to pore over the large old-fashioned type. But at four o'clock on a December afternoon there was not light enough in Loomborough to illumine the biggest type. The distant street-lamps shone redly across the intervening gulf of darkness. The Hexam scholars were whooping in the stony yard. The young man looked at them through a bit of ruby glass—the real old ruby—in the painted window, yawned, sat down in the comfortable old oak chair, leaned his head on his hands, and abandoned himself to troublesome perplexities—till sleep stole gently upon his wearied brain, and closed the book of care.

CHAPTER 2
THE HEXAM ESTATE

It was near the hour of closing, and that ancient student who devoted himself chiefly to the contemplation of the excellent sea-coal fire provided by the Hexam foundation paused in the dusky little vestibule for a chat with the chief librarian. There was no such thing as gas in the Hexam Library. A dim oil lamp illumined the low oak-panelled chamber where the librarian sat at his desk, with a large and ponderous tome before him, in which were recorded the names of the visitors and students of the library. There was a tradition that the autographs of Sir

Kenelm Digby and John Evelyn were to be found in those faded old pages, and that a later leaf bore the honoured signature of Samuel Johnson. But the custodian was chary of displaying his treasures. He loved the book, and dozed away many a quiet afternoon hour, with his gray head reposing affectionately upon the ancient binding.

'There's been a queer chap up yonder this afternoon,' said the fire-worshipper, 'very free and offhand in his manners. Who is he, and where does he come from?'

The librarian opened his book with a solemn visage, and pointed to the latest signature.

There, sprawling across the page, in careless youth's bold characters, appeared the stranger's name—

Hanbury Hexam,
At the Old Bell Inn, Loomborough,

'What does that mean?' asked the fire-worshipper.

'I don't know. Either it's meant for a joke, or he must be the son of that old clergyman who ruined himself and his family by going to law about the Hexam property—Sir Joshua Hexam's estate, you know. There was a Chancery suit that lasted ever so many years.'

'I remember. But it's ten years since that was over and done with. I've almost forgotten the story.'

'I haven't. My connection with this place made it almost a personal matter, you see; and I studied the case in all its bearings. This Michael Hexam was a clergyman, with a good living and a comfortable little estate of his own—a farm near Bilshott. That's about twenty miles from Loomborough, you know. The farmhouse was very old, almost as old as this library. There was the date under the cornice of the porch, 1603, as large as life; and a fine old place it was.

'But one day, in a tremendous storm of wind, down comes a chimney-stack—such a chimney-stack as they don't build now-a-days—bricks enough in it to build a house with; and behind the chimney Michael Hexham finds a kind of cupboard or strong-room, containing a lot of old plate and an iron box of old family papers, not one of them later than William the Third's time. Well, these papers, according to Mr. Hexam's view of the case, proved his right to the Hexam estate.'

'How did he make that out?'

'Why, you must know that Sir Hugh Hexam, our Sir Hanbury's son, who was created a baronet by James the First, died intestate, and without direct heirs, so that his estate passed to the next of kin. The next of kin who came forward to claim the property was a first cousin once removed, being the grandson of Sir Hanbury's younger brother. This young man was a second son, but he brought forward witnesses to prove his elder brother's death in foreign parts.

'So he got the property, and his descendants have held it from that day to this. Well, this Michael Hexam, the parson of Bilshott, had been taught by his father to consider himself the rightful heir to all the Hexam property in the possession of Sir Joshua—and of others, for the original estate had been divided and subdivided in the course of years—as well as to the baronetcy; but, till the falling of the chimney, there had been missing links in the documentary evidence, and he didn't see his way to putting forward any claim.

'The discovery of that box of papers altered the aspect of affairs. He submitted his case to a solicitor in Loomborough, who advised him to go in and win. He mortgaged his poor little estate to furnish the sinews of war, and he filed a bill in Chancery against Sir Joshua Hexam and several other defendants. It was like the mouse going to war with the elephant.'

'I remember the case,' replied the fire-worshipper. 'It was always dragging its slow length through the newspapers. The man was smashed, of course.'

'Well, the man was, but his case wasn't. Some people might have called the issue success—but it killed the litigant. After the case had been before the court for years, off and on, the judge, one of our greatest men, pronounced upon the merits of the claim. Michael Hexam had clearly proved his legitimate descent from the elder brother of Mark Hexam, who succeeded Sir Hugh as next of kin. He had proved that the witnesses brought forward by this Mark Hexam to establish the fact of his elder brother's death were lying witnesses—that the elder brother was then alive, trading as a merchant in Spain, and the father of several sons; no link was missing in the chain of evidence, nothing was wanting.

'But after acknowledging the justice of the litigant's claim, the judge declared that to redistribute a vast estate after a lapse of ages would be to commit a greater injustice than the wrong already done; and that, in his opinion, there was therefore no redress for that wrong, no appeal open to the claimant save to the generosity of the present possessors of the estate, of whom Sir Joshua Hexam was the largest and most distinguished.

'For the unhappy and mistaken gentleman who had put forward his claim the judge declared he had nothing but compassion; but to favour such claimants would be to introduce an element of confusion into the tenure of estates in the land, and to do harm to the multitude for the advantage of the individual. I know his speech pretty nearly by heart, I've read it so many times.'

'And did Michael Hexam appeal to Sir Joshua's generosity?' asked the other.

'No. He threw himself on the mercy of a greater tribunal than the Court of Chancery. He went straight home that dark December evening and cut his throat.'

'Did he leave any children behind him?'

'One—a son, a mere lad, called Hanbury. But he was abroad at the time, I believe—some said in a Jesuit college and nobody seemed to know where to find him. Sir Joshua Hexam wrote a letter to the papers professing his willingness to provide for this boy; but nothing ever came of the offer: the boy never came forward.'

'Curious boy!' exclaimed the fire-worshipper; 'I should come forward fast enough if any one offered to provide for me. And you suppose this is the very individual?' he said, laying his hand on the open page where that dashing signature showed darkly in the dim light.

'There's no other Hanbury Hexam that I know of,' answered the librarian, 'There are Hexams enough, but no Hanburys among them. The old name has died out.'

'Well, goodnight,' said the fire-worshipper, departing.

'Goodnight,' responded the custodian.

He closed his big volume, took his hat from its peg, and followed, locking various doors as he went, without a thought of the actual Hanbury, at that moment slumbering profoundly in the recess by the painted window.

CHAPTER 3

THE DREAM-PICTURE

Silence perfect and profound descended upon the shadowy old chamber where the stranger slept upon his open book. The ruddy fire still burned cheerily, banked up too liberally to be exhausted in an hour or two. And in the silence and solitude young Hanbury Hexam dreamed a dream.

Time had reversed his glass, and that foolish dreamer fancied himself the son of an age long gone by.

It was in the reign of good Queen Bess, and all Loomborough was like the Hexam library. The narrow streets were picturesque, with pointed gables and projecting upper stories, queer old mullioned windows, irregular pavements, open gutters through which the town sewage flowed merrily, like a rivulet. Loomborough was a small market town, with a cathedral that seemed ever so much too big for it, and a margin of fields and wooded hills encircling it. At this Christmas season the fields and hills were white with snow, and the black twigs of the trees bore only icicles.

Young Hanbury Hexam walked through the narrow streets, clad in trunk hose, the worse for wear, and a scarlet doublet in the same condition, and a small gray woollen cloak which hardly shielded him from December's searching blast He had come from beyond seas, where he had been trying to mend his fortunes with other adventurers, young, penniless and desperate, like himself. He had failed, and now returned to his native city, feeling himself altogether an unnecessary unit in the sum of existence.

Altogether unnecessary? Well, no; perhaps there was one person who might be just a little sorry if he were beaten down in the conflict. Yet even she might have changed. Three weary years had come and gone since he had gazed into those true fond eyes, and heard those sweet lips speak their promise. What might not those years have done?

Young Hanbury crossed the market-place and approached the tall gloomy-looking cathedral. There stood the low long pile, to the left of the holy edifice, just as it stands today—only instead of being a public library devoted to the worthy citizens of Loomborough, it was Sir Hanbury Hexam's private dwelling-house, with counting-house and warehouses adjoining; for Sir Hanbury was a great merchant, or a merchant who was counted great in those days. He had been knighted, as a reward for having made himself a handsome fortune, and was generally respected in the quiet old city of Loomborough. The young adventurer paused at the gate. There was a garden with a row of fine old elms where there is now only the wide stone-paved yard.

It is not a pleasant thing to beard the lion in his den, and Sir Hanbury had something leonine about him. His young kinsman paused, 'screwed his courage to the sticking place' as a popular dramatist of that period would have put it, and went in under the leafless elms, across the crisp white snow.

There sat Sir Hanbury, poring over his ledger, in a little room near the door, now the custodian's vestibule. Young Hanbury looked at him through the mullioned window. There he was, just as in the well-known portrait, with his pointed beard, stiff ruff, and black velvet skull-cap. Young Hanbury shivered in his slashed shoon, and then turned the handle of the door—how the old iron knocker rattled!—and went in, not courageous, but desperate.

Sir Hanbury looked from under his bristly iron-gray brows,

surveying the returned wanderer as coolly as if he had been only half an hour absent.

'You did no good yonder, I see, sirrah!' growled the merchant, returning to his ledger.

'No, sir. I have encountered great dangers, and many hardships, and have done no good for myself whatever.'

'Humph! and you come back like a piece of false money; and now that your pride has had a lesson I'll warrant you'll be glad to accept my offer to provide for you—the offer I made when your foolish father cut his throat, after trying to rob me of my fortune.'

'Not a word against my father, sir. If he was a mistaken man, he was at least an honest one, and had tight and justice on his side.'

'What are right and justice against centuries of possession?' exclaimed Sir Hanbury, contemptuously. 'Hearken, young Hanbury: when I offered you a stool in my counting-house—which meant a good deal more than you understood by it—and a seat at my chimney corner, you chose to refuse a fair offer, and to look upon me as the cause of your father's death. Yet, had your father been a wise man and brought his papers to me, instead of going to law, I would have given him more than the court awarded him; yes, sirrah, I would have freely given him a younger son's portion.'

'I come back to you, sir, to accept your protection, if you are still in the mind to give it,' said young Hanbury, in a manly and yet humble tone. 'There is no merit in my return—for I have tried my hardest to prosper without your help. Give me the lowest place in your counting-house, and let me labour for my wage. I ask no favour on the score of kindred.'

'And you shall have none,' said the old man, shutting his ledger with a bounce; 'but you shall have some reward for being an honest man and an affectionate son, and for having tried to live without my help, and for the sake of one that loves you.'

The young man's heart beat its fastest at this point. 'There are several reasons for you, sirrah.'

'One is more than enough, sir. 'Tis sweet for an exile to hear the word love.'

'Dorothy!' called the merchant, and lo! The door of an inner room opened—the dark old oaken door—and a girl entered who gave one look at the youth and then grew white as the snow in Sir Hanbury's garden. This was Dorothy Hexam, the old knight's only child; born in late wedlock, pure and pale as a winter rose.

'Dorothy, thy cousin has come home from beyond seas, and he is to live with us henceforward, and to work in the counting-house, and take my place by and by. Take him in, and give him a manchet and a tankard of October to stay his stomach till noon.'

The girl gave one happy cry, and drew near her kinsman like a startled bird. The young man grasped his patron's hand, stooped his handsome head to salute that iron fist with his lips, and then put his arm round Dorothy and led her through the grim old doorway. They went out of the counting-house together into the homely parlour beyond, and sat down side by side in the deep-recessed window, and sealed the beginning of their new life with a betrothal kiss.

CHAPTER 4
DOROTHEA

The sleeper awoke with a sense of chillness. The great cathedral bell was pealing the hour. He counted the strokes drowsily. Was the clock never going to leave off striking? Nine—ten—eleven—twelve.

Midnight. He had fallen asleep in old Sir Hanbury's reading-room, and had been locked in. There was no help for it but to finish the night here. The room was dark; but through the painted window came the friendly gleam of the distant lamps.

'What a fool I must have been to fall asleep in such a place!' he said to himself; 'but a man who has just come off a long sea voyage may be excused for being a trifle sleepy.'

He groped his way to the cavernous old fireplace, stumbling

over a heavy chair as he went. He had a box of vestas in his pocket, and striking one of these, took a brief survey of the scene.

A big iron box half full of coal stood on one side of the hearth, and behind it Hanbury Hexam spied some loose wood

'Good,' he said to himself. 'If I can light a fire, I shan't be so badly off after all.'

He had yesterday's *Times* in his pocket, and with this, the wood, cinders, and coal, he built up a pile, which he kindled with one of those useful vestas from his little tin box.

The old grate was still warm, and the fire burned bravely, the dry wood flaming up with a blue-and-yellow flare, lighting the stern countenance of the knight in his starched ruff and black skull-cap.

Hanbury the younger looked up at his great progenitor wonderingly. His dream came back to him, link by link; such a curiously graphic dream. He had seen the quaint old Elizabethan town by that mystic dream-light, as vividly as in the light of day. He had seen himself in his antique garments; seen the stern visage of the old knight melt into kindliness; and, last and best of all, had seen Dorothy's fair face—so like a living face he had looked on in the hopeless agony of parting three years ago.

'Perhaps you were not such a bad old fellow after all,' he said to himself dreamily contemplating, the portrait over the mantel-piece, which seemed to change its expression with every change in the flickering-light. 'If you were alive, and I were to appeal to you, I wonder whether you would help me. Would your proto-type and successor. Sir Joshua, help me, I wonder, if I were to go to him now, and remind him of his letter to the newspapers?'

The question made him thoughtful. He looked back at his brief and troubled past, and wondered how much of it had been foolishness. Ten years ago Hanbury Hexam had been a friendless young scholar in a great Continental school—a school where a good education was to be had at the lowest possible cost. It would hardly be possible to imagine a lad more utterly alone in the world at fifteen years of age than this young Hexam. His mother was dead. His father had given himself up body and soul to his fatal Chancery suit. Brothers or sisters he had none.

There was an aunt, a somewhat strong-minded maiden lady, Michael Hexam's sister, who cared a little for the desolate boy, and who wrote him an occasional letter telling him the progress of the Chancery suit, and who from time to time sent him a parcel of clothing

From his aunt, Sarah Hexam, the boy received the tidings of his father's miserable end. In the same letter—a bitter, passionate letter—she told young Hanbury how Sir Joshua Hexam had offered to provide for him.

'I do not know how you may look at the matter,' she said finally, 'but I consider that man your unhappy father's murderer.'

The boy wrote back indignantly to say that he would not accept a sixpence from Sir Joshua to save him from starving. Miss Hexam applauded his resolution. She had a little annuity of her own which she was ready to share with her nephew, taking it for granted that he would be on the high road to fortune before she died. She went over to Tours, where Hanbury was at school, and in that foreign city lived on a mere nothing during his final years of tutelage; and three years after her brother's death she set out with the lad of eighteen on a voyage of adventure,—she a hardy active woman of fifty-four; he an ardent poetic youth, full of high hopes and noble aspirations.

Very happy was the life these two led together; very moderate their desires, very simple their habits. They travelled through Switzerland and Germany, making long halts in quaint old towns, where the necessaries of life were cheap. Hanbury read a great deal, sketched from nature, and wrote not a little He sent bright, lively papers to the London magazines, and thereby gained a comfortable addition to his aunt's small income. However humbly they lived—with a simplicity that was almost Spartan—they always lived like a lady and gentleman, and were never mistaken for anything else.

They were at a quiet little water-drinking settlement near the Black Forest, a spring lately discovered by the German doctors, and only frequented by those who were indifferent to the allurements of fashion—when the event occurred which first introduced poetry and passion into Hanbury's life.

He had wandered somewhat far afield one bright September day with his sketch-book, when he came to an old quarry among the hills—a rough amphitheatre of stone embedded in the craggy hill-side. Above, on the hill-top, a grove of firs stood darkly out against the clear blue sky.

On the upper edge of the quarry, about forty feet from the ground on which he stood, Hanbury Hexam saw a fluttering figure in a white gown, with a scarlet scarf that made a patch of bright colour among the greens and grays of grass and stone.

'Rather a dangerous place,' he thought, 'for a lady to wander in; but I suppose she knows her ground.'

Just at this moment he became aware of the presence of a bony female in a lanky gray costume, a mushroom hat, and green spectacles, who was telegraphing wildly to the distant girl with a large buff parasol.

'Go back!' she screamed; 'go back the other way! The ground isn't safe where you're standing. Go back, Dorothea!'

The ground upon which that light figure was perched certainly had an insecure look. That edge of the hill had been partly undermined by the excavations below. It was an overhanging path, which might give way at any moment.

'What shall I do?' cried the lady in the green spectacles, tragically. 'I am sure Miss Hexam is in danger, and I don't know how to get at her up there, even if my breath would allow me to climb, which it will not.'

Miss Hexam! This was rather startling for Hanbury. But there was no time to be wasted upon surprise or interrogation.

'I'll find my way up to her,' he said cheerily; and, after one brief and comprehensive survey of the scene, began the ascent.

To the admiring eyes of Miss Limber, of the green spectacles, he seemed to bound from crag to crag with the practised grace of the chamois-hunter in *Manfred*—over the little patches of sunburnt slippery grass, now on a bit of blue-gray stone, now on a crumbling ledge of sienna-coloured clay, till with one bound he leaped upon the narrow verge, and stood beside the damsel in white.

'Allow me to lead you down by some more secure path,' he said, bareheaded. 'The lady below there is much alarmed for your safety; and, indeed, this is hardly a secure spot for your rambles.'

'My poor dear governess!' said the young lady, smiling. 'Was she really frightened? I am sure you are very kind to come after me. I climbed up here easily enough, but it does seem rather difficult to go down again; and I confess that I was beginning to feel just a little uncomfortable.'

How pretty she was! A fair and delicate prettiness; a pale oval face framed in dark-brown hair; soft dark eyes; a mouth like Cupid's bow.

'I feel sure there is an easier way down behind those firs,' said Hanbury, 'if you will let me take you that way.'

'You shall take me any way you like that is safe,' she answered easily, 'and that will make poor Miss Limber happy. Look at her waving that parasol at me. I haven't the faintest idea what she means.'

'She means that you are to trust yourself with me, Miss Hexam,' said Hanbury.

It cost him a slight effort to pronounce the name. Could this be Sir Joshua's only child, the great heiress of Hexam Park? Surely not. There were innumerable Hexams in Loomborough. Why should this fair girl be his enemy's daughter?

They crossed the hilltop, and on the other side, below the fir trees, beheld a winding path which was safe and easy enough. Down this Hanbury led Miss Hexam. How daintily she stepped from stone to stone! Now on the soft green moss, now on the rough crag. To watch the little feet in their neat buckled shoes was the pleasantest thing in the world; and then, how sweet to look up at the fair young face, with its happy, innocent smile! Hanbury wished that descent had gone ten thousand fathoms deep into the bowels of the earth.

If he had rescued her charge from the roaring sea or the raging flames. Miss Limber could not have thanked the young man with more enthusiasm than she displayed. They all three walked home to Gesundheitbrunnen together, a walk of nearly four miles; during the progress of which Miss Limber, to whom there was no music sweeter than the sound of her own voice, told Hanbury all about herself and her pupil.

The young lady was Miss Hexam, daughter and heiress of the great Sir Joshua Hexam, 'of whom you have doubtless heard,' said Miss Limber, pompously. She was travelling in the care of her governess; 'and attended only by a courier and maid,' added Miss Limber, with proud humility. She had come to Gesundheitbrunnen in quest of health, the place having been specially recommended by a distinguished Loomborough physician.

'Sir Joshua would have accompanied us,' said Miss Limber, 'but his enormous commercial responsibilities render his prolonged absence from Loomborough impossible; and Miss Hexam's medical advisers recommend a residence of three months at the springs.'

'Have you been here long?' asked Hanbury.

'We came at the beginning of August, and we are to remain till the end of October.'

It was now early in September. Nearly two months of bliss, thought Hanbury, if he could persuade his aunt to remain so long. Luckily she had a fancy for swallowing inordinate quantities of mineral waters, with a vague idea that she was benefiting her constitution.

They came to Gesundheitbrunnen at last, after a four-mile walk that had seemed as nothing to Hanbury. At parting it was incumbent upon him to tell Miss Limber his name. He had debated the advisability of giving a false name as he came along, but his frank mind revolted from the idea of deception, so he handed Miss Limber his card.

'Mr. Hexam!' she screamed. 'How extraordinary!'

'I have the honour to be a namesake of your pupil's. But I believe Hexam is not an uncommon name at Loomborough.'

'True,' replied Miss Limber, 'the original Hexam estate has been divided and subdivided among numerous branches of the family. Sir Joshua would not be the great man he is if he had not strengthened his position as a landed proprietor by commercial enterprise.'

They parted outside the one hotel of the place, a rambling wooden building, to which a room or two had been added from time to time as the reputation of the waters increased. Miss Hexam, her governess, and servants had a small annex to themselves, and were considered the most important residents at the hotel.

After this, Hanbury and Miss Hexam were continually meeting. Pedestrian exercise was an important feature in the regime prescribed by the young lady's medical advisers, and she spent the greater part of every fine day rambling in the forest or among the hills, Miss Limber toiling on beside her, or sitting by the wayside to rest while the younger lady explored some wild romantic spot near at hand.

In these walks Hanbury's attendance was freely permitted. Miss Limber had literary proclivities, read German indifferently, and finding Hanbury a master of the language, gladly availed herself of his assistance. They read *Faust* together; yes, valorously toiled through the bewildering second part of that mighty work. And then Miss Limber confided to Hanbury the secret of her own authorship. She had written a novel, and although no publisher had yet been found gifted with a mind wide enough to appreciate that great panorama of human life. Miss Limber's faith in her own genius was in no wise shaken.

She introduced Hanbury to her own particular fictitious world, read him chapters of the novel, and, in a word, derived so much pleasure from his society herself, that she entirely overlooked the danger there might be in such society for her pupil. Time glided pleasantly on. The two young people read together, sketched together, worshipped nature together, and lived as in a happy dream.

Hanbury was awakened awfully from that sweet dream-life by the sudden death of his good old aunt, who expired in a fit of apoplexy, brought on possibly by over-indulgence in chalybeate waters. This was a bitter blow to his affections, and it left him penniless. Miss Hexam's income died with her. Hanbury had neither trade nor profession. He had lived a careless holiday life, and now, in his two-and-twentieth year, had nothing better to look to than the pen of a ready writer for maintenance in the present and fortune in the future.

And how with such prospects as these was he to aspire to the hand of Sir Joshua Hexam's daughter?

He paid Dorothea one farewell visit after his aunt's death; told her all the truth about himself, and told her that he was going into the busy working world to seek his fortune.

'If I win in the great game of chance, you will hear of me again, Dorothea,' he said. 'If I lose ——'

'Whether you win or lose, I hope to see you again,' she said, tenderly. 'But oh, Hanbury, why not accept my father's offer? He would receive you as an adopted son; he would make your future so easy. I have often heard him speak of you, and regret his ignorance of your fate.'

'He is very good, but I had rather depend upon my own right arm than on any patron in the world, answered Hanbury, proudly.

He had taken his own way, and had tried what his right arm would do for him in America and in Australia, and had come back a failure; not for lack of energy, or of industry, or of talent; but fate had been against him, and he had never found a friend to give him a helping hand.

CHAPTER 5
How the Dream Came True

The cold winter night struggled through the thick winter darkness at last, and found Hanbury Hexam still seated before the wide old hearth, absorbed in thought. Long as the hours had been, they had not been too long for the struggle betwixt pride and fate. When the day dawned, Hanbury had made up his mind to apply to Sir Joshua Hexam for a stool in that commercial magnate's counting-house. Long ago common sense had taught him to acquit Sir Joshua of any blame in the matter of the fatal Chancery suit; yet pride had prevented his acceptance of the great man's help.

At nine o'clock the sub-librarian unlocked the door, and Hanbury was free. He walked straight to Sir Joshua's warehouse, a palatial building in one of the richest streets in the rich city of Loomborough. Very different was Sir Joshua's counting-house from the quiet little room where the dreamer had seen Sir Hanbury poring over his ledger. Sir Joshua's offices were like a bank: such shining mahogany desks; such glittering brass rails dividing the desks; such splendid stoves and glowing fires, and wonderful contrivances in the way of speaking-tubes; such well-dressed clerks, with pens behind their ears, and a general appearance of being weighed down by the magnitude of the business.

When Hanbury asked to see Sir Joshua, the gentleman to whom he had addressed himself looked as surprised as if he had offered to send up his card to Queen Victoria.

'Have you an appointment?' he asked.

'No.'

'Quite impossible, then; Sir Joshua never sees anyone except by appointment.'

'Be so kind as to take him my card, and ask him to favour me with an early appointment,' said Hanbury.

The clerk looked at the card and departed wondering. Five minutes afterwards Hanbury was closeted with Sir Joshua in a handsome apartment, Turkey carpeted, warmed by a huge fire, provided with all the luxurious appliances that embellish the dull labour of commercial life.

On the 27th of December, after a sorely desolate Christmas, spent for the most part in the snowy streets of Loomborough, Hanbury took his seat in his kinsman's office.

'Work honestly, and you shall be honestly rewarded,' the old man had said to him, not unkindly. He looked so like Sir Hanbury of the dream-picture as he made this little speech.

Hanbury did work honestly and well. Those three years of

hard fighting with ill fortune had sharpened wits that were originally bright. Before Hanbury had been a year in the office he had proved himself worth three ordinary clerks, and Sir Joshua had invited him to dine at Hexham Park every alternate Sunday.

In the second year of the young man's clerkship there came a great commercial crisis. House after house went down as with the shock of an earthquake; and for three awful days the great firm of Hexam and Co. tottered with the fall of its allies. In that crisis Hanbury Hexam displayed an energy and a firmness which went far to right the ship. Sir Joshua was ill at the time, and thus the master spirit of the firm was wanting when his presence seemed most needed. From that hour the young man was taken to his employer's heart, and became verily an adopted son.

Two years later he was a junior partner in the great house, and Dorothea Hexam's betrothed husband.

It was on one of the dark days before Christmas that the two lovers went together to the old library at Loomborough. An important purchase of books had just been made for the institution, and Hanbury wished Dorothea to see them.

Perhaps it was only an excuse for showing his betrothed the quaint old chamber where he had dreamed that curious dream.

The scene was almost the same as on his first visit. There was the old man hugging the fire, and there sat the compiler of prophecies, fenced in with books at his distant table. The local poet was absent.

Hanbury led Dorothea to the recess by the painted window, and they seated themselves there side by side.

'What a dear old place it is!' said Dorothea. 'It's ages since I've been here.'

'Yes, it's a nice old place,' answered her happy lover, 'I've reason to be fond of it I owe all my present happiness to a dream I had here. I had made up my mind to sail for New Zealand in the next emigrant ship, to work as a field labourer perhaps, when I got there; and I had written you a long letter of farewell, when I fell asleep, and had a curious dream about him,' pointing to Sir

Hanbury's portrait.

And then he told her his dream.

'Such dreams are sent by our guardian angels, Hanbury,' she said gently, 'to teach us faith in God.'

Sir Luke's Return

To say that Cadbury Hall had stood untenanted and dismantled within the memory of the oldest inhabitant of Cadbury village would be to say too much, for there were two or three aged men and women in Springfield Union who remembered old Sir Luke Cadbury, and the good old days when the hounds used to meet in front of Cadbury Hall, and old Sir Luke, steeped to the lips in debt, and with every acre of his estate encumbered, used to keep open house, and entertain the county in a liberal and large-hearted fashion, at the expense of the local tradesmen. Having mortgaged his last acre, and plunged as deep in debt as his creditors would allow, old Sir Luke found himself at the end of his tether; so he took the easiest way out of his difficulties by dying, and leaving the empty shell of his estate to his only son.

Young Sir Luke, not seeing his way to living luxuriously upon an estate whose revenues were swallowed up by the mortgagees, looked about him for some more promising mode of existence. He was nineteen years of age when he came into his property. He had been at an expensive public school, where he had learned to row, swim, and thrash boys of superior weight and size.

A little Latin and less Greek had been flogged into him, but, acquired thus unpleasantly, had oozed out of him very quickly. He took a day to learn a verb, with much tribulation of mind and sweat of brow, and he forgot it comfortably in half an hour. At home he learned to ride straight to hounds, and shoot his bird flying. Happily he was a young man of energetic temperament, an early riser, hardy, active, and simple in his tastes.

Feeling himself unfit for any of the learned professions, he turned his attention to commerce. People were beginning to look towards our antipodes as the source of fortune for adventurous spirits, and to associate Botany Bay with the wool trade, as well as with the exportation of our criminal classes. Sir Luke Cadbury made up his mind that Sydney was the place for him, and wool his way to fortune. He let off every rood of the land, except his mother's flower-garden, for agricultural purposes; shut up the good old house, with its insignia of death hanging on the wall above the hall door; put the property into the hands of the family lawyer and land agent, and left Cadbury within three weeks of his father's funeral.

'If I am ever rich enough to pay off the mortgages, I shall do it,' said Sir Luke to his solicitor. 'I think my father reserved power to liquidate by instalments?'

'In all cases,' replied Mr. Dragmore, the lawyer, with a smile, for it seemed to him that no event in the history of the future could be farther off than the redemption of the Cadbury mortgages.

Young Sir Luke went away, and had not been in Australia three years before he began to send home money. Year by year from that time forward the Cadbury mortgages underwent reduction, until in something over twenty years the estate was free. John Dragmore, the family solicitor, went down to his grave wondering.

'That a son of old Sir Luke should have paid forty thousand pounds to the mortgagees, and twenty shillings in the pound to all his father's creditors! 'He exclaimed on numerous occasions. 'To be sure, his mother was a Scotchwoman. That's the only way of accounting for it. It isn't in the Cadbury blood,'

Mr. Dragmore had been in his grave three-and-twenty years, and it was just forty-five years since young Sir Luke left Cadbury to make his fortune in wool. In all those years he had never returned to England. The fascination of wool, or of making money rapidly by that commodity, had kept him on the other side of the world. He had married early in life, and had lost his wife soon after marriage. That tie had never been renewed by him. He was a childless widower, and was supposed to be worth anything between a plum and a million.

He was, therefore, even in the distance, an object of considerable interest to the Cadbury people, who passed the old Hall daily when they took their walks abroad, and saw the old mansion day after day in exactly the same condition, shutters closed, grass growing on the threshold of the great iron gates, Farmer Mangle's cattle grazing in front of the Doric door. A tree or two had been blown down in the park, and the house had fallen into decay, but no other change had come over the old Hall; though Cadbury had expanded from a pastoral village into a smart little town, with plate-glass windows to its shops, and side streets of brand-new villas leading to nowhere.

Most of all was the great Australian wool merchant an object of interest to his next of kin. These were Mr. Grynde and his family at the Hollies, one of the neatest, most bandboxical places in the outskirts of Cadbury; and that reprobate young man. Waller Carlyon, who had very nearly brought his widowed mother's gray hairs in sorrow to the grave, by failing to pass his preliminary examination at the University of Oxford, or, in his own phraseology, being ploughed for smalls. He was not a brainless young man by any means, but was passionately fond of boating, and had given his attention to the geography of the Isis instead of the Scamander.

Samuel Grynde of the Hollies and Waller Carlyon stood in different degrees of relationship to Sir Luke Cadbury, Waller's being a very remote kindred of the third or fourth cousin order, while Samuel was first cousin to the reigning baronet, and considered himself heir-presumptive to the estate.

Samuel's father, a person of somewhat plebeian extraction, but distinguished for his success in the legal profession, had married old Sir Luke's sister, and Samuel was the fruit of that union. His father had left him twelve hundred a year, upon which income he had married and brought up a large family, with credit to himself and the neighbourhood he honoured by his residence. He had adopted no profession, except that of vestry-man and general busybody. He had a finger in every pie that was baked in Cadbury. Whatever project for the benefit of Cadbury was set on foot, Samuel Grynde was at the bottom of it.

There was not five hundred feet of drain-pipe put in the ground at Cadbury without Mr. Grynde making a speech about it. He was great upon sewage; he was a terror to the authorities of the Springfield, Bilbury, and Cadbury Union, always wanting to know about that odd half-pound of butter, and who eat those mutton chops, and whether the guardians' Worcester sauce and Bass's bitter were charged upon the parish. The luncheons of the guardians were always a stumbling-block to Mr. Grynde, and he would raise a whirlwind in the vestry by alluding to those mutton chops.

Mr. Grynde was spare in person, a man who eats very little himself, and objected to large appetites in other people. The young Gryndes had rather a hard time of it while they were growing and hungry—their father denouncing a fourth slice of bread-and-butter as an indulgence of the lusts of the flesh. Mr. Grynde had a long nose, sharp as a bird's beak, a long neck, and a habit of lifting up his coat tails as he hovered on the edge of a sewer, or bent over a drain-pipe, which suggested a resemblance to a stork on the edge of a marshy pool.

Mr. Grynde's private opinion was that he had made Cadbury; that it was through his fostering and paternal care the village had spread itself out into a town; that the plate-glass windows, the loop line from Springfield Junction, and the new railway hotel, all emanated more or less from him. He had talked about these institutions in the vestry until he believed in them as verily his own. Yet he was not a popular man in Cadbury. The blues had nicknamed him Sandy Stork, on account of the reddish tinge of his whiskers, and that propensity for hovering on the edge of open drains.

The yellows called him 'Those mutton chops,' in memory of those field-days in the vestry on which he had thumped the table, and perorated like a second Chatham—Pitt the younger was too mild for him—on the malfeasance and misappropriation involved in the guardians' luncheons.

To Waller Carlyon Mr. Grynde objected on so many grounds that his objections were hydra-headed, and if you had subjugated one, another would have cropped up in its place. He objected to Waller as a ne'er-to-do-well, who had squandered his money at Oxford, as an impudent pretender to Sir Luke's relationship, and above all as an admirer of Mr. Grynde's third daughter, Lucy, a giddy light-hearted damsel, whom all Mr. Grynde's paternal teaching had failed to improve into that pattern of maidenhood for which Mr. Grynde had in a manner taken out a patent.

The two elder girls were perfect specimens of Mr. Grynde's patent young woman. They played and sang duets like a pair of automaton performers, and were never out of time by so much as a demi-semiquaver. They read Racine, and nothing but Racine, in the French language. They had ploughed through Schiller's *Thirty Years' War*, in the original, of course, and found it interesting. They played croquet at proper seasons, which meant on a Wednesday afternoon, which was their At Home day, when they wore their clean muslin frocks, and received the *élite* of Cadbury.

Lucy was a wild weed among these flowers. In her nursery and schoolroom days her pinafores had always been torn, one tail of chestnut hair minus its ribbon, her French and German verbs all at sea in the subjunctive mood, and her bootlaces broken. She had always been what Mr. Grynde called 'an outrage' on his sense of decency. Now that she was grown into bright, impulsive, blushing, alternate smiling and weeping girlhood, she was still an outrage.

There was always something wrong—a bit of braid torn off the bottom of her dress, a new hat spoiled untimely by a shower, or she was late for prayers, or she was out when she ought to be at home, or she liked people whom Mr. Grynde disliked, or squandered her allowance on unworthy objects of charity. And now she had filled the measure of her iniquities by falling in love with her father's natural enemy, Waller Carlyon, whose widowed mother had, possibly with a malice aforethought, taken a pretty Gothic cottage next door to Mr. Grynde's square bay-windowed villa.

The villa possessed a large garden of the modem order, sunk croquet lawn, raised banks, geraniums in square, geraniums in single file, like soldiers; no trees, except plums and peaches skewered against the new walls. The cottage had an old-fashioned garden and orchard, all in one, full of queer crooked old trees, deep soft grass, all hillocks and hollows, a wilderness of hazel and elder for a boundary between cottage garden and villa 'grounds.'

There was an old tumble-down fence dividing the wilderness from Mr. Grynde's kitchen-garden, which that gentleman would assuredly have replaced with a ten-foot wall had he not cherished hopes of getting that cottage and garden a bargain some day, in which event he would have pulled down the cottage, and added the garden to his own domain.

Thus, in a laudable spirit of economy, he left the fence standing, and would not even lay out a sovereign on its repair.

'It's an eyesore, I admit,' he used to say, 'a blemish to grounds which I venture to think are otherwise perfect, but it would be folly to build a wall when I hope to enlarge in that direction by-and-by.'

This fence was at the bottom of all Lucy's troubles. She had torn her pinafores climbing it in the old nursery days, when the cottage was empty, and she and her brothers used to make raids into the orchard after half-ripened apples. It played the part of wall in the tragic story of Pyramus and Thisbe now. Waller and Lucy were cousins—cousins at any rate, however remote the cousinship—and they had been more or less acquainted all their lives. When Mrs. Carlyon came to live at the cottage that acquaintance expanded considerably. They began by wishing each other good morning across the broken old fence; they went on to exchange slips and cuttings; they developed from this into the interesting study of botany, and before they had got very deep into that science, they found their eyes wandering from calyxes and petals to each other's faces, losing themselves in a sweet entanglement; and a little later they confessed that they adored each other.

'Papa would never hear of it,' said Lucy, with a piteous face.

'Why not, love?'

'Oh, for ever so many reasons. He says you are wild.'

'Because I was weak enough to let myself be ploughed for smalls. That was boating, and not dissipation, my pet. I never was gated in my life, and I don't owe sixpence in Oxford. Besides which, I am working like a nigger at this present time.'

'Oh, Waller, when you waste whole afternoons talking to me!'

'Only necessary relaxation, dearest. I should very soon be in a lunatic asylum if I stuck to my books all day.'

Their fool's paradise had not lasted long before Samuel Grynde got to know of those meetings by the broken-down fence, and that his daughter's heart had been handed across that dilapidated boundary, together with the botanical specimens.

He was calm in the greatness of his anger.

'This is an outrage I was not prepared for he remarked to his contrite and weeping child, 'although your plebeian manners and slovenly habits have made your life one continued affront to me. I beg that you will consider yourself a prisoner in the house, except when your elder sisters are good enough to allow you to accompany them on their constitutional walks.'

Lucy gave a shuddering sob. If there was one thing she detested more than another, it was these constitutional walks. Three miles out and three miles home on the level high road to Springfield, with no landscape save an arable flat, bounded by an occasional stunted hedgerow. Her own rambles were sweet to her—unmeasured wanderings in Cadbury Park, or in the woods beyond the park, with her small brothers, nutting, blackberrying, spoiling her clothes, and cultivating a complexion that rivalled the roses and lilies in the old cottage garden. But these six miles by the milestones were an abomination to her.

All this happened during what Waller Carlyon called the long vac. It was the very end of the summer, and a glorious summer, the land overflowing with fertility, and the drainage of Cadbury not quite answering the expectations of its projectors. August was in its prime, and people had almost forgotten the sensation of a wet day.

'It's a very miserable summer,' complained Lucy, as she sat at her plain sewing—plain sewing was one of the accomplishments Samuel Grynde insisted on for his patent young woman—in the square, bare, sunny breakfast parlour at the Hollies. 'I wish it would rain torrents, or thunder, or lighten, or do anything instead of this perpetual broil, broil, broil.'

Waller Carlyon, cut off from that pleasant idlesse by the old fence, went harder than ever at his books, promising his mother that all should be well at the next examination; and the widow, who believed in him as a future Lord Chancellor, blessed him for his goodness and industry, and implored him to do justice to his splendid talents, which must have been designed by Providence to raise him to a pinnacle.

'Well, mother, I'll do what I can to swarm up the pinnacle,' answered the youth, in his sanguine style, 'or, at any rate, to get a fellowship before I'm thirty, so that I may be a help and not a burden to you.'

'Ah, Waller,' sighed his mother, 'I'm not thinking of money. I want you to be distinguished. Who knows whether you mayn't be rich some day, independent of your own efforts? Sir Luke Cadbury ——'

'Put Sir Luke and his fortune out of your mind, mother. Old Sandy Stork is a nearer relation than you or I; and, depend upon it, if ever Sir Luke comes back to Cadbury our next-door neighbour will wind round him like a serpent, lubricate him with soft sawder, and swallow him bodily, as a cobra swallows a rabbit.'

'Who knows?' said Mrs. Carlyon, with smiling significance.

She was an easy-tempered lady, and always made the best of the present, and hoped a great deal from the future. The idea that Sir Luke Cadbury might leave some of his money to her son had been the foundation of many an air-built castle. Waller would never admit that such a thing was likely.

'I dare say Sir Luke is a fiery-tempered old savage, and that if he comes home I shall hate him,' he used to say.

It was useless to think of stopping indoors in such an August as this, so, when the garden leased to be a paradise, Waller took Thucydides and his lexicon under his arm, and went into Cadbury Park. It was the loveliest place for a summer ramble. Neglect had beautified it. Instead of the well-kept orderly fairness of a prosperous gentleman's domain, it had the wild loveliness of untrodden woods. A painter would have revelled in such a wilderness. Oaks and beeches a thousand years old, bramble and fern that had flourished undisturbed for half a century, glimpses of a silvery trout stream that meandered in and out, and twined itself about the place as if it loved those shadowy deeps of foliage.

Here, on the margin of this silvern brook, Waller used to sit for hours, trying to grasp the spirit of the great historian as well as the letter; he used to sit and pore over the page, till it seemed to him that all the troubles of the Peloponnesian War were upon his shoulders.

He was getting rather sleepy over his book one particularly sultry afternoon, when he was startled from his drowsiness by a strident voice near at hand—a voice that had an overbearing and singularly caddish tone, he thought, sadly out of harmony with those tranquil woods.

'Too much timber,' said the voice; 'we must lay about with us the axe here, Blagrove.'

Another voice, very mild this one, murmured acquiescence.

'And we must have the roof off, Blagrove, and rebuild the stables. I never saw such a ramshackle old barrack. By Jove, sir, I wonder how my father tolerated it. But, to be sure, he hadn't a sixpence of ready money to lay out, poor old beggar. He couldn't write his cheque for fifty thousand, and feel none the poorer for it, as some people we know could, eh Blagrove?'

'By the beard of the thunderer,' ejaculated Waller, 'this must be Sir Luke.'

The voices were coming nearer to him, and the owners thereof now came in full view, on the opposite bank of the narrow stream.

The man with the big voice was portly and pompous. He had a rubicund nose, a keen gray eye, a coarse stubble of grey hair, and a fierce gray whisker. He carried his hat in his hand, and puffed and snorted a good deal, as if oppressed with the heat.

His companion was a small dark man, with an intelligent eye and a pleasant mouth—a mouth with a touch of good-humoured irony in its expression. He was about the same age as the stout man, his hair and beard iron-gray. He was rather shabbily dressed, and looked like a clerk, humble companion, or toady, Waller thought.

'Hi, you sir!' cried the big man. 'Do you know this place?'

'Pretty well,' answered Waller, still seated on the bank.

'Then you ought to know that you're trespassing. What's the use of people going to the expense of putting up boards, telling you that trespassers will be prosecuted, if you go on trespassing all the same?'

'I've been in the habit of using this park for the last ten years, and have never been told I was a trespasser till today,' said Waller.

'Nonsense! Don't the boards tell you so as plain as a pikestaff, if you can read?'

'Farmer Gibbs never told me so, and, as he rents the land, he has the best right to object to me.'

'Come, I say, young man, don't you be contumacious. You are trespassing upon my land, sir—my land. Do you understand that? I come home here after forty years' absence, and the first object I encounter is a trespasser. Pleasant state of things, sir, that, for a man who has made his fortune by the sweat of his brow on the other side of the world. Pleasant to come home and find his patrimonial acres made free with by a trespasser.'

'Make your mind easy, Sir Luke. I shan't intrude again.'

'Oh, you know me, do you?'

'Only by repute, sir, though I have the honour to be a distant relation of yours.'

'Distant relation. Yes, I expect I shall have distant relations cropping up at every hand's turn. And pray who may you be?'

'My name is Waller Carlyon.'

'Oh!' said Sir Luke. He surveyed Waller deliberately from head to foot, and then turned to his humble friend. 'Blagrove, you've a better memory than I have, and you've heard me talk about my family times and often. What relation is Waller Carlyon to me?'

'Third cousin,' answered Blagrove. 'Your father's first cousin, Sybilla Cadbury, married Squire Carlyon of Denzil Place, and this young man is their grandson.'

'Oh!' said Sir Luke, 'that's uncommonly distant. I can hardly be expected to recognise that as a claim, can I, Blagrove? Now look here, Mr. Waller ——'

But Waller had gathered up his books and was gone.

'Horrid old cad,' he said to himself as he went across the park. 'I dare say I've made an end of *my* chances in that direction; but I couldn't cringe to such an old savage as that for the chance of inheriting a million.'

Cadbury was convulsed. Sir Luke's return was the grandest event that had happened since the opening of the loop line from Springfield. Cadbury was on the tiptoe of expectancy. What was Sir Luke going to do? Would he rebuild the old Hall? To whom would he leave his money? Would Mr. Grynde, who had made a boast of his cousinship, be received into the great man's favour? Cadbury awaited the answer to these queries, breathless with curiosity and wonder.

Cadbury's doubts upon two points were speedily set at rest. Sir Luke did not rebuild the old Hall; he only restored it to its original solidity and splendour. And Sir Luke took Samuel Grynde to his bosom.

Mr. Grynde, spare of figure, and without an ounce of superfluous flesh about him, seemed bodily to expand after Sir Luke's return. He had always walked the streets of Cadbury as if the place belonged to him; but he contrived to impart increased arrogance to his walk—a superlative dignity to his figure—after Sir Luke's return.

He was at Sir Luke's right hand throughout the restoration of the Hall, which occupied all the autumn, and was more than ever stork-like in his motions and attitudes. He dipped his beak into every drain, climbed ladders upon perpetual journeys of inspection, peered into every gutter, and was continually whitening his coat with lime. He knew a good deal about building, and contrived to make the lives of bricklayers and other mechanics a burden to them, and to worry the architect into a low fever.

'I can save you hundreds. Sir Luke, *hundreds*,' he used to say. 'I know these fellows and the tricks they are up to.—Hi, you sir, what is that timber you are putting in? Let me see if you please. Do you call this free from sap? And those wall posts, are they stop chamfered, sir? Let there be no shirking here.'

This devotion was all the more creditable to Mr. Grynde as Sir Luke was by no means an agreeable person to serve. He was choleric, and in his choler made no distinction of persons. He would swear at his toady and dependant Jack Blagrove, and at Samuel Grynde, indifferently. He had an unpleasant way of telling people that they were fools, idiots, ignoramuses. He sent his dear Samuel on messages. He rounded on his dear Samuel to the architect, and let that gentleman know Mr. Grynde's very low estimate of his professional skill. He was a glutton and a gourmand, and made himself odious at dinnertime by quarrelling with the goods the gods had provided, and swearing at his cook. He was perpetually bragging about his wonderful career, and railing at the worn-out county families, which, he asserted, were lapsing to decay, slipping from stagnant respectability into absolute ruin, for want of the trader's energy and the trader's success.

'Suppose I had stayed at home, sir, and played the fine gentleman, just because I had a handle to my name, and let the mortgagees foreclose? Where would Cadbury Hall have been now, I should like to know?'

'Cadbury itself would be the poorer by one of the noblest examples ever offered to mankind,' exclaimed Mr. Grynde, feeling that his reply was at once appropriate and eloquent.

'Ah,' grunted Sir Luke, 'I wasn't afraid of trade because I was born in the purple. I dropped the handle to my name, and went in for wool, sir, and wool brought me through. Bring up your children to trade, Grynde, if you want 'em to be great men. Where would your Peels and your Gladstones be if they hadn't got trade at the back of 'em? That's the backbone, sir!'

Mr. Grynde winced. With the pride of a man whose forefathers had been commercial, he aspired to make his sons professional, to see their names by and by adorned with Q.C. , or supported by the prefix of Reverend. His sons, still in the hobbledehoy stage, were being ground into parsons and barristers, but had not yet got beyond a preliminary course of Æsop and Ovid.

'Trade is a fine thing,' he exclaimed gushingly. 'Trade is the quicksilver in the veins of society, which keeps all things moving. But, alas! I fear my poor boys lack that mental force needful to the trader. They have not the scope, the width, the breadth, the largeness of mind ——'

Here Mr. Grynde waved his arms like a thrashing machine.

'Humph!' muttered Sir Luke, 'that means to say you're going to make them respectable paupers in the learned professions. I'm sorry for 'em.—Blagrove, my camp-stool ——'

'Mr. Blagrove, the camp-stool,' repeated Mr. Grynde in a tone just a little more arbitrary than that of the tyrant himself.

Poor John Blagrove had rather a bad time of it that autumn. His patron was hard upon him always, but Samuel Grynde was harder. He pointed every joke of Sir Luke's against his toady by the frankness of his hilarity. If Mr. Blagrove had been a butt before, he was twice a butt now. Samuel Grynde never spared him.

'There doesn't seem to be much sympathy between you and me, Mr. Grynde,' the humble companion said once in meek remonstrance.

'Candidly, my good friend, there is none,' answered Mr. Grynde; 'I hate parasites.'

'And yet we both belong to the same family,' said Blagrove. 'You're much the sturdier plant, I admit; but we hang on the same tree.'

'What, sir, you presume to compare me, Samuel Grynde of the Hollies, a man of independent property, a man of illimitable influence in this parish, with your beggarly self?'

'I don't compare our persons or our social status, sir. I only say that our aims tend in one direction. You intend to be enriched by Sir Luke. I hope to be left a small competence by the same benefactor.'

'Oh, you do, do you, sir? You have the audacity to own that you anticipate a competence? A cool five thousand or so in the Three per Cents., I suppose, bringing you in something like two hundred a year?'

'I have served Sir Luke faithfully, and served him long.'

'And have been paid for your services, I'll warrant me. I am of Sir Luke's own flesh and blood, Mr. Blagrove; his first cousin, sir; couldn't be nearer unless I was his brother. What have you to say against that, sir?'

'Nothing,' answered Blagrove, with a touch of that manhood which was not quite extinct in him, 'except that Sir Luke might have had a more generous-minded cousin.'

The reparations and restorations at Cadbury Hall were completed just before Christmas, and a noble mansion the old house looked in its prosperity. Shining oak panelling, rich but sombre Turkey and Persian carpets, good old furniture, renovated, but in no case modernized. Despite his ingrained snobbishness, Sir Luke had shown excellent taste in all details, most of all in resisting Mr. Grynde's advice, and suffering himself to be guided by his toady Blagrove, who had a wonderful appreciation of the beautiful and the harmonious.

Christmas was to be a grand time at the Hall, for Sir Luke had taken it into his head to gather all his relations round him at that festive period. He would have them all in the house, he declared, from Christmas Eve till Twelfth-night.

'I want them all about me,' he said; 'I want to know of what stuff they're made of. They're pretty sure to turn themselves inside out in a fortnight. Let 'em all come. There are rooms enough for the whole biling.'

'Whole biling!' echoed Samuel, admiringly. 'That's what I call our racy English humour.'

Now this Christmastide hospitality was all very well, as regarded the Grynde tribe; but the worthy Samuel distinctly objected to Waller Carlyon and his mother—that weak-minded widow who insisted upon being alive and cheerful when her gray hairs ought to have been brought down in sorrow to the grave by her son's ill conduct.

Upon this point, however, Sir Luke was inflexible. 'Pig-headed,' Mr. Grynde called him inwardly.

'That Carlyon fellow is an insolent blackguard,' said the baronet; 'but I'll have him here all the same, and let him turn himself inside out.'

On this Mr. Grynde tried to make excuses for his daughter Lucy, whose peace of mind and ultimate destiny would be alike jeopardized by her being thrown into Waller Carlyon's society for a fortnight on end.

But here again Sir Luke's pig-headedness exhibited itself.

'If Lucy doesn't come, I won't have any of your brood,' replied the baronet, savagely.

So the brood came, and Lucy among them. Poor Lucy was not elated at the idea of spending a fortnight at the great house, where she would doubtless outrage those proprieties with which Mr. Grynde surrounded and fenced himself in, as with a particularly spiky *chevaux de frise*. Many a wound had Lucy given herself against those spikes.

No one told her that Waller was to be at the Hall, and it was a tremendous surprise to her when that young gentleman appeared at the great door and handed her out of the fly, in which she arrived with her sisters, at about four o'clock in the afternoon of Christmas Eve, light snow flakes sprinkling them as they alighted.

'Capital Christmas weather!' as Waller remarked, cheerily. The two elder girls, Caroline and Amelia, gave him only a distant bow in return for his civility; but he contrived to get hold of Lucy's hand and keep it for ever so long, while the bags and portmanteau were being carried in, the young ladies having brought all their fine raiment for the subjugation of 'dear uncle Luke.'

'Come, Lucy,' cried Caroline severely, directly her attention was withdrawn from her bonnet-boxes; and Lucy was led off like a state prisoner to the bedchamber which Mr. Grynde had contrived to secure for her—a room inside her sister's apartment—a funny old room, small, low, and with three closets in it, so that there was more closet door than wall-paper. There was a neat little brass bedstead, and a muslin-draped toilet table, with a lot of little Japanese boxes for pins, rings, and such small gear, and Lucy exclaimed that it was 'a duck of a room.'

'I wouldn't be so gushing if I were you, Lucy,' remarked Amelia; 'it's extremely vulgar. You know how papa admires repose of manner.'

Sir Luke received his young relations with a kind of bearish good-nature—loud, gruff and rough. The dinner was a profuse and splendid banquet, and poor little Lucy, who sat next her father and remote from Waller, felt that the whole thing was an ordeal. She would have been altogether miserable if it had not been for Mr. Blagrove, who sat on her left hand and talked to her, a good deal, telling her about his Austrian experiences in a very pleasant way. She thought him quite the nicest old gentleman she had ever met, and was absolutely enjoying herself, when her father's heavy boot came down savagely upon her poor little satin shoe.

'Oh!' she cried.

'What do you mean by encouraging that old sycophant?' whispered Mr. Grynde in Lucy's affrighted ear. 'Am I forever to be outraged by your vulgar instincts?'

After this Lucy's answers grew faltering and embarrassed. She was too tender-hearted willingly to let Mr. Blagrove see that she had been reproved for talking to him; but there was a palpable change in her manner, and the old man soon lapsed into silence.

'What has Mr. Blagrove done, papa, that I mustn't be friendly with him? 'Lucy asked later in the evening, when she found herself next her father for a minute.

'What has he done? Have you no sense? Are you utterly devoid of discrimination? Don't you understand that this old man is a sordid flatterer, who hopes by licking the dust under Sir Luke's feet to ingratiate himself into my cousin's favour, and succeed to some portion of—if not all—his money?'

'But don't you do the same, papa? I don't mean lick the dust; but don't you hope to succeed to Sir Luke's fortune?'

'Don't presume to address another word to me, girl,' exclaimed Mr. Grynde, beside himself. 'You're a born idiot, and I think you were created to annoy me. Look at your sisters.'

He pointed to those young ladies, who at this moment offered a back view to their admirers. They had just seated themselves at the piano to execute their grand duet, 'The Waking of the Lion.' There was quite a military precision in their attitudes—elbows, shoulders, chignons at exactly the same angles.

'Look at your sisters, and blush,' whispered Mr. Grynde to poor Lucy. 'Blush as you reflect how the advantages by which they have profited have been thrown away upon you.'

Lucy had a fine ear for music, but had never been able to overcome the mechanical difficulties of that art so as to excel in the performance of showy fantasias, and the only kind of music which impressed Mr. Grynde was music of the skyrocket school.

The lion growled—the lion bellowed—the lion stretched himself—shook himself—exploded into savage roars, as the Miss Gryndes scampered up and down the keys at a lightning pace, or threw all the power of their elbows into a volley of prodigious chords, which exploded in a sudden and alarming manner like musical torpedoes. Samuel hovered stork-like over the new grand piano, and rubbed his hands complacently, glancing round the assembly occasionally, as much as to say, 'This is my work. *I* taught them—or paid for their tuition, which is much the same thing.'

Sir Luke walked up and down the drawing-room throughout that performance, looking rather like a newly awakened lion himself. When it was all over he wiped his perspiring forehead with his Mandarin yellow bandanna, and exclaimed,—

'What an infernal row!'

Mr. Grynde's jaw dropped as he stared aghast at his kinsman.

'Will somebody play, "The Last Rose of Summer," or "Wapping Old Stairs"?' cried the baronet. 'That's the sort of music I like.'

'Caroline! "Wapping Old Stairs" immediately!' said Mr. Grynde, smiling amiably.

'I am sorry to say I have not that melody amongst my music, papa,' replied his dutiful eldest.

'Amelia,' then.'

'Nor I, papa.'

'Nonsense! What do you want with music to play a simple air like that?'

'We do not play by ear, papa,' replied Caroline and Amelia simultaneously, as if that incapacity were rather a virtue than a defect.

'Lucy does,' cried Andrew, the youngest boy. 'Lucy can play anything she has once heard.'

'Then let Lucy play as many good old tunes as she can remember,' commanded Sir Luke.

Lucy, blushing to the roots of her hair, took her seat at the piano. Her fingers faltered a little just at first, but very soon the delight of touching that deep-toned Broadwood overcame every other feeling, and she breathed her pure young soul into the familiar old melodies. 'Wapping Old Stairs,' 'The Last Rose of Summer,' 'My lodging is on the cold ground,' 'Auld Lang Syne,' 'Robin Adair,' 'Love's Young Dream' followed, like the beads of a necklace, strung together with tender untaught modulations. It was 'Love's Young Dream' with which the girl finished, and there was a young Oxonian in the corner by the wide old hearth whose eyes were wet with tears.

When Lucy rose, trembling a little at the silence her melody had made, Sir Luke marched straight to the piano and gave her a sounding kiss.

'Thank you, my dear,' he said; 'that's what I call music'

Caroline and Amelia were rather short in their tempers that night at hair-brushing time, and Lucy was glad to have her funny little cupboardy room all to herself.

Christmas Day was very much like Christmas Eve, except that everybody went to church in the morning, and that the afternoon was devoted to a general exploration of the house. The walk to and from church, and the perambulation of the spacious old house, with its various corridors and darksome lobbies, gave Waller and Lucy several opportunities for a *tête-à-tête*, in spite of the Miss Gryndes' vigilance.

'Now,' exclaimed the stentorian voice of Sir Luke at dessert, 'I want you young people to have an old-fashioned Christmas evening—blindman's buff, forfeits, puss-in-the-corner, acted charades, kissing under the mistletoe, and lots of it.'

'Vulgar old barbarian,' said Samuel Grynde inwardly; but in his outward and audible voice he cried, 'Dear Sir Luke, how your expansive nature delights in the pleasure of your youthful guests!'

'I should like to see some of 'em rather more youthful,' replied Sir Luke; 'those sons of yours look as if they were cased in whalebone from top to toe. I never saw such young prigs.'

'They have been carefully educated, I admit,' murmured Mr. Grynde.

'Carefully educated, sir! They've been drilled into anatomies!' cried Sir Luke. 'I should like to see them unbend, if it's in 'em to do it.'

Anxious to gratify his wealthy cousin, Mr. Grynde got near his sons, one by one, as the evening progressed, and whispered into their ears,—

'Be lively, sir, can't you? Jump, jig, be boy-like, vivacious. Give loose to your animal spirits, boy.'

But the animal spirit of Mr. Grynde's sons had been flat-ironed out of them, or was at best a very tame animal. They went about the old oak-panelled hall on tiptoe in the game of blindman's buff, grinning with a stereotyped grin, and looking as dapper and as *blasé* as Government clerks at a second-rate evening party.

Lucy—that perpetual offender against propriety—was the sole member of the Grynde family whose liveliness had not been brayed out of her in the paternal mortar. She skipped, she danced, she gave loose to girlhood's long pent-up mirth; she was always catching Waller Carlyon, or being caught by him. It was dreadful to see her going on so, her sisters remarked, with long faces.

But their remonstrances would have been useless, for Lucy was the heroine of the evening. Sir Luke took her under his wing, praised her pretty face, her flowing hair, her light step, her silver laugh, her sweet touch on the piano, by-and-by, when they had magic music, and Lucy played for them, interweaving a new garland of old melodies, from 'Hope told a flattering tale' to 'Cherry Ripe.' Yet this girl, out of very perversity, seemed to take more interest in that old toady John Blagrove's conversation than in Sir Luke's outspoken compliments.

Mr. Blagrove sat by the piano, and she talked to him softly while she played. He was very fond of music, he told her; and she felt that it was a real affection, and that the good old melo-dies went straight from her heart to his. It was quite the hap-piest evening Lucy had ever spent in her life, so different from Christmas evenings at the Hollies, which had been respectable and ceremonial occasions, enlivened with sacred music, and a solemn rubber for the elders.

The old hall was only lighted by the great roaring Yule log, which left shadowy corners unilluminated; and somehow, after the music, Waller and Lucy were always getting into these shad-owy corners, and that dear old Mr. Blagrove made it his business to keep off intruders from these dusky retreats. He had taken the lovers under his protection, though they hardly knew it as yet.

Poor Waller was very far gone that evening, and felt it his bounden duty to make another appeal to Mr. Grynde next morning. That gentleman referred him to Sir Luke.

'You are apprised of my sentiments upon this subject, Mr. Carlyon,' he said. 'They are not likely to undergo modification; but Sir Luke is my first cousin, the next best thing to being my brother, and he has in a manner taken my humble destiny and that of my children under his wing. If Sir Luke considers you a fitting match for my daughter Lucy, I withdraw my objections, and lay down my personal opinion as a sacrifice to that superior mind.'

'Sir Luke is in the library,' said Waller; 'will you say as much to him, and without delay?'

Mr. Grynde assented, and they went together to the library, where Sir Luke was lounging luxuriously in an armchair before the fire, reading yesterday's *Times*, while his humble companion, John Blagrove, wrote letters at a table by the window. A hardy man, Mr. Blagrove, with no self-indulgent habits.

'May I ask for a few words with you in private, Sir Luke?' said Waller.

'Talk away, sir, we are as much in private as we need be,' answered the baronet, curtly; 'Blagrove doesn't count.'

Waller urged his pretensions to Lucy's hand; he spoke of their mutual attachment, his hopes for the future—spoke with manliness and modesty.

Sir Luke flew in a passion.

'What, sir,' he cried, 'you come into my house only to seduce my favourite cousin's affections! You make love to her under my nose in a sneaking underhand way!'

'No, Sir Luke; Lucy and I came to an understanding last summer, and Mr. Grynde knew all about it.'

'Knew and disapproved, sir—disapproved, as you are aware, Mr. Carlyon; but I was willing to submit myself to Sir Luke—I was willing to be overruled by his superior judgment.'

'No fear of my overruling you, sir!' exclaimed Sir Luke. 'Marry my cousin to a jackanapes, who thinks he is going to set up housekeeping on a little Greek and Latin, and sponge upon me for the rest.'

This was unbearable. Waller lost his temper, and answered Sir Luke roundly. The baronet blustered and swore, and it ended in Waller going to his mother to tell her to pack her trunk, while he went down to the 'White Lion' to order a fly.

Mrs. Carlyon shed tears, and bewailed her adverse fate. 'After our spending such a happy evening and all,' she lamented. 'I am sure I thought you had made such a favourable impression on Sir Luke.'

'His hide is too thick to be impressed, mother, except by a sledge-hammer. Silly old lady, you're crying over your best cap and taking the starch out. Don't be downhearted, mother. You know I never counted on the old man's favour.'

'Perhaps not, Waller,' answered the widow piteously, 'but I did.'

Waller got the fly and went off in sullen state with his mother, feeing the servants handsomely, but taking leave of no one. The news of his departure got about very soon, however, and Lucy came down to luncheon with red eyelids and without any appetite.

Her father demanded a private interview with her that afternoon, and called upon her solemnly to renounce that Oxonian reprobate Waller Carlyon. She was to pledge herself there and then to hold no further communication with him, never to speak to him, look at him, or even think of him again. Goaded thus, poor Lucy plucked up a spirit. Perhaps it was the high living at Cadbury Hall which made her so bold.

'No, papa,' she said, with gentle firmness. 'This is a question that concerns all my future life, and I cannot give way until I have reason to think myself wrong. My youth has not been particularly happy since poor mamma died. You and I have not seemed to understand each other very well; and I cannot renounce the hope of happiness all at once, because you tell me to do so.'

Samuel Grynde broke out furiously at this defiance. The waking of the lion was nothing to him; he quoted King Lear, and declared that such ingratitude as this was sharper than a serpent's tooth; and then he ordered Lucy off to her room, there to remain in durance till the end of the visit. Her sisters would take care of her, Mr. Grynde added, significantly.

This seemed an arbitrary proceeding on a father's part; but the fact is, Mr. Grynde was beginning to feel just a little jealous of his youngest daughter. Sir Luke had bestowed a degree of notice upon Lucy which, although flattering to Samuel Grynde's pride as a parent, was alarming to his self-interest as a legatee. Money left to Lucy, for her separate use and maintenance, would be almost as much alienated from Lucy's father as if left to a stranger. She was just of age too; there would be no need of guardianship or trusteeship.

If Sir Luke were to die tomorrow, she would pass at once into possession of any fortune he might leave her, and would doubtless bestow it on that reprobate Waller Carlyon. Sir Luke was pig-headed, self-willed, and illogical enough to be capable of leaving his entire fortune to Lucy if it pleased his fancy to do so.

'He hasn't the faintest sense of justice,' Mr. Grynde told himself; 'he must be ruled by a stronger mind than his own, and that pert chit of mine must be kept out of his way.'

So Lucy was relegated to the little cupboardy room inside the spacious bedchamber occupied by her sisters, and Sir Luke was told that she was suffering from acute neuralgia.

It was curious what a blank was made in the circle that evening by the absence of Waller and Lucy. All the Christmastide mirth was gone. Caroline and Amelia played their finest pieces, and sang the last fashionable Italian songs about nothing particular, but gloom hung over the assembly as a curtain. Sir Luke fell asleep in his big chair by the fire; John Blagrove stole out of the room; the four Grynde boys played whist with the air of middle-aged fogies at the Cavendish Club; Mr. Grynde felt that things were going badly.

Lucy cried herself to sleep before it was dark, and woke to find the cold winter moon shining upon her white bed; a very awful-looking moon it seemed to her in the stillness of her chamber. She was a long way from all the sitting-rooms, quite at the end of a corridor, and she felt as if she were an inmate of some lonely tower in a great feudal castle. She began to be rather hungry too. One of the maids had brought a tray with chicken and other daintinesses at dinnertime, but Lucy had been too fast asleep just then to hear the knock at the door.

She struck a match and lighted the wax candles on the dressing-table, which made things a little better, but hunger still prevailed. She had been too nervous to eat anything at breakfast that morning, knowing that Waller was going to speak to her father, and now it was ten o'clock, and she had been fasting all day.

'Oh dear,' said Lucy, 'how I should like a biscuit, a common hard biscuit even!'

She had hardly breathed this desire when she heard a curious sound in one of the cupboards.

'Goodness!' she screamed, 'it is a rat. I never can stay in this room if there are rats;' and she jumped on the bed to escape the horrid intruder.

Happily this was no rat, for a voice in the cupboard said gently, 'May I come in for a few minutes. Miss Lucy?'

It was poor trodden-upon Mr. Blagrove.

'Oh yes,' cried Lucy, 'please come in. I thought you were a rat.'

A key turned in a lock, and the cupboard door opened to admit Mr. Blagrove.

'You haven't been in that cupboard all day?' asked Lucy.

'No, my dear. This cupboard has two doors, as you may see if you look inside, the inner one opening on the servants' staircase at the east end of the house. You may often find such closets in old houses. I don't think your papa knows of this.'

'I'm sure he doesn't,' said Lucy.

'Well, my poor child, how's the neuralgia?'

'Whose neuralgia?' asked Lucy; 'I never had neuralgia in my life.'

'Indeed! Then why are you up here?'

Lucy told him her troubles, artlessly as a child.

'Ah, I thought how the land lay. And so you two children are very fond of each other?'

'We adore each other.'

'And you think Waller would make you a good husband?'

'How could he be anything else? He is so good, so clever, such an affectionate son, so honourable, so industrious.'

'What a string of virtues! Well, my dear, without being quite so enthusiastic as you, I really believe he is a good honest-hearted young fellow. I only wish I could help you.'

'I wish you could,' said Lucy. 'I took to you from the very first, Mr. Blagrove; you made me feel more at my ease somehow, and when I saw how rude the others were to you—except Waller and his mother, of course—I liked you all the more. I thought you were an outrage, like me.'

'An outrage?' inquired Mr. Blagrove.

'Yes. Papa always says I am an outrage against his sense of propriety.'

'How old are you, Lucy?'

'Twenty-one last November.'

'And you hardly look nineteen. And how old is Mr. Carlyon?'

'Twenty-one last May.'

'Humph,' muttered John Blagrove. 'If he were to elope with you it wouldn't be abduction. Poor little girl! I'm sorry I'm such a useless, dependent creature. Is there any small way now in which I could be of service?'

'Oh yes,' cried Lucy, eagerly; 'if you'd be so very kind as to get me something to eat; I'm positively famishing.'

'Famishing! Why, didn't you eat that wing of a chicken I sent you, with a mince pie to follow?'

'No, indeed; no one has brought me anything.'

John Blagrove opened Lucy's door, and looked outside.

There was the tray just as the maid had left it, on a table in the next room—a silver cover over the plate of chicken, which was flanked by a pint of champagne, the cork drawn, and the wine rather flat by this time.

Lucy was delighted to find she had not been forgotten.

'You dear, good soul,' she exclaimed, 'how sweet of you to think of me when I was in disgrace!'

'Neuralgia,' said Mr. Blagrove.

'No, sir, disobedience; and you must have known it.'

John Blagrove put the tray on a little table by the fire, which he had brightened up into a blaze. He and Lucy sat opposite each other, and hobnobbed with the champagne and shared the mince pie. It was quite a merry little *tête-à-tête* supper. Mr, Blagrove had locked the door, to make sure against interruption.

'Now, Lucy,' he said, 'I am not going to have you shut up in this room much longer. If your father doesn't let you out in the course of tomorrow I shall let you out the morning after. Let me see, this is Thursday. Put on your best frock and your prettiest bonnet at nine o'clock on Saturday morning, while they all are at breakfast downstairs, and hold yourself in readiness to take a walk with me.'

'But what will papa say? He will never forgive me.'

'Nonsense, child! I think I know how to manage Mr. Grynde, with Sir Luke at my back. I can do anything with Sir Luke, you know.'

'Can you?' asked Lucy, wonderingly. 'I shouldn't have thought it; he seems to snub you so.'

'Only manner, my dear. But I must be off, or we shall have your sisters here, and then you'll get into trouble.'

So Mr. Blagrove gave Lucy a paternal kiss on her pretty white forehead, and let himself out by that mysterious old cupboard in which she had suspected rats.

The next day seemed very long to Lucy, though it was one of the shortest in the year. Her sisters had supplied her with a strip of embroidery to be worked, and a very dull book, but neither work nor book could beguile her thoughts from the one subject of wonder that occupied her mind. What did Mr. Blagrove intend by such an audacious step as he had talked about last night? And how would he succeed in pacifying her father? Her meals were brought her quite regularly today, but wonder had taken away her appetite.

She obeyed her old friend implicitly, however, next morning, and was arrayed in her pretty dove-coloured silk dress, her black velvet jacket, and brown straw bonnet lined with sky-blue, by the time the great breakfast-bell rang.

She was putting on her gloves—a new pair to match her dress—when John Blagrove knocked at the closet door.

'Come in,' cried she.

'Ready, I see,' said he, 'and looking your prettiest. What's the day of the month?'

'What a funny question!' said Lucy; 'why, the 28th of December, to be sure.'

'That's a date which you must remember all your life, little one,' said the old man. 'Come along.'

He took her hand, and led her down a darkish and narrowish stair till they came to a stone lobby that opened into the stable-yard. Grooms were hissing ferociously at their horses, and coachmen were squirting water at carriage wheels, but no one noticed Lucy and her companion. They went from the stable-yard to the park, and across the park, in the clear winter morning. The grass was frosted, and glittered in the sunshine.

'I am glad the sun shines, Lucy, for your sake,' said Mr. Blagrove. This remark, following on that about the date, seemed go odd that Lucy began to fear her old friend was not quite right in his head. A dear, good, pleasant old gentleman, but a little childish at times, perhaps.

They walked on till they came to the park gates, where there was actually a carriage waiting for them, Sir Luke's family coach, and into this they got. It drove them to the door of the old parish church.

'Is it a saint's day?' asked Lucy.

Mr. Blagrove answered never a word, but drew her little hand through his arm, and led her into the church. Just then the organ began to play a lively march of Mendelssohn's; and, gracious! here was Waller Carlyon coming down the aisle, with his mother on his arm, and Mrs. Carlyon had her best gown on, the lavender moire she wore at all the Cadbury parties.

'Now, Lucy, you are my little girl today, and you are going to be married,' said Mr. Blagrove.

'Oh!' cried Lucy, 'I couldn't possibly—I couldn't fly in papa's face like this. He'd never forgive me.'

'Yes, my dear, he would. He'll forgive you when he knows that I've adopted you, and that I can twist Sir Luke round my finger.'

Waller offered Lucy his arm now, and somehow she took it without quite knowing what she was doing, and they went up to the altar.

The good old vicar came out of the vestry, and the marriage service began, Lucy trembling very much; but when it came to her turn for responding, she spoke out more boldly than could have been expected. That glad young soul of hers burst its bonds of discipline just then, and she forgot all about her father's anger.

After they had all signed their names in the vestry, Mr. Blagrove asked permission to put a ring over the symbolic circlet which Waller had just placed on Lucy's finger, and he slipped on a diamond half-hoop, whose lustre made the spectators wink, so brilliant were the big white stones in the morning sunshine. Such a present could hardly have been expected from a poor dependent like Mr. Blagrove, and Lucy wondered more and more.

And now the organ burst out again with Mendelssohn—the 'Wedding March' this time—and to the sound of that pompous music they walked down the aisle, and to the door where Sir Luke's coach was waiting for them.

They all four got into the carriage and drove back to Cadbury Hall—yes, entered audaciously by the park gates, and drove boldly up to the great Doric door. Everybody had gone mad,

Lucy thought: yet she trembled no longer: she was no longer afraid of her father's wrath. She sat by her husband's side, and felt that safety and protection were there.

'Where is Sir Luke?' asked Mr. Blagrove as they went in.

'In the library, sir, with Mr. Grynde.'

'Come this way, then,' said Sir Luke's humble follower; and Lucy, Waller, and Mrs. Carlyon accompanied him to the sombre old room, with its long narrow windows and high walls lined with brown-backed books.

Sir Luke sat in his big armchair. Mr. Grynde stood in his favourite attitude in front of the fire, his coat tails over his arms. He faced the door as Lucy and her companions entered.

'Merciful powers! What does this mean?' he cried. 'Lucy, I thought I had desired you to keep your chamber.—Young man,' to Waller, 'I think that Sir Luke and I made our views pretty clear to you the day before yesterday.'

'Happily for me, sir, I had a friend of another way of thinking,' answered Waller, with respectful boldness; 'and, with his aid, I have ventured to take the law into my own hands. Lucy is of age and her own mistress, and within the last half-hour she has become my wife. She need be not the less your dutiful daughter on that account.'

Lucy was on her knees at her father's feet.

'Blow, blow, thou wintry wind,
Thou art not so unkind,

as this kind of thing,' cried Mr. Grynde, in a paroxysm of indignation. 'Go away, you base, undutiful child. Go and be a pauper with the pauper you have chosen for your husband. I renounce you!'

'And I adopt her,' said Mr. Blagrove, taking the weeping girl to his breast. 'I have given her away this morning; but I mean to keep her all the days of my life, and I shall leave her and her husband master and mistress of Cadbury Hall.'

'*You!* 'cried Samuel Grynde. 'What have you got to do with it?'

'Only this much,' answered the old man, quietly: 'I am Sir Luke Cadbury. When I came home from Australia after forty years' exile, it was suggested to me by my good friend and chief clerk here, John Blagrove,' pointing to the stout gentleman in the armchair, 'that, as a wealthy and childless man, I was likely to be the cause of much meanness and mercenary feeling in my next of kin, the object of a great deal of flattery and sycophancy, and that I should hardly succeed in seeing my next of kin in their true colours, so thick would be the coat of varnish they would put on to dazzle and deceive me.

'Out of this suggestion grew the idea that I, Luke Cadbury, should assume the person of my clerk and dependant John Blagrove, making that personification a great deal more subservient and dependent than the real Jack Blagrove, who is a truculent scoundrel, by the way.'

Here the two old men laughed heartily. Lot's wife, after that unlucky backward look of hers, must have been an image of cheerfulness as compared with Samuel Grynde at this juncture, so abject was the despair depicted on that gentleman's countenance.

'So I came as the clerk, and Jack took the character of the baronet, and very well he has acted it, barring a little exaggeration. He has made himself as disagreeable as he could, in order to test the fortune-hunting mind, and I must say he has found that order of intellect very elastic. You have put up with a good deal from my friend, Mr. Grynde, and you have not been particularly civil to me. But I hope you will forgive Jack Blagrove as heartily as I forgive you.'

'You are a set of —— impostors,' exploded Samuel; and he stalked out of the room and away from Cadbury Hall without another word, or so much as a look to the right or the left.

Sir Luke kept the rest of the family till Twelfth-night, with the exception of Waller and Lucy, who went off to Malvern in the baronet's carriage, and there were gay doings at the Hall. The news soon spread through Cadbury, and Samuel Grynde had a bad time of it while the story of Sir Luke's return was fresh in the minds of men, women, and children. The street boys laughed at him openly. That Christian-like spirit which was one of the ornaments of his character ultimately prevailed, however, and a month after Lucy's marriage he accepted an invitation to dine at the Hall.

'If I had been a fortune-hunter, I should have taken this trick of yours more keenly to heart,' he said to his cousin, in a tone of mild reproachfulness, 'but as I was utterly without ulterior views, I can afford to laugh at the little comedy, now that my first sense of irritation at Lucy's disobedience is over.'

'Quite without ulterior views?' said Sir Luke, slily; 'you told me a different story one day when I was John Blagrove.'

'Sir, I addressed you then as John Blagrove, and ventured to reprove what I considered your presumption in that character. I may have displayed a mistaken zeal, but my independence of mind never wavered.'

'I am glad of that, Samuel,' said the baronet;. 'I have not many years to live, and I should like to be friends with all my kith and kin, and to see them happy round me. When I am dead and gone it will not be found that I have dealt unjustly by anyone.'

This, though somewhat vague, was comforting.

A Very Narrow Escape

It was not quite a year since Mr. George Hartfield, the leading solicitor in the market town of Norbury, had returned from his honeymoon tour, bringing with him the prettiest little wife that the good old town had boasted for a long time. George was only thirty years of age, but his wife looked a mere girl, and was at least eleven years his junior, much to the disgust of more mature damsels, who would have been very willing to step into the proprietorship of the good-looking young lawyer and his prim respectable old house, which was one of the most conspicuous dwellings in the upper and more rural part of the High Street. Mr. Hartfield had inherited an excellent business from his father, and was altogether a person of some importance in the opinion of the Norbury world at large, and of himself in particular.

The wife was a shy girlish creature, who seemed scarcely fit to be mistress of that big formal house, with its shining wainscoted walls and grim old furniture—furniture that had been fashionable in the days of George's grandfather—gloomy old mahogany four-posters and walnut-wood presses, in the polished panels whereof sentimental little Alice Hartfield' whose head was a kind of branch depot of the circulating library, used to fancy she saw ghosts in the gloaming.

In honest truth, she did not take much to the house in the High Street, and looked back with fond regretfulness to the bright country home from which George had won her; but Mr. Hartfield being of an arbitrary temper, and convinced that the old house was perfection, she had never ventured to hint her dislike. It must be owned that the evenings were long and dull for so girlish a matron. George Hartfield was often out—sometimes at a public dinner at the Crown Hotel, sometimes at a social club held at the same prosperous tavern, sometimes playing billiards with bachelor clients—all in the way of business, of course, as he told his wife; but the evenings during which he was absent were not the less lonely on that account.

Mr. Hartfield employed three clerks: a gentlemanly young man, who was articled; a stripling, for copying and out-of-door work; and a grey-haired old man, with a face upon which there was a look of settled melancholy. Mr. Bestow, the articled clerk, and Thomas Dregger, the stripling, had christened him Old Dismal, and spoke of him commonly by that disrespectful sobriquet. If he ever heard the name, it apparently troubled him very little. He rarely spoke, except so far as his business required him to speak; and, in the two years that he had been with Mr. Hartfield, he had not advanced by so much as one step towards intimacy with his fellow-workers. He lived three miles out of Norbury, walking to and from the office in all weathers, and no one had ever seen the inside of his home.

Her first year of married life closed in sorrow and disappointment for Alice Hartfield. The baby-stranger, from whose coming she had expected so much pleasure, only opened its eyes upon this world to close them again for ever. She dwelt upon this loss with a grief which seemed to her husband just a little exaggerated, and it is possible that her tears and sad looks drove him to his club at the 'Crown' rather more often this year than in the previous winter. It was not that he was unkind or indifferent to his pretty young wife. He fancied that she was perfectly happy with her books and work and piano, in the interval between six o'clock and eleven, at which hour he punctually returned to his abode, as sober as when he left home, well pleased with himself and with the world at large.

The two younger clerks commented very freely upon the solicitor's conduct in his domestic capacity.

'If I had such a pretty wife, I wouldn't leave her alone evening after evening as our governor does,' remarked the stripling, pertly; 'I wonder he isn't ashamed of himself.'

'He ought to take her more into society certainly,' replied Mr. Bestow, the articled clerk, who was in much request in that brilliant circle which constituted Norbury 'society.'

Mr. Morgan, the old clerk, looked up from his desk with a sigh.

'What, my funereal friend,' cried Bestow, 'do you mean to say you are interested in the subject?'

'I am very much interested in Mrs. Hartfield,' the old man answered quietly; 'she is always kind to me. It is a good sign when a woman of her age takes the trouble to be polite to an old man like me—a sign that the heart's in the right place. I wish her husband understood her better. I don't think she wants to be taken to tea parties, Mr. Bestow; but I do think she wants a little more sympathy.'

This was a long speech for Mr. Morgan. The two younger men stared at him superciliously, and then went on with their work. From the first day of her coming to be mistress of the old house William Morgan had shown himself interested in his master's wife. He was always pleased to perform any little service for her, and seemed needlessly grateful for the smallest kindness at her hands. His way home took him the whole length of the town; and Mrs Hartfield used to entrust him with her books ,to change at the circulating library, an office which he performed with much taste and discretion.

'I take the liberty to carry a volume home with me for the night, at odd times,' he said to her one day.

'What, Mr. Morgan, do you read novels?'

'No, madam; but I have a niece living with me who is glad to skim the volumes of an evening.'

'Indeed! You never spoke of her before. Is your niece married?'

'She—she is a widow—to all intents and purposes. Her husband deserted her three years ago, and left her and her boy on my hands. But we are very happy together, I thank God.'

'The husband must have been a bad man.'

'He was a most consummate scoundrel!' answered the old clerk, with suppressed intensity.

'How hard it must be for you to work for all three!' said Alice.

'It will be harder for the two that are left when I am gone. My niece is able to earn a little money at her needle, but very little. It is a dark lookout for the future.'

One morning, early in the spring, Mr. Hartfield came into the office with a very dashing gentleman, a new client, who had just come into a handsome fortune by the death of old Squire Comberford, of Comberford Hall, seven miles from Norbury. Edgar Comberford, the new proprietor, was a nephew of the old man, and had been a schoolfellow of George Hartfield's fifteen years before. Since that time he had disappeared from the ken of Norbury, and was supposed to have led a wild life in foreign lands. He was eminently handsome, and in high spirits at his accession to the Comberford Hall estate.

'There are the papers, title-deeds, leases, and so on,' said George Hartfield, pointing to three japanned boxes on a shelf in the office; 'do you want to see them?'

'Not I, George,' answered Mr. Comberford, gaily; 'it is quite enough for me to know that the lands are free from mortgages, and that the rents come in briskly. The papers couldn't be in better hands. Holloa! What's that?'

It was Mr. Morgan, the old clerk, who had put his head in at the door of the office, and suddenly withdrawn it.

'Only one of my clerks,' answered George Hartfield. 'Come in, Morgan!' he bawled; but the clerk did not reply, and the two young men left the office—Mr. Comberford to be introduced to his friend's wife.

He was not a little surprised by her grace and beauty; not a little fascinated by her shy, girlish manners. He stayed to dinner, and contrived to make himself agreeable to both his host and hostess, giving an animated account of his adventures in Mexico during the last two years.

'I should never have come from there, George, but for my uncle's death,' he said. 'I was thoroughly cleaned out when I left England, and meant to live and die abroad.'

After this social dinner Mr. Comberford dropped in very often at his friend's house. He seemed to have some perpetual reason for seeing the solicitor on business, and happened, by a kind of fatality, to call when the master of the house was out. Would he leave a statement of his business with the clerk?

No, he would wait; and he strolled unannounced into the little sitting-room at the back of the offices, where Mrs. Hartfield spent her mornings. It was the prettiest room in the house, opening into a small garden, at the end of which there was a narrow creek—an inlet from the river that flowed through Norbury. By and by Mr. Comberford took to approaching the house by this way. He was an expert waterman, and spent a good deal of his time on the river.

So it was an easy and natural thing for him to moor his boat at the bottom of George Hartfield's garden, and step on shore. He always found Alice in her sitting-room, and he found a look in her face which told him his visits were not unwelcome. He was a thorough man of the world, and knew the danger of the game he was playing, nor did he yield without a struggle to the temptation that had overtaken him Such a heart as he had was hit harder than it had been of late years. The outside world of Norbury had not yet been awakened to the scandal of Mr. Comberford's frequent visits to the lawyer's house, nor was the lawyer himself alarmed by them; but the younger clerks were quick to remark upon the length and frequency of these morning calls, and on George Hartfield's blindness to the fact.

Edgar Comberford had been settled at the Hall for six months, when George Hartfield had occasion to go to Paris on business. He had intended to take his wife with him for the trip, but the weather was sultry and oppressive, and he went alone. Mrs. Hartfield seemed very little disappointed by this change in his plans. Mr. Comberford had assured her that Paris was quite unbearable in July. It was upon his business that George Hartfield was engaged. He went to make a settlement with a Parisian money-lender who had advanced money to the young man in the days of his insolvency, and who now put in an exorbitant claim for interest.

The first day of Mr. Hartfield's absence went by without any visit from Mr. Comberford, but in the evening, when the clerks were gone and Alice was sitting alone and very low-spirited, the familiar sound of the boat grating against the woodwork at the bottom of the garden struck upon her ear, and brought a sudden blush into her cheeks. She looked up with a movement of surprise as Edgar Comberford came across the garden. He came in at the open window with the air of a person who had a perfect right to be there, and seated himself opposite to Alice, at the little table where she was drinking tea.

'I thought you would give me a cup of tea after my row, Mrs. Hartfield,' he said, 'and I could not pass the creek without begging for one. I dread going home to the desolation of the Hall—empty rooms and a cross old housekeeper. I think I shall go back to Mexico before the year is out.'

Alice gave a little start.

'What!' she said, 'leave the Hall forever?'

'In all probability forever. A man seldom comes home a second time from such a place as Mexico.'

'But why should you go back there? Why should you be tired of the Hall so soon?'

'Why should I be tired of life altogether? Why should I wish to run away from myself—from you?'

And then he went on to speak of his love for her, in dark hints rather than in plain words. She tried to reprove him, tried to show him that she was angry, but the attempt was a very feeble one. She could only insist that he should leave her immediately. He did leave her, but not immediately, and not till she had changed insistence into piteous entreaty.

The boat had scarcely shot away in the twilight when the door between the sitting-room and the office opened, and the old clerk, Morgan, appeared on the threshold.

'You here, Mr. Morgan!' exclaimed Alice, making a vain attempt to conceal her tears; 'I thought all the clerks had gone.'

'I had some letters to copy, Mrs. Hartfield. Can I do anything for you in the town tonight?'

'Nothing, thank you.'

He lingered, twisting the brim of his shabby old hat round and round in his thin wrinkled hands.

'I wish to heaven I might speak to you freely,' he said at last, 'without offending or wounding you.'

'About what?'

'About the man who has just left you.'

'Mr. Comberford, my husband's friend?'

'Your husband's direst, deadliest foe—and yours,' answered the old man, passionately.

'What right have you to say that?' asked Alice, trembling with indignation.

'The right given me by my knowledge of mankind, and, above all, by my knowledge of Edgar Comberford.'

'What knowledge can you have of Mr. Comberford? Did you ever see him before he came to this office?'

'Never; but his name is a word of dire meaning in my life. Ask him what became of the girl he stole away from an honourable home and left in a wretched London lodging four years ago. Ask him to tell you the fate of Bessie Raynor?'

'Why should I trouble myself about his affairs? And who is this Bessie Raynor?'

'Never mind who she is, Mrs. Hartfield. She was a good girl before he met her. She will never be a happy woman again. Ask him about her if you doubt what I tell you, and you will see by his countenance whether he is innocent or guilty. Knowing what I do, I am bound to warn you of his real character.'

'I do not require any such warning,' replied Alice, coldly; 'Mr. Comberford is no more to me than any other client of my husband's. And I beg that you will not trouble yourself to dictate my conduct to him.'

'I see that I have offended you.'

209

'I do not like spies.'

'I am no spy, Mrs. Hartfield. I am an old man, and have had bitter cause to know the wickedness of the world. Your sweet face has been a kind of light to me ever since your husband brought you home to this house. God forbid that light should ever be clouded by the shadow of disgrace!'

He bowed and left her—left her standing in a reverie, looking absently out upon the dusky fields beyond the little garden and the winding creek. She was angry, unhappy, bewildered.

'I wish George had taken me to Paris,' she thought. 'He ought not to leave me alone in a dreary old house like this, to be insulted by a clerk.'

After this evening she passed Mr. Morgan without speaking to him, much to the old man's concern. The days went by, and not one passed without a visit from Edgar Comberford, although in that first evening Alice had expressly forbidden him to call again during her husband's absence. He was not easily to be put aside. He knew the weakness of the girl's unschooled nature, and knew how to trade upon it.

His tender talk of the life that might have been had Alice been free—his glowing descriptions of distant lands which those two might have seen, side by side, of countries where the commonest life was a kind of poetry—charmed her in spite of herself. She knew the guilt involved in this dangerous pleasure, and hated herself for her weakness, and yet looked forward with a dull sense of dread to her husband's return. Nothing could tempt her to sin against George Hartfield, she told Edgar, however unsuited they might be to each other. She was his wife, and would do her duty to the end of her life. But the tempter was not convinced.

One day she ventured to ask him about Bessie Raynor. He looked startled, Alice thought, at the sound of the name, but he declared that it was strange to him; and Alice was weak enough to believe his assertion. It had been a mere ruse of the old clerk's to frighten her, she thought. The poor dismal old creature had tried to make her miserable about the only acquaintance that gave her any pleasure.

Mr. Hartfield had been away ten days, when Mr, Comberford came in upon Alice suddenly one morning with a very grave countenance. The neat little parlour-maid was only just clearing away the breakfast-things when he came, and lingered inquisitively to hear the meaning of this early visit.

'I am sorry to say I have rather bad news of your husband, Mrs. Hartfield,' he said in answer to Alice's expression of surprise. 'He has been taken ill with some kind of low fever, which is a good deal about in Paris just now. Don't be alarmed; it is nothing very serious; but he wants you to go across to him. His doctor, a Frenchman, has written to me, but there is an enclosure for you from the patient.'

He handed her a slip of foreign paper, on which there were a few lines in her husband's hand:

Dear Alice,—Please come over to me at once, if you are not afraid of the journey. Comberford can escort you, as he is wanted over here.—Yours, &c.. G. H.

'You'll not be afraid of the journey?' asked Mr. Comberford.

'Not at all; I should not mind going alone.'

'But, you see, I am due there, so you cannot deny me the pleasure of being your escort'

'It is not a very pleasurable occasion,' said Alice, with some embarrassment, as she twisted the slip of writing round and round her fingers. She was wondering whether the strict moralists of Norbury would altogether approve of such an escort.

Mr. Comberford gave her little time to think. He went into the clerks' office to tell Mr. Bestow of his employer's illness, and to make inquiries about the London trains. William Morgan looked up from his desk and watched his master's client thoughtfully as he lounged against the mantelpiece reading the timetable.

There was no possibility of going to Paris earlier than by the night mail. Mrs. Hartfield would have to go first to London—a three hours' journey. There was a train left Norbury at a quarter to four in the afternoon, which would take the travellers in ample time for the Dover mail. Mr. Comberford decided upon going by this, and left Alice in order to make his preparations for the journey.

He did not, however, go back to the Hall, but fidgeted in and out of the lawyer's house several times in the course of the day on some pretence or other, spending the interval at the 'Crown,' where he drank brandy and soda-water to an extent that astonished the waiters. But in spite of all he had drunk, he looked pale and anxious when he came at three o'clock ready to take Mrs. Hartfield to the station.

Alice was just stepping into the fly, when William Morgan came out of the house, with a carpet bag in one hand and a morocco office bag in the other.

'Why, where the deuce are you going?' asked Mr. Comberford.

'I am to be your fellow-traveller, sir; at least, I am going second class by the same train.'

'To London?'

'No, sir, to Paris. Mr. Bestow sends me across with papers.'

'Why, what consummate folly of Bestow's! Your master is not fit for business. He won't be able to attend to anything for days to come.'

'I hope he may be better than you think, sir. In any case, I am bound to obey Mr. Bestow's orders.'

He spoke in a mechanical kind of tone, nor did his countenance express the faintest interest in his work.

Mr. Comberford laughed grimly to himself as they drove away with the old man on the box.

'That old fool's company can make very little difference,' he muttered, and then grew moodier than he was wont to be in Alice Hartfield's company.

He brightened considerably by and by, when they were alone in a first-class compartment, flying Londonwards at express rate; and he succeeded in making Alice believe that her husband's illness was only a trifling matter, and that she had no occasion to be anxious about him.

'Men think so much of the slightest touch of illness,' he said, 'and are always in a hurry to summon their wives. We are such helpless creatures, you see, and so miserable without the comfort of a woman's presence.'

And then he went on to speak of his own solitary position.

'What is to become of me in the hour of sickness, Alice,' he asked, 'with no one but a gloomy old housekeeper to care for me?'

'You will marry by and by, I dare say, and have a wife to care for you.'

'Never, Alice. There is only one woman on earth I care for; and if she cannot be my wife, I will go down to my grave a bachelor.'

'You must not talk to me like that; it is taking a mean advantage of my position. You know that I am with you at my husband's wish.'

'Yes, you have his order for the journey. Poor dear George, what a fine bold hand he writes, doesn't he?'

Mrs. Hartfield did not see the sardonic grin which accompanied this trivial remark, nor did Mr. Comberford again offend her by any allusion to his hopeless passion. It was pitch dark when they reached Dover, not a star in the sky, and a high wind blowing. There was considerable confusion in getting on board, and Mrs. Hartfield scarcely knew where she was till she found herself standing on the deck of a steamer arm-in-arm with Edgar Comberford, while the lamps of Dover receded rapidly from her vision. Her companion persuaded her to remain on deck.

'There is an atmosphere of seasickness below that would inevitably make you ill,' he said. 'Let me find you a comfortable corner, where you can be secure from wind and weather.'

He found a sheltered nook by one of the paddle- boxes, and. here Mrs. Hartfield sat comfortably wrapped in shawls and railway rugs, and amused by her fellow-traveller's conversation. He seemed now in the highest possible spirits, and did his uttermost to entertain her; but well as he succeeded in doing this, he could not make her quite unconscious of the passage of time.

'I thought the steamer crossed in an hour and a half,' she said; 'but we have surely been more than two hours on board.'

'Oh dear no, I think not. There's a good deal of wind tonight, however; so I dare say the passage will take a little longer than usual.

Mrs. Hartfield questioned him about the time more than once after this, but he was unable to give her any definite answer.

It was all right, he said vaguely, and his spirits mounted as the boat plunged gaily through the waters.

With the first gleam of morning they neared the shore. Their luggage was ready for landing among the first, only a couple of carpet bags and a portmanteau, which were pounced upon speedily by officials, and borne off to a building in the distance.

Mr. Comberford led Alice up the steps, and put her at once into a fly that loomed duskily out upon them in the chilly atmosphere. He came back to her presently with the luggage, and seated himself by her side; but before he could rejoin her she had asked the driver the name of the place, and he had told her that she was in Ostend.

She looked at Edgar Comberford with a face full of terror. 'What a wretched mistake!' she said; 'we have come by the wrong steamer. Why did you not tell me the truth on board? But of course we can go from here to Paris. It is only the loss of time that annoys me.'

'My darling Alice, you are as innocent as a baby,' exclaimed Mr. Comberford, with a triumphant smile. 'We are no more going to Paris than we are going to the moon. All stratagems are fair in love and war, George Hartfield is as well as ever he was in his life, and the little note you so implicitly believed in was only a specimen of imitative penmanship by your humble servant. I wanted to get you away from that dreary old town without *esclandre*, my love. We are bound for the sunny Rhineland, there to forget that there is such a place as Norbury, or such a person as George Hartfield.'

'And you think that I will go with you?'

'My dearest, I do not think you so foolish as to resist your fate. The Rubicon is passed, and return utterly impossible. We gave your husband's old clerk the slip at Dover. He will be in Paris at seven o'clock, with the story of your journey, which will be at once set down as an elopement.'

'I am not so weak or so wicked as you think,' cried Alice, snatching her hand indignantly from his grasp. 'Foolish and guilty as I have been in listening to you, I am not so base as you seem to have thought me. You must take me on to Paris by the first train, Mr. Comberford, or I must go alone.'

'Impossible!'

'Where are we going now?'

'To an hotel I most get you some breakfast. There is no train for Paris till seven; there is one for Cologne at the same hour, and it is by that we are to travel.'

Alice looked at him in despair. Whatever love she had felt for him died a sudden death in this moment of agony. How gladly would she have welcomed her husband's honest face! How bitterly she reproached herself for her neglect of the old clerk's warning!

'He was my truest friend,' she thought, 'and I refused to listen to him.'

They were at the door of an hotel by this time. While the driver was ringing, a second fly drove up, and an old man alighted. It was Morgan, the clerk.

Alice gave a cry of delight, and called him to the door of the vehicle.

'There has been a mistake,' she said; 'Mr. Comberford brought me by the wrong boat. But, thank Heaven, you came the same way. You can take me on to Paris.'

'Or back to Norbury, whichever you prefer, madam,' answered the old clerk, respectfully. 'Mr. Comberford has an unfortunate habit of making mistakes. This is not the first time he has signed another man's name by mistake. There was an awkward business about a forged accommodation bill, some years ago, which in-

215

duced Mr. Comberford to cross the Atlantic.'

'What do you mean, sir?' cried the younger man, indignantly.

'I mean that there is no one in the world who knows you
better than Bessie Raynor's uncle,' answered William Morgan. 'I
never set eyes on your false face till you came into my master's
office, but I have heard your history from the lips of a woman
who loved you, and who would willingly have made the best
of it. You have not changed for the better since your days of
poverty, and you have not taken the trouble to ascertain what
became of the girl who shared your hardships and disgrace. She
is living with me, sir, three miles from Norbury, where you are
now so grand a gentleman. I told this lady to beware of you, but
she was too confiding to doubt you, and not confiding enough
to believe me. I think, however, you have thrown off the mask
too soon.'

'Don't lecture me, sir. The lady must decide between us.
Whatever wrong I have done has been done for her sake. I had
reason to think she loved me.'

This was said with a tone of bitter reproach, and then the
young man stood awaiting his fate with a moody countenance.

'I think I had better take you on to Paris, Mrs. Hartfield,' said
the clerk. 'It would set Norbury folks talking if we went straight
home. You can tell your husband the whole truth, and he can
settle the score with this gentleman.'

'I am going straight on to Germany,' said Mr, Comberford. 'If
Hartfield wants me, he must follow me there.'

He walked into the hotel, the door of which had just been
opened by a sleepy-looking waiter, leaving Alice under the care
of the old clerk. She went to Paris with him, and there made
the best story she could to her husband, humbly confessing her
own errors.

'I suppose I must have flirted with him a little, George,' she
said shyly, 'or he would never have done such a wild wicked
thing.'

And this confession had a very good effect upon George

Hartfield, who felt that he had been wanting in due care and consideration for his pretty young wife. He withdrew himself from the club at the 'Crown,' left off billiards, and took to rowing Alice on the river in the summer evenings, and reading to her or playing chess with her in the winter. He did not follow Mr. Comberford to Germany, but contented himself with writing a formal letter, relinquishing the conduct of that gentleman's affairs.

Mr. Comberford came back to the Hall three years afterwards, with an aristocratic but by no means agreeable wife. Before returning he took steps to settle a modest annuity upon Mr. Morgan's niece, Bessie Raynor; an annuity which was accepted by the young woman, but the quarterly payments of which were carefully banked against that rainy day when William Morgan should be no more. The old man scorned to touch a penny of Edgar Comberford's money.

The Little Woman in Black

There was hardly anything talked about in the clubs and the coffee-houses that November of 1753, but the approaching marriage of Miss Sarah Pawlett and Lord Bellenden. My lord was one of the finest gentlemen in England, a statesman and a diplomatist, a man of great learning, eight-and-thirty years of age, honoured and favoured at Court, on terms of friendly intimacy at Strawberry Hill and Marble Hill, where Lady Suffolk swore he was the one honest man in his Majesty's dominions. He was owner of a splendid estate in Hertfordshire, and a fine house in St. James's Park; he had a castle in Ireland, and a deer forest in North Britain. In a word, he was the best match in all London.

Had the beautiful Sarah been about to marry some lordling of the fribble and fop tribe, instead of this splendid gentleman, the town would doubtless have had a good deal to say about her promotion; for it is not an everyday incident for an actress to be raised to the peerage, albeit Polly Peacham, after more than twenty years of probation, had lately been made Duchess of Bolton; but for the Covent Garden actress to carry off the finest gentleman in London was another matter, and folks were greatly amazed at her high fortune.

She herself bore her success calmly, was said, indeed, to have a somewhat melancholy air when she showed herself in her coach in the park, or attended a fashionable auction to bid for some old delft jar or Indian monster. But a pensive air best became that statuesque loveliness of hers, and rollicking and blithesome as she was in a comedy part, she had ever in society the look of a tearless Niobe, pale as marble, and with large violet eyes full of a strange pathos.

'She had not always that doleful air,' said little Tom Squatt, the critic, an early admirer of Sarah's; 'I remember the time when she was as gay as a bird—ready to jump over the moon—and that was when she was not always sure of her dinner.'

'Ah, that was before she took the town,' said another literary gentleman at the Little Hell Fire Club, a room over a tavern in Covent Garden, where a choice circle of garretteers and hireling wits met every night after the play. 'Success sobers 'em all. They begin to think of saving money, and turn religious. Besides, that was before she fell in love with Ned Langley.'

At this there was much head-shaking and elevation of eyebrows in the little assembly, and divers pinches of snuff were taken with an air and a shoulder-shrug, as who should say, 'We could, an' if we would,' and so on. Yet scandal had hardly breathed its venom over the young actress's fair fame. She had never left the wing of the old half-pay Major, her father, who had fought with King George at Dettingen, and who was punctiliousness itself upon all points of honour; and she was known to have supported a brood of younger sisters, down-at-heel slatterns, with pretty faces and towzled heads, out of her earnings as an actress.

True! But she was also known to have been for at least one brief season—the girl's dream-land time—over head and ears in love with handsome Ned Langley. Langley the irresistible, the *beau*-ideal lover and reprobate of the dear old reprobate-drama, the Wildair, the Lovelace, the Mirabel, the Ranger of fashionable comedy; polished, elegant, supple, villainous, bewitching.

Ned could hardly help carrying some of his comedy characteristics into real life. The town would not have had him otherwise. Society began by giving him his diabolical reputation, and poor Ned had to live up to it. He must be Don Juan or nothing. His fashion would have waned in a season had it been hinted that he lived soberly and had ceased to intrigue with women of quality. In dress, and manner, and morals, he must needs be as the heroes of Wycherley and Vanburgh, if he would keep his vogue. And Ned was vain, and loved to be the fashion; and he deemed it his first duty to himself and society to ruin the peace of any beautiful woman who came within his ken.

Sarah Pawlett came into Covent Garden Theatre innocent, fresh, warm-hearted, pure-minded, pious even, in an age when unbelief was the last fashion. She came from her humble training in booths and barns, and queer little provincial theatres, and took the town by storm. Her beauty, her youth, her buoyancy came upon the jaded London playgoer as a surprise. It was long since so bright and spontaneous a being had flashed and sparkled on those boards. She seemed the very spirit of comedy; and to see her act a love scene—half sentiment, half mockery—with Ned Langley, was to see the very perfection of acting.

The town flocked to hear these two interchange the joyous banter of Wycherley or Congreve, charmed with their sparkle and fire, their dash and exuberance.

Of course, stage-lovers so delightful must be lovers off the stage and in earnest. The tumultuous love scenes of that broad, bright comedy must find their counterpart oft' the stage in a deeper and more fatal love. This is the universal belief of the playgoer.

For once in a way the audience were right in their guesswork. Those stage-lovers had not wooed and bantered each other in the shine of the oil lamps for half a year before they had fallen deeper in love than ever Wycherley or Congreve dreamed of in their gamut of passion. She gave up heart and soul to the gallant lover, surrendered her young fresh lips to his stage-kisses, melted in his arms, heart beating against heart, sweetest eyes lifted confidingly to his, while the audience applauded and cried, 'How exquisite, how natural!'

She was to be his wife. No shadow of any other thought had ever crossed the unsullied surface of her mind. As yet there had been no word spoken of their marriage. They two had been but seldom alone together. The old Major was at his post behind the scenes every night, and carried his daughter off to their lodgings in Holborn directly after the performance. He attended rehearsals, took snuff with the actors and actresses, and bored them exceedingly with his prosy old stories of Dettingen, or the forty-five. He had been stationed at Derby when the young Pretender turned back with his rabble army. He was Hanoverian to the marrow.

No, there had been no word of marriage. The wooing had been all stage-wooing— tender embraces, eyes entangling themselves in eyes, swooning sighs, impassioned kisses, hearts beating to suffocation, but all stage-play. If the Major complained that these love scenes were too natural, the town was enraptured, and greeted those two young lovers as if the pair had made but one perfect whole. Applause given to her was sweetest laudation for him. He looked down at her fondly, proudly, as they stood hand in hand at the fall of the curtain. He was much more experienced in stage-craft than she; and it may be that he fancied he had taught her to act. Those who know genius when they see it, knew that with her acting was as the gift of song to the bird, God-given, spontaneous.

After that first half-year of stage courtship there came a time when little hints and faint breathings of venom began to be heard in the side-scenes and green-room: shrugs, innuendoes, a suggestion that the prosy old Major was being hoodwinked by those fiery spirits; that the lovely girl who walked off to her dingy lodgings so meekly every midnight, muffled and hooded, and clinging to the father's arm, had begun to be experienced in the ruses by which ladies of quality overreach a tyrannical parent or a jealous husband; that the frank smile and the sparkling eye now served to mask a secret.

'Why don't they marry?' asked the comic old man.

'The old Major would never consent to throw away his clever, beautiful daughter upon an extravagant wretch like Langley,' answered the lady who played the heavy mothers. 'Why, her salary has to keep the whole family—yes, feed and clothe all those hulking sisters, and find the old man in grog. She is the milch-cow; and if she were to marry Langley they must all starve.'

'If Ned were a man of spirit he would run away with her,' said the actor; 'or get himself spliced by one of your May Fair parsons.'

'Ned has too many strings to his bow,' answered the lady, with her tragic air; 'half the women of quality in London are in love with him. He has the *ton* at his beck and call. Ned would be a fool to marry.'

'Not to marry Sarah Pawlett, my good soul. That girl is a fortune in herself. She is a genius, madam, a genius. Ned must be a man of snow if he can resist such charms, such graces. When she comes on the stage it is like the sun breaking through a cloud. The whole scene—nay, the whole theatre brightens.'

But time went on, and there was no hint of marriage between those ideal lovers. The old Major was laid up with gout, and unable to haunt the side-scenes as of old; but he was represented by a *duenna* of Irish extraction—an old servant who had nursed all the towzle-haired girls, including Sarah herself. This dragon was of a mild nature, and the lovers enjoyed each other's society very freely while the demon Podagra laid the old soldier by the heels. They seemed to move in a paradise of their own, regardless of those around them, thoughtless of the morrow, forgetful of yesterday, infinitely happy in the present hour.

Their careless joy gave occasion for more shoulder-shrugging among their worldly-wise comrades. There were some who gave the lovely Sally over for lost, some who denounced the handsome Ned as an arrant scoundrel—behind his back, mark you; but if this beautiful butterfly creature were hovering on the brink of a precipice, there was no hand stretched forth to hold her back from the abyss.

Suddenly the stream of gossip was turned into a new channel, and the only talk of wings and green-room, club and coffee-house, was of the wonderful conquest Sarah Pawlett had made in my Lord Bellenden—no light-minded haunter of play-houses and French taverns, but one of the magnates of the land, a gentleman of the purest water, a gem without a flaw, white and perfect as the Regent's diamond. While Ned Langley had trifled and fooled, this most estimable gentleman had stooped from his high estate to make the actress an honourable offer of marriage.

Old Major Pawlett was on his legs again by the time this happened. His gout had fled before the magic wand of supreme good luck. He proudly accepted his lordship's generous offer. The girl was but a child—not nineteen until next April—and she had all a child's waywardness. Yet she could not be otherwise than deeply grateful, moved and melted to her heart's core by his lordship's generosity.

The girl herself said nothing of gratitude, or any other feeling. She stood up in the midst of the shabby lodging-house parlour, thin and straight and pale, like a tall white lily, and allowed herself to be given away to this stately nobleman as if she had been a chattel.

He looked down at her with his grave, grand face, smiling calmly; confident in his power to hold that which he won, strong in past triumphs over the hearts of women, strong in the consciousness of his own worth. He put a diamond hoop on the third finger of the cold, unresisting hand—so cold albeit so yielding.

'Let our wedding bells sound as soon as may be, dear one, he said; 'we have nothing to wait for.'

'Oh, not too soon, not too soon,' she pleaded piteously; 'your lordship is almost a stranger to me.'

'Never again lordship, and not long a stranger,' he answered gently.

He saw that look of anguish in the lovely face, and knew that her heart was not his; but he saw the pure and candid soul shining out of the sorrowful eyes; and he told himself that such a heart was worth winning.

There was a painful scene between Sally and her old father as soon as the nobleman's back was turned. The girl grovelled at the Major's feet, vowed with passionate sobs that she would do anything for her father and her sisters, except this one thing that was wanted of her. She would work like a pack-horse. She would bring them every guinea she earned—she would wear one old grogram gown from year's end to year's end. She would live on bread and cheese. But the Major upbraided her with basest ingratitude to him and to Providence—to Providence for having given her such a lover as Lord Bellenden, to her father for his having been clever enough to bring such a lover to honourable proposals.

'Do you suppose if I had been anything else than an officer and a gentleman, and a man of the world to boot, his lordship would have offered you marriage?' he demanded indignantly.

'Nay,' answered the girl, with a touch of pride that ennobled her—pride in the man who loved her, albeit she could not return his love, 'his lordship is a man of honour, and would not have made dishonourable proposals to the lowliest orphan in the land. He is like King Cophetua in the old ballad.'

'I wonder you have the impudence to praise him after the fuss you have been making,' said the old man angrily, and he emphasised his speech with sundry forcible epithets common to the conversation of military men in those days.

He watched his daughter like a lynx that night at the theatre. Not a word could Ned Langley and she say to each other in the green-room or at the side-scenes; but there was one opportunity on the stage when they two were standing together at the back of the scene, while the low comedian and the comic old woman were fooling in front of the footlights.

She told him what had happened, clasping his hands in hens, looking up at him with divine love and confidence.

'You must marry me, and quickly too,' she said. 'There is no other way out of it. If you don't I shall be married to Lord Bellenden, willy nilly. My father's heart is set upon it, and all the girls were in tears this afternoon beseeching me. If you love me, Ned, as you have sworn you do, ah, so often—so often, you must make me your wife without a day's delay.'

He looked at her with passionate earnestness, betwixt love and pain. 'My dearest, it can't be,' he said, 'it can't be.'

'But, why not?'

'Don't ask me, love, it can't be— and only reflect, sweet one, what a chance you are throwing away. Such a match as Lord Bellenden is not offered to an actress twice in a century. You would be doing better than either of those Gunning girls about whom we have all heard so much—and indeed you are handsomer than either; and what,' he whispered in her ear, drawing close to her as the serpent to Eve, 'what is to prevent us loving each other till the end of the chapter, even if you are Lady Bellenden?'

Her hands grew cold as death, and she wrenched them from his, as she would have snatched them out of a fiery furnace. She recoiled from him, stood apart from him for the rest of the scene, neither looked at him nor spoke to him, save when the business of the stage compelled her.

Three days afterwards Ned Langley went over to the enemy, accepted an engagement at the rival house, and the manager was left in despair.

'What the plague am I to do?' he asked piteously, with his wig pushed on one side, from sheer vexation. 'There is no comedian like him in London—not in the world, perhaps—in spite of their talk of those frog-eating jackanapeses in the Rue St. Honoré.'

'Play tragedy,' said Sarah, 'and then you won't miss him. You have Mr. Deloraine, who took the town in Romeo. I am dying to act tragedy.'

'What, you, Mrs. Madcap? Do you think that you, who have kept the town laughing so long, will ever set them crying?'

'Try me!' she answered, fixing him with those beautiful eyes of hers, so large, so limpid in their exquisite azure. 'I can cry myself, mark you, sir; and that's half the battle.'

She stood a little way from him, threw her head slightly backward, and lifted up her eyes to heaven, in a Carlo Dolci attitude. Slowly, gradually, the beautiful eyes tilled, and slowly overflowed. Pearly drops chased each other down the delicate cheeks; not a contortion disfigured the chiselled features; no flush disturbed the pure pallor of that ivory skin. 'Yes, you will do it,' cried the manager. 'What a face to prelude Juliet's potion scene, when mother and nurse have left her, and she stands alone, like Niobe, fixed in despair. Yes, you shall play Juliet next week. Deloraine is at his best in Romeo, and at forty looks an admirable twenty-five.'

The manager kept his word, and mistress Sarah's Juliet was the mode for a month. The town was all agog about her matrimonial engagement, and flocked to see her act with ever increasing fervour. She had refused to leave the stage till the eve of her wedding; refused with a charming feminine obstinacy which delighted her lover, though he would have had it otherwise. A man so deep in love is all the more smitten by having his every wish denied. Sarah was the coyest, proudest, most tormenting of mistresses; and there was that shadow of sadness, which came and went like the clouds that drift across the moon on a windy autumn night, and only made her more beautiful.

Mr. Deloraine was plain and pock-marked, and lacked all the graces of handsome Ned Langley; but he contrived to make himself handsome on the stage, by the aid of white lead and ceruse, and he was a highly respectable gentleman, who paid his way and went to church on Sundays. He had a dull wife and eleven children, so Lord Bellenden had no cause for jealousy about this Romeo, even when he saw Juliet in his arms at the passionate hour of parting, what time the lark carolled above the olive woods beyond Verona. Little by little—by infinitesimal stages of days and hours—Sarah learnt, first to honour, and then to love her noble wooer.

He was a man worthy to be loved—generous, chivalrous as that lover in the old ballad which Sarah knew by heart—nobler than the ideal of her girlish dreams. She surrendered her heart to him almost unwillingly, deeming herself unworthy to be loved by him, unworthy even to love him; but she could not withhold her love. He commanded her affection, as he had first commanded her respect.

She loved him, and in a few weeks she was to be married to him. The most fashionable mantua-maker at the West End was busy with her gowns and *falballas*: the Bellenden diamonds were being remounted for her: a chariot of the newest shape and style was being built for her: and ladies of the highest ton stood up in their carriages to stare at her as she drove through the Park in a hired Berlin with her father. With all this she was not happy, and she had more than one reason for her unhappiness.

First, there was the thought of Ned Langley's treachery, and the love she had wasted upon him. This rankled like a green wound. Then there was the stinging memory of certain girlish half-mad letters she had written to him, when she had believed him noble as a Greek god. Thirdly, there was the haunting presence of a little woman in black, who dogged her in the street by day, now following her, now lurking at corners to watch her, and who sat on the same bench, in the same spot—the third seat from the end near the door on the prompt side, in the second row of the pit—every night.

At first, Sarah had been interested, amused, flattered by the lady's constant attendance. She had pointed her out to Ned Langley, solitary, silent, intent upon the play; evidently a friendless creature, alone in the desert of the town, with no amusement but the play-house.

'She looks a poor little shabby-genteel creature, but a lady all the same,' Sarah had said to Langley, 'and how she watches you and me, and hangs upon every word we utter. I am quite taken with the poor harmless soul. I wish you would find out who she is!'

'Impossible, child! a stranger from the country, most likely. A waif thrown up by the ocean of change— a widow who has lost her fortune and her husband, and has come to London to seek new one.'

On another occasion, when Sarah talked of the little woman in black, Ned had a vexed air.

'I believe she is a political spy,' he said; 'the Government is still suspicious of dealings with the Pretender, and has all sorts of agents.'

And now, when she and Ned Langley were strangers for evermore, Sarah found herself watched more closely than ever by the little woman in shabby black—a pale, sharp-featured little woman, who might, perchance, have been pretty in girlhood, but who had lost all her beauty at five-and-thirty, which was about the age Sarah gave her. She had a restless, lynx-eyed look, as of one who had worn herself out with watching other people.

One night that the Major had stayed late at a convivial party, Sarah, walking home with her maid, was overtaken by a pair of lightly-tripping feet in Lincoln's Lin Fields, and was startled by the tap of a hand on her shoulder.

She turned and fronted the little woman in black, whose pale, pinched face seemed ghostly in the dim light of the oil-lamp overhead. They had just turned the corner by his Grace of Newcastle's big stone mansion.

'What do you want, woman?' asked Sarah haughtily.

'Five minutes' conversation with you, madam; and it is for your welfare that you should grant me the interview.'

'You can fall a little in the rear, Margaret,' said Sarah to the old servant. 'This lady wishes to talk with me in private.'

The Irishwoman looked doubtful, and fell back only a few paces. The woman in black seemed too small a person to be dangerous. Her head hardly reached the queenly Sarah's shoulder.

'You are going to make a great match, madam,' said the stranger; 'all the town is full of your good fortune.'

'I hope you have not stopped me so solemnly in order to tell me that!' retorted the actress. 'I have noted you in the pit many an evening, madam, and as you seem an admirer of the drama I should be sorry to deem you crazy.'

'No, madam, I am not crazy, though I have had more than enough to make me so. A father's anger, aye, and the loss of every friend I had in youth, a fortune forfeited, and, for a crowning mercy, an unfaithful husband—yes, unfaithful— though it was for him I sacrificed father and fortune, friends and position. I was the only daughter of a bishop, madam, and kept the best company before I was married.'

'Those facts are interesting, madam, to yourself or your personal friends, but hardly so to me. I wish you goodnight,' said Sarah hastily, assured that the lady was a lunatic. But the little woman pressed upon her steps.

'I shall find means to awaken your interest presently, madam,' she said. 'You are about to be married to the best match in London, as I was saying, and your fortune is to be envied by all your sex. I have heard wagers in the pit as to whether the marriage would or would not come off.'

'The people who made such wagers were monstrously insolent.'

'No doubt, madam; but insolence is the order of the day. Now, I myself would not mind wagering that your engagement with Lord Bellenden would be off tomorrow if he knew as much as I do; and if he were favoured with the perusal of certain letters which you wrote—and by the dozen—to handsome Ned Langley, your stage-lover, madam, and your very earnest lover off the stage.'

'My letters!' cried Sarah, aghast. 'What do you know of my letters?'

She was utterly unskilled in deceit, unpractised in denial, and admitted her folly as freely as a child would have done.

'What do I know of them? They are my daily reading; they are my morning service. I know them by heart, madam. Yes, and I know of your meetings, too; your stolen kisses in the old house by the river—among the rats and the spiders, and the ghosts, madam—yes, the ghosts. You were scared by a ghost once, I think, when you and Ned were standing side by side in the twilight in that empty house which you chose for your rendezvous.'

'Yes,' cried Sarah, 'there was a figure flitted by—noiseless—shadowy. It turned my blood to ice—a figure in black. It was you!'

She stood gazing at the little woman in the moonlight—so pale, so attenuated. Yes, that was the form which had flitted past on the shadowy landing by the open door of the room in which she and Ned were standing, hand clasped in hand, pouring out their tale of love.

She had taken the little black figure for a visitant from the other world; and now she knew that it was even worse than a ghost—a woman, mad, or it might be, only jealous—a woman with a bitter, unscrupulous tongue bent on doing her mischief.

This creature would betray her to her lord, whom she reverenced, whom she loved. It was of Bellenden she thought as she faced her foe in the corner of the square by the turnstile, the moon shining down upon them, the shadows of the houses making great blots of darkness here and there.

She had done this foolish thing, she, Sarah Pawlett, whom Lord Bellenden deemed the purest of women. She had compromised herself deeply for that false lover of hers, consenting to stolen meetings in an old empty house by the river, between the Temple and Blackfriars, a house that had been in Chancery for fifty years, and which was supposed to be haunted. Ned Langley had procured a key somehow; and here they had met with impunity between the morning rehearsal and the evening performance. When Sally was late in returning to the family dinner or the family tea, she had but to say that the rehearsal had been longer than usual.

There had not been many such meetings, a dozen at most, and the rendezvous had been of a perfectly innocent character; but the mere fact of such secret stolen interviews would have been quite enough to compromise or to condemn Sarah in the opinion of such a man as Lord Bellenden.

Her letters were full of allusions to these meetings; she had dwelt with all a girl's romantic fondness upon the delight of being alone with her idol; of touching his soft silken locks, of looking up into his eyes. The letters were written with all the self-abandonment of a young heart, written to one who was to be the writer's husband, who was her all in all, the beginning and end of her universe; written to one whom she would no more have suspected of falsehood or meanness than she would have doubted the purity of the blue ether far away above the common earth, in a region where defilement cometh not. She had not asked for the return of her letters, for, until that never-to-be-forgotten night when she had told Ned Langley that the time had come for their marriage, she had lived in the assurance that she was to be his wife.

He had not definitely spoken of their union, but it had seemed to her a thing of course from the hour in which they confessed their mutual love. What else had they to live for, either of them, but to love and wed? they who seemed made to be mated; like two flowers on one stem, turning to each other naturally as the wind of fate blew them. After that bitter moment in which her lover had revealed his worthlessness, Sarah had been too proud in her deep anger to approach him, or communicate with him in any form, even for the sake of regaining her letters. She had hardly thought of those letters, indeed; thinking of the whole love story as a chapter in her life that was closed for ever; a vault sealed and secret, in which lay the dead corpse of her first passionate love.

And now she was learning that there might be a second love, sweeter even than the first; graver, deeper, truer; less romantic, but more ennobling; she was learning this and forgetting everything else, when this new trouble came upon her. Those letters, those foolish, wildly sentimental letters, were in the keeping of this strange woman.

'How came you by my letters, madam?' she asked indignantly. 'Are you a thief?'

'No, madam. I am a much injured woman; and you ought to take it kindly that I have borne my wrongs so patiently, and not disgraced you in your theatre, where you fire like a queen. But stage queens have had mud thrown in their faces before today.'

'*You*, disgrace me! You!'

'Yes, I, madam; Ned Langley 's wife.'

'Ned—Langley's—wife!'

Sarah repeated the words slowly, almost in a whisper.

'Oh! he did not tell you that he was a married man, did he? he never does. You are not the first he has deluded. He does worse than that, for he tells villainous lies about me; he tells his fellow-actors that the poor little crack-brained woman at his lodgings is not his wife, but his mistress—a young lady of quality whom he ran away with, and who has been a burden to him ever since. That's what he tells his friends, madam; because that story leaves him at liberty to make love to the last fashionable actress, and to promise her marriage.

'And I am fool enough to stay with him and to slave for him, knowing all this; to warm his slippers of a night before he comes home, and mix his grog for him, and bear with him when he staggers home drunk from his Hell Fire Club, and hear his boasts of women of ton who are over head and ears in love with him. It was one night when he was in liquor that I found the first of your letters in his pocket; and after that I watched him, and picked them up everywhere. You've no notion how careless he is of such letters; and, madam, the women all write alike, and lovers get tired of so much honey. I've heard him say, "More of their precious scribble." We wives have the best of it, perhaps, with such fellows; for, at least, we are behind the scenes, and we see them with their masks off.'

'And you have my letters—all of them?'

'Three-and-twenty, madam. I doubt that's all, for I ransack every corner in quest of such things. I know my gentleman's ways!'

'Will you give them me back, tonight?' asked Sarah, eagerly.

'No, madam, neither tonight nor tomorrow. I will not give them back to Sarah Pawlett; I will only return them to Lady Bellenden. When you are his lordship's wife, madam, the letters shall be yours."

'I see,' said Sarah, gloomily, 'it is the old story. I have heard of such things. You mean to keep the letters, and hold them over me as a continual threat after I am married. You will make me pay you to be silent about them.'

'Pay me! No, madam, I am not so base as that. I have no grudge against you. I cannot even blame your conduct, though it was somewhat imprudent. You are but one of many whom handsome Ned Langley has deluded. I am not a double-dealer. The letters shall be yours when you are Lady Bellenden. On your wedding-day, if you like.'

'Why wait till then! Give me the letters tomorrow, and I shall be your grateful debtor for life. There is nothing in my power, as an honest woman, that I would not do for you.'

'You promise fair, madam, but I have my fancy. I will only surrender those letters to Lord Bellenden's wife.'

'But you must have your price—you must want something of me.'

'Well perhaps I do. Yes, every man has his price, and I suppose every woman has hers too. I shall tell you mine when I give you back your letters on your wedding-day.'

Sarah tried, even with tears, to argue Ned Langley's wife out of this rigid determination. The three women—Irish Margaret in the rear—walked round Lincoln's Inn Fields twice in the moonlight, Sarah pleading—the little woman as firm as a rock.

'On your wedding-day, madam, and no sooner,' she said at parting; 'I shall be in the church, with the letters in my pocket. I wish you a very goodnight.'

She made a low curtsey as ceremoniously as if she had been at Ranelagh, and tripped lightly off towards Clare Market; leaving Sarah and the maid to go on to Holborn together.

After this midnight interview, came a period of keenest anxiety, nay, almost of mental torture for Sarah Pawlett. Three weeks had yet to pass before she would be my Lady Bellenden. How she regretted her own persistency in having postponed the wedding—her obstinacy in having insisted upon acting until the eve of her marriage. She acted now in fear and trembling, expectant of some demonstration from the little woman in black. The little woman never missed a night in her accustomed seat in the second row of the pit. She had acquired a prescriptive right to that seat by her constant attendance, and by being always one of the first to enter the theatre. Regular pit-goers knew her by sight, and gave way to her—a dramatic enthusiast, doubtless, a little distraught, but harmless.

Sarah's first look when she came on the stage was to that seat in the pit.

She acted the potion scene in Juliet with her eyes fixed on the little woman in black, fixed as if she had been face to face with Nemesis. It was a wonderful expression: people remembered it, and quoted it a quarter of a century afterwards as a marvel of finished art and high-wrought feeling.

Driving with Lord Bellenden in the park, or attending a fashionable auction with him, or at an afternoon water-party, Sarah was tortured by the expectation of the same haunting presence. The little woman seemed ubiquitous. Small, active, insignificant, neatly dressed, and with lady-like manners, she was able to push herself in anywhere. She tripped about auction-rooms and looked at china monsters. She had her seat in the park, as she had in the pit.

She might even be seen on the river, alone with her waterman, shooting about among the crowded wherries and gaily-clad people—a creature of no more significance than a blot of ink on a gaudy flowered wall. Sarah was always dreading an explosion; and her future husband was so devoted to her, so chivalrous, so true. His love lifted her to a calm heaven of proud contentment. To be beloved by him was to enter into a state of tranquil blessedness; just as she had pictured to herself the condition of the elect in the world to come.

Sometimes she had a mind to fall at his feet and confess everything: her romantic passion for Ned Langley, and the way she had been fooled by him—even their secret meetings in the deserted house—yes, she would have confessed all that, she would have endured the shame of it; but the idea that those letters of hers, written in all the intoxication of a first love, should be read in cold blood, read by a man of cultivated mind—those foolish, rambling sentences and reiterations, the poor little stock of words so repeated and misused, and, worst of all, the bad spelling.

Yes; Sarah had been educating herself severely since her engagement to Lord Bellenden, and in the course of her studies had discovered how sorely she had erred in that matter of orthography. To think that throughout those fatal letters she had spelt affection with one f, and rapture with sh, instead of t. Orthography is such an arbitrary thing; has neither rhyme nor reason in it, Sarah thought, submitting her old lax notions to the rigid schooling of the dictionary.

And now came the wedding-day. She was to be married at St. Martin's-in-the-Fields, his lordship's house being in that parish. The wedding was to be a very quiet ceremonial. His lordship's mother, a dowager of seventy years of age, and of great dignity-, of whom Sarah lived in awe, was to be the only relative present on the bridegroom's side. His best man was an old friend. On Sarah's side there were the four sisters, and an oafish brother. The Major was to give his daughter away, and was to have a new coat for the occasion. The eldest of her sisters was to be bridesmaid.

After the wedding, bride and bridegroom were to step into a travelling carriage, and drive off as fast as six fine horses could take them to Tunbridge Wells, where they were to spend the honeymoon at the dowager's secluded villa near Leeds Castle. It was said to be one of the prettiest seats in Kent, on a small scale—gardens, fountains, shrubberies all perfection. It had been the lady's delight in her thirty years of widowhood to create and beautify the grounds and gardens.

'We shall be vastly quiet there, Sally,' said his lordship, when he was describing the beauties of the place 'I hope you will not get tired of me.'

'Tired of you !' She looked up at him with worshipping eyes—how strangely different from that despairing look with which she had once entreated him to delay their marriage!

He felt ineffably proud of his conquest. He had told himself that he could win her, and sworn to himself to make her his in heart and soul before the law bound her to him.

'When we are very sick of each other we can go to the Rooms or the Pantiles to see the modish people,' he said, smiling at her.

'I would rather stay at home and hear you read to me,' she

answered gravely. 'Think how much I have to learn before I shall be worthy to be your wife!'

'I think you have learnt the only lesson I shall ever care about teaching you,' he said.

'How do you mean?'

'I think you have learnt to love me, Sarah. That's the only wisdom I ask of you.'

'Yes, I have learnt that with all my heart. Yet when you first came to this house I almost hated you.'

'That was because you loved another. Nay'—as Sarah tried to speak—'neither deny it nor confess it, my dear. I want to learn nothing about the past. I am happy in the present, and confident about the future.'

Sarah changed from red to pale and was silent.

How could she speak of those accursed letters after this? How could she ever let him look into the depth of her past fully?.

She was as white as sculptured marble next morning—as white as her ostrich feathers, but a bride has a privileged pallor. Nobody wondered at Sarah's colourless cheeks.

'You look frightened, my dear,' said the outspoken dowager as she kissed her in the church. 'I hope you don't repent what you are doing.'

'No, madam. I love your son with all my heart, and am proud with all my heart of his love.'

Then the organ played a psalm, and the little procession went up to the altar rails, or the rails which defended that table which should have been an altar.

Very clear and firm and full were Sarah's accents as she gave the responses that made her George, Lord Bellenden's, wife.

'There is some advantage in having been taught to speak,' thought the dowager, as she heard those rich, round tones.

Anon came the business in the vestry. The old Major was weeping for very pride that his daughter was now one of the nobility. Sarah signed herself Sarah Pawlett for the last time in her life, kissed her husband, and went out of the church leaning on his arm, happy, since he was verily hers now, and yet painfully expectant.

So far there had been no sign of the little woman in black. Sarah had looked about the church expecting to see her in the corner of a pew, or lurking behind a pillar; but she had descried the pinched little face nowhere. 'How could I suppose that she would keep her promise?' thought Sarah despairingly; 'she will treasure those letters as a weapon to use against me whenever the fit takes her.'

But in the church porch the little woman in black pressed forward to speak to the bride, with a small brown paper parcel, very neatly packed, in her hand.

'Mr. Jones, the glover, was anxious that you should have this ere you started, my lady,' she said. 'He could not execute your order sooner.'

'Give it to one of my servants, madam,' said his lordship, but Sarah snatched the parcel.

'I thank you, madam, from the bottom of my heart,' she murmured, with an earnest look, while her bridegroom was giving an order to one of the outriders who were to escort them to Tunbridge Wells.

Another minute and she was in the chariot, sitting by her husband's side, the brown paper parcel in her lap.

'Shall we open it and see what the gloves are like, which the man sends you at the eleventh hour?' asked Lord Bellenden.

'No,' she said, 'I know all about them; I want to talk to you.'

So they talked, and the parcel was not opened, and the streets and the new bridge, and the long suburban road, which in those days so soon became rustic, fleeted by them like a dream that is dreamt, a happy vision of sunlight and glancing leaves, white houses, cottage gardens—now and then a carriage, now and then a cart—and on to the woods and pastures, orchards and hop-gardens of Kent.

Before the bride dressed for dinner she burnt every one of those foolish letters—burnt them without reading a line in any of them.

'If I were to read them I should hate myself too much for

my silliness in ever having written such trash,' she said to herself, as she thing them into the fire, and thrust them down among the blazing coals, and held them there with the poker till not a vestige of that romantic bosh remained.

Three days afterwards Lady Bellenden received a prim little letter with the London postmark, written in a niggling hand, and beautifully spelt:

Honoured Madam—
When we were talking together that night you asked me if I had a price for your letters, and I said perhaps I had.
'You are now Lady Bellenden. You will be a leader of fashion before long, if you play your cards cleverly. Ask me to your parties. I have long languished for modish society. The loss of that is a greater deprivation to me than any of the troubles of my married life—wretched as that is. Ask me to all your parties. I shall not disgrace you. I know how to behave in company, and I shall always come in a chair. God bless you. I am very glad you are happily married, and have escaped that scoundrel, my husband. Be sure you send me a card for your first rout.

Lady Bellenden readily complied with this request, and Mrs. Edward Langley, of Castle-street, Leicester-square, received a card for her ladyship's first reception, and with the card a parcel of black Genoa velvet for a gown, and Spanish lace to trim the same. The little woman looked to advantage in her velvet gown, and mingled in the throng of English and foreign nobility, men about town, wits and authors, without attracting any adverse criticism. But as the years went by the little woman in black became as familiar an object in Lady Bellenden's drawing-room as the looking-glasses which her ladyship had brought from Venice, or the statues which his lordship had brought from Rome.

She was very harmless; she listened to the music, and looked on at the dancing, and never obtruded herself upon anybody's attention. But it was observed that Lady Bellenden was always particularly kind to her, and by-and-by, when there came a bevy of sons and daughters, the little woman in black acquired the position of a maiden aunt or a godmother, among these young people, and spent the greater portion of her life with the Bellendens either in town or country.

Ned Langley had vanished from the stage of the world long ere this, after having dropped into disrepute as an actor in consequence of his intemperate habits.

He died in a sponging house, very suddenly, struck down by cerebral apoplexy, after a midnight drinking bout. Most people had heard the little woman in black spoken of as Mrs. Langley; but very few people knew that she was the widow of handsome Ned Langley, the famous comedian.

The Dreaded Guest

A bleak December night nearly a hundred years ago. Hard frost, and a keen biting wind blowing the snowflakes into the faces of those few foot-passengers who still tramp the half-deserted City streets; a frost so hard, that the fast-falling snow does not change to mud and slush all in a moment, after the usual manner of London snow, but lies crisp and white upon road and pavement, and crowns the steep roofs and gables with mountainous heaps of whiteness, which overhang the parapets, and threaten pedestrians with the fall of miniature avalanches.

There are retired nooks and corners of this crowded London city where the snow might lie almost as pure and undefiled as in some silent Alpine gorge known only to the eagle and the chamois—notably one narrow little street, scarcely better than a court or alley, in its way, tenanted by two or three working jewellers, a Dutch merchant in some small way of trade, the chief clerk in a great colonial house under the shadow of the monument, and Dr. Prestwitch.

One feeble oil-lamp glimmers at the entrance to this quiet little street—which leads nowhere, by the way, Dr. Prestwitch's house facing the explorer, and barring his farther progress, except through Dr. Prestwitch's hall-door—one dim blear-eyed little lamp, which does not do much towards the illumination of the street in a general way. But tonight there is the lightness and brightness of the snow, which lies thick upon the paved footway between the two rows of tall narrow houses, unmarked by a single footfall. The occupants of Little Bell-street are a sober steady-going people, and there has been no traffic, not so much as the opening or shutting of a door, since eight o'clock this evening.

It is now eleven.

As an auxiliary to the public lamp, Dr. Prestwitch burns a little coloured lamp of his own under the wooden shell that surmounts his doorway—a relic of former splendour, when great people lived in the City, and fashionable bachelors or small gentry with large pretensions may have occupied Little Bell-street; a lamp which announces his profession to the world at large, keeps him in the eye of the public as it were, and which has more than once brought him a chance patient—some ruffian bruised and mangled in a street-fight, a child run over in a neighbouring thoroughfare, a black eye, or a sprained ankle.

There is one tall narrow window upon each side of Dr. Prestwitch's tall narrow door, and in the extreme left corner of Dr. Prestwitch's house there is a passage, scarcely wide enough to admit one person of bulky figure, leading to Dr. Prestwitch's back premises—the surgery where he compounds his medicines and spreads his plasters, and a bleak bare room, with a long deal table on tressels, and a smaller leaden-topped table fitted with a sink. This room is very rarely used by the doctor, never entered by the doctor's family, and has a mould odour.

In the time of the December snowstorm Dr. Prestwitch was quite a young man; a young man with a bright eager face, dark curling hair, which he did not often disguise with powder and pomatum, and a bright eager manner; a man who had given hostages to Fortune in the shape of a pretty little wife and three small children, and who was perhaps rather too anxious to succeed in life. It is doubtful whether this young surgeon had any legal right to the title of doctor, but the neighbourhood of Little Bell-street had made him a doctor by common consent. The brass plate upon his stout oak door described him simply as 'Mr. Prestwitch, Surgeon.'

He had not a large practice, and the task of supporting that small household was a hard one, simple as were the needs of the pretty little wife and the three small children. They had one servant, a fat over-grown girl, with a shock of red hair, and a countenance in which good temper did duty for all other charms; a stupid honest creature, who heartily loved the doctor's wife and children, and thought the doctor himself the greatest man of his age. The daily meals in that respectable house in Little Bell-street were apt to be meagre in quantity and inferior in quality; but Barbara Snaffles—commonly called Bab—was a faithful soul, who would have shared the diet of Count Ugolino and his sons without a murmur, if fidelity had demanded such patience. As it was, she had a fair share of whatever was eaten or drunken in the house, and was treated more like a member of the family than was perhaps consistent with the dignity of a professional man's household.

On this particular December night she was sitting darning stockings upon one side of the hearth in the everyday parlour—a small panelled chamber, furnished in the scantiest way, but with a certain air of neatness and even comfort nevertheless—while her mistress occupied the other. A handful of fire burnt cheerily in the old-fashioned grate—such a roomy old grate, with such a capacity for the consumption of fuel, but pinched and contracted by an artful contrivance of brickwork upon each side. The red-worsted curtains, a trifle scanty even for the narrow window, but very comfortable-looking notwithstanding had been drawn to their extremest stretch; the honest mahogany table had been vigorously polished by Bab after the removal of the tea-things; the one candle was kept carefully snuffed; the cat reposed luxuriously against the open-work side of the bright brass fender; and this room, altogether humble as it was, bore the unmistakeable aspect of home.

The doctor was in his surgery reading. He was a studious young man, and in the dearth of more profitable employment devoted his evenings to the study of medical science. It had been a matter of no small regret to him that he had been unable to advance very far in the practical study of that branch of his profession which seemed to him the most important, the study of

242

anatomy. The cost of a subject for his experiments rendered this part of his science almost a sealed book to the poor and hard-working student, who could not afford to avail himself of the services of those gangs of desperate ruffians who were continually violating the sanctity of the grave by their unholy traffic.

Martin Prestwitch had a friend, however, in the house-surgeon of Newgate, and that gentleman, who had a surfeit of subjects sometimes, had promised to send him the first defunct criminal he should be able to dispose of on his friend's favour. There were outstanding claims to be considered first, for the jail was in those days the only legitimate resource for the student; but whenever there should be a subject *to spare*, it was to be for Martin Prestwitch.

He had been reading hard in an old book upon anatomy this evening, and his fingers itched to be using the scalpel.

'I'm afraid Jack Tylney has forgotten his promise,' he said presently with a sigh.

He was wrong. Mr. Tylney, the Newgate surgeon, had not forgotten the obligation that was upon him. His promise was destined to be kept that very night. The first footsteps to defile the snow that had remained untrodden through all the quiet evening hours were the footsteps of two men carrying a ghastly burden.

They took it first to the hall-door, where one of them stooped to read the name upon the brass plate, and then knocked—a cautious, mysterious-sounding knock.

The door was opened almost immediately by the faithful Barbara, who scented a possible patient in this untimely summons; but at the sight of that ghastly burden—it was muffled in a sack, but there are some things that will not be hidden—she fell back with a start.

'Lord save us! What's that?' she cried.

'A subject for Dr. Prestwitch—the man that was hung for coining at Newgate this morning.'

'What!' exclaimed Bab, 'do you mean to say it's a dead body?'

'Yes, miss,' one of the bearers answered with a grin; 'not to make too many bones about it, it's a stiff un—with Mr. Tylney's compliments to Dr. Prestwitch.'

'Take the dreadful thing round to the surgery,' said Barbara, aghast. 'Master's in there reading.

Take it down that passage; I'll come and open the door directly minute.—And to think that anyone can wish to have such a thing!' she ejaculated, as she shut the front door.

She had heard her master talk of that subject which Jack Tylney was to send him.

She opened the surgery-door and told the doctor what had come for him, and then opened the door leading into the passage, where the men were waiting. Martin Prestwitch was all on the alert in a moment. He took his candle, led the way into that damp-smelling room set apart for such a purpose as this, and so rarely used. The horror was carried in there, and laid upon the deal table, Barbara Snaffles standing on the threshold all the time and peering in, fascinated by the ghastly sight. Then Martin Prestwitch and the men came out, and the doctor dismissed them with a shilling to buy drink—one of his few shillings.

He locked the door of his dissecting-room, while Barbara stood a little aloof, open-mouthed, devouring the scene with her big round eyes.

'Ask your mistress to make me some of her good coffee, Bab,' said the doctor—'I shall sit up late tonight; and be sure she knows nothing of this business,' he added pointing to the locked door.

'Lord bless you! No, sir; not for the world. I don't want to turn that poor dear's whole mask of blood, as mine was turned just now when I saw that orful thing in a sack.'

Barbara gave a gulp and made a wry face as she spoke.

'You'd better come and say goodnight to missus, sir, if you want her to go to bed.'

'Ay, to be sure,' answered Martin Prestwitch, at all times an affectionate husband, but just at this moment somewhat distracted by the thought of that inanimate clay lying upon his table.

He went into the parlour, where his industrious little wife was singing softly to herself, as she put the finishing touches to a triumph of ingenuity and economics in the shape of a frock for the biggest of the three small children, made out of a cast-off petticoat of her own.

'See, Martin,' she cried, looking up at him with her bright loving face, 'won't Molly look nice in that?'

'Very nice, dear; but you oughtn't to sit up so late, sewing for Molly. It's nearly twelve o'clock.'

'That's the very last stitch, Martin; and it's just as late for you as it is for me; and you've not had a morsel of supper either. There's the bit of beef-steak pudding that was left at dinner. Bab has warmed it nicely, and there it is, waiting for you, down in the fender.'

'I'll eat it by and by, dear; but I've no appetite for supper just yet. I want you to make me a cup of coffee—as strong as you like.'

'What. Martin! You're not going to sit up over your fusty old books again?' cried the little wife dolefully.

It was a common thing for the doctor to sit poring over his medical books deep down into the night, and Mary Prestwitch had often crept downstairs in the gray morning, to find him still studying one of those dismal volumes, with his candle burned down to the socket.

'Yes, Mary, my dear; I want to sit up an hour or so longer. There's a very interesting case I'm reading up, a case that will be useful to me in my practice; and you know love, how much depends on my getting on in my profession.'

Mary gave a little nod and a sigh. Yes, indeed, it was vital to that small household that the surgeon's efforts should be crowned with success. Only that evening, Mrs. Prestwitch and Bab had been calculating the amount of the Christmas bills—Christmas brings so little for struggling householders except bills—and wondering whether the trades-people would be content with such small sums as Dr. Prestwitch could give them, on account.

'They know that we are honest, Bab,' said the anxious wife;

'thank Heaven they know that. We have lived in this house for five years, and paid our way somehow. I don't think they will find it in their hearts to be hard upon us.'

Martin Prestwitch kissed his wife, and sent her off to bed directly she had made the coffee, during which operation there was heard a great clattering of bolts and bars as the indefatigable Barbara, who took as much pains to secure all these fastenings as if her master's house had been the most tempting field for an enterprising burglar. It was just midnight when the little woman tripped upstairs, with Barbara behind her, and all the clocks of the City seemed to booming out the hour as Dr. Prestwitch went to his dissecting-room, carrying a steaming jug of coffee in one hand and a candle in the other. He had to put his jug on the floor while he unlocked the door, for there were no superfluous tables or sideboards in the passages of that sparsely-furnished abode.

The room struck cold as some ice-bound region on that bleak winter night, and the doctor's first labour was to light a fire. There were happily some wood and coals in a cupboard near the fireplace, and with these and an old newspaper Martin Prestwitch set to work. The task was not an easy one; the grate was damp, the smoke came down the chimney, and well-nigh choked him; but the doctor's patience and energy got the better of these difficulties, and when he rose up from his kneeling position before the dingy hearth the fire was burning cheerily.

He refreshed himself with a cup of coffee before proceeding to his more serious labour, and set the jug down upon the hearth, to keep the remainder of that comfortable beverage warm. Then he set to work in real earnest.

There is no need to enter upon the details of that ghastly performance. Before he had reached more than the preliminary stage of his labour, Dr. Prestwitch came to a full stop, suddenly, with the knife in his hand, arrested by a conviction that had come upon him like a flash of lightning, and set his heart beating with an awful fear.

Another moment, one rapid movement of that skilful hand

which held the knife, and he might have been a murderer.

The creature was not dead!

Martin Prestwitch bent down with his ear against the felon's naked chest, and listened.

Yes, there it was, weak and suppressed, but still palpable to the professional ear—the action of the heart.

In the next moment the doctor was at work with the approved means of those days for the revival of suspended animation. It was a slow business, but he was rewarded at last. The coiner gave a great sigh, muttered something that sounded like an oath, and then opened his bloodshot eyes, and stared with a bewildered gaze at his benefactor, the man who had given him back his forfeited life.

'Where the —am I?' he asked; 'I thought they were going to hang me. Was there a reprieve?'

'No, there was no reprieve. Mr. Ketch must have bungled over his work, I suppose.'

The coiner sat upright, and looked about him; and at this moment it occurred to Martin Prestwitch that he had perhaps been guilty of a kind of felony in giving back life to a man whom the law had doomed to death. The law was a critical thing in those days, involving such a large amount of capital punishment, that Dr. Prestwitch was by no means sure that such an act as assisting in a felon's evasion of the gallows might not be in itself a hanging matter.

But the deed was done; and there sat the coiner, a stalwart square-built ruffian of near six feet high, a man who could have annihilated the slim surgeon.

'Can't you give a man something to drink?' asked the coiner. 'My throat's like a lime-kiln.'

Dr. Prestwitch handed him the coffee-jug, which he emptied at a draught.

'Cat-lap!' said the coiner contemptuously; 'but it's done me good. And now, do you mean to tell me as they hung me this morning? I remember standing on the drop, and feeling the sleet and hail pelting against the blessed night-cap they'd pulled over my face; and I think, of all the blessed cold days I can call to mind, this blessed morning was the coldest. Do you mean to tell me as they made a botch of it, and let me off?'

'So it appears,' replied Dr. Prestwitch gently; for although a man of some moral courage, he felt himself at a disadvantage in this *tête-à tête*,—'so it appears. All I know is that you were brought here about an hour ago, and introduced to my notice as an individual who had paid the last penalty of the law.'

'Brought here? What for?'

'Well—for—in short, for scientific purposes. My name is Prestwitch, and I am a professor of medicine and surgery.'

'*What!*' roared the restored sufferer; 'were you going to cut me up?' The coiner looked so ferocious as he asked the question, that Dr. Prestwitch felt as if his last moment had come.

'Don't excite yourself, my good friend,' he remonstrated mildly. 'If things had been as I had every reason to suppose you would not have felt the slightest inconvenience. The legitimate ends of science would have been promoted without any suffering on your part. How much happier would you have been in that respect than the dogs and rabbits, whose vivisection has served to demonstrate the theories of some of our great anatomists! As it is, however, you have some reason to be grateful to me, as you owe me your life.'

Dr. Prestwitch glanced towards the door, thinking there was no real necessity that this interview should be prolonged farther, and that this terrible guest of his might be going. Then all at once, it dawned upon him that there was an obstacle to the coiner's departure. With the exception of the sacking that had muffled him when he was brought to Little Bell-street, he was garmentless; and the sacking was scarcely a costume for a cold winter's night in the streets of London.

'Grateful!' muttered the man. 'I don't know as life's much of a favour to a poor devil that doesn't know where to get a morsel of bread; that's marked down by a pack of bloodhounds, and if he doesn't get hung today, is pretty safe to get hung tomorrow. You can't give me back my tools, I suppose? I had a pretty set of moulds and presses as was ever seen, in a cellar down by Lambeth Pallis, for my business, which was a good un till a pal peached upon me. Howsomedever, I make no doubt you meant kindly, and here's my hand upon it.'

With that the scoundrel extended a dingy-looking paw, very broad and muscular the doctor observed, and Martin Prestwitch was fain to accept the friendly invitation, and shake hands with the coiner.

'And now, doctor,' said the man, wrapping the sacking round him as closely as he could, and planting himself in the single chair by the fire, which he stirred in a manner that showed no mercy to the doctor's coals,—and now, doctor, since we begin to understand each other, I'll trouble you for something to eat. I had some breakfast at six o'clock this morning—for I wasn't a-going to be put off my feed by Jack Ketch—but I've had nothing since.'

'I'll go and see,' said Dr. Prestwitch doubtfully, knowing the slender resources of his larder.

He remembered the beefsteak-pudding, which had been put aside for his own supper, and which he could gladly have eaten just now, and he presently returned to the dissecting-room with this savoury mess, and a great hunch of bread and a slice of cheese. The coiner devoured these, and then looked about him with the air of a man who could have eaten half an ox or so, and to whom this light refreshment seemed about as substantial as a handful of lollipops.

'You haven't got any more of that there puddin', I suppose?' he asked dolefully.

'Not a morsel.'

'Nor a slice of cold beef, or anything in that way?'

'I am sorry to say there is no cold joint in the house.'

'And I'm sorry to hear it. You ain't out of bread and cheese, though, I daresay; and I must make up with that. So if you'll bring me the loaf and the cheese, I shall be thankful. Don't take the trouble to cut it. It ain't likely as a gentleman such as you would be able to take the measure of *my* appetite.'

Dr. Prestwitch sighed as he went away to comply with this request, distressed to think how bare a look the larder would have next morning at breakfast-time. The quarter loaf was shrunk already, the family cheese was only the remnant of a pale-complexioned specimen of the Dutch kind; but it was impossible to refuse submission to the demands of such a guest! So Martin Prestwitch carried these provisions to the coiner, and laid them on the table before him, with a plate and knife.

'Your house don't seem to be too well supplied with victuals, doctor,' said the man, eying the pale-faced Dutchman with no special favour.

'I am not a rich man,' Martin Prestwitch answered humbly. 'I find it a hard thing to live.'

'Humph!' muttered the coiner; 'that's a common complaint I suppose. I've had my ups and downs—the fat of the land to-day, and a dry crust tomorrow; and now I've got to begin life again, with the brand of the law upon me, and every man's hand against me, and no more mercy to expect from any of 'em than if I was a hunted rat. I should like to know how I'm to set about getting my living when I leave this house tomorrow morning.'

Dr. Prestwitch breathed a little more freely. It was some relief to him to learn that this unexpected visitor did contemplate departing in the morning. What a blessed thing it would be to have him gone! It seemed to the perplexed surgeon as if the burden of this nameless criminal's presence had been weighing him down for months.

The coiner made a fierce dart at the pale cheese, and hewed alternate wedges from that and the loaf, in a half-absent manner, until both were demolished, grumbling to himself the while about the hardness of life, when a poor creature might not manufacture a few guineas for his own use and maintenance, without becoming liable to the stiffest penalties of the law.

'And how I'm going to work again, with all my tools gone, and not a pal as I can trust in, is more than I know,' muttered the coiner audibly.

'I really think, my good friend,' Dr. Prestwitch suggested gently, 'that in your case I should emigrate. A foreign country—a new country especially, like Nova Scotia—might offer a fair field for—' Dr. Prestwitch did not like to say 'coining,' but concluded with a polite periphrasis—'your particular line of business.'

'Emigrate!' exclaimed the coiner contemptuously 'How the deuce'—his actual expression was considerably more forcible; but Dr. Prestwitch, who was always a mild man, used to tell this story in the mildest language, only hinting that his guest's vocabulary had been something beyond the common in the way of rude vernacular vigour—'how the deuce is a man to emigrate who hasn't sixpence towards his passage-money? And a nice outfit I've got for emigration!' added the coiner, with a shiver, looking down at the sacking in which he was hugging his burly limbs. 'If you want me to emigrate, doctor, you must find me the rhino.'

'I!' cried Martin Prestwitch, turning a shade paler, though he had been pale enough before. 'My good man, what are you dreaming of?'

'Yes, *you;* you brought me back to life, and you're bound to provide for me. I didn't ask you to come any of your reviving dodges over me, did I? I was brought here to be dissected, and it was your duty to dissect me. But you scientific parties are never satisfied without trying your blessed experiments!'

'Good gracious me!' exclaimed Dr. Prestwitch, completely confounded by this blatant ingratitude. 'Here is an extraordinary creature! I restore him to life, and he looks upon me as his enemy!'

'I didn't ask to be restored, did I?' grumbled the coiner. 'Life's no favour to such as me! Howsomedever, you've revived me, and now you must keep me going; and in the first place, I'll trouble you for a suit of clothes.'

'A suit of clothes!' murmured the surgeon in a helpless tone.

'Yes. I can't walk about like this; it's against the law.'

' I have not an extensive wardrobe,' said Martin Prestwitch; 'and even if I had, my garments would scarcely fit you.'

'Well, you are but a poor thread-paper of a man, certainly,' answered the coiner, who had perhaps devoured more beef in a week than the surgeon was in the habit of consuming in a quarter; 'but any clothes are better than none, and I must screw myself into 'em somehow; so turn 'em out, Mr. Doctor.'

'Good gracious me!' exclaimed Dr. Prestwitch again dolefully; 'it's like an awful dream.'

He went away to do his visitor's bidding. It did really seem to him almost as if he had been walking in his sleep, the victim of some gruesome vision. A cold perspiration bedewed his forehead as he crept upstairs, candle in hand, to search for garments wherewith to clothe that midnight intruder.

He chose the biggest thing he could find—a bottle-green riding-coat with a fur collar, that had belonged to his father (a good and substantial garment, which he had cherished with care, intending to have it cut down and adapted for his own wear on some convenient occasion). It went to his heart to part with this treasure, and he felt the fineness of the cloth with a slow regretful hand, as he flung the garment over his arm. he found a pair of leather knee-breeches that had belonged to the same esteemed parent—a bulkier man than himself—and with these, a clean linen shirt, and a rusty black brocaded waistcoat of his own garnished with copper lace, he went downstairs.

'I can only *lend* you the coat,' he said, as he laid the garments before the coiner; 'the breeches and waistcoat you are welcome to keep.'

The unknown looked at the things with a somewhat contemptuous expression of countenance, and then proceeded to invest himself in them, splitting the shirt-sleeves with his brawny arms, and straining the leathern breeches of the defunct Prestwitch senior with his ponderous legs. The waistcoat he split up the back with a knife, and then laced up the opening dexterously with a bit of whipcord which the doctor procured for him. The coat fitted him comfortably, and concealed all deficiencies; but even then there remained his extremities still unclad—his great bare feet and muscular legs—for which Martin Prestwitch must needs find shoes and stockings. With that bottle-green coat and fur collar the man was too well dressed to go out barefoot.

'As soon as the shops are open, I'll slip out and buy you a pair of shoes and stockings,' said the doctor; 'but for mercy's sake, man, keep quiet while I'm gone. I wouldn't have my wife know of your being in the house for worlds.'

'I'll keep quiet enough,' growled the coiner. 'These togs are no great shakes; but I feel myself more like a Christian in 'em than I felt in that old sack; and, I say, doctor, you'll give me a trifle of money to set me going again won't you?'

'Money!' exclaimed Martin Prestwitch. 'Why, my good creature, I'm as poor as a church mouse!'

'Come, that won't do,' said the coiner. 'You doctors make no end of money, helping your patients out of this world. It is only fair you should spend a little on a patient that you've helped *into* the world.'

The doctor again urged his poverty, but it was no use. His arguments, however reasonable, prevailed nothing against that direful visitant.

'It's no good humbugging, doctor,' said the man. 'I don't leave this house without a fi'-pun note.'

It did happen that Martin Prestwitch possessed the sum of seven pounds ten, amassed by what supreme efforts of economy he and his narrow household only could have told, and honestly set aside for the payment of the Christmas quarter's rent. To part with any of this would be like shedding his heart's blood; but he felt himself utterly unable to cope with this dreadful creature whom he had given back to this living world; and if the coiner had asked him for his heart's blood instead of a five-pound note, it seemed to Martin Prestwitch that he must needs have given it.

So, after a longish parley, and a desperate endeavour to defend his treasure on the doctor's part, Martin Prestwitch stole upstairs once more in the dead night-time, and crept like a robber to his little hoard, from which he took the five-pound note demanded by his tormentor. He looked at a little Dutch clock in the kitch- en before he went back to the dissecting-room—watch he had none—and saw that it wanted still a quarter to three o'clock. The long dismal winter's night was not half gone yet, and Dr. Prestwitch did not know how much more that resuscitated felon might ask of him before it was done. To think of going to bed was worse than idle; sleep or rest was an impossibility with that baleful creature upon the premises. Dr. Prestwitch seated himself by the fire opposite his visitor, and prepared to wait for the morning with what patience he had.

Fed and clothed, the intruder was inclined to be social, and expanded considerably as the night wore on, favouring Dr. Prestwitch with numerous glimpses of his past history, exhibiting a career at once adventurous and felonious. Sense of right and wrong seemed altogether wanting to this creature, whose real name, he told the doctor, was Jonathan Blinker, but who had been known to fame by several aliases, the most familiar of which was Captain Flashman

Day dawned at length—a dull gray winter's morning, the atmosphere heavy with unfallen snow, the bright white ground looking even whiter than it was against the dense leaden sky. When the little Dutch clock in the kitchen struck seven, Martin Prestwitch turned the key in the dissecting-room, and conjured Mr. Blinker to keep silence; and for one whole hour the two men sat without speaking, Mr. Blinker dozing by the expiring fire, the surgeon listening to Barbara Snaffles's movements as she bustled about, performing her morning duties. Then came the shrill small voices of the children, and then his wife's gentle tones inquiring for the doctor at the dissecting-room door.

'You don't mind being locked in here for half an hour or so, while I go and get those shoes and stockings do you?' asked Martin of Mr. Blinker, in a whisper.

The coiner looked at him doubtfully.

'You ain't going to sell me, are you?' he said. 'You wouldn't go and peach upon a poor devil that you've brought back to life? You won't let me swing a second time for the sake of the reward?'

'Do you take me for a scoundrel?' exclaimed Martin, with

suppressed indignation

'No, I don't, and I'll trust you,' answered the other promptly.

So Dr. Prestwitch went out, and locked the door behind him, to secure his secret from the exploring eyes of Barbara Snaffles.

He had to answer his wife's remonstrances and tender up-braidings. How could he sit up all night, to the peril of his precious health? He told her that his studies had been especially interesting, and the night had slipped away unawares.

'What! Didn't it seem long, Martin,' she exclaimed, 'all those hours down in that cold dreary room?'

'No, indeed, my love; I never was more comfortable,' answered the doctor, with audacious mendacity.

'You eat a good supper, anyhow, sir,' said the familiar Barbara. 'Only think, mum; there isn't a mossel of yesterday's quartern, and the Dutch cheese is clean gone!'

Martin Prestwitch slunk off without attempting an answer to this accusation. He muttered something about seeing a patient in the next street, put on his hat, and went out.

It would not do to trifle with Mr. Blinker. The shops must be open by this time, and the coiner might be shod and despatched. The doctor cheapened a pair of roomy second-hand shoes on a cobbler's stall, and bought a pair of comfortable worsted stockings, of the size which his anatomical eye taught him was likely to suit Mr. Blinker. The half-hour had scarcely expired when he turned the key in the dissecting-room door. The coiner was asleep, with his head reposing comfortably upon the operating table.

The shoes and stockings were an admirable fit; and when Dr. Prestwitch had farther provided an old hat, Mr. Blinker presented a tolerably respectable appearance. There was still the question of disguise; but the doctor, after some little search in his surgery, found a pair of green spectacles, which made a considerable alteration in Jonathan Blinker's physiognomy. When these had been assumed, the doctor looked out, saw that the ground was clear, that no inquisitive Barbara or anxious wife was lurking in the shadow of an adjacent doorway, and then ushered Mr.

Blinker into the court, rejoiced beyond all measure to be rid of him, even at the cost of a five-pound note and that excellent bottle-green coat.

On the threshold Mr. Blinker turned round.

'I shall give you a look-in soon, doctor, to tell you how I get on.'

'O, don't if you please,' the surgeon cried piteously. 'It would never do for you to come here. You see, my family look upon you in the light of a body, and I don't see how they are to be brought to regard you from any other point of view.'

'I shan't come to see your family,' replied Jonathan Blinker; 'I shall come to see you.'

With this awful threat he stalked away, looking gigantic in the narrow alley. The doctor closed the door with a groan, and went to the parlour, where the meagre breakfast was neatly laid on the round table by the small bright fire, and where the anxious wife was ready to take alarm at Martin's haggard face.

But Mary Prestwitch's anxious looks were not half so embarrassing as the searching glances of Barbara Snaffles, who regarded the surgeon with a morbid curiosity, as a man who had just left an abnormal employment. She lingered in the room while he ate his breakfast, handing him his coffee-cup and hovering over his solitary egg.

'Is *it* there still?' she asked him in a stage whisper, while Mrs. Prestwitch was engaged with the three hungry children, the youngest of which was still dependent upon the maternal breast for the most primitive kind of nourishment.

'What do you mean by *it*?' Dr. Prestwitch asked impatiently.

'Him! The body.'

'No, girl; it's gone.'

'Gone? What! You've done with it already?'

'Yes.'

'And they've fetched it away?'

'Yes, they've fetched it away.'

'Well, I never!' exclaimed Barbara, with an injured air; 'they must have been in a hurry. I thought I should have seen it this morning. I've seen a many in my time—drownded and other-wise—and I never missed one before. I make no doubt I shall dream of him.'

'Dream of him? Nonsense girl!'

'Not having seen him, I make no doubt I shall dream of him,' said Barbara, with an air of conviction. 'I never missed one be-fore—not if it was three streets off and the family as it belonged to a'most strangers to me; and to have had one in the same house, and not seen him, seems right-down stupid-like.'

'Good gracious me!' cried the doctor; 'the girl is a perfect vampire!'

'Was it them two as brought him as fetched him away?' Miss Snaffles inquired curiously.

'Of course,' answered the doctor.

'And are they going to bury him in Newgate?'

'I suppose so. There Bab, go and mind your work and don't worry me any more about the man. He's gone; that's enough for you.'

Heartily did Martin Prestwitch wish that his visitor of last night had indeed been carried away to be safely interred with-in the prison-walls. That farewell threat of Jonathan Blinker's weighed heavy on his soul.

For the first time since he had lived in Little Bell-street, Dr. Prestwitch was behind-hand with his Christmas rent, to the be-wilderment of his faithful wife, who had helped him to save the seven pounds ten so carefully scraped together against the landlord should claim his due.

'It's gone, Mary,' the doctor said dismally, 'or at least five pounds ten out of it. You see, my dear, I was obliged to part with it.'

'But what for, Martin? What could you want five pounds ten for?—you, who never spend money?'

'Surgical instruments, my love; a man's first duty is to his profession.'

And again Martin Prestwitch hated himself for having lied to the wife of his bosom.

The landlord was displeased but not implacable. Dr. Prestwitch was a careful tenant, and had shown himself an honest man; so, after grumbling a little, the landlord gave him a month's grace, and went his way.

Jonathan Blinkers kept his promise. In the wintry gloaming a great hulking man in a bottle-green coat with a fur collar might have been often seen entering the doctor's surgery from the narrow side-alley, with a furtive surreptitious air. Here Dr. Prestwitch held converse with him, and was fain to provide some small sum of money against his coming. In time these donations took the form of a weekly allowance, and the accomplished Captain Flashman became a regular pensioner upon the doctor. He always used the same argument when claiming this bounty—Dr. Prestwitch had revived him of his own volition, and was therefore bound to aliment him—to keep him 'going', as the Captain called it.

Dr. Prestwitch submitted to this imposition with much bitterness of spirit, and many a groan breathed in the solitude of his surgery. He was a man of a gentle and somewhat timorous nature, and he felt himself unable to resist such a claimant; so week by week the struggling surgeon's brain was racked by the consideration of how he was to provide for Jonathan Blinker. Nor was it money only that his tormentor demanded from him.

The ex-coiner was of a hungry temperament, and took it in bad part if there was not some trifling snack provided for him when he paid his weekly visit; whereby the surgeon was fain to have recourse to divers small stratagems in order to set aside the remains of a beefsteak-pie or to secure the bladebone of a shoulder of mutton for the refection of his oppressor. The devoted Barbara did not fail to note the disappearance of these viands, and to remark upon the fitfulness of her master's appetite.

For a long time this secret burden weighed Martin Prestwitch down to the dust. Life had been a hard struggle before, but it was infinitely harder now, when the small weekly scrapings which he might have saved were absorbed by the omnivorous Blinker. He woke sometimes in the dead of the night, startled from sleep by the memory of his tormentor, and lay broad awake for hours brooding over his difficulties.

Mr. Blinker had taken care to impress upon him that the thing he had done was against the law, and that he was liable to some severe penalty for having assisted in the evasion of a condemned felon. Being too benevolent a man to betray his incubus, and not valorous enough to face the difficulties of the case, Dr. Prestwitch submitted to be imposed upon, and received his pensioner as meekly as if Jonathan Blinker had been a creditor armed with a righteous claim against him.

Things went on in this dismal manner for some time, and then there came a gradual change for the better in the doctor's circumstances. Patients dropped in upon him or sent for him much oftener than of old. Now it was a summons to attend the birth of a slum in St. Giles's, anon he was called to the deathbed of some ancient inhabitant of the Mint; sometimes he was sent for to repair the damages caused by a faction-fight in the purlieus of Field-lane, or to operate upon the fractured ribs of some muscular member of the dangerous classes in Bedfordbury.

On all these occasions he found that he had been recommended by Jonathan Blinker, who had described him as a perfect master of surgery and physic; and on all these occasions Dr. Prestwitch had reason to suspect that his new clients belonged to the criminal classes. But patients are patients, and these people paid the doctor promptly and liberally when flush with money, and showed themselves honourable whenever he gave them credit. The juvenile population in these quarters was perpetually being increased; and the ladies being uniformly pleased with gentle Mr. Prestwitch, one matron recommended him to another until the gentleman who was usually described amongst them as 'Blinker's doctor' found his practice was really picking up, and his financial position becoming easier.

There were still, however, those dreaded visits of Jonathan Blinker; and it seemed to Dr. Prestwitch as if his whole life was pervaded by that bulky figure in the bottle-green coat, very shiny about the cuffs and elbows, and very mangy as to the fur collar, by this time. And yet he felt that, on the whole, he was bound to be grateful to his tormentor, for the ultimate result of the business had been advantageous to himself. He did even try to make some show of gratitude; while Jonathan on his part was positively affectionate to his benefactor, declaring himself ready to serve him in any manner, at the hazard of a second suspension *per col.* even.

'There's nothing I wouldn't do for you doctor,' he said. 'I'd coin for you if I had a new set of tools, or the money to buy 'em There!'

The doctor, of course, entreated him to dismiss all ideas of coining from his brain, and to set about leading an honest life; but on this Mr. Blinker would only shake his head dubiously, as not perceiving the relevance of the proposition.

So things went on for nearly three years. The doctor's three small children had been recruited by an infantine brother, and now numbered four, with the possibility of a fifth looming in the distance. The doctor's practice was better, but it was not a good one, and could not by any means be called an aristocratic or even a genteel practice; nor had the doctor any prospect of being able to remove to a more fashionable locality than Little Bell-street. He could pay the butcher and the baker, however, and had no need to worry himself about his rent; and this to a man of such modest desires was enough for contentment.

Mr. Blinker had been his pensioner all this time, and Barbara Snaffles had become quite familiar with the weekly visitor in the bottle-green coat, dimly visible in the gloaming; for whatever the season of the year, Mr. Blinker came only in the twilight. She believed in him firmly as a patient in the corn-chandlery line—Dr. Prestwitch had told her he was a corn-chandler—afflicted with some chronic disease, and one of her master's most profitable customers.

The third year was closing in when the evening and hour of Mr. Blinker's accustomed visit came round without bringing that gentleman to Little Bell-street. It was the first time he had failed to appear with Tuesday evening's dusk since the foundation of this institution, and Dr. Prestwitch passed the remainder of the evening in a state of feverish restlessness, with the ex-coiner's allowance in his pocket. Could anything have happened to Jonathan Blinker? Could it be this affliction had come to a sudden end?

A second Tuesday came round, and again Mr. Blinker was missing; a third, and then a fourth, with the same result. Dr. Prestwitch felt a wild half-guilty hope that he should never see Jonathan Blinker again. Yet he was somewhat sorry to think that evil had befallen the missing man, nevertheless; for the surgeon was of a kindly disposition, and the creature had loved him.

Six weeks went by, and there were still no tidings of Mr. Blinker. The surgeon read the police news, expecting to see some record of calamity to his felonious acquaintance; but the scanty news-sheet of the day contained no information of the missing Jonathan. If he had suffered, he had suffered under some alias unknown to the doctor. At the end of the six weeks, and while Dr. Prestwitch's wonderment was yet at its height, there came a mysterious brown-paper parcel, addressed to the doctor in a queer cramped hand that he had never seen before. It was a small oblong package, very carefully corded and sealed, yet in a somewhat clumsy manner; and it arrived in the evening, while Martin Prestwitch was enjoying a pleasant interval of repose in the bosom of his family.

The surgeon of Little Bell-street was not the recipient of many parcels. Gifts and offerings of friendship were not showered upon him, even at the most festive season. Christmas brought him no monster turkeys, the New Year no costly frivolities for his children in the way of sugar-plums; and his little ones had grown out of infancy without so much as a sponsorial fork and spoon amongst the four of them. The advent of a parcel, therefore, was a sufficient cause for excitement in the small family circle. The loving little wife's bright eyes grew brighter with pleasure, the two elder children hustled each other at their father's knees in their eagerness to see the parcel opened; and Barbara Snaffles stood open-mouthed and open-eyed at her master's elbow.

The parcel felt very heavy—almost like a plate, Dr. Prestwitch thought—and, O, what an acceptable gift a dozen or so of silver forks and spoons would have been in that humble household! He broke the seals and unfastened the cord with hands that were tremulous with excitement. Inside the brown paper there was a small deal box, roughly made, and with the lid nailed down. There was some work and some delay in raising the lid; but when it was lifted, Mary Prestwitch thought the sight she beheld an all-sufficient reward for a hundred times as much trouble.

Comfortably reposing between two layers of cotton wool appeared a quantity of gold guineas, their yellow brightness pleasingly relieved by a background of crown pieces, fresh from the Mint.

'O Martin,' cried the little woman, with clasped hands, ' who can have sent us so much money? Thanks be to God, whoever it is.'

For a few moments Dr. Prestwitch did indeed believe that some unknown benefactor had taken compassion upon his poverty, and that the glistening counters before him were genuine coin of the realm. Only for a few moments, and then the image of Jonathan Blinker arose before his dazzled eyes, and he felt assured that these bright reproductions of King George's image were the handiwork of the coiner.

He pushed away his wife's hand as she stretched it out to take one of the guineas.

'Don't excite yourself, Molly,' he said gently. 'It isn't real money. It's only someone playing off a practical joke upon me.'

'Not real money? O Martin!' exclaimed the wife, with something like a sob.

'No, my love. They look very well, certainly, but there's not a genuine guinea amongst them; and if you or I were to try to pass one of them, it would be at the hazard of our necks.'

'I wouldn't mind trying, though,' said the reckless Barbara, 'at Bartlemy Fair.'

'Bab, I'm ashamed of you!' cried the doctor.

He took up one of the elusive coins between his finger and thumb, and felt the edges with the air of a man learned in metallurgy.

'Examine the milling, my dear,' he said, handing the false guinea to his wife. 'That is the test.'

Mary Prestwitch burst out crying as she looked at the bright simulacrum. It was a bitter disappointment. Five minutes ago she had fancied that a shower of riches had descended upon them; and now it seemed as if the thought of their poverty was a keener pang than it had ever been before.

'Are they really false, Martin?' she asked piteously.

'As false as any that ever a man was hung for coining,' replied the doctor.

He had just come upon a scrap of paper that lurked at the bottom of the box—a brief scrawl from Jonathan Blinker.

'Honerd Sirr,' wrote the felon, 'I ave gott sum tooles and biggun wurk agen. I send a fu spessiminits, wich may bee yusefull. Thay wold parse in yer nayburode—Yers to command, J. B.'

Martin Prestwitch tossed this missive into the fire.

'O Martin, who is it that has played this wicked trick?' asked his wife; 'and what was there in that note?'

'nothing that I could make out, Molly. Don't fret, my darling. I don't suppose the person meant unkindly.'

'Not meant unkindly! And to disappoint us like that! O Martin!'

The Christmas snow lay in the retired nooks and byways of the great City once more, and the doctor was fourteen years older than at the beginning of this story. But he still lived in Little Bell-street, and still worked very hard to provide for his wife and children. The fact was, he had so many of them, that his household expenses for the last fourteen years had been steadily on the increase. He did not grumble at this, however. He could ill have spared one of that merry band.

His circumstances had improved somewhat year by year, but

never so much as to justify his removal to a more fashionable neighbourhood. His patients belonged to the lower classes, and if he had left Little Bell-street he must have left his practice behind him. So a whole nosegay of blooming flowers had grown up in that dingy old house, more or less under the dominion of Barbara Snaffles. '*Old servants are such hard masters*,' says Charles Reade, and certainly Barbara ruled the doctor's household with a rod of iron.

There was a great commotion in the family this Christmas. The eldest girl, her mother's namesake Molly, was going to be married; going to be transplanted into a sphere of life much loftier than that in which her father and mother had their being, for she had been lucky enough to win the affections of a fashionable young doctor, whose father was a physician with a large West-end practice; a very proud and pompous gentleman, not a little disposed to consider that his only son was throwing himself away upon pretty Molly Prestwitch.

They were to be married upon the last day of the old year, and poor Molly had had hard work to prepare her simple wedding outfit, with the aid and counsel of Barbara Snaffles. Gentle little Mrs. Prestwitch was something of a cipher in the household, like most mild-tempered women whose lives are taken up with the rearing of children. She was content to look on and see the indefatigable Barbara manage for herself and her family, and it seemed to her that everything Mistress Snaffles did was wise.

On Christmas-day there was to be a great festival in Little Bell-street. Young Mr. Clemmory—Molly's intended—was to dine with his future father-in-law; and the great Dr. Clemmory himself, of Savile-row, had condescended to accept Martin Prestwitch's invitation to partake of his modest Christmas fare. The fare was to be by no means unworthy of the distinguished guest, however; for Barbara had been up to her eyes in preparations for the last week, and had cheapened one of the finest geese in Leadenhall-market for the feast, which, with a haunch of mutton, a boiled round of beef, and a veal-pie, the doctor and his wife agreed would make a very pretty little dinner.

They were to dine at three in the afternoon—quite a patrician hour—but young Clemmory had informed them that his father never dined earlier; and as the appointed time drew near, Barbara's nervousness increased to a feverish intensity. She felt that her reputation as a cook and a manager was staked upon this cast.

A little before three Dr. Clemmory and his son arrived, the West-end physician a ponderous man, with a fat voice, a powdered wig, a pair of handsome legs in black-silk stockings, and a gold-headed cane. The small wainscoted parlour seemed hardly capacious enough for such grand company; and Mrs. Prestwitch was quite fluttered by the importance of her guest.

It was nearly dinner-time, and they were all assembled in the parlour: Molly the younger radiant and blooming in a white-muslin frock, with a coral necklace round her slender throat; two younger girls, who looked like smaller repetitions of Molly; three boys, more or less in the hobbledehoy stage of existence, all in clean shirt-frills, but showing a little more bony wrist below their coat-cuffs than was in accordance with the reigning fashion—poor people's children grow so fast.

It was on the stroke of three; Mrs. Prestwitch was wondering how the goose would turn out; whether the haunch of mutton would be roasted to that perfection of culinary art which such a man as Dr. Clemmory had a right to expect in any joint set before him; and whether Barbara would emerge triumphantly form the plum-pudding ordeal, and walk unscathed through the mince-pie furnace. The house was small, and the narrow entrance-hall had been odorous with dinner for the last hour or more.

Before the neighbouring clocks began to strike the hour, there came a loud double-knock at Dr. Prestwitch's door. The surgeon and his wife started and stared at each other aghast. They had invited no other guest; and the advent of a dropper-in upon such an occasion would be an unmixed calamity. Every fork and spoon had been pressed into the service of the day, every inch of the dinner-table was engaged.

The West-end surgeon was laying down the law in his pomp-ous voice, talking about the King, and My Lord North, and these contumacious Americans; but every other tongue was silent, and Dr. And Mrs. Prestwitch were straining their ears to the utmost to hear the opening of the street-door, and Barbara's parley with the unexpected visitor. There was a long pause: it was not an easy thing for Bab to leave her dinner at the supreme moment of 'dishing up', and it would be ill-manners for a member of the family to leave the room in order to open the street-door. There was a prolonged pause, therefore, during which the church clocks chimed three with a solemn sound, and the individual who had knocked gave a loud husky h'm, a sound that sent a cold shiver through Martin Prestwitch, he scarce knew why.

At last the door was opened, and a voice that turned the surgeon's blood to ice was heard inquiring for Dr. Prestwitch. Then a pair of creaking shoes walked down the passage, the par-lour-door was flung open, and Barbara announced Mr. Jonathan Blinker!

It was the coiner, dressed in a bran-new bottle-green coat and breeches, and a scarlet waistcoat elaborately adorned with gold lace; the coiner grown stout and red-faced and prosperous-looking; the coiner in a snow-white frilled shirt, and with a new hat under his arm.

There was dead silence. Martin Prestwitch's countenance as-sumed a sickly hue; the great man from Savile-row stopped sud-denly in his lecture, and stared at the newcomer, as if waiting for an introduction. Mrs. Prestwitch and the children stared also; but were inclined to consider Mr. Blinker's jovial red face in a favourable aspect. He looked an eminently respectable gentle-man of the agricultural class.

'How d'ye do, doctor?' he said, unabashed by the assembly in which he found himself. 'I've just come back from America, and I thought I'd give you a look up before I went away anywheres else, even though it was Christmas-day; and I don't mind cutting my Christmas beef with you, if you've no objections.'

What could Martin Prestwitch do—a weak soul at the best,

and especially feeble where Jonathan Blinker was concerned? He faltered out a half-audible introduction, 'Dr. Clemmory, Mr. Blinker; Mr. Clemmory, Mr. Blinker.' The physician bowed with an urbane stateliness; good-natured George Clemmory shook hands with the stranger.

'Your arrival is somewhat of a coincidence,' said Dr. Clemmory; 'we were discussing the aspect of American affairs when you knocked.'

Barbara announced dinner before Mr. Blinker could reply. By a rapid and judicious manoeuvring of the knives and forks she had contrived to prepare a cover for the uninvited guest; and the coiner took his place amongst the rest of the company to the horror of Martin Prestwitch, who knew not what revelations might be made before the meal was finished, and who felt that his face was palpably bedewed with cold perspiration.

The banquet was a success. Dr. Clemmory ate like an alderman, and praised the goose and the haunch until Barbara's countenance glowed with an honourable pride. Mr. Blinker made himself eminently agreeable, talking jovially with the youngsters at his end of the table, and leading the laughter for all Dr. Clemmory's jokes with a stentorian peal. It is true that he put his knife in his mouth a good deal, an supped his gravy in a painfully audible manner; but people were not so refined in those days, and a prosperous agriculturist might do as much as this without causing a scandal. Altogether, things were much better than Martin Prestwitch had expected, and as the evening wore on he began to breathe more freely.

After dinner there was a dessert of nuts and oranges. How happy George Clemmory and pretty Molly Prestwitch seemed roasting chestnuts at the fire in the dimly-lighted parlour, with all those young brothers and sisters, while their parents conversed more gravely in the dining-room, where there was a steaming bowl of punch! Under the influence of punch, the West-end physician became wonderfully expansive, and patronised Jonathan Blinker in the most genial manner.

'I like a man of that stamp,' he said afterwards in confidence to Martin Prestwitch; 'an honest jovial fellow, cast in a good mould, sir, cast in a good mould. There's genuine metal there, Dr. Prestwitch; you can hear the ring of it. The man is sterling coin, sir.'

Martin Prestwitch shivered, and could only reply with a sickly smile.

Before the night was out Dr. Clemmory was obviously the worse or the better for liquor, and had become almost maudlin in his expressions of regard for the ex-coiner. Mr. Blinker had drunk more, but the strong drink had no effect upon him. When the physician's coach came to fetch him away from Little Bell-street, he volunteered to set Mr. Blinker down at his inn before driving home; and offer which was accepted to the horror of Martin Prestwitch.

If Dr. Clemmory had taken a fancy to Mr. Blinker, that worthy, on his part, had taken a fancy to the junior members of the Prestwitch family. He insisted upon kissing the three girls under the mistletoe when he wished them goodnight, and wound up by kissing Barbara Snaffles in the passage. He squeezed Martin Prestwitch by the hand upon the threshold, and said in a confidential voice,

'I think you've been glad to see me, doctor; and I take it kindly. I've not forgotten past favours. I've made a bit of money out yonder in the shipping line, and I've left every penny of it to you.'

It was the truth; and the bit of money turned out to be a large fortune, which Dr. Prestwitch inherited three years afterwards from the grateful Blinker, who expired in the odour of sanctity at his own house at Clapton, sincerely regretted by the young Prestwitches, to whom he had been a kind of fairy god-father, showering benefits and gifts upon them during those concluding years of his life. To the last day of his existence Dr. Clemmory was wont to speak of Mr. Blinker as a model of probity, and the very flower of successful traders and self-made men.

The True Story of Don Juan

When the citron groves of the Alcazar were in their ripest glory, and the gilded palace of the Moors yet wore the freshness that had made it splendid in the days of its first masters, there lived a certain Sevillian *hidalgo* whose entrance to the Plaza de Toros was the signal for a hum and a whisper among the multitude that filled that bloody arena; whose rare presence at vespers in the dusky aisles of the great cathedral boded ill to some fair worshipper within the solemn fane; a man from the touch of whose infidel fingers the priest withdrew his holy-water brush as from contact with the foul fiend himself; a man behind whose steps followed ever the smothered anathema of the pious and the weak.

This man was Juan Tenorio, one of the twenty-four, the best hated and the most feared among the inhabitants of Seville. Handsome, proud, brave—with a desperate brutal courage— false, and cruel, he was all these, and known to be all these, for he came of a race in which these qualities had been hereditary since the Mahometan was driven out of Spain.

Don Juan's wealth was even greater than his rank. He was master of many a square mile of vineyard between Seville and Jerez, and owner of a delicious oriental villa on the banks of the Guadalquiver, built in the true Moorish style, with airy barbaric colonnades, and pierced pavements of coloured marble through which a hundred jets of limpid water rose to cool the sultry southern atmosphere, and a quadrangle where a fountain played all day and night amidst a wealth of exotic blossoms, beneath the

269

shade of a wide silken awning. Here, in the idle summer noon-tide, the noble Sevillian loved to bask, and here, beneath the tender light of the southern moon, were held revels of which all good citizens spoke with a shudder.

Dancing-girls and *matadors* had told strange stories of ban-quets given in those marble-paved chambers -banquets at which Lucifer himself might have taken the chair; of dances performed in that Moorish quadrangle which might have delighted the Prince of Darkness and his chosen courtiers; of deeds scarcely less terrible than those by which Pedro the Cruel had given the Alcazar a hideous renown. Don Juan Tenorio had elevated vice into a kind of poetry, and refined sin into a science. From his boyhood his name had been a terror to husbands and fathers and brothers; but of late the good people of Seville had crossed themselves as they spoke of him, as when they pronounced the name of the fiend. His latest crime had surpassed his former vil-lainies, for on this last occasion he had added murder to seduc-tion.

Amongst those weak enough or bold enough to countenance this man, in spite of his infamous repute, was the Commander Gonzalo de Ulloa, with whose young and beautiful daughter Don Juan Tenorio professed himself eager to form a matrimonial al-liance. The Commander was influenced by the rank and wealth of the suitor; the terms of the contract were arranged, and the con-tracted parties were allowed to meet in the most ceremonious man-ner on certain rare occasions—the promised bride attended by her *duenna*, and supported by her proud old father.

Whether Juan entered upon this engagement in good faith at first was only known to himself. Certain it is that, after a very short court-ship, the idea of matrimonial bondage in the future, and the wea-risome attendance of father and *duenna* in the present, became alike obnoxious to him. The habit of evil-doing had grown with his growth and strengthened with his strength. He was practiced in the corruption of *duennas*, versed in all delusive arts for the conquest of a weak inexperienced girl, and the end in this case came but too soon.

One morning the gossips of Seville were startled by the tidings of Donna Octavia's elopement with Don Juan; and before nightfall a great terror came upon the city with the knowledge that the Commander Don Gonzalo de Ulloa had been found stabbed through the heart on a lonely road twenty miles from the gates.

He had discovered his daughter's disappearance within one hour of the wretched girl's flight; had extorted some half-confession from the unwilling *duenna*, and had followed the fugitives, attended by one servant, who saw his master overtake a travelling-carriage, in which were a lady and gentleman, both masked. The Commander had dragged the gentleman from the carriage, and a sharp encounter had followed on the spot, with fatal result to Don Gonzalo, the lady shrieking piteously all the while. The gentleman had not once removed his mask, and had sprung into the carriage directly after his opponent's fall, crying to the postillions to drive like a thousand devils.

The servant was an inexperienced rustic, who had been but a few weeks in the service of the Commander, and he was unable to identify the masked traveller, but had a kind of idea that it was no other than Don Juan Tenorio, who had graciously sworn at him for a base-born dog more than once upon the occasion of his visits to Don Gonzalo.

The Commander's family were furious against the libertine, scarcely knowing whether to hate him most as the seducer of their kinswoman or as the murderer of their kinsman. Shame was new to their house, and was so much the more bitter to bare. They urged their wrongs in the ears of legal authority, and demanded that the seducer and assassin should be brought before the tribunal of justice; but as the *duenna* had contrived to disappear from Seville during the confusion that followed her employer's death, there was no direct evidence against Don Juan Tenorio.

And besides this difficulty there was another in the fact that Don Juan was not to be found. It was reported that he and his frail companion had embarked at Cadiz on a vessel bound for the East. Don Gonzalo's remains were brought to Seville and interred with much solemnity in the church of the Franciscan monastery, where the house of Ulloa possessed a mortuary chapel, and of which order the only son of the late Commander was a superior; and after affording gossip and excitement for all Seville, the monstrous scandal gradually died away, and, if not forgotten, at least ceased to be a common subject of conversation.

But there was one gloomy mind from which no time could efface the memory of Don Juan's iniquities, there was one chief member of the holy brotherhood of St. Francis from whose thoughts the fatal image of the murderer and seducer was only banished during the supreme service of the altar, and scarcely banished then.

Father Onofrio of the Holy Sepulchre, whose name in the world had been Paez de Ulloa, cherished the memory of his father's death and his sister's disgrace as other men cherish the image of a lost love, or wasted wealth, or long-departed happiness. By day and night his prayers arose to heaven, imploring justice from Him who claims the divine right to avenge all earthly wrongs.

"Thou hast said '*Vengeance is mine,*'" cried the monk. "Surely Thou wilt not suffer this libertine to go unpunished; and if Thou needest an earthly instrument, behold, Thy servant is ready."

Months grew into years, and it seemed as if the brother's pleading was unheard at the supreme tribunal. A marble effigy of the murdered Commander was executed for the mortuary chapel in the church of the Franciscans, a noble image of the dead, "in his habit as he lived," erect and sword in hand, as if standing guardian over the vault below, awfully life-like in the obscurity of that solemn shrine.

Three years had passed since Donna Octavia's flight, and in all that time the Moorish villa on the banks of the Guadalquiver had been deserted by its master. Suddenly as he had disappeared Don Juan Tenorio came back to his native city; and again his very name was a terror in all virtuous households.

He reappeared with a bold and dauntless front, expressed himself profoundly grieved to hear of Don Gonzalo's death and his daughter's elopement, declared that he had quarrelled with and parted from the damsel on the very day before her flight, having reason to suspect her of a low intrigue with one of the *matadors* of the circus, and had left Seville quietly and alone immediately after this quarrel, since which departure he had been travelling in the Holy Land.

The story was rendered somewhat plausible by the fact that a celebrated *matador* had disappeared from Seville about the time of Donna Octavia's flight; but the Sevillians were not the less convinced of Juan Tenorio's guilt, and regarded him with a gloomy interest as he stalked among them at bullfight and festival, shunned yet admired, splendid and lonely.

Unhappily the very fact of his evil reputation rendered him an object of interest in the eyes of foolish women; and from the hour of his return he grew bolder and more successful in crime. The rumour of his return and his new iniquities penetrated to the sombre retreat of the Franciscan monks, and Father Onofrio declared that the hour had come in which the offended majesty of Heaven must be vindicated by an earthly champion. This blasphemous libertine, whose career was devastating as the progress of some dragon of fabulous story—this hardened sinner, whose rank enabled him to defy the law, and whose infidelity mocked the dangers of divine wrath—had come back to the scene of his guilty deeds, and had come to expiate them.

"The hour has arrived," said the superior, in solemn conference with the holy brotherhood. "When the cowardice of venal man shrinks from the duty of chastising the high-born sinner—when the outraged law is powerless, it is time that the Church should assert its authority. This man is an incarnate vice, and it is the office of the Church to vanquish sin. Juan Tenorio must die."

The superior spoke with a tone of conviction that seemed inspiration. His pale careworn face brightened with an awful radiance; so might look the avenging angel, as he proclaims the doom of a sinner.

"There should be no scandal," faltered one of the brotherhood. "The—deed—must be done secretly."

"The Church can keep her secrets and can answer for her acts to God," replied Father Onofrio, calmly. "For the safety of Seville, for the glory of Heaven, it is expedient this man should perish."

"And the means by which he shall die?" nervously interrogated Brother Ildefonzo.

"Leave the means to Heaven—and to me," replied the Superior.

"I want to put the question of the righteousness of this deed to the vote. Let those of the brotherhood who are opposed to this act of justice hold up their hands."

There was a solemn silence of some minutes, during which Father Onofrio waited with calm inflexible countenance. No hand was uplifted, no voice pleaded for the abandoned libertine, Juan Tenorio.

"Enough," said the superior; "it is decided. Diximus."

The suppers and dances at the Moorish villa had been gayer than ever since Don Juan's return from his wanderings,—unholy festivals, to which men and women stole between dusk and midnight in a stealthy, secret manner. But to have partaken of one of those banquets was to be a lost creature in the sight of all good men and women, and over the gates of that barbaric paradise might have been written, "Who enters here leaves honour and good name behind." The distant flash of many lamps, the fitful sound of gay dance-music or snatches of song floating Seville-wards on the still night-air, were all that respectable people knew, or sought to know, of Don Juan's festivities. But 'twas said the morning sun beheld the close of revelries more disgraceful than that fair orb had shone upon since Commodus and his venal favourites greeted the god of day with their drunken chorus of jubilee.

It was at the close of one of these infamous orgies that Juan Tenorio strolled alone on the broad terrace-walk, from which he looked across groves of orange and citron, myrtle and arbutus, to the fair winding river glorified by the morning sun. The festival just ended had wearied and disappointed the giver of the feast. That dread hour had come in which the cup of pleasure begins to pall upon the lips of the libertine, and in which for the first time he asks himself the fatal question, "And is this happiness?" Is this all? Is it to be always the same: lovely eyes with the same fond flattering looks, soft round arms wreathed in the same caresses; music and song as old as life itself; wines that have lost their power to warm the blood; dances whose voluptuous enchantments have ceased to enchant; the mere dull mechanism of profligacy, the dreary *coulisses* of vice?

"Is this all that life has left for me?" cries the libertine drearily. "O for some intrigue which shall thrill every sense with the old fire; something mysterious, awful, perilous; something which shall outstep the limits of earthly bliss, and carry my jaded soul into the domain of the supernatural! I am weary of women. Is there no fair fallen angel among the ranks of the damned who will take pity on a soul as lost as her own?"

"A packet for his highness Don Juan Tenorio."

The address was so sudden as to seem like an answer to that blasphemous invocation; but it came only from a messenger who had approached the musing *hidalgo* with stealthy foot. He handed Don Juan a small packet, carefully sealed with a blank seal, bowed, and disappeared before there was time to interrogate him.

The packet contained a letter and a miniature. Don Juan first examined the miniature. It was exquisitely painted, and it represented a lovelier face than any that Juan Tenorio had ever seen out of his dreams. Dark eyes of marvellous bewitchment, parted lips of ripest crimson, and a smile that was of almost diabolical beauty.

The letter was brief.

"One who has long cherished your image, and watched your career, would fain see you alone. If you are bold enough to venture an interview with a stranger, and in a place not often devoted to such meetings as you attend, come, two hours after midnight, to the Franciscan church, where you will be waited for in the chapel to the left of the high altar."

This was all. The writer made no allusion to the portrait; but could Don Juan doubt that those delicate feminine characters were hers upon whose image he gazed with new hope and passion?

"A rendezvous two hours after midnight in a church!" exclaimed the *hidalgo*. "This savours of the diabolic. Yes, fair fallen angel, I will come, though the foul fiend himself should make a third at our meeting. The church of the Franciscan monastery? It is surely there that Don Gonzalo was buried; yes, I remember."

This association was scarcely an agreeable one even to Don Juan, who held all things lighter than his own pleasure; but it nowise deterred him from attending the rendezvous. He looked at the miniature twenty times during the day, wondering how it was he had never beheld the lovely original.

There were no revels that night at the villa, and at one o'clock Don Juan left his house alone, and on foot. It was a somewhat memorable departure; for he was destined never again to cross that familiar threshold.

The monastery of the Franciscans was situated in a dreary spot upon the outskirts of the city. Beyond lay the open country, wild and solitary. All was dark and silent, even in the city; but beyond those deserted streets and squares reigned an unspeakable gloom. Intrigue affects darkness, and the unknown senorita had chosen a moonless midnight for her assignation.

As the *hidalgo* approached the lofty walls of the monastery, he began to wonder how he should gain admittance to the church at this dead hour of night. Did the pious Franciscans leave their gates open for the faithful and the penitent all night long? The customs of the pious were not familiar to Don Juan Tenorio, and he could not answer this question.

"My fallen angel has made all things smooth for me, no doubt," he reflected, with an insolent smile; "but a church is a strange place for a post-midnight rendezvous; and if nothing but a church will suit my unknown mistress, I should have been better pleased had she chosen any other fane than that which hallows the ashes of the Commander."

He was close under the walls by this time. The western door of the church stood before him. It was ajar, and he saw a faint light burning within. He pushed the door open gently, and entered the sacred building with stealthy steps. There was no such feeling as fear in his mind. He was not even awe-stricken by that solemn, time-hallowed solitude. He felt only a chill, unpleasant sense of repugnance to the place, and a vague sentiment of vexation against the folly of the fair one who had selected such a spot and such an hour.

"She must be of a rank to render extreme caution necessary," he thought, "or she would scarcely bring me to such a place."

He walked slowly along the southern aisle, looking to the right and the left. Solitary tapers burned dimly before the images of Virgin and saints. No living creature was to be seen within the solemn precincts. The cautious footsteps of Don Juan Tenorio sounded loud upon the broad stone flags, beneath which reposed the ashes of many a penitent brother whose feet had paced them living.

The chapel to the left of the high altar was in deepest shadow. Don Juan's footsteps quickened as he drew near that appointed spot. His heart beat loud and fast with the old eagerness for triumph and conquest. He entered the chapel, and stood face to face with-Don Gonzalo de Ulloa.

It was only the Commander's statue, the noble marble effigy of that murdered gentleman, which confronted Don Juan, sword in hand, with—but that was a trick of light and shadow—a vengeful frown upon its lifeless brow.

"St. Jago! if this be meant for a jest, the *senorita* shall pay dearly for it," muttered Don Juan, when he recovered his breath.

He turned his back on the statue and the mortuary chapel, and looked along the shadowy aisles in search of the person who had summoned him.

At an insignificant door in the opposite aisle he saw a slight black-robed figure, beckoning to him with uplifted hand. He crossed the church, and followed this figure through the open door into the grounds of the monastery. Here he would fain have arrested the black-robed stranger; but the unknown kept in advance of him, and pointed onward with commanding gesture.

They crossed a cypress-grove, and entered a small enclosure surrounded by high walls. It was the ground which had been used as a burial-place for the brotherhood since the vaults below the church had been filled.

Here Juan Tenorio saw a group of monks encircling an open grave. The scene was illumined by torches stuck in the newly-dug earth, that made a bank upon one side of the grave; and the picture had something of the diabolic in the fitful glare of torchlight.

"If this be a jest," cried Don Juan, "it is a sorry one, and the Franciscans shall answer to the king for such an insult to one of the noblest among his servants."

He grasped the loose garment of his unknown guide, who turned towards him with uplifted hood, and showed him the boyish countenance of a young novice.

"It is no jest," said one of the hooded monks, in a voice that was strangely familiar to the libertine; "you have been summoned hither, Don Juan Tenorio, to expiate your many crimes."

"Before what tribunal?"

"The tribunal of the Church. When a sinner of your rank outrages heaven and man, and defies the law of his country, it is time that a superior power should take upon itself the punishment of his iniquities. It is better that one man should perish than that the souls of many should be destroyed. You have been the incarnate scourge of your native city; you have sinned with an impunity that is a lasting witness against the cowardice of your fellow-citizens; but you shall do evil no more. Prepare yourself for death, guilty brother; your grave is ready."

Don Juan drew his sword; but a strong hand snatched the weapon from his grasp, and flung it to the bottom of that dismal yawning grave. Other hands seized him at the same instant, and bound his arms to his sides with rope. Bound thus, amidst that circle of solemn, black-robed figures, the sinner knew that he was doomed.

"You are allowed half an hour to prepare for death," said the calm voice of the superior. "Kneel, brother, and pray that your guilty soul may be finally purified in the flames of purgatory."

"I believe as much in purgatory as I believe in heaven or hell," answered Don Juan, "and have no breath to waste in prayer. I conclude this performance is some priestly practical joke, or a stratagem for the extortion of money. If it be the latter, you had better name the price of my liberty at once. I am prepared to be liberal, and I deserve to pay dearly for my credulity in coming here at the behest of a lady who exists—"

"Only in a picture of Joseph's Temptation, by Leonardo da Vinci, from which one of our brotherhood, skilled in miniature-painting, copied the head of Potiphar's wife. We knew the style of beauty calculated to attract Don Juan Tenorio," said the superior. "Once more, wretched man, I tell you this is no jest, but solemn earnest; no trick to extort money, but a tribunal to execute summary justice on a villain. And in order that you may believe this the more easily, know that I, who within these sacred walls am called Father Onofrio

of the Holy Sepulchre, bore, in the world from which I have withdrawn myself, the name of Paez de Ulloa, only son of the man you
murdered, and brother of the woman you seduced.—Now, let the
Dies Ires be sung, and the sinner prepared for death."

The solemn hymn was chanted, the funeral service was performed.
Juan Tenorio stood by, motionless as the statue of the Commander
in the mortuary chapel. White as that marble effigy was the face of
the condemned, but the haughty lip curved in a defiant sneer, as if in
scorn of death itself.

The coffin was brought forward to the brink of the grave, and the
victim was lifted in the arms of four stalwart monks and laid living in
that last habitation of mortality.

"We would not inflict unnecessary torture even on a criminal,"
said Father Onofrio; "a draught has been prepared which will short-
en the pangs of death— Brother Ignatius, let the cup be offered to
the lips of the condemned."

A monk advanced with a metal goblet in his hand, knelt by the
side of the coffin, and offered the vessel to the lips of Don Juan. He
drained it in silence. This being done, the lid of the coffin was adjusted
and nailed down by two other monks, and then the funeral service
proceeded.

The first faint streak of day glimmered in the east as the last shovel-
ful of earth was thrown into the grave; and in that faint morning light
the procession of monks moved with slow and solemn step from the
burial-ground. A bird began its gay carol as they crossed the monastic
garden, beneath the dark cypress avenue, and the bell for matins
sounded from the gray church-tower.

The disappearance of Juan Tenorio was the subject of much
wonderment to the Sevillians; but their wonder was speedily changed
into horror upon the arising of a strange rumour as to the manner
of his death.

It seemed that Don Juan had gone at midnight to the Church
of the Franciscans, and had there insulted the statue of the Commander, Don Gonzalo. And lo, horror of horrors! the statue had been
endowed with life and motion, and had invited the insulter to mortal
combat; which ghastly challenge being accepted, the effigy had led

the way to a waste place beyond the convent garden, and suddenly a great chasm in the earth had opened, and Juan Tenorio was devoured alive.

This story was vouched for by the monks of the Franciscan Monastery; certain members of that holy brotherhood having witnessed the awful doom of the profligate. And on such indisputable evidence the story of Don Juan passed into the records of Seville, a never-to-be-forgotten legend of human guilt and supernatural retribution.

The Winning Sequence

The house is silent—a roomy, old-fashioned house in the Royal Village, that old-world Richmond to which King and Queen and Dukes and Duchesses, wits and politicians, and lovely loose-lived ladies, used to come a century and a half ago, and where Royalty still inhabits, and loyal joy-bells often ring loud.

The house is silent in the quiet grey hour betwixt night and morning. Through the tall window on the staircase a horizontal rift in the sky, a streak of pale light between two banks of black cloud, tells that day is near.

Not a sound but the faint patter of mice, like the trickling of water, behind the worm-eaten panelling. Not a sound? Yes, there is a sound; a sound which has been heard often in that house, on that landing, at just that grey hour which is neither night nor morning—the sound of a footfall that is lighter than tread of human foot; the sound of a sigh that breathes from the far distance of an unknown grave.

A door opens gently, slowly, and a scared face looks out into the dimness. It is the mistress of the house, who has heard that footfall before tonight, and who knows the story of it, and wants to see and hear more than mortal lips can tell her. She steps softly in slippered feet, as if her footsteps would disturb a ghost. She sees, or fancies she sees, in that grey twilight—first two high-heeled shoes, standing on the threshold of the door opposite her own door; embroidered velvet shoes, with red heels; next, turning her eyes towards the staircase, she sees, or fancies she sees, a figure slowly descending—the figure of a woman, handsome, past her first youth, but still young,

281

tall, commanding, dressed in a loose gown of Indian silk curiously patterned, a dull red, with a yellow scroll figured over it. The woman of the house sees, or believes she sees, all this—every particular of the tall figure, the loose flowing hair, the bare white arm, even to the delicate modelling of the hand which lightly touches the broad oak banister rail.

★ ★ ★ ★ ★

Slowly, softly, she follows that silent figure, treading so stealthily With its bare feet; slowly, stair by stair, with cautious pauses and lingering movements, to the hall below, which is darker than that upper corridor and, after noiseless opening of a door, into the dark drawing-room, where the woman of the house sees, or thinks she sees, that shadow-woman strike a light with flint and steel and clumsy process of burning tinder, and so light a candle.

Then the shadow-woman sets down the tall silver candlestick on a phantasmal card-table, and the house-mistress sees that other woman, who has been dead a century and a half, kneel on the carpeted floor, which is scattered with cards thick as fallen leaves in November woods—kings and queens and aces, cards that turn the fortune of a game; she gathers them up in heaps, and kneeling by the table, in the dim candlelight, she sorts pack after pack with infinite pains, assures herself, with earnest eyes and puckered brow, of numbers and of suits, each pack complete, and with nothing to spare, and then after this patient labour, which lasts a long time, she lays one small pack of cards on the table, and flings all the rest upon the ground again—flings them pell-mell about the floor and under the card-table.

The little pack of selected cards she thrusts into the bosom of her red and yellow bed-gown; and then she blows out the candle and creeps out of the room and across the hall and upstairs again, her figure lighted by an unearthly light—a bluish glimmer, faint and dim and fitful, which the woman of the house fancies must be the light that hangs above an unhallowed grave, a light which that shadow-woman carries about and around her, a light of which that ghostly being is unconscious, and so must needs grope for a candle to assist her stealthy march.

Slowly and softly she steps with pale naked foot from stair to stair, and at the top of the staircase melts and is absorbed into the growing dawn, and lo, when the living woman looks at the ground by the door of the empty bedchamber, the velvet shoes are gone. There is nothing left but a fancy or a dream. The old eight day-clock ticks in the dark hall below, the mice scamper, a bird sings in the little suburban garden outside, a cool breath of the morning blows in at an open window. The new-born day has begun, in all its freshness of awakening bird and opening flower.

★ ★ ★ ★ ★

THE STORY

"Dearest, if you would make me happy, you would give up high play," said the Colonel.

"I would go further than that," answered Mrs. Fermor, "If it would make you happy, I would give up cards altogether. What are they worth? An hour's excitement, the brief triumph of a winning hand, the misery of losing more than one can afford to lose, and having to make light of one's losses, and sit smiling, while one thinks of servants' wages overdue and black looks from one's milliner."

"Indeed, my love, this passion for play, so common in your charming sex nowadays, is a folly that touches near the edge of sin. And if you would make so great a sacrifice for my sake, if you would indeed abandon a practice which fashion has made almost a necessity—"

"What trumpery worldly pleasure would I not sacrifice for you? Why I would give up more than cards. I would give up eating and drinking, and starve to death, smiling in your face all the time, were we ship-wreaked on a desert island. I would give up my friends and home, change my religion—"

"Thou shalt give up nothing, but a passion which verges on a vice. I know your losses at cards have vexed you."

"True! But I have been luckier lately—I won enough last week to pay all my poor domestic debts. You will see only smiling faces among my household."

"My dear Sibylla, to my mind it is more degrading to win than to lose; and that good luck, as you call it, exercises a worse influence on a woman-gamester than ill-fortune."

"Yet severely as you condemn the passion, you sometimes play yourself."

"I never venture more than I can afford to lose. I am a man; and I cannot always refuse to share the amusements of my friends."

They were in the first raptures of affianced love. She was young and beautiful; a widow, who had married a man considerably her senior, and whose marriage had proved a disappointment, since the husband's fortune was less than people thought when the matrimonial bargain was struck. She had been left with an income just large enough to make a show with, and insufficient for comfort and show. She might have lived comfortably and avoided debt, had she consented to exist without a couple of footmen, and to ride in a hired coach. But the coach and the footmen seemed to her as essential as the air she breathed; and when she played high it was with the hope of supplementing her income by a run of luck at *quadrille* or *faro*.

She had been a gamester for years, and with varying fortunes; now lifted to the empyrean, now sunk as low as Hades, hourly expecting to be hauled off to the Sponging-house, and to see dress-coach and gilded chair, abigail and footmen, vanish like Cinderella's cavalcade at the stroke of midnight.

For this last season, since her engagement to Ralph Challoner, her star had been in the ascendant, and she had enjoyed a run of luck which her friends had begun to wonder, not without an occasional curled lip and shrugged shoulder, not without an occasional *innuendo*.

It was one of those innuendoes, carelessly uttered in a crowded card-room and overheard by Colonel Challoner, which had made him urge her to play no more. Not for worlds would he have repeated the sneer, the scornful hint, which had it not fallen from a woman's lips would have been accounted for with blood. He told her only that he had observed the pernicious influence of the gaming-table. He had seen her feverish and excited at cards, *ennuied* and absent-minded when she was away from the card-table. He had seen her haggard countenance and worried look, even during a run of luck which her friends had called miraculous.

He was a poor man, a soldier in a line regiment; but he had fought with Wolfe at Quebec, and his name had figured advantageously in the *Gazette*. He knew that to marry the beautiful widow would be to hazard the peace and happiness of his future life; but he was still young enough to be desperately in love, and he turned a deaf ear to the whispers of prudence when asked, "What have you, with scarce two hundred a year beyond a lieutenant-colonel's pay, to do with an expensive wife?"

He knew that the lady was living beyond her means, and had ventured to expostulate with her upon her extravagance; but she put him off with a kiss.

"When I am your wife I will live as you bid me," she said; "in a cottage by Kensington Gravel-pits, with one red-elbowed servant wench. Do you remember the cottage we passed that day we rode out westwards after we had visited the Princess? A wooden hovel smothered with roses and honeysuckle. Well, Ralph, I would be content to live there—with you."

"Why, your hoop would not pass through the doorway, love."

"I would live without a hoop, without fine clothes or jewels," she protested, with a sigh at the thought of the jewels which might be seized by her creditors tomorrow, were they ill-natured enough to take the law of her.

"Then live without cards, Sibylla. Make that sacrifice, and I will hold myself the happiest of men."

"Let me get out of debt first," she urged.

"What? Are you so sure of winning?"

His head was bent low to kiss the small hand that he was wont to clasp and fondle throughout their confidential talk, seated side by side on the Louis Quatorze sofa. Had he been looking at her he must have seen the sudden terror in her eyes, and the sickly whiteness under her rouge as he asked that question.

"Sure? No, of course not," she answered fretfully. "Who can be sure of winning? Only I believe in luck; and it seems foolish to leave off play until my luck changes."

His prayers prevailed, and she gave him her promise, but she did not give up her card-parties. She had her "day" and her "night" and once a week the tables in her spacious drawing-room were going all day and till after midnight; and she insisted upon Challoner's playing for at least an hour or so at her parties.

"My future husband has puritanical ideas about women gamesters," she said lightly, "and I am his obedient slave, so he must take my place and help to amuse my friends."

She would hang over his shoulder sometimes as he played, and her flashing eyes and flushed cheeks showed that she had lost none of her interest in the game. The perfume of her hair, the soft touch of her cheek as it brushed against his, even the light pressure of the restless hand which fluttered and trembled on his shoulder, distracted his attention from the cards in his hand, and his play would have been careless and automatic, had she not advised, and even commanded him.

He usually sat in her favourite place, at an oblong table that stood in front of two long, narrow windows. Voluminous curtains of gold and amber brocade covered the windows and wall space between them, and these rich draperies made a splendid background for powder and diamonds, brilliant eyes and complexion; and her visitors, who noticed Mrs. Fermor's preference for this particular table, were wont to ascribe the choice to vanity.

The game affected at that time, and in that particular circle was an improvement, or at least a modification of faro. Challoner, as deputy host, took the bank and did his utmost to keep the play low: such play as would have provoked the scorn of those fine gentlemen Horace Walpole writes about, who could make love at one end of the room, while they were risking thousands on the turn of a card at the other end. Sibylla's luck seemed to have passed to her lover. Moderate as the play was, his winnings were not altogether despicable. He handed them to his mistress, to dispose of among those insatiable creditors who made her life a burden.

"Another sop for Cerberus," she would say, laughingly, as she put his money in her apron pocket. "You really ought to play a bolder game, since Fortune is so kind to you."

"I doubt I am wise to play at all, Sibylla; for after all it is only letting you gamble behind a mask."

"Pshaw, child, somebody must play for politeness' sake; or people would leave off coming to my house. They would fancy themselves reproved by my self-denial. No, as long as I have my 'day' and my 'evening' in this Court suburb, somebody must make my house pleasant."

She teased her lover until one night he consented to play high, still at her favourite table with the background of voluminous brocade.

A circular mirror, surmounted by a brazen eagle, occupied the only wall space between the amplitude of the curtains; but the candles in the brazen sconces on either side of the glass were never lighted. Mrs. Fermor declared they threw the players' cards into shadow. There were only a pair of candles on each card-table, and people often complained to one another that Mrs. Fermor's drawing room was "too ill-lighted for anything but a *camera obscura.*"

"If the play is to be serious, love, you had best seek some other amusement than to watch my cards," Challoner said, before he took his seat. "Your presence makes all other things seem trivial." "What, may I not be your councillor?" she asked. "I would rather play my own hand."

"As you will," she said, and turned from him with a vexed air, to lavish her attentions upon a witling of seventy, whose conversation so amused her that a ripple of youthful and aged laughter was wafted to Colonel Challoner's ear as he sat at cards, and distracted him greatly. Indeed he soon found that he was no better off for having got rid of his advisor, since his glances were continually wandering towards that distant corner where the ancient jest-maker was lolling across the spinet, looking up at Mrs. Fermor, and where a brace of younger sparks had joined them.

He knew that he was playing wildly, backing weak cards,

doubling the stakes just when he ought not. His luck had turned. "She is my luck," he thought, "and without her I am nothing." He tried to catch her eye; but she did not look his way till the end of the hand, when as he flung his losses on the table, she turned suddenly and looked at him across all the length of the room, as if the jingle of his guineas had attracted her.

He beckoned her with a look. She left her friends instantly and came gliding to his elbow.

"Well," she whispered, "have you lost much?"

"Only a month's pay, not worth speaking of so long as you are pleased."

"I am not pleased. You should let me advise you. Fairy Good-luck was not at your christening."

She established herself in her old place, hung over his chair, cut the cards for him, and with a pretty impetuous movement flung the cards that were done with from the table to the floor. The perfumes that hung about her lace and frippery, the ivory whiteness of her arm, the tapering hand, the music of her *sotto voce* speech, these were the ingredients in the intoxicating cup which she brewed for him nightly. He was not master of his wits, he was not master of himself, when she hung over him, when her hair touched his brow and her breath fluttered on his cheek; and he scarcely knew what he dealt or to whom he dealt, scarcely knew whether he was winning or losing, had but one desire, one impulse, and that was to draw the lovely head down to his breast and lose himself in the witchcraft of her kisses.

The game was played with two packs shuffled together, and the banker might have the cards cut by whomsoever he chose; by the black footman handing chocolate if he thought Blackie would bring him luck. Colonel Challoner's luck was at his el-bow, in the dazzling white hand which scarce needed the spar-kle of diamonds—the restless, impetuous hand, which swooped upon the cards like a white bird, quick and eager. It was growing late, and pack after pack had been thrown down since the game began, till the floor about the table was scattered thick with cards. The losers had begun to look at their watches and yawn ostentatiously. The bank was winning steadily, when one of the men who had been losing cried out:

"I protest against that Queen of Hearts. It is the third time that has been played since the pack was cut. I swear 'tis not the first time I have suspected an interloping honour. No wonder you are so fortunate a banker, Colonel Challoner. Some good fairy doctors your cards. I'll wager that previous packs will prove as rich in winning cards as the last Mrs. Fermor flung on the floor; if anyone will take the trouble to hunt for them."

If anyone will take the trouble? All the losing players were down on their knees within the next minute, gathering up the scattered cards, counting, sorting, arranging. And oh! that terrible array of honours, damning evidence of somebody's dishonour, which Sir Lomax Treherne, the man who had given the alarm, laid out on the card-table. A King of Spades not accounted for; an Ace of Diamonds not accounted for; and so on; and so on. The packs which had been gathered up and sorted were complete without those cards.

Colonel Challoner stood in the midst of the excited babblers, white as marble, silent, till the last card had been picked up.

"This matter concerns you and me primarily, Sir Lomax," he said, "and I think we can settle it without any fuss. My friend shall wait upon you."

He walked out of the room without another word, without one look at the woman who stood with her powdered head against the blue and gold brocade, her tall slim figure leaning against the curtained wall, smiling at the company with tremulous lips, that convulsive smile accentuated by carmine, fanning herself vehemently, and saying over and over again:

"'Tis all vastly absurd. I protest not one of you knows how to count a pack of cards."

★ ★ ★ ★ ★

Mrs. Fermor's black footman had little rest that night; but was kept trudging about upon his lady's service. He carried a letter to Colonel Challoner's suburban lodging, and was told there was no answer; but on going back to his mistress she stormed at him, wrote another

289

letter, longer, more passionate than the last, and despatched him again, bidding him not to return to her without Colonel Challoner's reply, if he valued his life.

"I shall kill you if you come back empty-handed," she cried.

Day was dawning when he brought his mistress Challoner's letter, for which he had waited more than an hour, sitting in darkness on a bench in the entrance hall in a fashionable lodging-house on the Green. Mrs. Fermor's hands shook as she broke the seal, and her scowling brow told poor Scipio that she was not much better pleased with her lover's letter than she had been by his silence. She stared at the letter with heaving breast and quivering lips, then crushed the paper suddenly, and turned on the weary African as if he had offended her.

"Go to bed, fool!" she said. "But be sure you are up and dressed before eight o'clock, and ready to go on an errand."

It was now five, a summer morning, and the birds were singing in the hawthorn and lilacs that screened Mrs. Fermor's garden from the High Road. She snatched up her hood, with a sudden design of going to her lover's lodgings to fling her arms about his neck and hold him back from death, as Circe might have held him; for though his letter contained nothing but an icy farewell, she knew that a duel between him and Treherne was inevitable. She would have gone to him, secure in her power to mould him to her will, but as she stopped automatically before her looking-glass to put on her hood, the reflection she saw there in the clear morning light made her change her mind. Was that haggard countenance, plastered with white lead and ceruse, with drawn features and purple lips, a face to work Circean spells? To see her as she looked this morning in the searching eastern light would be enough to break love's spell at its strongest. No, she would not try to see him. She would write to him again, and again, and again—passionate protestations of love, piteous entreaties, fervid words blotted with her tears. Could he resist such an appeal?

"For my sake, for my sake, refuse to meet the man. Tell him that I, and I alone was the cheat; that you have done with me forever. I care not what shame I have to endure. I can hide myself from the world: turn Papist and bury myself alive in a Convent; but, oh! if you have a spark of mercy in your nature, let me not suffer the agony of knowing that I killed you—that you flung away your life because of my sin. My love, my husband that was to be, have pity upon me. I will never ask to see you again, if you would have it so. Live a stranger to me, if you will; only live, live, live, and save the woman who adores you from madness."

Those were the closing sentences of a long letter, a letter of passionate reiteration: such a letter as distracted women write, drowning meaning in a torrent of wild words, a letter which generally fails in its purpose.

Scipio carried the letter to Challoner's lodgings at eight o'clock, and brought home the fatal news. Colonel Challoner had left the house in a coach at half-past seven, with two other gentlemen. He had been heard to tell the coachman to drive to Ham Common.

Mrs. Fermor went about the house all day smiling and talking to herself, as she had talked to her departing guests last night. "So vastly absurd! Was there ever such a ridiculous mistake?" Dear Mrs. Fermor could not conceive that she tampered with the cards. If there were too many honours it was the card-maker's error. The cards came into her house in sealed packets, and she never touched them until the game began. She still smiled her strange artificial smile, still talked to herself or to any rare visitor in the same strain; long after Colonel Challoner had been lying in Petersham Churchyard, shot through the heart by Sir Lomax Treherne.

★ ★ ★ ★ ★

She was quite mad, but quite harmless. She lived for many years in this piteous condition, and used to walk about Richmond with an attendant, pointed out as the poor lady who had lost her wits after the tragical death of her lover, who had been discovered cheating at cards, and had fallen in the duel which followed that discovery.

Wild Justice

SCENE 1. THE INN YARD

It was two days after the great coming of age ball at Hanbury Manor, and there had been a lull in business and traffic and in the minds of men after that great event, which had given employment to every man, boy, and horse in the little town of Ledford, in the Fens. Masters and servants, men and boys, had yawned through the drowsy tomorrow of the festival, getting up late after coming home in the chill darkness before dawn, half asleep and half drunk some of them. They had got through the broken day in a somnolent and semi-consciousness, relieved by gossip and occasional drinks.

And now work-a-day life was beginning again. The great heiress's coming of age dance was a thing of the past, and the thread of dull daily toil in a dull little town set in the midst of a landscape of level dullness had to be taken up again.

"A fly to be had at Dr. Parker's door in good time for the 11.15 train."

That was the message which came from the bar to the stable yard at nine o'clock on Thursday morning. Coachman, ostler, and lads were washed and wakeful and in their right minds. Miss Hillborough's coming of age belonged to history.

The coachman went to his coach-house. There had been no orders yesterday in the general stagnation. He and his underlings had cleaned three out of the four vehicles which fetched and carried the gentry to and from Ledford and the civilised world; but there was a fourth fly, a spacious and venerable landau, the oldest vehicle on the premises, which had come in about five o'clock in the morning, driven by an occasional helper, and had been dragged ignominiously into a shed, and left to moulder in its dirt.

"Fetch out Noah's ark," said the coachman to his slave, a bare-armed boy whom very few people had ever seen in a coat; "she'll do for Parker. She wasn't cleaned t' other night. Thou'd best gi' her a wash down, lad."

The lad dragged out the leathern monstrosity, which emerged wobbling upon its worn springs. He opened the door with a burst and a tug, pulled out the blue sheepskin rug, and flung it on the ground with a cry that startled everybody in the yard and made the scullery wench look up from her sink yonder by the scullery window. "What's t'row?" "Blood! Mat's all over blood, and bottom o' carriage, too."

The men clustered round. Were those dark stains that steeped and blackened the carpet and the sheepskin rug verily blood? Yes, blood! Wet, still some of it, among the fleecy wool. Wet enough to stain the coachman's hands hideously.

"It's as bad as if somebody had been killing a pig."

"His nose must ha' bled," said the boy, who was a chronic sufferer in that line.

"Noses don't bleed enough to rot a carriage floor," said the coachman, grimly looking round at the eager, awe-stricken faces crowding at the carriage door, open mouths, scared eyes, and a speechless horror everywhere.

"Who was it had this carriage?"

There were enquiries, assertions, contradictions, and finally the head of the livery yard arrived at these facts.

A gentleman had arrived in the station bus late on Tuesday night, the bus that met the last down train; a tall good-looking man, in a long overcoat and a soft felt hat that hid all the upper part of his face. He wanted a fly to take him to the Manor, and the three respectable carriages being all engaged, the old Noah's ark had been dragged out of its penthouse, dusted and made ready for the stranger, who paid his guinea in advance, and who waited in front of the inn while the horse was harnessed, walking about and smoking a cigar.

The man who took his order remembered nothing more about him than this.

The man who drove the fly was an outsider, employed occasionally when there was a press of business at the "George"- an elderly man-of-all-work, out of a place after the death of an old mistress, in whose service he had been gardener, groom and coachman—a man who, while professing general handiness, did nothing well, and was, moreover, not without suspicion of inebriety.

"Dorks drove, did he?" said the landlord of the George, brought from his bar parlour by the clamour in the yard, "and of course, Dorks was drunk."

No dissentient voice pleaded for Dorks. Who could doubt that on an occasion of general relaxation Dorks would have had more than his proper share of alcohol?

One of the boys was sent to fetch Dorks from the cottage where he lodged in inglorious idleness, interrupted by odd jobs. He came looking half asleep, and less than half washed, and this was the burden of his tale.

Yes, he had driven the stranger to Hanbury, and the stranger had gone in among the rest of the visitors. Dorks had seen the footman taking off his coat in the hall. It was late, and there were people coming away, and very few going in. He told Dorks to wait for him. When Dorks suggested that much waiting might be injurious to the horse, the stranger used bad language about that respectable animal, and repeated that Dorks was to wait for him in the avenue. "I'll send for you, or come to you when I want you," said the stranger.

After this Dorks waited—it might be an hour, it might be two, or indeed as evidenced by the time of his return to the George it must have been at least three hours—but the coldness of the night air had induced slumber, and Dorks confessed that his mind had been a blank till he was startled by the stranger opening the door of the landau.

He had just time to see that another gentleman got into the carriage before the rightful fare, who told him to look sharp and drive to Fairfield.

"You know your way there, I suppose?" said the stranger, and another voice came from the inside of the carriage directing him.

"I told him I know'd the way before either of them was born," said Dorks.

Fairfield was a village on a cross road between Ledford and the nearest market town. To pass by Fairfield on the way back to the George Inn would lengthen the journey by about two miles.

The road from Hanbury Manor to Fairfield was as bad a road as could be found in that part of Lincolnshire. It crossed one of the dreariest bits of that dreary district—a broad ditch on one side, open and unguarded, a copse on the other, habitations few and far between—a deep stream and a wooden bridge to be crossed—a bridge that was generally out of order, and on which many a horse and cart had come to grief.

It was dismal in broad daylight, what of gloom and loneliness might not brood over the long monotonous level in the dark grey interlude betwixt night and morning, when one ragged rip in the low eastern sky adds to the sense of dullness by that pallid suggestion of a day that seems immeasurably remote.

Dorks, not particularly sensitive or impressionable, shuddered as he recalled that long cold drive.

He thought they were having high words inside, but he couldn't hear much, for there were stones newly put down for half a mile on the Hanbury side of the stream, and the carriage made too much noise for him to hear what was going on inside of it. Once he fancied there was a bit of a scuffle, for the carriage jolted more than it need have done, even over that rough bit of road. He had no doubt both gentlemen had taken a drop, and they were a little quarrelsome; but his business was to watch his horse and take care he didn't pull them all into the ditch; that horse was a bad one for bearing to the left, and wanted a deal of driving.

"Driving!" cried the landlord, losing patience, albeit eager to hear all that Dorks could tell. "Why you don't know the meaning of the word. You never drove a horse in your life. Well, go on, can't you, and tell your story a little straighter than you drive, or we shan't hear the end of it this side of dinner."

There was a laugh at this—a laugh that relieved overcharged bosoms, weighed down by the silent horror of those dark stains in the carriage. What a fine gentleman was this landlord of the George, who could jest in the face of the most gruesome suggestions.

"There ain't much more to tell," growled Dorks, waxing surly, "one of the gents, him as hired the fly, called to me to stop, just arter we crossed the bridge, and got out. 'Get back to your stable as fast as you like,' says he; 'I'm a going to walk with my friend.' "

"Was the other man with him when he spoke?"

"Not unless he was inwisible. I never laid eyes on him from the time he got into the carriage in the avenue."

★ ★ ★ ★ ★

Nothing came of those ugly stains in the old landau, that dark and ghastly pool which had soaked through the floor in the carriage.

The local policeman came, and scrutinised and listened, and asked questions. He tried to look wise, but could make nothing of it, inclined to think it a case of nose bleeding. The gentlemen were in liquor, had come to blows, and one had suffered severely in the fray, but not mortally.

To satisfy the doubts of the innkeeper and the doctor, this authority walked over the ground by which the fly had driven, accompanied by Dorks, to show where it was he had felt the carriage lurching and jolting more than usual—where his fare had alighted and left him.

The innkeeper went with them on this detective expedition, but neither he nor the constable could extract any exact information from Dorks, who admitted, when hard pressed, that he had been more than half asleep while they were going over the stones, and that he had only been thoroughly awakened when the stranger called to him to stop.

Whatever drops of blood might have oozed from the carriage to the road had been washed away in the muddy drift, after a long day of autumnal rain. Whatever secret the dyke could have told them there was no clue to point the spot where it lay, and the constable, relying on his own theory, proposed no further investigation.

"If them there stains means murder, why there'll be a reward offered, and then it will be time enough for you and me to come forward and tell what we know about this here business," said the constable, eagerly appointing himself partner in the discovery made at the George. "But I don't believe there's no harm done, Mr. Jocock, except to your carriage," he told the landlord; and the landlord shook his head, and went home burdened with unsatisfied doubts, which he discussed with his wife, over an old-fashioned night-cap of fierce brandy and water, "Hot with," which fiery mixture he stirred with a miniature glass baton instead of a spoon.

"It bothers me, Jane," he told his wife, "and I feel as if I should have to burn that old landau, though it's a useful conveyance for family work. Painting the bottom, and putting in a new rug, which will run to a pound at least, won't do away with the uncomfortableness of it."

"Lor', Tom, why should you bother about it? If there was anything wrong—anybody hurt—or anybody missing, shouldn't we have heard of it before now?"

"Well, I suppose we should, my girl. News do fly about so fast nowadays. I don't say as there's anything remarkable in a stranger coming at close upon twelve o'clock at night, to go to the ball at the Manor. There must have been plenty of strangers there, but where was he going to put up for the night? and who could the other man have been; and how was it Dorks only saw one man leave the carriage and walk away?"

"Why, because Dorks was as per usual," replied his spouse smartly; "the wonder is he didn't see four men. And as to where the gentlemen were going, why, to Fairfield, of course, where they were on a visit to friends, as the way is when there's a ball in the neighbourhood."

"Ah, but where now? From the style of the gent that paid for the landau, they would be a cut above visiting in a farmer's house. And except farmers and the parson, there's nobody at Fairfield."

"Well, then, they were going to the Vicarage. Why not?"

"Ah, why not?" echoed the landlord, relieved but not convinced. "If I was acquainted with Mr. Challoner, I should go and ask him all about it."

SCENE 2. THE BAR-PARLOUR.

There was nobody missing—no hint of a mysterious disappearance in the neighbourhood of Ledford. Certainly there was no hint of trouble at Fairfield Vicarage, as the landlord of the George discovered by a side-wind, before his mind was at rest.

The landlord's next-door neighbour was Tyley, the baker, whose daughter was parlour-maid at the Vicarage, and this young person, taking her afternoon out and dropping in at the George to see her old school fellow, the landlord's daughter, was warmly pressed to stay to tea in the bar-parlour.

While enjoying Mr. Jocock's hospitality, and in reply to his questioning, she told him that there was nothing in the way of trouble in her master's house, and that the young ladies were all as merry as grigs. "Did any of you go to the ball t'other night?" asked the landlord. "None of us went; our young ladies are not 'out,'" the parlour-maid answered grandly, having educated herself by dinner-table talk; "but master's nephew went."

"Oh," said the landlord, "that good-looking young chap that was at the vicarage last Easter. What may he be now?"

"He's a barrister up in London."

"Oh, so he went up to the ball, did he? What time may he have got home?"

"Well, he didn't come back to the Vicarage. He met a friend at the Manor, and they went up to London together by the early train—the one that leaves soon after five."

"The 5.25 up?" assented the landlord. "That was rather a queer start, wasn't it?"

"Oh, I don't know. Mr. Desborough was always a bit wild in his ways; late in the morning, late at night, late for dinner. 'Ratick, the vicar used to call him. 'Harold is dreadfully 'ratick,' I've heard master say times and often. He telegraphed to my mistress next day to apologise for giving trouble. But there was nobody sitting up for him. The hall door key was hidden under a laurel bush where he'd be able to find it."

"Oh, he telegraphed, did he? He ain't written to your missus since, I'll lay," said the landlord, rubbing a whisker with a meditative movement of a large fat hand.

"No, he ain't much of a one to write letters. He was always one to telegraph, never troubling that every telegram costs a shilling for the messenger." The landlord had lapsed into deepest thought by this time. "Ah, you seem to know all about this here young gent, Mariar," he said, after a longish pause. "I suppose he was rather attentive to you, now?"

"Never to me," answered Maria promptly. "He held his head much too high for that. But he was very attentive to someone in our house."

"Come, Mariar, it couldn't have been your missus. She's a handsome woman still, but there's too much of her to take a young man's fancy."

"*In the spring a young man's fancy lightly turns to thoughts of love,*" quoted Maria, from the fourth standard reading book. "It was the spring when Mr. Desborough was staying at the Vicarage, and him and the young ladies and the governess was—"

"What, that sandy-haired young 'ooman with short petticoats and flat feet. He must have been uncommon high if he preferred her to you, my lass."

"No! no, Mr. Jocock. That sandy young person is Miss Pepper. She's only been with us six weeks. It was Miss Heron that used to be about with Mr. Desborough. Miss Heron is very pretty, a delicate little thing with dark eyes, and very young looking. She never told her age to any of us servants, but I don't believe she was out of her teens."

"So there was a bit of a flirtation between them two," said the landlord.

"It was more than flirtation, I'm afraid. I believe she was half heart-broken when he went away, poor thing, though she never let anybody see she was fretting—except a servant like me. Sometimes when I went into her room with the water for her bath of a morning, I could see by her poor pale face and red eyelids that she'd been awake half the night and had cried herself to sleep. But she would come downstairs an hour afterwards looking fresh and light, and as neat as a new pin. She's a young lady that knows how to respect herself."

"Why did she leave her situation?"

"Her health gave way. It's not what you can call an easy place—four strong, active girls to teach, and look after, and walk out with, and expected to mend their under-linen into the bargain. She got through the work well enough for the first six months, and she was a real good worker, never idle for a quarter of an hour, always active, and bright and ready to run about with the children just like one of themselves. But after that young man had left us she gave way; and one day when the children had all been very naughty about their lessons, and Mrs. Challoner was cross to her at lunch, making out that it was her fault, she burst into tears and ran away from the table, and when missus sent me to look after her, I found her running down the shrubbery walk like a wild thing, and she threw herself on the seat in the summer house in a fit of the violentest hysterics I ever saw—and I've seen many a fit of hysterics, and had 'em too, dreadful bad."

"Poor thing," replied the landlord, "I'm afraid it's the old story—a silly young woman and a double-faced young man."

"Oh, I hope not," said the girl, with a shocked look. "She was such a little lady. I never heard her speak a vulgar word; and so neat, so pretty in all her ways—everything about her from her comb-bag to her umbrella quite the lady—and religious too—her *New Testament* on the table by her bed. And she read it too, every morning. No, I couldn't think any harm of her."

"The harm wouldn't be in her but in him, Mariar. Nobody thinks any harm of the lamb, it's the butcher we hate."

SCENE 3. THE VICARAGE

"That foolish woman has sent Harold's letters back—the packet I sent him last Tuesday—and ever so many more, John," Mrs. Challoner said to her husband, on the morning after Maria's conversational tea-drinking at the George. "He is evidently not at his chambers. Poor fellow, I daresay he finds life very dreary there, without the prospect of a brief!"

"He ought to sit in his room and read law till the briefs come," said the vicar, grimly. "I found my first curacy very dreary, but I didn't cut it till I got something better. I'm afraid that young man will never do any good; he's too fond of himself."

"I'm afraid his smart friends spoil him. He is so good-looking—and so altogether nice. The world is too crowded for that kind of thing. Nobody is really wanted; nobody is ever missed."

"Nonsense, Lucy. Nobody spoils anybody in London. A young man of Harold's calibre lives in a fool's paradise. He looks in his glass and thinks he is such a pretty fellow that the world can't do without him."

"It's very worrying to have these letters sent back," moaned Mrs. Challoner. "I don't know what I ought to do with them."

"Keep them till he turns up here, or send them to the dead letter office," answered the vicar, as he went off to his poultry yard, thinking a great deal more of some new Chochin Chinas than of his nephew.

He was not very fond of that good-looking, high-handed nephew—a young man who made it so unpleasantly clear that he felt his superiority to his surroundings, especially when those surroundings were limited to a rural vicarage and a dinner table served by a parlour-maid and her attendant sylph from upstairs.

He had a shrewd idea, too, that there had been some fooling of that pretty little governess—the nice, little, motherless girl whose father was keeping sheep on the other side of the world, working to make a home for his only daughter in another hemisphere. Yes, the vicar feared there had been some fooling; trivial enough and innocent enough, no doubt; but bad for the poor, pretty, little thing, who looked paler and lost her happy smile after Desborough's visit.

Mrs. Challoner made an inclusive packet of Desborough's letters and posted it to his Temple address, with a line on the envelope—

"Mr. Desborough has left Fairfield. Keep letters till you hear from him."

Two days later there came a laborious, epistolary effort from the laundress.

Honerred Madamm,—Your nevew not bean hat is roomes sense he pade yew a vesset, I doan no wot to do abowt hes leters or thinks. Peepel kawls and arsts four hem, and 1 gent ad a napintmint and wors verry putt hout hat nott fynden hem. Mi weaks kash nott to 'and as korsed ilcawnwenence wich mi 'usband's hilnes maks worst, hand munny lade howt likways,—Your 'umble survent,

Mrs. Tilton.

The unexplained absence of a briefless barrister from his chambers might in some cases occasion anxiety; but having long ago summed up his nephew's character and conduct as erratic Mr. Challoner was not easily alarmed. He was going to London in a week or two; so he sent the distressed laundress a sovereign on his nephew's account, and told her he would call at the chambers in about a fortnight, by which time Mr. Desborough would no doubt have returned.

Even the fact that he had not sent for his luggage awakened no unpleasant suspicions, for the luggage consisted only of a good-sized Gladstone bag containing the young man's night gear, and the suit of clothes in which he had arrived at the Vicarage. He had come for a couple of nights only, on purpose for the heiress's ball.

Scene 4. The Manor House

On the very day she received the letter from the laundress Mrs. Challoner made her ceremonial call at the Manor, the visit of a lady who had been invited to an entertainment, and who, having refused the invitation, deemed herself not the less beholden.

"What good shall I be at a dance, Laura?" she said, when Miss Hanbury reproached her for her absence. "I am not wanted as a chaperon while my girls are in the nursery. I could only be a useless consumer of the atmosphere."

"Oh, but we had plenty of atmosphere. We could have spared you the proper allowance or cubic feet, and we had nice rooms and comfortable chairs for our non-dancing friends. I was dreadfully disappointed at not having you and the vicar."

Miss Hanbury was almost alone in the world, and had all the

independence of a young woman brought up by governesses and trustees, and never having known parental authority.

"You had our nephew, and he is a good dancer. I think you had the best of the bargain," said Mrs. Challoner, smilingly.

There had been playful odds and ends of flirtation between the heiress and Harold, and it was the vicar's opinion that the young man, by taking pains, might make himself partner in Miss Hanbury's splendid fortune; but then, this young man was a person who never could be depended on to take pains about anything, a young man so bereft of common sense that he was not even desirous of marrying an heiress.

"Your nephew was very little use to us," the young lady answered, blushing a little as she spoke of him; "for after two or three dances he contrived to elude us all. Mummie ran after him," smiling at the faithful old governess, "and I scolded him, but he wouldn't let me lead him to the sacrifice, though there were really pretty girls sitting smiling at vacancy and waiting for partners; girls in new frocks ordered on purpose for my ball. I felt myself responsible."

"That is not like Harold," said Mrs. Challoner.

"No, it ain't a bit like him. I'm afraid he was feeling awfully ill. I don't think he liked that friend of his coming uninvited, though he said it was quite in accord with Colonial manners."

"A friend of Harold's at your dance!"

"Yes, somebody from Australia—Queensland, I think he said. I forget the person's name—indeed I don't think I heard it properly, for Mr. Desborough looked rather flurried when he introduced him and didn't speak very distinctly. A tall, handsome looking man, sunburnt, middle-aged. No doubt you know him?"

"I don't think I do. I don't recall any Colonial friend of Harold's."

"No? Well, it don't matter a bit, only I'm afraid his appearance in that—Colonial—way, spoilt your nephew's evening. They sat in the conservatory together talking."

"They were in the supper room together, and I'm told the Colonial gentleman drank half a bottle of brandy," said the old governess, without looking up from her knitting.

"Butler's gossip, Mummie. You oughtn't to listen to such nonsense," remonstrated Miss Hanbury.

Mrs. Challoner was stricken with shame. Her nephew's appearances at me ball which should have been a turning-point in his destiny—which might, ought, could, should have led to such a grand result—had been a *fiasco*. He had introduced a brandy-drinking Australian. How could Harold have done such a thing?

"I can't imagine who the man could be, or what could have induced Harold to take such a liberty," she said, with troubled brow.

"Oh, but it wasn't Mr. Desborough's liberty. Pray don't worry about it, dear Mrs. Challoner; and don't on any account mention the nonsense to your nephew when you next see him. The man was evidently an old acquaintance. I did not see them go, but I am told they left together. There was something rather grand in the man's appearance, and he looked anything but a vulgarian!"

"Still it was a great impertinence."

"No, no, no, dear Mrs. Challoner, only Colonial."

★ ★ ★ ★ ★

The vicar went to London in the following week. Nothing had been heard of Harold Desborough at his chambers. No one whom the vicar knew, or knew of, in London, as an acquaintance of his nephew's, had seen the young man since the date of Miss Hanbury's ball. Nor to this day has the young man been seen or heard of at Fairfield or in London.

Investigations were made. The landlord of the George told all he had to tell of the hiring of the fly overnight, and the ghastly condition in which it was found afterwards. The driver's story was told, and the dyke was searched for the missing man, but besides the mile and a half of dyke that bordered the road, there was the wide expanse of fen beyond it, and there was the running water below the bridge with many a deep hole where murder might lie hidden till the day of judgement.

The vicar and his wife tried to persuade themselves that Harold Desborough had for some sufficient reason chosen to abandon his friends and country and had accompanied the unknown guest of the ball to the other side of the world. The fact that he had left all his goods and chattels in his chambers might prove nothing except that this disappearance was of the nature of a flight. He had done something —got himself entangled in some financial web—gambling, bill-discounting, who knows?

"Harold was always erratic."

And the ghastly witness of the carriage? A quarrel, a scuffle—an accident of no importance, perhaps.

EPILOGUE

From James Heron, Brisbane, to Sir John Blake, Barberry, Hereford.

Dear Sir John,

Do not think me ungrateful for leaving England without see-ing you and Lady Blake, or thanking you in person for your goodness to my poor girl. I was only three weeks in my na-tive country, where everything looked strange and unfriendly, and where I was too unhappy to meet the face of an old friend.

I found my daughter—alone—in a London lodging, broken-hearted, a life spoilt, a name blighted. Not your fault, my good friend, nor Lady Blake's. You both did all that friendship could do when you transferred my poor child from the excellent school where she was happy and well-cared for to the country vicarage, where she would have been just as happy, and just as safe, if it had not been for—

Perhaps you guess the rest, which I can't write.

You know something of my temper, and something of my views about the right of every man to settle certain debts in his own way.

The man who broke her heart will break no more hearts.

She knows nothing except that she is here in a new world with a father who idolises her, and whose sole task in life henceforth is to make her forget the past.

God bless you and yours,
Goodbye,
J.H.

Herself

CHAPTER 1

"And you intend to keep the Orange Grove for your own occupation, Madam," interrogates the lawyer gravely, with his downward-looking eyes completely hidden under bushy brows.

"Decidedly," answered my friend. "Why, the Orange Grove is the very best part of my fortune. It seems almost a special Providence, don't you know, Helen," pursued Lota, turning to me, "that my dear old grandfather should have made himself a winter home in the south. There are the doctors always teasing me about my weak chest, and there is a lonely house and gardens and orange groves waiting for me in a climate invented on purpose for weak chests. I shall live there every winter of my life, Mr. Dean."

The eminently respectable solicitor allowed a lapse of silence before he replied.

"It is not a lucky house, Miss Hammond."

"How not lucky?"

"Your grandfather only lived to spend one winter in it. He was in very good health when he went there in December—a strong, sturdy old man—and when he sent for me in February to prepare the will which made you his sole heiress, I was shocked at the change in him—broken—wasted—nerves shattered—a mere wreck."

"That was very sad; but surely you would not blame a lovely villa in Italy," smiling down at a photograph in her lap, the picture of the typical southern villa, French windows, verandah, balconies, tower, terraces, garden, and fountain, "for the sudden break-up of an elderly constitution. I have heard that old men of very active habits and a hardy way of living, like my dear old grandfather, are apt to grow old suddenly."

"It was not merely that he was aged—he was mentally changed—nervous, restless, to all appearance unhappy."

"Well, didn't you ask him why?" demanded Lota, whose impetuous temper was beginning to revolt against the lawyer's solemnity.

"My position hardly warranted my questioning Mr. Hammond on a matter so purely personal. I saw the change, and regretted it. Six weeks later he was gone."

Poor old gran'pa. We were such friends when I was a little thing. And then they sent me to Germany with a governess-poor little motherless mite—and then they packed me off to Pekin where father was Consul and there he died, and then they sent me home again—and I was taken up by the smartest of all my aunts, and had my little plunge in society,

and always exceeded my allowance; was up to my eyes in debt—for a girl. I suppose a man would hardly count such bills as I used to owe. And then gran'pa took it into his head to be pleased with me; and here I am—residuary legatee. I think that's what you call me?" with an interrogative glance at the lawyer, who nodded a grave assent, "and I am going to spend the winter months in my villa near Taggia. Only think of that, Helen, Taggia—Tag-gi-a!"

She syllabled the word slowly, ending with a little smack of her pretty lips as if it were something nice to eat, and she looked at me for sympathy.

"I haven't the faintest idea what you mean by Tag-gi-a," said I. "It sounds like an African word."

"Surely you have read Dr. Antonio."

"Surely I have not."

"Then I have done with you. There is a gulf between us. All that I know of the Liguria comes out of that delightful book. It taught me to pine for the shores of the Mediterranean when I was quite a little thing. And they show you Dr. Ruffini's house at Taggia. His actual house, where he actually lived."

"You ought to consider, Miss Hammond, that the Riviera has changed a good deal since Ruffini's time," said the lawyer. "Not that I have anything to say against the Riviera *per se*. All I would advise is that you should winter in a more convenient locality than a romantic gorge between San Remo and Alassio. I would suggest Nice, for instance."

"Nice. Why, someone was saying only the other day that Nice is the chosen rendezvous of all the worst characters in Europe and America."

"Perhaps that's what makes it such an agreeable place," said the lawyer. "There are circles and circles in Nice. You need never breathe the same atmosphere as the bad characters."

"A huge towny place," exclaimed Lota. "Gran'pa said it was not better than Brighton."

"Could anything be better than Brighton?" asked I.

"Helen, you were always a Philistine. It was because of the horridness of Nice and Cannes that gran'pa bought a villa—four times too big for him—in this romantic spot."

She kissed the white house in the photograph. She gloated over the wildness of the landscape, in which the villa stood out, solitary, majestic. Palms, olives, cypress—a deep gorge cutting through the heart of the picture—mountains romantically re-mote—one white crest in the furthest distance—a foreground of tumbled crags and threads of running water.

"Is it really real?" she asked suddenly, "not a photographer's painted background? They have such odious tricks, those pho-tographers. One sits for one's picture in a tidy South Kensington studio, and they send one home smirking out of a primeval for-est, or in front of a stormy ocean. Is it real?"

"Absolutely real."

"Very well, Mr. Dean. Then I am going to establish myself there in the first week of December, and if you want to be very careful of me for gran'pa's sake all you have to do is to find me a thoroughly respectable *major-domo*, who won't drink my wine or run away with my plate. My aunt will engage the rest of my people."

"My dear young lady, you may command any poor services of mine; but really now, is it not sheer perversity to choose a rambling house in a wild part of the country when your ample means would allow you to hire the prettiest *bijou*-villa on the Riviera?"

"I hate *bijou* houses, always too small for anybody except some sour old maid who wants to over-hear all her servants say about her. The spacious rambling house—the wild solitary landscape—those are what I want, Mr. Dean. Get me a butler who won't cut my throat, and I ask no more."

"Then madam, I have done. A wilful woman must have her way, even when it is a foolish way."

"Everything in life is foolish," Lota answered, lightly. "The people who live haphazard come out just as well at the end as your ineffable wiseacres. And now that you know I am fixed as fate, that nothing you can say will unbend my iron will, do, like a darling old family lawyer whom I have known ever since I began to know one face from another, do tell me why you object to the Orange Grove. Is it the drainage?"

"There is no drainage."

"Then that's all right," checking it off on her forefinger. "Is it the neighbours?"

"Need I say there are no neighbours?" pointing to the photograph.

"Number two satisfactory."

"Is it the atmosphere? Low the villa is not; damp it can hardly be, perched on the side of a hill."

"I believe the back rooms are damp. The hill side comes too near the windows. The back rooms are decidedly gloomy, and I believe damp."

"And how many rooms are there in all?"

"Nearer thirty than twenty. I repeat it is a great rambling house, ever so much too large for you or any sensible young lady."

"For the sensible young lady, no doubt," said Lota, nodding impertinently at me. "She likes a first floor in Regency Square, Brighton, with a little room under the tiles for her maid. I am not sensible, and I like lots of rooms; rooms to roam about in, to furnish and unfurnish, and arrange and rearrange; rooms to see ghosts in. And now, dearest Mr. Dean, I am going to pluck out the heart of your mystery. What kind of ghost is it that haunts the Orange Grove? I know there is a ghost."

"Who told you so?"

"You. You have been telling me so for the last half-hour. It is because of the ghost you don't want me to go to the Orange Grove. You might just as well be candid and tell me the whole story. I am not afraid of ghosts. In fact, I rather like the idea of having a ghost on my property. Wouldn't you Helen, if you had property?"

"No," I answered, decisively. "I hate ghosts. They are always associated with damp houses and bad drainage. I don't believe you would find a ghost in Brighton, not even if you advertised for one."

"Tell me all about the ghost," urged Lota.

"There is nothing to tell. Neither the people in the neighbourhood nor the servants of the house went so far as to say the Orange Grove was haunted. The utmost assertion was that time out of mind the master or the mistress of that house had been miserable."

"Time out of mind. Why, I thought gran'pa built the house twenty years ago."

"He only added the front which you see in the photograph. The back part of the house, the larger part, is three hundred years ago. The place was a monkish hospital, the infirmary belonging to a Benedictine monastery in the neighbourhood, and to which the sick from other Benedictine houses were sent."

"Oh, that was ages and ages ago. You don't suppose that the ghosts of all the sick monks, who were so inconsiderate as to die in my house, haunt the rooms at the back?"

"I say again, Miss Hammond, nobody has ever to my knowl-

310

edge asserted that the house was haunted."

"Then it can't be haunted. If it were the servants would have seen something. They are champion ghost-seers."

"I am not a believer in ghosts, Miss Hammond," said the friendly old lawyer; "but I own to a grain of superstition on one point. I can't help thinking there is such a thing as 'luck.' I have seen such marked distinctions between the lucky and unlucky people I have met in my professional career. Now, the Orange Grove has been an unlucky house for the last hundred years. It's bad luck is as old as its history. And why, in the name of all that's reasonable, should a beautiful young lady with all the world to choose from insist upon living at the Orange Grove?"

"First, because it is my own house; next, because I conceived a passion for it the moment I saw this photograph; and thirdly, perhaps

because your opposition has given a zest to the whole thing. I shall establish myself there next December, and you must come out to me after Christmas, Helen. Your beloved Brighton is odious in February and March."

"Brighton is always delightful," answered I, "but of course I shall be charmed to go to you."

Chapter 2. An Earthly Paradise

I was Lota's dearest friend, and she was mine. I had never seen anyone quite so pretty, or quite so fascinating then: I have never seen anyone as pretty or as fascinating since. She was no Helen, no Cleopatra, no superbly modelled specimen of typical loveliness. She was only herself. Like no one else, and to my mind better than everybody else—a delicately-wrought ethereal creature, all spirit and fire and impulse and affection, flinging herself with ardour into every pursuit, living intensely in the present, curiously reckless of the future, curiously forgetful of the past.

When I parted with her at Charing Cross Station on the first of December it was understood that I was to join her about the middle of January. One of my uncles was going to Italy at that time, and was to escort me to Taggia, where I was to be met by my hostess. I was surprised, therefore, when a telegram arrived before Christmas, entreating me to go to her at once.

I telegraphed back: "Are you ill?"

Answer: "Not ill; but I want you."

My reply: "Impossible. Will go as arranged."

I would have given much, as I told Lota in the letter that followed my last message, to have done what she wished; but family claims were too strong. A brother was to marry at the beginning of the year, and I should have been thought heartless had I shirked the ceremony. And there was the old idea of Christmas as a time for family gatherings. Had she been ill, or unhappy, I would have cancelled every other claim, and gone to her without one hour's delay, I told her; but I knew her a creature of caprices, and this was doubtless only one caprice among many.

I knew that she was well cared for. She had a maiden aunt with her, the mildest and sweetest of spinsters, who absolutely adored her. She had her old nurse and slave, a West Indian half-caste, who had accompanied her from Pekin, and she had—"Another, and a dearer one still."

Captain Holbrook, of the Stonyshere Regiment, was at San Remo. I had seen his name in a travelling note in the *World*, and I smiled as I read the announcement, and thought how few of his acquaintance would know as well as I knew the magnet which attracted him to quit San Remo rather than to Monte Carlo or Nice. I knew that he loved Violetta Hammond devotedly, and that she had played fast and loose with him, amused at his worship, accepting all his attentions in her light happy manner, and giving no heed to the future.

Yes, my pretty, *insouciante* Lota was well cared for, ringed round with exceeding love, guarded as faithfully as a god in an Indian temple. I had no uneasiness about her, and I alighted in a very happy frame of mind at the quiet little station at Taggia, beside the tideless sea, in the dusk of a January evening.

Lota was on the platform to welcome me, with Miss Elderson, her maternal aunt, in attendance upon her, the younger lady muffled in sealskin from head to foot.

"Why Lota," said I, when we had kissed, and laughed a little with eyes full of tears, "you are wrapped up as if this were Russia, and to me the air feels balmier than an English April."

"Oh, when one has a hundred guinea coat one may as well wear it," she answered carelessly. "I bought this sealskin among my mourning."

"Lota is chillier than she used to be," said Miss Elderson, in her plaintive voice.

There was a landau with a pair of fine strong horses waiting to carry us up to the villa. The road wound gently upward, past orange and lemon groves, and silvery streamlets, and hanging woods, where velvet dark cypresses rose tower-like amidst the silvery grey of the olives, and so to about midway between the valley, where Taggia's antique palaces and church towers gleamed pale in the dusk, and the crest of the hill along which straggled the white houses of a village. The after-glow was rosy in the sky when a turn of the road brought our faces towards the summer-like sea, and in that lovely light every line in Lota's face was but too distinctly visible.

Too distinctly, for I saw the cruel change which three months had made in her fresh young beauty. She had left me in all the bloom of girlhood, gay, careless, brimming over with the joy of life and the new delight of that freedom of choice which wealth gives to a fatherless and motherless girl. To go where she liked, do as she liked, roam the world over, choosing always the companions she loved—that had been Lota's dream of happiness, and if there had been some touch of self-love in her idea of bliss there had been also a generous and affectionate heart, and unfailing kindness to those whom Fate had not used so kindly.

I saw her now a haggard, anxious-looking woman, the signs of worry written too plainly on the wan pinched face, the lovely eyes larger but paler than of old, and the markings of nervous depression visible in the droop of the lips that had once been like Cupid's bow.

I remembered Mr. Dean's endeavour to dissuade her from occupying her grandfather's villa on this lovely hill, and I began

313

to detest the Orange Grove before I had seen it. I was prepared to find an abode of gloom—a house where the foul miasma from some neighbouring swamp crept in at every open window, and hung grey and chill in every passage; a house whose too obvious unwholesomeness had conjured up images of terror, the spectral forms engendered of slackened nerves, and sleepless nights. I made up my mind that if it were possible for a bold and energetic woman to influence Lota Hammond I would be that woman, and whisk her off to Nice or Monte Carlo before she had time to consider what I was doing.

There would be a capital pretext in the Carnival. I would declare that I had set my heart upon seeing a Carnival at Nice; and once there I would take care she never returned to the place that was killing her. I looked, with a thrill of anger, at the mild sheep-faced aunt. How could she have been so blind as not to perceive the change in her niece? And Captain Holbrook! What a poor creature, to call himself a lover, and let the girl he loved perish before his eyes.

I had time to think while the horses walked slowly up the hill-road, for neither the aunt nor the niece had much to say. Each in her turn pointed out some feature in the view. Lota told me that she adored Taggia, and doted on her villa and garden; and that was the utmost extent of our conversation in the journey of more than an hour.

At last we drove round a sharpish curve, and on the hillside above us, looking down at us from a marble terrace, I saw the prettiest house I had ever seen in my life; a fairy palace, with lighted windows, shining against a back-ground of wooded hills. I could not see the colours of the flowers in the thickening gloom of night, but I could smell the scent of the roses and the fragrant-leaved geraniums that filled the vases on the terrace.

Within and without all was alike sparkling and lightsome; and so far as I could see on the night of my arrival there was not a corner which could have accommodated a ghost. Lota told me that one of her first improvements had been to install the electric light.

"I love to think that this house is shining like a star when the people of Taggia look across the valley," she said.

I told her that I had seen Captain Holbrook's name among the visitors at San Remo.

"He is staying at Taggia now," she said. "He grew rather tired of San Remo."

"The desire to be nearer you had nothing to do with the change?"

"You can ask him if you like," she answered, with something of her old *insouciance*. "He is coming to dinner tonight."

"Does he spend his days and nights going up and down the hill?" I asked.

"You will be able to see for yourself as to that. There is not much for anyone to do in Taggia."

★★★★★

Captain Holbrook found me alone in the salon when he came; for, in spite of the disadvantages of arrival after a long journey, I was dressed before Lota. He was very friendly, and seemed really glad to see me; indeed, he lost no time in saying as much with a plainness of speech which was more friendly than flattering.

"I am heartily glad you have come," he said, "for now I hope we shall be able to get Miss Hammond away from this depressing hole."

Remembering that the house was perched upon the shoulders of a romantic hill, with an outlook of surpassing loveliness, and looking round at the brilliant colouring of an Italian drawing-room steeped in soft clear light, and redolent of roses and carnations, it seemed rather hard measure to hear of Lota's inheritance talked of as "a depressing hole;" but the cruel change in Lota herself was enough to justify the most unqualified dislike of the house in which the change had come to pass.

Miss Elderson and her niece appeared before I could reply, and we went to dinner. The dining-room was as bright and gracious of aspect as all the other rooms which I had seen, everything having been altered and improved to suit Lota's somewhat expensive tastes.

"The villa ought to be pretty," Miss Elderson murmured plaintively, "for Lota's improvements have cost a fortune."

"Life is so short. We ought to make the best of it," said Lota gaily.

We were full of gaiety, and there was the sound of talk and light laughter all through the dinner; but I felt that there was a forced note in our mirth, and my own heart was like lead. We all went back to the drawing-room together. The windows were open to the moonlight, and the faint sighing of the night wind among the olive woods. Lota and her lover established themselves in front of the blazing pine logs, and Miss Elderson asked me if I would like a stroll on the terrace. There were fleecy white shawls lying about ready for casual excursions of this kind, and the good old lady wrapped one about my shoulders with motherly care. I followed her promptly, foreseeing that she was as anxious to talk confidentially with me as I was to talk with her.

My eagerness anticipated her measured speech. "You are unhappy about Lota," I asked.

"Very, very unhappy."

"But why haven't you taken her away from here? You must see that the place is killing her. Or perhaps the dreadful change in her may not strike you, who have been seeing her every day—?"

"It does strike me; the change is too palpable. I see it every morning, see her looking a little worse, a little worse every day, as if some dreadful disease were eating away her life. And yet our good English doctor from San Remo says there is nothing the matter except a slight lung trouble, and that this air is the very finest, the position of this house faultless, for such a case as hers, high enough to be bracing, yet sheltered from all cold winds. He told me that we could take her no better place between Genoa and Marseilles."

"But is she to stop here, and fade, and die? There is some evil influence in this house. Mr. Dean said as much; something horrible, uncanny, mysterious."

"My dear, my dear!" ejaculated the amiable invertebrate creature, shaking her head in solemn reproachfullness, "can you, a good Churchwoman, believe in any nonsense of that sort?"

"I don't know what to believe; but I can see that my dearest friend is perishing bodily and mentally. The three months in which we have been parted have done the work of years of declining health. And she was warned against the house; she was warned."

"There is nothing the matter with the house," that weakbrained spinster answered pettishly. "The sanitary engineer from Cannes has examined everything. The drainage is simply perfect—"

"And your niece is dying!" I said, savagely, and turned my back upon Miss Elderson.

I gazed across the pale grey woods to the sapphire sea, with eyes that scarcely saw the loveliness they looked upon. My heart was swelling with indignation against this feeble affection which would see the thing it loved vanishing off the earth, and yet could not be moved to energetic action.

CHAPTER 3. "SOMETIMES THEY FADE AND DIE"

I tested the strength of my own influence the next day, and I was inclined to be less severe in my judgement of the meek spinster, after a long morning in the woods with Lota and Captain Holbrook, in which all my arguments and entreaties, backed most fervently by an adoring lover, had proved useless.

"I am assured that no place could suit my health better," Lota said, decisively, "and I mean to stay here till my doctor orders me to Varese or home to England. Do you suppose I spent a year's income on the villa with the idea of running away from it? I am tired to death of being teased about the place. First it is auntie, and then it is Captain Holbrook, and now it is young Helen. Villa, gardens, and woods are utterly lovely, and I mean to stay."

"But if you are not happy here?"

"Who says I am not happy?"

"Your face says it, Lota."

"I am just as happy here as I should be anywhere else," she answered, doggedly, "and I mean to stay."

She set her teeth as she finished the sentence, and her face had a look of angry resolve that I had never seen in it before. It seemed as if she were fighting against something, defying something. She rose abruptly from the bank upon which she had been sitting, in a sheltered hollow, near the rocky cleft where a ruined oil mill hung mouldering on the brink of a waterfall; and she began to walk up and down very fast, muttering to herself with frowning brows:

"I shall stay! I shall stay!" I heard her repeating, as she passed me.

★★★★★

After that miserable morning—miserable in a climate and a scene of loveliness where bare existence should have been bliss—I had many serious conversations with Captain Holbrook, who was at the villa every day, the most wonderful and devoted of lovers. From him I learnt all that was known of the house in which I was living. He had taken infinite pains to discover any reason, in the house or the neighbourhood, for the lamentable change in Lota, but with the slightest results. No legend of the supernatural was associated with the Orange Grove; but on being questioned searchingly an old Italian physician who had spent his life at Taggia, and who had known Ruffini, confessed that there was a something, a mysterious something, about the villa which seemed to have affected everybody who lived in it, as owner or master, within the memory of the oldest inhabitant.

"People are not happy there. No, they are not happy, and sometimes they fade and die."

"Invalids who come to the South to die?"

"Not always. The *Signorina's* grandfather was an elderly man; but he appeared in robust health when he came. However, at that age, a sudden break up is by no means wonderful. There were previous instances of decay and death far more appalling, and in some ways mysterious. I am sorry the pretty young lady has spent so much money on the villa."

"What does money matter if she would only go elsewhere?"

She would not. That was the difficulty. No argument of her lover's could move her. She would go in April, she told him, at the season for departure; but not even his persuasion, his urgent prayers, would induce her to leave one week or one day sooner than the doctor ordered.

"I should hate myself if I were weak enough to run away from this place," she said; and it seemed to me that those words were the clue to her conduct, and that she was making a martyr of herself rather than succumb to something of horror which was haunting and killing her.

Her marriage had been fixed for the following June, and George Holbrook was strong in the rights of a future husband; but submissive as she was in all other respects, upon this point she was stubborn, and her lover's fervent pleading moved her no more than the piteous entreaties of her spinster aunt.

I began to understand that the case was hopeless, so far as Lota's well-being depended upon her speedy removal from the Orange Grove. We could only wait as hopefully as we could for April, and the time she had fixed for departure. I took the earliest opportunity of confiding my fears to the English physician; but clever and amiable as he was, he laughed all ideas of occult influence to scorn.

"From the moment the sanitary engineer—a really scientific man —certified this house as a healthy house, the last word was said as to its suitableness for Miss Hammond. The situation is perfect, the climate all that one could desire. It would be folly to move her till the spring is advanced enough for Varese or England."

What could I say against this verdict of local experience? Lota was not one of those interesting and profitable cases which a doctor likes to keep under his own eye. As a patient, her doctor only saw her once in a way; but he dropped in at the villa often as a friend, and he had been useful in bringing nice people about her.

I pressed the question so far as to ask him about the rooms at the back of the house, the old monkish rooms which had served as an infirmary in the seventeenth and eighteenth centuries. "Surely those rooms must be cold and damp?"

"Damp, no. Cold, yes. All north rooms are cold on the Riviera- and the change from south to north is perilous—but as no one uses the old monkish rooms their aspect can make little difference." "Does not Miss Hammond use those rooms sometimes?" "Never, I believe. Indeed, I understood Miss Elderson to say that the corridor leading to the old part of the house is kept locked, and that she has the key. I take it the good lady thinks that if the rooms are haunted it is her business to keep the ghosts in safe custody—as she does the groceries."

"Has nobody ever used these rooms since the new villa was built?" I asked.

"Mr. Hammond used them, and was rather attached to that part of the house. His library is still there, I believe, in what was once a refectory."

"I should love to see it."

"You have only to ask Miss Elderson."

I did ask Miss Elderson without an hour's delay, the first time I found myself alone with her. She blushed, hesitated, assured me that the rooms contained nothing worth looking at, and fully confessed that the key was not come-atable.

"I have not lost it," she said. "It is only mislaid. It is sure to turn up when I am looking for something else. I put it in a safe place."

Miss Elderson's places of safety had been one of our stock jokes ever since I had known Lota and her aunt; so I was inclined to despair of ever seeing those mysterious rooms in which the monks had lived. Yet after meditating upon the subject in a long ramble on the hill above the villa I was inclined to think that Lota might know more about that key than the good simple soul who had mislaid it. There were hours in every day during which my friend disappeared from the family circle, hours in which she was supposed to be resting inside the mosquito curtains in her own room. I had knocked at her door once or twice during this period of supposed rest; and there had been no answer.

I had tried the door softly, and had found it locked, and had gone away believing my friend fast asleep; but now I began to wonder whether Lota might not possess the key of those uninhabited rooms, and for some strange capricious motive spend some of her lonely hours within those walls. I made an investigation at the back of the villa the following day, before the early coffee and the rolls, which we three spinsters generally took in the verandah on warm sunny mornings, and most of our mornings were warm. I found the massive Venetian shutters firmly secured inside, and affording not a glimpse of the rooms within. The windows looked straight upon the precipitous hill, and these northward-facing rooms must needs be dark and chilly at the best of times. My curiosity was completely baffled. Even if I had been disposed to do a little house-breaking there was no possibility of opening those too solid looking shutters. I tugged at the fastenings savagely, but made no more impression than if I had been a fly.

CHAPTER 4. SUNSHINE OUTSIDE, BUT ICE AT THE CORE

For the next four days I watched Lota's movements.

After our morning saunter—she was far too weak now to go further than the terraced paths near the villa, and our sauntering was of the slowest—my poor friend would retire to her room for what she called her afternoon rest, while the carriage, rarely used by herself, conveyed her aunt and me for a drive, which our low spirits made ineffably dreary. Vainly was that panorama of loveliness spread before my eyes—I could enjoy nothing; for between me and that romantic scene there was the image of my perishing friend, dying by inches, and obstinately determined to die.

I questioned Lota's maid about those long afternoons which her mistress spent in her darkened room, and the young woman's answers confirmed my suspicions.

Miss Hammond did not like to be disturbed. She was a very heavy sleeper.

"She likes me to go to her at four o'clock every afternoon to do her hair, and put on her teagown. She is generally fast asleep when I go to her."

"And her door locked?"

"No, the door is very seldom locked at four. I went an hour earlier once with a telegram, and then the door was locked, and Miss Hammond was so fast asleep that she couldn't hear me knocking. I had to wait till the usual time."

On the fourth day after my inspection of the shutters, I started for the daily drive at the accustomed hour; but when we had gone a little way down the hill, I pretended to remember an important letter that had to be written, and asked Miss Elderson to stop the carriage, and let me go back to the villa, excusing my desertion for this afternoon. The poor lady, who was as low-spirited as myself, declared she would miss me sadly, and the carriage crept on, while I climbed the hill by those straight steep paths which shortened the journey to a five minutes' walk.

The silence of the villa as I went softly in at the open hall door suggested a general *siesta*. There was an awning in front of the door, and the hall was wrapt in shadow, the corridor beyond darker still, and at the end of this corridor I saw a flitting figure in pale grey—the pale Indian cashmere of Lota's neat morning frock. I heard a key turn, then the creaking of a heavy door, and the darkness had swallowed that pale grey figure.

I waited a few moments, and then stole softly along the passage. The door was half open, and I peered into the room beyond. It was empty, but an open door facing the fireplace showed me another room—a room lined with bookshelves, and in this room I could hear footsteps pacing slowly to and fro, very slowly, with the feeble tread I knew too well.

Presently she turned, put her hand to her brow as if remembering something, and hurried to the door where I was standing.

"It is I, Lota!" I called out, as she approached me, lest she should be startled by my unexpected presence.

I had been mean enough to steal a march upon her, but I was not mean enough to conceal myself. "You here!" she exclaimed.

I told her how I had suspected her visits to these deserted rooms, and how I had dreaded the melancholy effect which their dreariness must needs exercise upon her mind and health.

"Do you call them dreary?" she asked, with a curious little laugh. "I call them charming. They are the only rooms in the house that interest me. And it was just the same with my grandfather. He spent his declining days in these queer old rooms, surrounded by these queer old things."

She looked round her, with furtive, wandering glances, at the heavy old bookshelves, the black and white cabinets, the dismal old Italian tapestry, and at a Venetian glass which occupied a narrow recess at the end of the inner room, a glass that reached from floor to ceiling, and in a florid carved frame, from which the gilding had mostly worn away.

Her glance lingered on this Venetian glass, which to my uneducated eye looked the oldest piece of furniture in the room. The surface was so clouded and tarnished that although Lota and I were standing opposite it at a little distance, I could see no reflection of ourselves or of the room. "You cannot find that curious old glass very flattering to your vanity," I said, trying to be sprightly and careless in my remarks, while my eyes were watching that wasted countenance with its hectic bloom, and those too brilliant eyes.

"No, it doesn't flatter, but I like it," she said, going a little nearer the glass, and then suddenly drawing a dark velvet curtain across the narrow space between the two projecting bookcases.

I had not noticed the curtain till she touched it, for this end of the long room was in shadow. The heavy shutters which I had seen outside were closed over two of the windows, but the shutters had been pushed back from the third window, and the casements were open to the still, soft air.

There was a sofa opposite the curtained recess. Lota sank down upon it, folded her arms, and looked at me with a defiant smile.

"Well, what do you think of my den?" she asked.

"I think you could not have chosen a worse."

"And yet my grandfather liked these rooms better than all the rest of the house. He almost lived in them. His old servant told me so."

"An elderly fancy, which no doubt injured his health."

"People choose to say so, because he died sooner than they expected. His death would have come at the appointed time. The day and hour were written in the *Book of Fate* before he came here. The house had nothing to do with it—only in this quiet old room he had time to think of what was coming."

"He was old, and had lived his life; you are young, and life is all before you."

"All!" she echoed, with a laugh that chilled my heart.

I tried to be cheerful, matter of fact, practical. I urged her to abandon this dismal library, with its dry old books, airless gloom and northern aspect. I told her she had been guilty of an unworthy deceit in spending long hours in rooms that had been especially forbidden her. She made an end of my pleading with cruel abruptness.

"You are talking nonsense, Helen. You know that I am doomed to die before the summer is over, and I know that you know it."

"You were well when you came here; you have been growing worse day by day."

"My good health was only seeming. The seeds of disease were here," touching her contracted chest. "They have only developed. Don't talk to me, Helen; I shall spend my quiet hours in these rooms till the end, like my poor old grandfather. There need be no more concealment or double dealing. This house is mine, and I shall occupy the rooms I like."

She drew herself up haughtily as she rose from the sofa, but the poor little attempt at dignity was spoilt by a paroxysm of coughing that made her glad to rest in my arms, while I laid her gently down upon the sofa.

The darkness came upon us while she lay there, prostrate, exhausted, and that afternoon in the shadow of the steep hill was the first of many such afternoons.

From that day she allowed me to share her solitude, so long as I did not disturb her reveries, her long silences, or brief snatches of slumber. I sat by the open window and worked or read, while she lay on the sofa, or moved softly about the room, looking at the books on the shelves, or often stopping before that dark Venetian glass to contemplate her own shadowy image.

I wondered exceedingly in those days what pleasure or interest she could find in surveying that blurred shadow of her faded beauty. Was it in bitterness she looked at the altered form, the shrunken features—or only in philosophical wonder such as Marlborough felt, when he pointed to the withered old form in the glass—the poor remains of peerless manhood and exclaimed: "That was once a man."

I had no power to withdraw her from that gloomy solitude. I was thankful for the privilege of being with her, able to comfort her in moments of physical misery.

Captain Holbrook left within a few days of my discovery, his leave having so nearly expired that he had only just time enough to get back to Portsmouth, where his regiment was stationed. He went regretfully, full of fear, and his last anxious words were spoken to me at the little station on the sea shore.

"Do all you can to bring her home as soon as the doctor will let her come," he said. "I leave her with a heavy heart, but I can do no good by remaining. I shall count every hour between now and April. She has promised to stay at Southsea till we are married, so that we may be near each other. I am to find a pretty villa for her and her aunt. It will be something for me to do."

My heart ached for him in his forlornness, glad of any little duty that made a link between him and his sweetheart. I knew that he dearly loved his profession, and I knew also that he had offered to leave the army if Lota liked—to alter the whole plan of his life rather than be parted from her, even for a few weeks. She had forbidden such a sacrifice; and she had stubbornly refused to advance the date of her marriage, and marry him at San Remo, as he had entreated her to do, so that he might take her back to England, and establish her at Ventnor, where he believed she would be better than in her Italian paradise.

He was gone, and I felt miserably helpless and lonely without him—lonely even in Lota's company, for between her and me there were shadows and mysteries that filled my heart with dread. Sitting in the same room with her—admitted now to constant companionship—I felt not the less that there were secrets in her life which I knew not. Her eloquent face told some sad story which I could not read; and sometimes it seemed to me that between her and me there was a third presence, and that the name of the third was Death.

She let me share her quiet afternoons in the old rooms, but though her occupation of these rooms was no longer concealed from the household, she kept the privilege of solitude with jealous care. Her aunt still believed in the *siesta* between lunch and dinner, and went for her solitary drives with a placid submission to Lota's desire that the carriage and horses should be used by somebody. The poor thing was quite as unhappy as I, and quite as fond as Lota; but her feeble spirit had no power to struggle against her niece's strong will. Of these two the younger had always ruled the elder. After Captain Holbrook's departure the doctor took his patient seriously in hand, and I soon perceived a marked change in his manner of questioning her, while the stethoscope came now into frequent use. The casual weekly visits became daily visits; and in answer to my anxious questions I was told that the case had suddenly assumed a serious character.

"We have something to fight against now," said the doctor; "until now we have had nothing but nerves and fancies."

"And now?"

"The lungs are affected."

This was the beginning of a new sadness. Instead of vague fears, we had now the certainty of evil; and I think in the dreary days and weeks that followed, the poor old aunt and I had not one thought or desire, or fear, which was not centred in the fair young creature whose fading life we watched. Two English nurses, summoned from Cannes, aided in the actual nursing, for which trained skill was needed; but in all the little services which love can perform Miss Elderson and I were Lota's faithful slaves.

I told the doctor of her afternoons spent in her grandfather's library; and I told him also that I doubted my power, or his, to induce her to abandon that room.

"She has a fancy for it, and you know how difficult fancies are to fight with when anyone is out of health."

"It is a curious fact," said the doctor, "that in every bad case I have attended in this house my patient has had an obstinate preference for that dull, cold, room."

"When you say every bad case, I think you must mean every fatal case," I said.

"Yes. Unhappily the three or four cases I am thinking of ended fatally; but that fact need not make you unhappy. Feeble, elderly people come to this southern shore to spin out the frail thread of life that is at breaking point when they leave England. In your young friend's case sunshine and balmy air may do much. She ought to live on the sunny side of the house; but her fancy for her grandfather's library may be indulged all the same. She can spend her evenings in that room, which can be made thoroughly warm and comfortable before she enters it. The room is well built and dry. When the shutters are shut and the curtains drawn, and the temperature carefully regulated, it will be as good a room as any other for the lamp-light hours; but for the day let her have all the sunshine she can."

I repeated this little lecture to Lota, who promised to obey.

"I like the queer, old room," she said, "and, Helen, don't think me a bear if I say that I should like to be alone there sometimes, as I used to be before you hunted me down. Society is very nice for people who are well enough to enjoy it, but I'm not up to society, not even your's and auntie's. Yes, I know what you are going to say. You sit like a mouse, and don't speak till you are spoken to; but the very knowledge that you are there, watching me and thinking about me, worries me.

"And as for the auntie, with her little anxious fidgetings, wanting to settle my footstool, and shake up my pillows, and turn the leaves of my books, and always making me uncomfortable in the kindest way, dear soul—well, I don't mind confessing that she gets on my nerves, and makes me feel as if I should like to scream. Let me have one hour or two of perfect solitude sometimes, Helen. The nurse don't count. She can sit in the room, and you will know that I am not going to die suddenly without anybody to look on at my poor little tragedy."

She had talked longer and more earnestly than usual, and the talking ended in a fit of coughing which shook the wasted frame. I promised that all should be as she wished. If solitude were more restful than even our quiet companionship, she should be sometimes alone. I would answer for her aunt, as for myself.

The nurses were two bright, capable young women, and were used to the caprices of the sick. I told them exactly what was wanted: a silent unobtrusive presence, a watchful care of the patient's physical comfort by day and night. And henceforth Lota's evenings were spent for the most part in solitude. She had her books, and her drawing-board, on which with light, weak hand she would sketch faint remembrances of the spots that had charmed us most in our drives or rambles. She had her basket overflowing with scraps of fancy work, beginnings of things that were to have no end.

"She doesn't read very long, or work for more than ten minutes at a time," the nurse told me. "She just dozes away most of the evening, or walks about the room now and then, and stands to look at herself in that gloomy old glass. It's strange that she should be so fond of looking in the glass, poor dear, when she can scarcely fail to see the change in herself."

"No, no, she must see, and it is breaking her heart. I wish we could do away with every looking-glass in the house," said I, remembering how pretty she had been in the fresh bloom of her happy girlhood only six months before that dreary time.

"She is very fond of going over her grandfather's papers," the nurse told me. "There is a book I see her reading very often—a manuscript book."

"His diary, perhaps," said I.

"It might be that; but it's strange that she should care to pore over an old gentleman's diary."

Strange, yes; but all her fancies and likings were strange ever since I had entered that unlucky house. In her thought of her lover she was not as other girls. She was angry when I suggested that we should tell him of her illness, in order that he might get leave to come to her, if it were only for a few days.

"No, no, let him never look upon my face again," she said. "It is

328

bad enough for him to remember me as I was when we parted at the station. It is ever so much worse now—and it will be—oh, Helen, to think of what must come—at last!"

She hid her face in her hands, and the frail frame was convulsed with the vehemence of her sobbing. It was long before I could soothe her; and this violent grief seemed the more terrible because of the forced cheerfulness of her usual manner.

Chapter 5. "Seek Not To Know"

We kept early hours at the villa. We dined at seven, and at eight Lota withdrew to the room which she was pleased to call her den. At ten there was a procession of invalid, nurse, aunt, and friend to Lota's bedroom, where the night nurse, in her neat print gown and pretty white cap, was waiting to receive her. There were many kisses and tender goodnights, and a great show of cheerfulness on all sides, and then Miss Elderson and I crept slowly to our rooms-exchanging a few sad words, a few sympathetic sighs to cry ourselves to sleep, and to awake in the morning with the thought of the doom hanging over us.

I used to drop in upon Lota's solitude a little before bedtime, sometimes with her aunt, sometimes alone. She would look up from her book with a surprised air, or start out of her sleep.

"Bedtime already?"

Sometimes when I found her sleeping, I would seat myself beside her sofa, and wait in silence for her waking. How picturesque, how luxurious, the old room looked in the glaring light of the wood, which brightened even the grim tapestry, and glorified the bowls of red and purple anemones and other scentless flowers, and the long wall of books, and the velvet curtained windows, and shining brown floor. It was a room that I too could have loved were it not for the shadow of fear that hung over all things at the Orange Grove.

I went to the library earlier than usual one evening. The clock had not long struck nine when I left the drawing room. I had seen a change for the worse in Lota at dinner, though she had kept up her pretence of gaiety, and had refused to be treated as an invalid, insisting upon dining as we dined, scarcely touching some things, eating ravenously of other dishes, the least wholesome, laughing to scorn all her doctor's advice about dietary. I endured the interval between eight and nine, stifling my anxieties, and indulging the mild old lady with a game of *bezique*, which my wretched play allowed her to win easily, Like most old people her sorrow was of a mild and modified quality, and she had, I believe, resigned herself to the inevitable. The careful doctor, the admirable nurses, had set her mind at ease about dear Lota, she told me. She felt that all was being done that love and care could do, and for the rest, well, she had her church services, her prayers, her morning and evening readings in the well-worn *New Testament*. I believe she was almost happy.

"We must all die, my dear Helen," she said, plaintively.

Die, yes. Die when one had reached that humdrum stage on the road of life where this poor old thing was plodding, past barren fields and flowerless hedges—the stage of grey hairs, and toothless gums, and failing sight, and dull hearing—and an old fashioned, one *idead* intellect. But to die like Lota, in the pride of youth, with beauty and wealth and love all one's own! To lay all this down in the grave! That seemed hard, too hard for my understanding or my patience.

★★★★★

I found her asleep on the sofa by the hearth, the nurse sitting quietly on guard in her armchair, knitting the stocking which was never out of her hands unless they were occupied in the patient's service. Tonight's sleep was sounder than usual, for the sleeper did not stir at my approach, and I seated myself in the low chair by the foot of the sofa without waking her,

A book had slipped from her hand, and lay on the silken coverlet open. The pages caught my eye, for they were in manuscript, and I remembered what the nurse had said about Lota's fancy for this volume. I stole my hand across the coverlet, and possessed myself of the book, so softly that the sleeper's sensitive frame had no consciousness of my touch.

A manuscript volume of about two hundred pages in a neat firm hand, very small, yet easy to read, so perfectly were the letters formed and so evenly were the lines spaced.

I turned the leaves eagerly. A diary, a business man's diary, recording in commonplace phraseology the transactions of each day, Stock Exchange, Stock Exchange—railways—mines—loans—banks—money, money, money, made or lost. That was all the neat penmanship told me, as I turned leaf after leaf, and ran my eye over page after page.

The social life of the writer was indicated in a few brief sentences.

Dined with the Parkers: dinner execrable; company stupid; talked to Lendon, who has made half a million in Mexican copper; a dull man.

Came to Brighton for Easter; clear turtle at the Ship good; they have given me my old rooms; asked Smith (Suez Smith, not Turkish Smith) to dinner.

What interest could Lota possibly find in such a journal—a prosy commonplace record of losses and gains, bristling with figures?

This was what I asked myself as I turned leaf after leaf, and saw only the everlasting repetition of financial notes, strange names of loans and mines and railways, with contractions that reduced them to a cypher. Slowly, my hand softly turning the pages of the thick volume, I had gone through about three-fourths of the book when I came to the heading, "Orange Grove," and the brief entries of the financier gave place to the detailed ideas and experiences of the man of leisure, an exile from familiar scenes and old faces, driven back upon self-commune for the amusement of his lonely hours.

This doubtless was where Lota's interest in the book began, and here I too began to read every word of the diary with closest attention. I did not stop to think whether I was justified in reading the pages which the dead man had penned in his retirement, whether a license which his grand-daughter allowed herself might be taken by me. My one thought was to discover the reason of Lota's interest in the book, and whether its influence upon her mind and spirits was as harmful as I feared.

I slipped from the chair to the rug beside the sofa, and, sitting there on the ground, with the full light of the shaded reading-lamp upon the book, I forgot everything but the pages before me.

The first few pages after the old man's installation in his villa were full of cheerfulness. He wrote of this land of the South, new to his narrow experience, as an earthly paradise. He was almost as sentimental in his enthusiasms as a girl, as if it had not been for the old-fashioned style in which his raptures expressed themselves these pages might have been written by a youthful pen.

He was particularly interested in the old monkish rooms at the back of the villa, but he fully recognised the danger of occupying them.

"I have put my books in the long room which was used as a refectory," he wrote, "but as I now rarely look at them there is no fear of my being tempted to spend more than an occasional hour in the room."

Then after an interval of nearly a month

I have arranged my books, as I find the library the most interesting room in the house. My doctor objects to the gloomy aspect, but I find a pleasing melancholy in the shadow of the steep olive-clad hill. I begin to think that this life of retirement, with no companions but my books, suits me better than the pursuit of money making, which has occupied so large a portion of my later years.

Then followed pages of criticism upon the books he read-history, travels, poetry—books which he had been collecting for many years, but which he was now only beginning to enjoy.

"I see before me a studious old age," he wrote, "and I hope I may live as long as the head of my old college, Martin Routh. I have made more than enough money to satisfy myself, and to provide ample wealth for the dear girl who will inherit the greater part of my fortune. I can afford to fold my hands, and enjoy the long quiet years of old age in the companionship of the master spirits who have gone before. How near, how living they seem as I steep myself in their thoughts, dream their dreams, see life as they saw it! Virgil, Dante, Chaucer, Shakespeare, Milton, and all those later lights that have shone upon the dullest lives and made them beautiful—how they live with us, and fill our thoughts, and make up the brightest part of our daily existence."

I read many pages of comment and reverie in the neat, clear penmanship of a man who wrote for his own pleasure, in the restful solitude of his own fireside.

Suddenly there came a change—the shadow of the cloud that hung over that house:

I am living too much alone. I did not think I was of the stuff which is subject to delusions and marbled fancies—but I was wrong. I suppose no man's mind can retain its strength of fibre without the friction of intercourse with other minds of its own calibre. I have been living alone with the minds of the dead, and waited upon by foreign servants, with whom I hardly exchange half a dozen sentences in a day. And the result is what no doubt any brain-doctor would have foretold.

I have begun to see ghosts.

The thing I have seen is so evidently an emanation of my own mind—so palpably a materialisation of my own self-consciousness, brooding upon myself and my chances of long life—that it is a weakness even to record the appearance that has haunted me during the last few evenings. No shadow of dying monk has stolen between me and the lamplight; no presence from the vanished years, revisiting places. The thing which I have seen is myself—not myself as I am—but myself as I am to be in the coming years, many or few.

The vision—purely self-induced as I know it to be—has not the less given a shock to the placid contentment of my mind, and the long hopes which, in spite of the Venusian's warning, I had of late been cherishing.

Looking up from my book in yesterday's twilight my casual glance rested on the old Venetian mirror in front of my desk; and gradually, out of the blurred darkness, I saw a face looking at me.

My own face as it might be after the wasting of disease, or the slow decay of advancing years—a face at least ten years older than the face I had seen in my glass a few hours before—hollow cheeks, haggard eyes, the loose under-lip drooping weakly—a bent figure in an invalid chair, an aspect of utter helplessness. And it was myself. Of that fact I had no shadow of doubt.

Hypochondria, of course—a common form of the malady,—perhaps this shaping of the imagination into visions. Yet, the thing was strange—for I had been troubled by no apprehensions of illness or premature old age. I had never even thought of myself as an old man. In the pride bred of long immunity from illness I had considered myself exempt from the ailments that are wont to attend declining years. I had pictured myself living to the extremity of human life, and dropping peacefully into the centenarian's grave.

I was angry with myself for being affected by the vision, and I locked the door of the library when I went to dress for dinner, determined not to re-enter the room till I had done something—by outdoor exercise and change of scene—to restore the balance of my brain. Yet when I had dined there came upon me so feverish a desire to know whether the glass would again show me the same figure and face that I gave the key to my *major-domo*, and told him to light the lamps and make up the fire in the library.

Yes, the thing lived in the blotched and blurred old glass.

The dusky surface, which was too dull to reflect the realities of life, gave back that vision of age and decay with unalterable fidelity. The face and figure came and went, and the glass was often black—but whenever the thing appeared it was the same—the same in every dismal particular, in all the signs of senility and fading life.

'This is what I am to be twenty years hence,' I told myself, 'A man of eighty might look like that.'

Yet I had hoped to escape that bitter lot of gradual decay which I had seen and pitied in other men. I had promised myself that the reward of a temperate life—a life free from all consuming fires of dissipation, all tempestuous passions—would be a vigorous and prolonged old age. So surely as I had toiled to amass fortune so surely also had I striven to lay up for myself long years of health and activity, a life prolonged to the utmost span.

★★★★★

There was a break often days in the journal, and when the record was resumed the change in the writing shocked me. The neat firm penmanship gave place to weak and straggling characters, which, but for marked peculiarities in the formation of certain letters, I should have taken for the writing of a stranger.

The thing is always there in the black depths of that damnable glass—and I spend the greater part of my life watching for it. I have struggled in vain against the bitter curiosity to know the worst which the vision of the future can show me. Three days ago I flung the key of this detestable room into the deepest well on the premises; but an hour afterwards I sent to Taggia for a blacksmith, and had the lock picked, and ordered a new key, and a duplicate, lest in some future fit of spleen I should throw away a second key, and suffer agonies before the door could be opened.

'*Tu ne quaesieris, scire nefas—*'

Vainly the poet's warning buzzes and booms in my vexed ear—repeating itself perpetually, like the beating of a pulse in my brain, or like the ticking of a clock that will not let a man sleep.

'*Scire nefas—scire nefas,*'

The desire to know more is no stranger than reason.

Well, I am at least prepared for what is to come. I live no longer in a fool's paradise. The thing which I see daily and hourly is no hallucination, no materialisation of my self-consciousness, as I thought in the beginning. It is a warning and a prophesy. So shalt thou be. Soon, soon, shalt thou resemble this form which it shocks thee now to look upon.

Since first the shadow of myself looked at me from the darker shadows of the glass I have felt every indication of approaching doom. The doctor tries to laugh away my fears, but he owns that I am below par—meaningless phrase—talks of nervine decay, and suggests my going to St. Moritz. He doubts if this place suits me, and confesses that I have changed for the worse since I came here."

Again an interval, and then in writing that was only just legible.

It is a month since I wrote in this book—a month which has realised all that the Venetian glass showed me when first I began to read its secret.

I am a helpless old man, carried about in an invalid chair. Gone my pleasant prospect of long tranquil years; gone my selfish scheme of enjoyment, the fruition of a life of money-getting. The old Eastern fable has been realised once again. My gold has turned to withered leaves, so far as any pleasure that it can buy for me. I hope that my grand-daughter may get some good out of the wealth I have toiled to win.

Again a break, longer this time, and again the handwriting showed signs of increasing weakness. I had to pore over it closely in order to decipher the broken, crooked lines pencilled casually over the pages.

The weather is insufferably hot; but too ill to be moved. In library—coolest room—doctor no objection. I have seen the last picture in the glass—Death—corruption— the cavern of Lazarus, and no Redeemer's hand to raise the dead. Horrible! Horrible! Myself as I must be—soon, soon! How soon?

And then, scrawled in a corner of the page, I found the date- June 24, 1889.

I knew that Mr. Hammond died early in the July of that year.

★ ★ ★ ★ ★

Seated on the floor, with my head bent over the pages, and reading more by the light of the blazing logs than by the lamp on the table above me, I was unaware that Lota had awoke, and had raised herself from her reclining position on the sofa. I was still absorbed in my study of those last horrible lines when a pale hand came suddenly down upon the open book, and a laugh which was almost a shriek ran through the silent spaces around us. The nurse started up and ran to her patient, who was struggling to her feet and staring wildly into the long narrow glass in the recess opposite her sofa.

"Look, look!" she shrieked. "It has come—the vision of Death! The dreadful face—the shroud—the coffin. Look, Helen, look!"

My gaze followed the direction of those wild eyes, and I know not whether my excited brain conjured up the image that appalled me. This alone I know, that in the depths of that dark glass, indistinct as a form seen through turbid water, a ghastly face, a shrouded figure, looked out at me—

As one dead in the bottom of a tomb.

A sudden cry from the nurse called me from the horror of that vision to stern reality, to see the life-blood ebbing from the lips I had kissed so often with all a sister's love. My poor friend never spoke again. A severe attack of haemorrhage hastened the inevitable end; and before her heart-broken lover could come to clasp the hand and gaze into her fading eyes, Violetta Hammond passed away.

His Oldest Friends

Maxime De St. Vallier was no longer a young man when he succeeded to the family estate of St. Vallier le Roi, which had belonged to his race from the time of the Fronde, when a certain Hector St. Vallier commanded a regiment of light cavalry in Condé's army, and in the course of an adventurous career, including two wealthy marriages, managed to accumulate a considerable fortune, and to leave behind him the *château* and lands of St. Vallier le Roi, adjoining the insignificant Bourg of that name, which lies ten miles from a station on the Lyons railway and in the heart of a richly wooded district.

There is no more beautiful *château* in France of its size than this of St. Vallier, with its four tall towers under steep conical roofs, its carved balconies and oriel windows, its decorated gables and floriated ironwork; a *château* planted on a knoll that lifts the dainty edifice just high enough above the rolling woods and fertile valley to make it a picturesque point in the landscape.

Maxime inherited the estate and a handsome fortune in stocks and shares from an eccentric bachelor to whom he was but distantly related, but who had been passionately in love with his mother before her marriage, and who had been refused by her in favour of a much poorer man. It may be that Maxime de St. Vallier's early manhood would have taken a different and a better course had he known all about this good fortune which was waiting for him in the future; if he had known that at nine and thirty years of age he would be rich in wealth and lands, and endowed with all that weight and respectability which dignify the possessor of a fine estate.

"I should have tried to educate myself up to my fortune," he said, "and instead of wasting my nights in singing-cellars and dancing-gardens I should have been studying scientific agriculture and the landed interest. But the old fellow never took any notice of me, and I thought no more of him than of the Grand Lama of Thibet or the Khan of Tartary."

Yes, he would have shaped his life differently, and might have shaped it better had he but known. The vision of a sweet pale face and pathetic violet eyes rose before him in the first hour of his new and unexpected fortune. That lovely face had vanished forever, as he thought, from Maxime St. Vallier's adoring gaze, even years before the coming of his inheritance. He had loved the only daughter of one of Napoleon the Third's generals, had modestly offered himself and the possibilities of a journalistic career, which had been full of golden opportunities, all flung to the winds. He had enlarged upon the great things he might and would do in literature and politics if he were but urged by the noblest incentive to labour, the responsibilities of a husband who idolized his wife.

General Leroux listened to his fervid harangue with calm politeness, and smiled the bland pitying smile of age that has forgotten the sensations and dreams of youth.

"I cannot marry my daughter to possibilities, however brilliant," he said. "I am an old man. I should die before your efforts had begun to realize these great rewards which you say are within your power to gain. I should die harassed by the apprehension that my daughter and her offspring would starve. I am a poor man, remember. Lucie's *dot* would not do more than furnish an apartment in a respectable street. And you, sir, admit that you have saved nothing, though you tell me your earnings on the press have been considerable."

"No, I had no motive for hoarding."

"No more had Balzac, or Alexandre Dumas, or Gerard de Nerval, or Alfred de Musset, or a good many more whom I remember—geniuses all; and since you have lived to the age of two and thirty without having put by anything out of your earnings, you can hardly ask me to believe in your capacity for saving money in the future, when your expenses are to be increased by the maintenance of a wife and a possible family."

"I have flung away as much money as would support a wife and a home every year of my life, since I was five-and-twenty."

"Yes, you have had a brilliant career, I know, and you have taken life at breakneck time, as if it were a waltz at the Mabille. I admire your talents, my dear St.Vallier, and I like you, in any other relation of life than as a possible husband for my daughter. Frankly, too, the question of her future has long been quietly settled between her mother and me on the one part, and a couple of old friends of ours on the other part."

"Does Lucie know? Is Lucie content?" questioned St.Vallier, with pallid lips and fast-beating heart.

No, he was sure she had been told nothing of this parental scheme, even before his question was answered. He knew that she loved him, and would many no one else of her own free will.

"Lucie will know all in good time, and she is too dutiful to oppose the wishes of her parents," replied the general.

He added some friendly words, he grasped the lover's cold hand, and Maxime went out into the streets of Paris, feeling as if he had a stone in his breast in the place where his heart had beaten with glad emotions when he entered General Leroux's house an hour earlier.

He knew Lucie Leroux well enough—knowing her soft pliable nature, her love of father and mother, her severely religious training at an Ursuline convent—to be very sure that she would obey her parents and marry the suitor they had chosen for her. It was hopeless to fight against his fate; the *bourgeoise* Nemesis called Prudence barred his path to happiness. He went off to Algiers with one of the most brilliant imaginative writers of the day, and in the society of that gifted young man, and amidst scenes of romantic beauty, he tried to live down his love, and at least succeeded in Finding life endurable, and full of inspiration for his pen.

He was still in Africa when he saw the announcement of Lucie's marriage. The bridegroom was Charles Colnet, the junior partner in Colnet & Cie., a firm of iron-founders of established position and large wealth. Looked at from the materialistic standpoint of modern Paris the match was a good one, and General Leroux and his wife were to be congratulated upon having done remarkably well for their daughter.

Maxime's business in life was to forget her. He was not able to do that all at once, but he was able to fling himself heart and soul into his literary work—embittered and hardened, but also strengthened by the one honourable passion of his life, a stronger and a better man for having loved nobly and in vain. From being known as one of the cleverest journalists of his day, he became famous as the author of a novel which struck a new string upon the seven-stringed lyre of earthly passion and heavenward-looking hope.

It may have been this sudden blast of Fame's trumpet which made the childless old sybarite's eyes turn towards his distant kinsman; anyhow, his latest will was dated after the success of St. Villier's first and most remarkable story. When a man has been writing for eighteen years, and then in the maturity of his powers takes upon himself to write a book, it is probable that this first book will be better than anything he produces afterwards.

St. Vallier found himself a landowner of some importance, and furnished with means which justified his taking life exactly as his own inclination suggested. He might spend the greater part of his days as a man of fashion in Paris, where he could afford to set up a bachelor establishment on the most splendid scale. He might have courted notoriety in twenty different ways in the city of pleasure; and might have won for himself that ephemeral renown which is the most brilliant and the most intoxicating of all earthly glories, while it lasts.

All this he might have done, and would have done, perhaps, had fortune dropped her favours into his lap just ten years ear-

lier. But he had lived his life, had been famous in Bohemia as
the scribbler of the squib and the entre-filet, pungent criticisms
and risky stories, famous in the great world as the writer of the
cleverest book of the season. He had no vanities or ambitions
which Paris could gratify. He told himself that he wanted restful
days, the tranquil autumn of a life whose summer was faded and
sped; so he settled quietly down in the Louis Treize Château, and
for the first year of his possession devoted himself to the almost
impossible task of improving upon perfection.

If he could not exactly improve he could at least elaborate.
The old man who was gone had prided himself on his library,
had deemed himself a *connoisseur* in books and bindings; but his
taste, though excellent, had been old-fashioned, and new genera-
tions are in advance of the old. So the wonderful collection of
books new and old grew under the hand of the new lord, and a
taste which was simpler and yet more splendid prevailed in the
new acquisitions. As in the library, so in every room in the *château*, in gardens and stables, in home-farm and falcon-house, the
improving hand was seen, the artistic taste was at work. Maxime
St. Vallier made his *campagne,* as he called it, the religion of his sober middle-age. He told his friends that he only lived to expand
and beautify St. Vallier le Roi.

It has been said by a French classic that the greatest luxury is
that which is least observable. The perfection of the Château St.
Vallier was a perfection in those minor details which in many
splendid houses are neglected. Maxime's guests found themselves lapped in luxury, but were never oppressed with a too
obvious splendour or profusion. Every desire, every need of humanity, was foreseen and provided for. An unsleeping *prévoyance*
attended the guest from his arrival at the station till his departure
from the same place.

Not till his friends were comfortably seated in their railway
carriage did Maxime's care, personal or vicarious, cease in their
behalf; and were the journey long his attentions followed to the
very end, in the shape of a carefully provided *piquenique* basket,
and as much light literature as the book-stall would furnish in

the way of novelty. Hence it came to pass that a visit to St. Vallier le Roi was among the choicest privileges of the few who yet survived of that gallant band with whom Maxime had begun life at the Sorbonne and on the "Boul Mich." He had not the temperament which makes new friends, and he clung with a warm affection to those he had known in the freshness of his morning hours.

Alas! They were so sorely diminished a crew. Life on the "Boul Mich" uses itself quickly. Of Maxime's bosom-friends one had hanged himself in a blind alley; another had cut the knot of a difficulty with his razor in a miserable garret behind the church of St. Sulpice; and more than one had been sacrificed to the demon absinthe. Three had been killed in the war and the siege, and pulmonary complaints had accounted for others.

The list of those who had fallen by the wayside in that march of life from twenty to forty was appalling. St. Vallier, who was of a thoughtful temper, had many a gloomy hour in which he pondered over the days that were gone, and the friends who were numbered with the dead. It seemed to him in these hours of despondency that fortune had come too late to be of any real value.

He might perhaps have fallen into a habit of settled melancholy but for a new and most unlooked-for happiness that came to him three years after his inheritance. Charles Colnet, of Colnet & Cie., went the way of all flesh with an awful suddenness early in the spring of that year; and in the following summer Maxime met his old sweetheart at La Bourboule, ill, nervous, and fragile as a pale March primrose—shaken and scared by the shock of an unloved husband's death, childless and despondent.

There could be but one result of such a meeting. To Maxime's eye the pensive and ailing woman was more interesting, if less lovely, than the girl he once had hoped to win. And then what exquisite delight it was for him to watch the return of the old loveliness, like the gradual glow and glory of a summer sunrise, as the widow's heart reawakened to the old love! Yes, she had loved him always, she confessed, when they parted late in September, she to return to Paris to arrange her affairs and prepare for a second wedlock, he to go back to the woods and gardens of St. Vallier, and to elaborate that which he had been elaborating for the last three years. He had to prepare the apartments of the new *châtelaine*. Everything had been pronounced complete from garret to cellar; but nothing in existence could be good enough for the new mistress of his home and the old mistress of his heart.

The wedding was solemnized in Paris a year after Charles Colnet's death. It was a very quiet ceremonial, an arrangement in a minor key; yet the newspapers had a great deal to say about the bride and bridegroom, the wealth of the iron-foundry, the historical associations of St. Vallier le Roi; but most of all about the lady's bridal gown and *trousseau*, her jewels and wedding gifts.

This was the beginning of a new existence for Maxime St. Vallier. All things took brighter colours in the sunlight of domestic happiness. But youth that is spent is spent. No man can make himself young again, least of all the man who has taken those strong years of manhood between twenty and forty at a swinging pace. The later years of that man are like the tired hunter's return stablewards after a grand run with the hounds. The horse may have done prodigies between noon and sundown; but he has had his day, and must creep quietly home to rest. The most famous physician in Paris told St. Vallier to be careful of himself.

"You have burnt the lamp of life rather too fiercely," he said; "there is, however, oil enough left for a good many years to come if you will only husband it."

This was a sage warning, but it is difficult for a man who has won the fruition of his fondest hopes to remember the shadow on the dial, creeping on with slow, inevitable progress. St. Vallier gave himself up to the gladness of his new life, and to the delight of his wife's society. She was charmed with her surroundings at the *château*, pleased at the idea of spending the greater part of every year in that tranquil home, far from the excitements and

345

dissipations of Republican Paris. Her husband's friends were her friends; and although there was a faint flavour of the Quarter Latin and the Bal Bullier still clinging to those old comrades, they were all of them men of intellect, and some of them men of mark—poets, romancers, painters, who had made themselves famous or at least fashionable; advocates whose florid eloquence had but too often made the forger or the parricide appear rather the victim than the criminal, and had found extenuating circumstances in the darkest story of crime.

It was in the second autumn of St. Vallier's wedded life that a party of these friends arrived at the *château*, intent upon enjoying all the sports and pleasures which St. Vallier le Roi could afford—hawking, shooting, hunting, yea, even the music of village Orphéonistes, and the dances at the village fairs. Maxime's friends were all men. Lucie supplied the feminine element, and brought around her half a dozen of the most elegant women in Paris: widows, or wives on furlough, fresh from their seaside holiday, or their "cure" in Auvergne or Savoy, Schwalbach or the Pyrenees.

Everyone was charmed with the *château*. Pretty women went buzzing up and down the corridors, peering into the grim seventeenth-century turrets, fluttering up and down the corkscrew staircases, with much music of light laughter, and *frou-frou* of silk and lace.

Madame's friends were delighted with everything, but perhaps most of all to find that very audacious painter of Parisian *boudoirs*, Tolpâche, and that daring analyst of the female heart, Vivien the novelist, on the premises. "There is something very awful in the idea of living for a fortnight in the same house with two such men," said Madame Evremonde, the banker's widow; "one feels one's principles in danger of being gradually undermined. If Vivien's conversation is anything like his books—"

"Thank Heaven it isn't!" said St. Vallier, "or M. Vivien would be intolerable. Social analysis is a very good thing to dream and doze over, with a cigar between one's lips, and one's feet on the fender, but to have to listen to the analyst expounding his theories—*quelle corvée!*

One of the first inquiries from the lady visitors was for the family ghost.

"Of course there is a ghost—some sad story of a jealous husband and a murdered lover, perhaps, or a faithless wife shut up in one of those too delicious turrets?" said Madame Belfort, who was stout and sentimental—a kindly adipose creature, who offered to the fashionable *faiseur* the problem of how to make me best of a jelly-fish. "Unhappily, *chère dame*, there is no ghost."

"What! In a *château* built in the middle of the seventeenth century—a *château* built when men wore long hair, and velvet doublets, and cannon sleeves, and Point d'Alençon ruffles. That cannot be! There must be a ghost. You have not hunted up the family traditions. A house without a ghost story, a family without traditions, would be hardly respectable."

"I said there is no ghost, but I did not say there are no family traditions."

"There are traditions, then?" asked the stout lady. "Yes."

"Ghostly ones?"

"There is one that savours of the supernatural; but as I never yet believed in a story of that kind when I heard it told of another man's family, I am not likely to believe in this legend because it is told of my own ancestors."

"A legend! The very word has a fascination!" cried Madame Evremonde. "Please let us hear it."

"Then you own to a ghost!" exclaimed Madame Belfort, who had the density of large bodies. "Pray show us the haunted room. I feel sure it is one of the turret-rooms, so quaint, so historical, so uncanny."

"Again, *chère dame*, must I protest that no ghost—not the shadow of a shade—had ever been asserted to walk these corridors, or harbour in any room, garret, or cellar of this *château*. If you good ladies will graciously wait till after dinner, I will tell you the story of St. Vallier le Roi while we take our coffee."

"It is a long story, then?"

"Not very long, but too long to be told in this passage while your maids are running about with your luggage, and while my chef is doubtless in a fever of impatience lest the dinner should be delayed so long as to spoil his best efforts."

His guests took the hint, and ran off to their various rooms, Madame St.Vallier and her housekeeper going about with them to show them where they were lodged. Lamps were being lighted in the corridors; many wax candles were burning upon toilet tables and mantelpieces. As the great clock chimed the half-hour after six, all the windows in the *château* gleamed and twinkled through the October twilight. It was still early in the month. The evenings were soft and grey. The woods were still green.

The dinner was excellent. The guests were full of vivacity and light airy talk. The dining-hall, with its dark oak panelling, family portraits, Gobelin tapestry, and Henri *deux* pottery, was a picture which delighted the eye of Adolphe Tolpâche, the painter—a background which he was likely to use in many a little pictured *tête-à-tête,* confidential, *risqué,* suggestive. On the appearance of coffee and liqueurs, Madame Evremonde turned to her host, by whose side she was sitting.

"Your family tradition, *Monsieur,*" she said. "The moment has come."

Maxime bowed a smiling assent.

"We'll get rid of the servants first," he murmured in her ear. "That will do, Robert," to the *major-domo;* "you and Jacques can put your salvers on the table yonder," pointing to a table in a recess.

The well-trained servant understood the dismissal, and at once withdrew with his underlings. As the heavy oak door closed upon them, Maxime leant forward with his folded arms on the tablecloth.

"Now then for the ghost story," he said. "It is a ghost story, but, I am happy to say, the ghost has nothing to do with this house. We have no haunted room from which the too-daring guest emerges, after a self-imposed ordeal, with his hair blanched and his brain turned. Our ghosts are out-of-door ghosts. The legend of St.Vallier is the legend of the phantom *char-à-bancs.*"

"A phantom *char-à-bancs*. A new manner of ghost, *par Dieu*. What does it do, this *char-à-bancs*?"

"Very little. It is supposed to be seen driving through the woods in the evening dusk; seen by the owner of the estate. A curious old-world carriage, a carriage belonging to a period in which coaches were a novelty, and when a Court beauty was known to barter her reputation for a gilt coach; a beauty of rank and social status, mark you, who had resisted every other lure,"

"We know our de Grammont, *merci*," laughed Vivien; "*revenez à votre char-à-bancs.*"

It is seen in the gloaming, somewhere along that wooded road which leads to the home-farm; at least, that is the traditional place. It is seen by the owner of the estate; and in that strange antiquated vehicle he sees a strange set of passengers-the friends he cared for in his youth, the friends he valued most, the friends who have gone before."

"*Que diable!* Your estate is well provided," exclaimed Tolpâche. "Not a single ghost, not the old-established family spectre, but a whole company of apparitions, a coach-load of phantoms. *Après, Mon ami?* When the lord of the soil has seen the spectral char-a-bancs, what then?"

"He is forewarned of his approaching death. If the legend is to be believed, no man ever long survived the apparition of that vehicle, the passing of those noiseless wheels."

"India-rubber tyres," said Tolpâche; "a carnival trick of some *roué* St. Vallier's fast and furious friends. A thing done once, perhaps, in the wild days of the Regency, and exaggerated by rumour into a family custom. *Histoire de rire.* That is the way ancestral ghosts are made!"

"My dear Tolpâche, if you are a sceptic, so am I. I no more believe in my family apparition than you do; only these ladies wanted the story, and there it is for them."

"These ladies" were charmed with the story, and were inclined to believe in the phantom *char-à-bancs.*. Madame Belfort insisted upon being told in what direction the road lay by which the *char-à-bancs* was supposed to travel, in order that she might take her morning constitutional on that very road.

PART 2

When a man has a beautiful wife and a circle of intimates, however well he may have chosen his friends, and however long he may have known them, there is always a traitor among them. There is always one man who holds no law sacred where a lovely woman's favour is, or may be, the reward of treachery. There is always one man who disbelieves in woman's chastity, and who thinks every man's wife a possible prize, if not for other men, at least for himself.

There was one such traitor in Maxime de St. Vallier's circle, and that traitor was Vivien, the novelist, a writer who had painted duchesses from models picked out of the Parisian gutter, who had dissected and analyzed, and poetized and bedevilled his own idea of woman, evolved out of his own very nasty inner consciousness, and who could not recognize purity when he saw it.

Hector Vivien was neither a shooting nor a hunting man, cared for neither foxhounds nor falconry. He would have bored himself to death at St. Vallier le Roi if he had been without an object. Every man who lives in the country must hunt something, even if that something be only a beetle or a butterfly. Vivien hunted Lucie St. Vallier. The calm, high-souled, beautiful woman was the quarry which he had chosen; and he fully believed that he should succeed in the chase.

"If not today, tomorrow." That was his motto where women were concerned. Elated by a succession of facile conquests, he thought all conquests easy. Lucie's matronly dignity was, to his mind, only the mask worn by all well-bred women. Behind the Roman wife there was always a potential Messalina.

He pursued his accustomed arts very carefully, varying his tactics in accordance with his surroundings. He was so subtle that neither husband nor wife suspected his motives. St. Vallier apologized to him for the monotony of life at the *château*. "You, who care neither for hawk nor hound, must find it a very dull business," he said.

"My dear Maxime, you forget that I have to finish my novel, and find a title for it, before the end of the year. Nothing could suit me better than the repose of this uneventful life."

"I fear you did not make much progress with your story yesterday, *Monsieur*," said Lucie, gaily; "you were loitering about the gardens and the farm all the afternoon."

"Dear *madame*, I was thinking of my title. That is the hardest work of all."

It was to be observed that Vivien spent day after day in the same leisurely meandering between garden and farm, park and *pleasaunce*, or in accompanying the ladies of the party to distant ruins or rustic villages, or, indeed, in any direction that Madame de St. Vallier proposed for the day's drive. He was not averse from riding, was a light weight, and rode fairly well for a literary man; so, having found a mount of St. Vallier's that suited him to perfection, he took to accompanying his hostess and Madame Evremond in their morning rides, and thus familiarized himself with every path and glade in the extensive woods.

Lucie showed him the spot where the phantom *char-à-bancs* was said to have appeared; a point where the footpath branched off from the road, and where a giant oak spread his gnarled and withered limbs, alive and flourishing on one side, and dead on the other—fitting landmark for a haunted spot.

Vivien was very jocose about the *char-à-bancs*, but Lucie checked him with a sigh.

"What if the legend were true!" she said gravely; "what if some day Maxime were to tell me he had seen the phantom carriage!"

"You would guess, dear Madame, that he had supped with the widow Cliquot overnight," the novelist answered gaily. He was not going to encourage sentimentality about a husband.

October wore towards its close. A pack of English foxhounds had been brought over to a neighbouring *quasi*-royal *château* by an Irish nobleman, a man in whose family sport and fine riding were a tradition. The hounds afforded splendid sport, and the peer was a social success, dined at St. Vallier le Roi twice in a fortnight, and made himself particularly agreeable to the ladies of the party. It was curious that, coming upon the scene as a stranger, he should have been the only visitor who saw threatened mischief in Hector Vivien's languid saunterings and close attendance upon Madame de St. Vallier and her friends.

"If I were a little more intimate with St. Vallier, I should try to open his eyes about that particular friend of his," said the peer, communing with himself as he drove home after his second dinner at the *château*. "A fellow who is able to sit a horse, and yet does not care for riding to hounds in such a splendid country as this, must have some darker game in view. I think I know pretty well what the Parisian novelist is aiming at."

Maxime had been completely happy during those short autumn days. He had not been husbanding his strength, for he had ridden as hard as anybody else, yet he had felt in better health than he had enjoyed for the last ten years, full of life and vigour, and with an appetite which made him think with a pitying smile of the days when he had trifled fretfully with the choicest *entrée* at Bignon's, and disdainfully rejected the costliest *primeurs* of the season. He felt that he was rapidly acquiring the hardy vigour of the genuine *campagnard,* and that henceforth he might laugh at doctors and diagnosis.

The month was waning, and several of the visitors had left the *château*; but the party seemed only cosier and more lively as the circle grew smaller; 'just the right number for sitting round the fire and telling stories," Maxime said, as they drew their chairs in a semicircle about the wide hearth in the central hall, a hearth whereon burned huge logs of red fir, exhaling aromatic odours; just the right number to appreciate Lucie de St. Vallier's low sweet voice as she sang Heine's ballads, or De Musset's passionate love-songs, in the pensive hour between daylight and darkness.

'Ninon, Ninon, que fais tu de la vie
Toi, qui n'a pas l'amour?

"What does she do with her life, this tranquil, dignified

chatelaine?"Vivien asked himself; she who seemed to know nothing of love—certainly not of love as he interpreted the passion—a transient fever, prompting to all manner of falsehood and treachery; a burning fiery furnace, from which a woman emerges scathed and seared, marked with the ineffaceable brand of infamy.

The meet had been more remote than usual, and the hounds had gone in a direction that led farther and farther away from St. Vallier le Roi; so on this particular evening Maxime was riding home alone, having left his friends, Tolpâche the painter, and the advocate Bartrond, to take their own line. He knew that his wife would be full of anxieties and morbid fancies about him, should he not return till long after dark, and to stay with the hounds this afternoon would mean a very late home-coming. He had left the hounds at three o'clock, by which time they had lost their first fox and were drawing a wood fifteen miles from St. Vallier le Roi. In all probability the fox would take them farther away from that point, and the day's sport might finish with death or disappointment thirty miles from home.

Maxime was riding a second horse, which took him homeward at the rate of seven miles an hour, and the sun was just beginning to set as he rode out of a bridle-track through a thickly planted fir wood, and came upon the carriage-road which Madame Belfort had christened the Phantom's Highway. Nothing was further from his thoughts than family traditions upon that particular evening. He was in excellent health and spirits, and was thinking how delightful it would be to get home in advance of the other men, and to enjoy a quiet hour with Lucie, *tête-à-tête,* in that quaint old turret-room which she had made her *boudoir.* How sweet it would be to sit beside the fire in the curious hooded chimney corner, talking confidentially, and all in all to each other, just for that one quiet hour before it was time to dress for dinner!

He rode slowly along, thinking of the woman he loved so dearly, with such a pure and placid affection; a love so strong in its unbounded faith; a love across whose brightness there had never fallen the shadow of change. He thought how blessed life had been made for him within the last three years, blest by earthly prosperity, blest how much more in this perfect and happy union, and his heart swelled with gratitude to Providence.

Lucie had reawakened in his mind the devout feelings of early boyhood, the faith learnt at his mother's knees; and now he told himself he might look forward to long years of this serene and full existence—years of prosperity, social influence, and wedded love—for all those threatening signs of nervous decay, fatigued brain, wasted strength, which had scared him when he consulted the famous doctor, had gradually disappeared, and he felt as fit for the battle of life as he had felt at five-and-twenty. Full of these self-congratulations, he rode slowly along the road, towards a sharp curve where the woodland opened upon a lovely glade, sloping down to a level stretch of marshy pasture, where the cows stood breast-deep in the flowering grasses.

The sun was dipping towards this grassy expanse at the bottom of the glade, a great crimson disk. As Maxime reached the turn of the road, and saw the glade in a slanting line before him, with that red orb facing him, he was startled by the sound of a horn, curiously faint, yet seeming near. Could the hounds have been following in his direction all this time? Had the fox, as if out of sheer perversity, set his nose towards St. Vallier le Roi?

While he was asking himself this question, turning in his saddle to look back and listen, a strange chill crept through his veins, colder and more sudden than the chill that comes after the sinking of the sun, and, looking straight before him, he saw a carriage approaching, and mechanically pulled his horse out of the narrow road to make way for it. The carriage was large and heavy-looking, drawn by four horses, and neither wheels nor horses' hoofs sounded on the hard gravel road.

It drove slowly past him as he stood watching it; a *char-à-bancs*, filled with men whose faces were all turned towards him, pallid in the grey faint light; the face of Gerard de Nerval, who hanged himself in the Rue de la Vielle Lantèrne; the face of Alfred de Musset, who wrecked his constitution by drink and dissipation; faces of men less famous than these two—all gone before. One, his oldest, dearest, trustiest friend in the long ago, stood up in the carriage, and, looking at him earnestly, pointed with solemn gesture to the setting sun. The red-gold edge of the orb dropped as he pointed, and the day was dead.

"*Ce char Horace,*" sighed Maxime, as the carriage vanished into the shadows of the wood. "That means a rendezvous. We are to meet soon."

He rode homeward very slowly. He had never believed in this legend of the *char-à-bancs*, and yet the fact of having seen it, and the faces of his dead friends, gave him no surprise. It seemed to him, now that the thing was over, as if he had known always that he should see those familiar faces, and receive this warning of approaching death. Yet only a few minutes ago he had been rejoicing in the idea of long and happy years lying before him, a quiet leisurely journey, hand in hand with his beloved, down the hill of life. The effect of that strange vision upon him was like the effect of a blow that produces brief unconsciousness. The man who has been stunned awakens with a confused sense of time; feels as if years had gone by in those few minutes of total oblivion.

Not for a moment did he try to reason away the vision, to think it a delusion of a mind prepossessed by that particular image. To him the thing was a truth, a positive indisputable fulfilment of the family legend. He was doomed shortly to die. In the midst of his calm delight in life the fateful summons had come, and he must obey. He could not misunderstand that look in his dead friend's face, the hand pointing to the sinking sun. For him, too, the sun of life was going down. He had fancied himself so much improved in health, so much stronger than of old. A fallacy born of a contented mind, perhaps. That decay which he had once dreaded was going on within the citadel of life. In brain, or heart, or lungs, somewhere there must be hidden mischief, and the finger of death had marked him.

"I'll see what science says of me," he thought, "and if the doctor's verdict coincides with the spectral warning, I shall know that my race is run. There is always some comfort in certainty. I will go to Paris by the Rapide tomorrow and let Bianchon overhaul me."

Having come to this decision, he put his horse at a trot, and rode rapidly home, arriving in time for a cup of tea, which Lucie called "*le* five o'clock," in the turret *boudoir*, and for that long cosy talk with his wife, which he had anticipated. She praised him for his devotion in leaving the hounds and coming home alone, lest she should spend uneasy hours after dark. She was gay, caressing, charming, and it was exquisite happiness to snatch this hour alone with her. Not by one word or sigh did Maxime reveal the mental shock he had experienced; yet, in the midst of their light talk and laughter, he was thinking of a day near at hand when she would be sitting lonely and widowed in that room; and he was recalling the provisions of the will which he had made directly after his marriage—a will which left his wife everything.

Before going to her *boudoir* he had despatched a mounted messenger with a telegram, asking Dr. Bianchon to expect him at a certain hour on the following day. He would take the omnibus train from St. Vallier le Roi to Dijon that night, in time to start from Dijon by the Rapide. After much happy talk, he told Lucie that he had to go to Paris on particular business, and that he meant to travel at night, both in going and returning, so that he might be absent for the shortest time possible.

"But you will fatigue yourself dreadfully by two night journeys!" said Lucie, growing sad at the prospect of even this brief separation.

"Not at all. I shall take a wagon-lit each way."

"Be sure you do. And you will be back—"

"The day after tomorrow, much too early for breakfast."

"I will have breakfast ready for you, however early you may be. I shall be at the station with the carriage."

"I beg that you will do no such thing. A long drive on a cold wintry morning might give you a dangerous chill!"

"I am too hardy a plant for that, Maxime. The life I lead in these delicious woods has made me as strong as a lioness!"

"My lioness!" he cried, smothering the fair bright face with kisses, "Queen of my forests and of my heart!"

The gong sounded loud in the vaulted hall, signal to dress for dinner. Maxime hurried off to change his clothes, and to give orders about his departure. A carriage was to be ready at ten to take him to the station. The omnibus train left St. Vallier le Roi at twenty minutes past eleven, reached Dijon in time for the Rapide, and he would be in Paris in the early morning, with two or three hours to waste before he could hope to be admitted to the great Bianchon's consulting-room.

He was full of talk and laughter at the dinner-table that evening, in the small, snug circle of seven, with the exaggerated vivacity of a man who is trying to hide a canker in his heart. Vivien, too, was unusually gay; told his best stories, flashed his brightest repartees, a shade more recklessly than usual; and it may be that if Maxime de St. Vallier had not been preoccupied with his own gloomy thoughts he might have taken objection to some of the novelist's sallies. As it was he talked and rattled on, scarce hearing, certainly not heeding what was said by others, and hardly knowing what he said himself. In this feverish state he sat over the coffee and liqueurs till the butler announced the carriage that was to take him to the station. His servant and his valise were ready.

He took a hasty farewell of wife and friends, and was gone.

Dr. Bianchon received M. de St. Vallier before any other patient, although even at nine o'clock the great man's waiting-room was crowded. He had met his patient often in society, and received him as a friend.

"My dear St. Vallier, I have to congratulate you upon the improvement of your appearance. You look ten years younger since you were last in this room. In what Medea's cauldron have you been stewing?"

"My only Medea is my wife. My only medicine had been a year and a half of supreme happiness!"

"Ah, that is a kind of physic we often prescribe; but there are no chemists who make it up. And so you have come to tell me how well you are, and to get a little friendly advice that will enable you to become a centenarian," concluded Bianchon laughingly.

A consulting physician has so often occasion to look grave

that he gladly snatches any excuse for being cheerful.

"I have come to ask you to make a thorough examination, and to find out if there is any hidden mischief in my constitution."

"Do you suspect anything?" asked the doctor, with his keen look—a look which suggested that for him the outward semblance of a man, coat and waistcoat included, was but a glass case through which he saw the inner machinery.

"No; I never felt better in my life."

"And you deliver yourself over of your own accord to the stethoscope and the sphygmometer! Prudent man. Kindly take off your coat and waistcoat."

Dr. Bianchon made a most studious examination of his patient, sounded, rapped, and listened, and then with a smile gave him a clean bill of health.

"Your pulse is capital, so we won't trouble the sphygmometer, which I find very useful with my alcoholic patients," said the doctor. "I told you when you were here last that there was nothing organically wrong. I can tell you now, in all good faith, that you are as sound within as you are well-looking without-no whited sepulchre here, *mon ami*," with a friendly tap on the patient's chest.

"And there is no fear of my dying suddenly, within the next three or four days?"

"Not unless you get yourself under the wheels of an omnibus, or by the side of some clever friend who will scrabble through a hedge with the muzzle of his gun pointed at your ribs. Death by internal disease you have no need to fear. Heart and lungs are as sound as a bell."

"Thank God!" exclaimed Maxime, fervently.

"What put these fears into your head? You must have felt nervous about yourself, or you would hardly have come all the way from your country place to see me."

"A foolish fancy. I am too happy in my surroundings not to fear. Goodbye; come and see me at St. Vallier if ever you can find time."

"That is just the thing I never can find; but I should like to spend a couple of days at your *château* when all Paris is out of town. Unfortunately, when all Paris is away, there are generally some very interesting cases at the hospitals; and I take that opportunity to go on with my education."

Maxime and his wife possessed a *pied-à-terre* in the Rue de Varennes. It had been Lucie's house during her widowhood—a dainty little house *entre cour et jardin*—and here a couple of old servants kept all things in order while their master and mistress were in the country. Maxime had sent his servant on before him, and found a comfortable breakfast, neatly set out in the well-furnished library, which his wife had given him as his own den.

Small as the house was, and although all things in it were in perfect order, the rooms had an aspect which weighed upon Maxime's spirits. There was an atmosphere of emptiness and desolation. He was glad to put on his hat, and go out and wander aimlessly about Paris, finding his way to the Champs Elysées, and the Bois, counting the hours till the eight o'clock Rapide would take him southward.

In spite of the physician's positive assurance he was not altogether at ease. He could not feel as calm and hopeful as he should have done, under the circumstances. That vision of his old friend pointing to the setting sun, and looking at him with solemn prophetic eyes, was with him wherever he went, came between him and every cheerful thought. His mind travelled back to those old days, under the shadow of St. Sulpice, fifteen years ago, when he and that dead friend had eaten the *vache enragée* together, and when in the midst of their struggles they had been hopeful and gay. Then had come literary successes—for him who was dead, the poet's laurel wreath, that withered all too soon, and left nothing behind it but the absinthe-madness, and a premature grave in Père la Chaise.

He had engaged places in the sleeping-car for himself and his valet. He was at the terminus half an hour before the train started, tired out with his rambles about Paris, and with the wakeful night in the express; so he took off coat and boots, and laid himself down under a fur rug which his servant arranged for him, and was soon asleep.

He must have slept some hours, for it was the voice of the porters shouting, "*Tonnerre!*" that awoke him, and most of the travellers were getting out for supper. He did not care to eat or drink—felt weary in limbs and head, and composed himself to sleep again. This time sleep did not answer to his call. Two men in berths near his were gossiping in a subdued murmur, which was more exasperating to St. Vallier's nerves than the loudest talking might have been.

"Know him?" said one of the speakers, "I should think I did know him much better than he knows the women he pretends to analyse in those sickly novels of his. I tell you he is a lump of vanities—thinks himself irresistible—thinks that where he is concerned there is no such thing as virtue or honour in a woman. A woman may have resisted every other tempter; but when he comes, he comes like Caesar, to see and to conquer."

"I don't believe he will succeed with Madame de St. Vallier, irresistible as he may consider himself," said the other man.

"Do you know the lady?"

"I knew her when she was Madame Charles Colnet, and knew her to be a perfect wife; and yet I believe she was married to Colnet by her parents, when she was very young. He was hardly the kind of man a beautiful girl would have chosen for herself—a rough diamond, *ce cher Colnet*—but she never allowed society to see that he was not the first man in the universe for her; and if this fellow, Vivien, brags of her favours, he must be an arrant scoundrel."

"He does not actually claim to be favoured; but he declares that he will be. You know his device: 'If not today, tomorrow.' I saw a letter he wrote to Julot, of the Sancho Panza, in which he vapoured as if tomorrow were near at hand."

They talked of other things, and by-and-by the murmuring ceased; but St. Vallier lay broad awake till the train steamed into Dijon, and he counted every minute that must pass before the tardy morning train would take him back, stopping at three village stations on the way, to St. Vallier le Roi.

His wife was at the station to meet him with a *coupe* and pair, more fur rugs, and a *bouillotte*.

She was there to meet him, radiant, loving; yet his soul sickened at the thought that her fondness might be a disguise to hide a heart that was already faithless. Yet no; he would not doubt her purity, even though the tainted breath of the seducer had passed across her name.

"Is Vivien still at the *château?*" he asked carelessly, as they drove away from the station.

He had lost so much time on the way with that accursed omnibus train that it was already daylight, and he could see his wife's face darken suddenly at the sound of the novelist's name, and he felt the arm within his own tremble slightly.

"Yes; but he leaves this evening, by the same train by which you travelled."

"That is rather sudden, isn't it? He talked of staying as long as we would have him, in order that he might finish his novel in the quiet of the country."

"He may have found that his novel made very little progress, and that the air of St. Vallier was not conducive to literary work."

"Lucie! I believe that man has been guilty of some impertinence to you."

"Not the least in the world," his wife answered, with a little laugh, which was meant to be reassuring; "only he has somewhat outstayed his welcome. Laure and I are of the same opinion in being tired of his company, and we ventured to let him perceive our sentiments—of course in the politest way—during your absence. Literary men are sensitive, and he was quick to understand the situation, and devise a sudden necessity to be in Paris."

"God bless you, my dearest!" cried Maxime, clasping his wife to his heart. "If Eve had been like you, the serpent would have crawled out of Eden baffled and humiliated."

"Dear Maxime, I really don't know what you are thinking about," his wife said gaily. "The whole business was as simple as

361

bonjour, and I hope you will be especially polite to M. Vivien on the last day of his visit."

Maxime had not the slightest doubt that Hector Vivien had taken advantage of the husband's absence to declare himself to the wife, and that he had been repulsed with the fearless scorn of unassailable purity. He took an opportunity to question Laure Evremonde in the course of the day, and though she would tell him very little, her admissions, and even her reservations, confirmed his belief.

Vivien and his host did not meet till dinner-time. The novelist was in his room all day, busy packing, and arranging his papers. He travelled without a valet, and refused all offers of assistance from St. Vallier's household. Consumed with rage and agitation, he felt that he could not trust himself in the society of another man's servant. His irritation might break out at any moment and wreak itself upon some rustic wretch who had only offended by sheer stupidity.

Yes, he had wooed his friend's wife. He had found his opportunity in the afternoon solitude of the *pleasaunce,* screened from the windows of the *château* by ten-foot hedges of ilex and yew, as secure from observation as in a forest labyrinth. He had brought to bear all those arts and fascinations which he had always found irresistible with duchesses—in his novels—and occasionally triumphant with middle-class matrons in actual life; and his reward had been the scorn of scorn: such scorn as a pure-minded woman who loves her husband must needs feel at the folly of any man who dares to suppose that he can supersede that husband in her affections.

The dinner-table was not so gay as it had been on many another evening. Vivien talked as much as usual; but an angry "light in his eyes, and a keener cynicism in his conversation, indicated latent irritation.

Maxime, who had been hysterically vivacious on the evening before his journey to Paris, was now grave and watchful. He and Tolpâche had talked together for half an hour before dinner, walking up and down the terrace on the edge of the moat, in the wintry darkness; and Tolpâche, like his host, was silent and *aux aguets.*

The dinner was long, and the carriage was announced while the men were still lingering over coffee and cigarettes. Madame de St.Vallier and her friends had retired to the music-room, whence came the sound of lightest opera-*bouffe* melodies played by Madame Evremonde, who was passionately fond of the music that lives for a Parisian season, to be as completely forgotten afterwards as the butterflies of last summer.

Vivien began his *adieux* with a cordial round of hand-shaking, taking the men at random as they happened to be standing. His host was the last to whom he came, with sinister smile, and outstretched hand.

Maxime stood straight and stern in front of him, and did not take the hand.

"You know the old saying, *Monsieur,* 'Speed the parting guest'?" he said grimly. "I have the utmost pleasure in speeding your departure, which I believe was hastened by the particular request of my wife."

A quiver of surprise shook Vivien for a moment; but in the next he collected himself, and accepted the situation with all its consequences.

"I am leaving hurriedly, I admit," he said; "but although I am in some haste to leave this part of the world, I can spare you an hour tomorrow morning, in the wood on the other side of the railway. I shall spend tonight at the inn in your village, and shall be at your service at whatever hour may suit your convenience, and that of your friends."

"Tolpâche, you were prepared for this. Loisin, I know I can rely on you?" said Maxime, turning to his two most intimate friends. "For my own part I have only one desire to express. Let our meeting be at sunset tomorrow: weapons as you please. That delay will give me time to arrange my affairs."

He turned on his heel, and went to the music-room, leaving Vivien to choose his own seconds, and settle details.

He felt, in his choice of the sunset hour, that he was obeying an old friend's summons, and accepting his fate.

The next day passed like a peaceful dream. Maxime and his wife were alone together for the greater part of their time, Lucie having excused herself from an excursion to a village racecourse in order to be her husband's companion. No cloud upon his brow forewarned her of approaching doom. He wanted that day to be cloudless—that day which he told himself would be his last of love and of life. He parted with her at half-past three o'clock, straining her to his breast, with one long passionate kiss, as he bade her goodbye.

There was despair in that embrace; and for the first time since his return she was startled from her happy security.

"Why goodbye?" she asked. "How pale you are, Maxime! Is there anything wrong?"

"Wrong? No. dearest, I am only going as far as the village, to settle some farming business with my bailiff."

"You will be back to dinner?"

"I hope so."

When the sun dipped at the bottom of that wooded hollow, where Maxime had seen it sink three days before, the augury of the earnest face and the pointing hand had been fulfilled.

The Ghost's Name

CHAPTER 1
WHAT PEOPLE SAID OF THE GHOST

The most singular feature of the Halverdene ghost was that it never appeared twice in the same shape and fashion. The main fact that a certain room at Halverdene was haunted, and a place of horror, had been borne witness to by so many conscientious people as to be placed beyond the regions of doubt. There were records of the ghost nearly a century old; there were histories as it were of yesterday, all vouched for by witnesses most unlikely to lie; but the ghost, though an old-established fact, verified by nearly a hundred years of varied experiences, was by no means a distinct personality of Shadowland.

The ghost was a very Proteus of ghosts; now man now woman; now old now young; but mostly horrible, and sometimes deriving its chiefest horror from a hideous indistinctness, a gigantic overpowering presence which weighed on the chilled spectator like a mountain of iron; a shapeless oppression to which he awakened shrieking, with icy water-drops upon his forehead.

Lucilla, Lady Halverdene's younger, lovelier sister, called the cedar-room at Halverdene the room of dreadful dreams. She had insisted on sleeping there once in a skittish Christmas mood, when the house-party at Halverdene overflowed every attic; but vowed afterwards that not to be sure of the best match in the county would she go through that ordeal again.

When pressed with questions as to what she had seen, she answered, "Caliban, ten times larger than life. He was there all night. I knew of him in my sleep, though I could not open my eyes to look. My eyelids were sealed with lead, and oh, I had such a headache! He gripped me by the throat, he sat upon my chest. Never, no, never again, Beatrice; not for twenty Halverdenes would I endure a night in that room!"

Everybody in Lucilla Wilmot's generation, a generation now mostly dust—for it was in the days when Lord Melbourne was minister, and railroads were a new thing in the land—everybody at Halverdene, in Beatrice Lady Halverdene's time, regretted that the ghost should have chosen so fine a room as the cedar-room for its head-quarters, since this cedar-panelled bed-chamber was one of the most spacious, if not one of the best rooms in the house. It was in the oldest part of the house, the Stuart wing, which comprised hall and library, a summer parlour, and this large cedar-room which was known as the garden bedroom.

The old wing was on a level with the most delicious old garden in Yorkshire; or so Beatrice Halverdene called it when she came as a bride with the husband of her choice to the old north-country manor. A garden needs perhaps to be two hundred years old in order to be perfectly beautiful. This was a garden planned in Bacon's time, and with many of the quaint features of that time still remaining, but without the sage's more fantastic and tea-gardenish ornamentation, the mere suggestion of which in the famous essay might convince any reasonable person that if Bacon wrote Shakespeare's plays, Shakespeare did not write Bacon's essays: for he whose lightest line can conjure visions of Arcadian beauty would never have recommended stately arches upon pillars of carpenter's work, crowned with little turrets containing bird-cages, or "broad plates of round coloured glass, gilt, for the sun to play upon," in his scheme of an English garden.

Beatrice in those early days of happy wedded love called that fair enclosure her Garden of Eden; but seven years of childless wedlock had sobered her enthusiasm, and the union between my lord and my lady seemed hardly that of the Miltonic Adam and Eve. There were those in the neighbourhood who said that my lord cared more for the health of his hounds than for the happiness of his wife; and that an outbreak of distemper in the kennel would have distressed him more than a threat of phthisis in the partner of his life.

There are men with whom love is only a transient fever; lovers to whom it comes natural to love and ride away, and who, when riding away is impossible, are apt to become churlish companions by the domestic hearth.

Those were days in which it was counted no disgrace to a man of high station to be a hard drinker. The memory of the Prince Regent, of Fox, of Sheridan, was still fresh in the minds of men. Brougham and other great intellectual lights were carrying on the old tradition. Port, Burgundy, Madeira, and other heady vintages were much more popular than Bordeaux and light wines from the Rhineland. Port was a part of an Englishman's patriotism, almost of his religion. It was a sound orthodox wine which churchmen loved. Rural benevolence found its best expression in port. Your Lady Bountiful no longer brewed unsavoury decoctions of healing herbs and called that charity. She sent strong soup and strong wine to the weak and ailing, and every villager in England smacked his lips at the name of the rich red vintage of Portugal.

Thus, it was counted no shame to Lord Halverdene that after a day in the saddle he recruited himself with a night over the mahogany and a couple of bottles of his famous wine. It was counted no shame if his valet had to help him up the slippery oak staircase now and again, and was occasionally sworn at for his pains. My lord was excused even for occasional rough language to my lady; for, as the village gossips said, "it was a sad pity she had no children, and it was only human natur' that his lordship should feel disappointed at the nonappearance of an heir."

Horses, hounds, and wine were my lord's idea of happiness. My lady loved her garden, her books, and her harp, and contrived to preserve an outward semblance of contentment under circumstances which might have driven a woman of lesser nature to open revolt against hard fate.

My lord had a house in Grosvenor Square and a park in Sussex, besides this manor and park of Halverdene, between York and Beverley. He was fondest of Halverdene, because of its accessibility from

York, Doncaster, and Pontefract, where the frequent race-meetings afforded him the amusement his soul loved best. He had a small racing stud at Halverdene, but his best horses were kept at Malton, under the invincible eye of John Scott. The chief ambition of his mind was to win the Leger, or for second best, the Great Ebor.

After three seasons in London, Lady Halverdene withdrew altogether from Metropolitan society, and was to be heard of only in Yorkshire or in Sussex, generally in Yorkshire, where for the first four years of her married life there were large house-parties, and where Lucilla Wilmot found life very enjoyable, attending all the county race-meetings with her sister, and riding to hounds. But for the last two years there had been very few visitors of my lady's choosing at Halverdene. Lucilla was always there, her sister's only companion in the long autumn evenings when his lordship was away at race-meetings; but, of the fashionable world, the dowagers and wives, the young men and maidens, who had once filled all the rooms and corridors with voices and laughter, there was nothing left but the memory of those days when Halverdene House had been hospitable and gay.

Visitors there were, it is true, racing men brought home by his lordship without word of warning to wife or housekeeper. Sometimes, after one of the northern meetings, three or four post-chaises would drive up to the door, late at night, and a bevy of half-intoxicated men would come reeling in. Some of these were underbred men whose talk was half made up of turf slang, and from whose society Lady Halverdene and her sister shrank as from a pestilence.

People shrugged their shoulders when they talked of Lord Halverdene.

"There is a mystery of some kind," said old General Palmer, to a little knot of men at the Rag.

"The mystery is that Halverdene beats his wife," answered Mr. Soaper-Snarle, the famous wit and reviewer. "We don't call that kind of thing a mystery in St. Giles'. There it's only wife-beating; but when an English nobleman turns brute and bully we call it a social mystery."

"Is that true?" cried an eager voice, strong and stern of accent. "Is it true that Lord Halverdene ill-treats his wife?"

The inquiry came from a tall broad-shouldered young man, with a sunburnt face and a cavalry moustache, a man just returned from the Punjab, and to whom most English scandals were new.

"I can only answer for what I saw myself when I was at Halverdene two years ago," answered Snarle, blandly. "Halverdene was uncommonly disagreeable to his wife then, and she looked as if she was used to it. There was nothing of the snivelling Griselda about her, mind you, but her resistance was quiet and dumb. She met his brutality with an icy scorn; but the house was no longer a comfortable house to stay in. One felt oneself on the crust of a volcano. Since then there have been very few high jinks at Halverdene. I saw her ladyship and her sister at York races last August, and they were both very nice to me, as they always were; only there was no talk of my going to Halverdene, although I was in their neighbourhood."

"I have heard things," said General Palmer; "but one never knows how much to believe. It was a love-match, wasn't it? I was told so when they were married."

"Yes, it was a love-match. Miss Wilmot was one of the beauties of her year—a *belle* in her first season—a ward in chancery, with a fortune that came very handy to Halverdene."

The sunburnt soldier from Kabul had left the group and was looking out of the window. His half-smoked cheroot lay forgotten where it had dropped from his hand, and his thoughts were in a Devonshire orchard, where he was a boy again, fresh from a military school, playing battledore and shuttlecock with two fair-haired girls in white frocks—girls whom, by some right of cousinship, he called by their Christian names. The Wilmots and the Donellys were very distant cousins, but still it was a cousinship, and Oscar Donelly had many privileges in the house of the jovial maiden aunt by whom these orphans were reared. He was a favourite with the elder lady, and the girls were frankly cordial to him. He brought them news of the great world, of which they knew absolutely nothing. Even Beatrice, the elder, would have to wait three or four years before she was to be presented and spend her first season in London, under the wing of a married aunt who had a house in Curzon Street, and was said to know only the best people.

The young cornet sailed for India with his regiment at the beginning of the Afghan war. The campaign had been a long and bitter one, and the subaltern came back to England a captain, but not altogether assured that the hero of Candahar was more to be envied than the cadet who played battledore and shuttlecock in the orchard between Starcross and Exeter. Home letters had told him of the Wilmots' appearance in society—the sisters had been presented at the same drawing-room, and made their *debut* in the great world side by side. There was only a year between them, and Beatrice had begged that they should go through the ordeal together, and had prevailed against her aunt's opinion.

"You will not be thought half so much of," she said, "if there are two of you."

The event proved her mistaken. The fact that there were two girls equally handsome and equally dowered, both bright and spirited and in the first freshness of youthful bloom, impressed people. The two Miss Wilmots were admired and run after wherever they went. No smart party was complete without them. When the two Miss Wilmots took influenza and were laid up together, Mayfair was in mourning.

Each had numerous offers between April and August. Both were difficult, but Lucilla was impossible. She refused some splendid opportunities of doing well for herself and improving the status of her family. Her aunt, Mrs. Montressor, who had married three portionless daughters with business-like celerity, was irate at this capriciousness.

"Do you expect to marry the Pope?" she asked.

"I believe a triple crown would tempt me; but then he would be old; they always are," said Lucilla, who had not been so severely educated as to trouble herself about the arrangement of nominatives in familiar conversation.

Everyone was surprised when Lord Halverdene was announced to the world as Beatrice's successful suitor. His reputation was by no means spotless; his passion for the turf was notorious; but he was handsome, and had that grand open manner and rather haughty bearing which a very young woman is apt to admire; especially when she has seen very little of the world, or of the dark abysses that may lie under that fine candid manner.

No doubt in the beginning of things Halverdene was deeply in love, and a sincere passion gave fire and force to his pursuit of the heiress.

They were married, and for the first year of her wedded life Beatrice was completely happy. Then came the shadow of trouble, and then the cold wind of a husband's indifference blew with deadly breath across the home paradise. Slowly and gradually the wife grew to understand the character of the man she loved. She heard stories of his past; she knew of damning facts in the present. Hymen reversed his taper, and the sacred flame went out for ever.

Beatrice was what is called a woman of spirit. She had made her choice matrimonial, and had stuck to it in the teeth of opposition, disregarding her London aunt's hints and insinuations, her country aunt's prejudices and cautions. Having taken her own course, she was too proud to complain of her disappointment even to her nearest and dearest. The world only knew of her troubles through the gossip of servants and rustic neighbours, and from the cessation of all pleasant hospitalities.

Lucilla, who insisted upon living with her sister, to the hindrance of all matrimonial opportunities for herself, alone knew what that sister had to suffer, and even to her Beatrice never opened her heart.

The affection between the sisters was of the strongest, or Lucilla would hardly have endured life in a house where she was subject to the rough insolence of a host for whom her presence was often an incubus; but Lucilla was not the kind of young woman to be scared by any man's rudeness, and she laughed his lordship's attacks to scorn.

"You don't suppose I stay at Halverdene to please you," she said, "or that I care whether you are glad or sorry to have me here?"

Beatrice had urged her sister to find a happier home, even if she did not care to accept any of those offers which would have ensured her a kind husband and a good social position. Any home would have been more congenial to a handsome young woman than Halverdene, where the dullness was only broken by an occasional irruption of noisy racing men. Lucilla was adamant.

"I don't mean to marry till I fall honestly in love," she told her sister; "and I don't want to set up a house of my own and establish myself in permanent spinsterhood. As for his lordship, *je m'en fiche*. It amuses me to quarrel with him. I am perfectly happy here. We have the horses and dogs, old servants who are fond of us, and a garden which we both adore. What more can we want for happiness? If you plague me about leaving you I shall order my goods to be taken to the garden bedroom, and establish myself there; and then perhaps I shall see the ghost, and die, as those poor children did."

This was an allusion to the earliest well-authenticated tradition of the ghost-chamber.

In the days when the garden bedroom had been a night nursery, two children of the first Lord Halverdene, a boy and a girl of nine and seven years old, had been frightened by some ghastly appearance in that fine old room, and had told their nurses vague stories of the something that brooded over their beds. The visions had occurred at longish intervals, and their vagueness had suggested childish dreams; but the death of the two children, which had happened within a year, had given a new aspect to the story in the minds of the superstitious and ignorant. The formless visions childishly depicted were placed on record as ghostly warnings foreshadowing doom, and the reputation of the garden bedroom as a ghost-chamber was firmly established. A century and a half of occasional appearances had maintained the traditions of the house, and to hint a doubt of the ghost in the village of Halverdene, or even in the vicarage drawing-room, was to be assured with gravest head-shakings that this particular case was established by indisputable evidence. Other ghost-stories might be foolishness; but the ghost at Halverdene House was fact.

"And nobody can tell me the nature and appearance of the thing," cried Lucilla, taking tea in the bosom of the vicar's family, which was not too grand to dine at three o'clock in summer and take tea at six, for the sake of an evening walk after tea. "That is what worries me about this particular ghost. Nobody seems to know anything about him. When I slept in the room myself—"

The two younger daughters—both in the pinafore period of then-existence—crowded upon her at this point, and nearly squeezed her off her chair, interrupting her with breathless interrogation.

"Did you—did you really sleep there, Miss Wilmot? How awful!"

"How lovely!"

"And did you see anything? Oh, did you see *it?*"

"No, Dolly, I didn't see it; but I knew it was there."

"Oh, tell us, tell us, do tell us!" with growing breathlessness. "How sweet of you, how brave of you to sleep there! Let me take your cup. Do tell us."

"There is very little to tell. It was Christmas-time, and we had a big house-party. I had been dancing all the evening, and I was dead beat. I slept like a top for two or three hours; and then I woke suddenly in the pitch darkness, and I felt that there was something—something holding me by the throat and strangling me—something huge and horrible, with red-hot claws that pressed into my chest. I don't know if I fainted, or fell into a dead sleep, or what happened to me; but when the house-maid brought me my tea in the morning, I woke with a splitting headache, and I felt ill, and shivering, and wretched for two or three days after; and then Beatrice insisted on carrying me off to Bridlington to get the ghostly feeling blown out of me by the North Sea."

"And you don't even know what the ghost was like?" said Dolly, disappointed.

"How could I? The room was pitch dark."

"How tiresome! There is generally some kind of light," pursued Dolly, falling back on her knowledge of the stories of Ghostland she had read in gorgeous half-guinea annuals, among the portraits of beautiful peeresses. "The moon suddenly shines in through an opening in the damask curtains; or the wood fire, which has burnt low, flames up with a last flash, and one sees the ghost's face, and dress, and jewellery."

"Ah, Dolly, that is the ghost of fiction; a lady in a *sacque*; a gentleman in a Ramillies wig. The thing that haunts Halverdene is a reality, and the fact that nobody has ever been able to describe the thing goes to prove that it is real."

Dolly and her sister listened open-mouthed as Lucilla soared into that region of the abstract where their young minds could not follow her.

The thing that haunts the room may be an unresting conscience burdened with a crime unatoned, or a wicked soul that died and made no sign, and even in the grave is tortured with its lust of sin, hate, jealousy, wicked love—who knows? Oh, my dears, forgive me! I am raving. Don't let me talk of that horrid room any more. When I remember what I suffered there I always get a little mad."

"It had red-hot claws," said Dolly, dwelling on the one descriptive touch which appealed to her juvenile ideality.

"Dolly, if you insist upon talking about it, I vow I'll make you sleep in the room," cried Lucilla, shaking herself free from the two pinafores. "I should like to sleep there," said Dolly, opening her eyes very wide. "Yes, and die like those other children who slept in the garden bedroom when it was a nursery. That room has always been fatal to children. It was not the first Lord Halverdene's children only—there were others who died ninety years afterwards, three children in one family—a younger son's family—three children in one summer."

"Had they seen the ghost—all of them?" asked Dolly, awe-stricken; while Cecily, the younger pinafore, could only shape the words dumbly with dry lips.

"I don't know; they had been frightened in the room. The old woman at the lodge told me about them. They were nervous, sensitive children—not great bouncing creatures like you and Cis—and they died in one summer. That's all the old woman could tell me about them, and she was nursemaid at Halverdene fifty years ago. But it's very wrong of me to talk to you of such horrors."

"We like it," said Dolly; "we dote upon ghosts."

"Silly, morbid little things! Why, all sensible people know that ghosts are nonsense. Come and show me your gardens."

"She has a lettuce in hers," said Cicely, pointing to the older pinafore. "It isn't very big yet, but we water it every evening."

"You'll drown it," Lucilla told them. "It will turn into a watercress."

They took hold of her, one hanging on to each hand, and dragged her out through the French window, and across the lawn to that obscure portion of the vicarage grounds where the children had their allotments. They were two funny little figures in long white pinafores, and plaited pig-tails tied with brown ribbon, and they really were children, which was not so wonderful a fact in the early part of the forties as it might seem now.

CHAPTER 2
HOW CAPTAIN DONELLY HEARD OF THE GHOST

Captain Donelly could not banish the thought of the Devonshire orchard and the girls whose bright faces had made the homely scene paradisaic. He was deeply moved at the notion of Beatrice's domestic troubles. That she should be ill-used by a husband, she whose love should have made the meanest of men great and noble, she whom he would have loved kneeling, as devout Romanists love the saints. She was only seventeen in those innocent boyish days, before ever his battle of life began, as fresh and as confiding as a child. He would have deemed it sacrilege to tell her of his love—selfish to ask her to wait for him. What of this world's gear could he ever have worthy to lay at her feet?

They had been boy and girl together, she seventeen, he under twenty, and his love had been but a boy's love. A lad just beginning life in a profession which he thinks the finest in the world, with his future all before him, and the novel delights of uniform, mess, and parade ground, is apt to think just a little more of himself and his own ambitious hopes than of the girl he loves. It was afterwards at a lonely hill-station, where the long evenings hung heavy on his hands, that Oscar Donelly began to discover how fondly he had loved that third or fourth cousin of his.

It was afterwards when a letter from his father's Irish vicarage brought him the news of Beatrice's marriage, that he knew how deep he had been in love with her, by the sharpness of his agony at knowing that she was lost to him. His happy-go-lucky Irish temper had made him ignore the probability of her marrying in her first season. He told himself that she would be difficult to please; he flattered himself that he had a corner in her heart which might help to keep out a stranger, and that after a few years of hard fighting he might go home to find her still free, and willing to be won He knew how daring had been his hopes now that all hope was over.

He had only been in London a few days when he heard his old friend General Palmer and Mr. Soaper-Snarle talking about Lady Halverdene. His first duty was to his father and sisters in the south of Ireland, where he spent the second half of July and the beginning of August. That visit finished he set his face towards Yorkshire, a long cross-country journey from Holyhead; but he contrived to arrive at York in time for the summer meeting. He had been told that Lord and Lady Halverdene were sure to be at the races.

It was brilliant weather, and the old city was full of gaiety, and overflowing with visitors. Beds, even in the shabbiest lodging-houses, over shabby shops, were at a premium. Happily Oscar had friends at the barracks who were able and willing to put him up for the three nights, and on their drag he went to the Knavesmire.

He did not stop with the party on the drag, but left them in order to look for his friends on the grandstand, after a careful review of the carriages had convinced him that the Halverdenes were not among that giddy and unbusinesslike part of the community to whom a race only means picnicking among a smartly dressed crowd, with all the troublesome accompaniments of gipsies, acrobats, itinerant musicians, and beggars of every description. The nigger minstrel—otherwise Ethiopian Serenader—had not been invented at that period of English history.

The comparative quiet of the grandstand, though it was pretty well filled, was positively soothing after the noise and racket of the course, and Captain Donelly had no trouble in finding the people he wanted. They were in the front seat at one end of the stand, two tall women dressed almost alike in lavender muslin gowns, straw bonnets, and black silk scarves, a style of dress which would seem very dowdy to the modern idea, but which was then graceful and elegant. The reader may refer to *Nicholas Nickleby*, or to the illustrations of Balzac's novels, where he will see a simplicity of drapery which is not unbecoming to a graceful figure.

Captain Donelly thought he had never seen a lovelier face than the one which smiled at him in the shadow of a cottage bonnet.

"Beatrice!" he exclaimed, holding out his hands, and seizing both of hers.

"No, Lucilla. Beatrice is so absorbed in the horses that she has not even seen you. How sunburnt you are! When did you come home?"

"Four weeks ago. I need not ask if you are well. Those blooming cheeks answer for themselves."

"If I were a milkmaid I should curtsy my thanks for your compliment, but blooming cheeks are about the last thing a young woman of *ton* would choose to be accredited with. Pallor and fragility are the essentials of a fashionable *belle*."

"I have had a surfeit of pallid beauty in India, and I am charmed to see health and good looks at home. How is Lady Halverdene?"

"You must ask that question for yourself. Beatrice, here is Captain Donelly waiting to be welcomed as a hero after his perils in the Punjab."

Beatrice rose and came towards them. She was changed from the happy girl he had known in Devonshire. Trouble had set its mark upon her. In the old days Lucilla had been an insignificant chit of sixteen, with hardly the promise of beauty, while Beatrice was radiant in budding loveliness; a rosebud just expanding into a rose. Now Lucilla was the rose, and Beatrice had a faded look, but withal so noble a carriage of head and throat, and so exquisite a smile, that she was to Oscar's eyes even more interesting than in the bloom of her girlhood.

She blushed as she welcomed him, and then sighed. The blush was for an innocent love-story that had long been ended and all but forgotten. The sigh came with the thought of all she had suffered since they two had parted. Then the woman of society asserted herself.

"Have you seen Halverdene? No! He is in the ring, or in the paddock, I dare say. He has two horses in the next race, both doomed to lose, I fear. Are you not glad to be back in England after that terrible war? What horrors, what suffering! My heart bled—every English heart bled—as I read of that awful tragedy."

They sat down side by side and talked gravely, frankly, as if they had been brother and sister—talked of himself and of his experiences; but of herself and of what she had done and suffered in the long interval of severance there was very little said.

"You have a place near here, I think?" he said, by-and-by, when the race was over.

One of Lord Halverdene's horses had come in a bad third, the other was nowhere. Beatrice looked distressed at the failure, though it had seemed inevitable before the race began.

"Nineteen miles. I don't know if you call that near."

"Do you go back tonight?"

"No. Lucilla and I are stopping at the hotel with Halverdene. We shall go back tomorrow evening; but I dare say Halverdene will stay for the last of the racing, and come home on the coach on Saturday."

Halverdene came up to the stand presently, very angry at the failure of his horses, but flushed with wine, and with a kind of savage mirth which showed itself in his effusive recognition of his wife's kinsman.

"You'll dine with us at the Royal, of course. Captain Donelly, seven sharp, and as good a brand of Moet as you need wish to drink."

The captain explained that he was staying at the barracks, and could hardly excuse himself from the mess dinner.

"D—n the mess! I know all those fellows, and they know me. Bring as many of them as you like. We'll make a night of it."

"I'd rather come in for an hour after dinner, if you'll allow me."

"Do as you like, my dear fellow," cried his lordship; and then swaggered away and was speedily absorbed into a group of rather disreputable looking men, and laughing and talking louder than the loudest of them.

His presence had silenced his wife, and Oscar could see that every tone of that loud voice, every peal of reckless laughter, was pain to her. She sat looking across the Knavesmire with eyes that took no delight in the varied crowd, the play of summer light upon the landscape and the people, the movement and the gladness of the scene.

Captain Donelly dined with his friends at the mess, and adjourned to the Royal Hotel at nine o'clock. He found Lady Halverdene and her sister in a dimly lighted drawing-room, while from the adjoining dining-room came the sound of several voices and frequent bursts of laughter.

"Halverdene asked some of his racing friends to dinner," Beatrice told him; "so Lucilla and I dined *tête-à-tête*, and have been moping here in the dark ever since. I think there is hardly anything so disheartening as an inn sitting-room for birds of passage, as we are. No belongings, books, work, anything. We have been looking at the engraving of the Queen's marriage as if we had never seen that work of art before."

"I should have asked the waiter to bring us a pack of cards if I had not been afraid he would laugh at me. We might have played Beggar my Neighbour or Casino," said Lucilla.

"Will you join Halverdene and his friends in the dining-room?" asked Beatrice.

"What, desert you when you own to being moped! No, Lady Halverdene, I mean to be as amusing—or at least as flippant as a walking gentleman in a five-act comedy. How I wish I were witty for your sakes! Or, a happier idea; you two who have lived in the world, while I have been living out of it, can amuse me with a few of the scandals that have been town-talk while I have been in the Indian hills."

A waiter brought in an urn and a tea-tray, and Lucilla made tea, and the talk soon drifted out of an artificial channel to the days that were gone, when these three had been happy without fear or even thought of the future. Oscar and Lucilla were the chief talkers. Lady Halverdene sitting in the shadowy region beyond the light of those candles which made so formidable an item in an old-fashioned hotel bill, and yet left a room so dark. Once there came a faint sigh from among the shadows, but there was for the most part silence.

Presently the doors burst open and Lord Halverdene and his boon-companions poured into the room, most of them like the sons of Belial, "flown with insolence and wine." The talk became noisy almost to riotousness. Halverdene had obviously been drinking, and if his guests seemed less affected by liquor, it was only because they were hardened by longer habit, and that while he had been gradually degenerating into a drunkard, intemperance was with them a second nature.

Tonight he was good-natured in his cups, and he treated Donelly with boisterous friendliness.

"You must come to Halverdene," he said; "you can go post with me tomorrow. We'll manage to put you up: the old house will bear a good bit of squeezing, though my lady and her sister contrive to absorb a whole wing. Your fine lady is a bird that must have a very roomy cage, nowadays. Let me see," advancing an uncertain finger and pointing first at one of his companions and then at another; "there's you, and you, and the major, and Parson Bob," here the wavering finger indicated a seedy man in a clerical neckcloth, "and the rest of you," half a dozen in all, but to Halverdene's blinded vision they may have seemed half a score; "but we can find a shake-down for her ladyship's cousin; yes, old file, even if we have to put you in the haunted room."

He stood in front of the empty fireplace, with his coat-tails under his arms, swaying backwards and forwards, laughing long and loud at what he thought a capital joke. No one noisier than my lord when he took his wine good naturedly.

This was the first that Oscar Donelly had heard of the haunted room.

"What, have you a ghost at Halverdene?" he exclaimed lightly.

"Dozens of 'em. Not that I ever saw anything; but the ghosts have been there time out of mind, and the room they haunt is a plaguey unlucky room. It may be only a coincidence," said Halverdene, sinking from loud joviality to a solemn whisper; "but any young people who have slept in that room have come to an untimely end. It used to be a nursery! A nice nursery, by Jove! The children saw something, took it to heart, and died. If Providence—gave me an heir—wou'dn lerr him sleep in that nur-er-y," concluded Halverdene, becoming suddenly unintelligible.

Captain Donelly thanked him in general terms for his invitation, and declared his intention of profiting by it, not immediately, but at some future time.

"When your house may not be quite so full," he said; "though I am not afraid of a night or two in your haunted room. I always carry a pistol-case; and I think your ghost would come off second best."

"Ah, that's a dangerous dodge, popping at ghosts," said the seedy parson; "generally turns out badly. You may shoot the footman who brings you your shaving-water, or a sportsman who has got up at three o'clock for cub-hunting, and happens to look into the wrong room. No use shooting at a ghost! If he is a ghost you can't hurt him, and if he isn't it may mean manslaughter."

Captain Donelly did not court conversation with the cleric whom his friends addressed as Parson Bob. The old clock on the stairs struck eleven, and Oscar bade his cousins good night, and slipped out of the room while Halverdene's back was turned. His lordship was standing at a card-table with his friends clustered round him betting on the cut, in that highly intellectual game known as Blind Hookey. The captain's heart ached for the lady whom he remembered so lovely and light-hearted, with life and its chances of happiness all before her.

Yes, he meant to avail himself of Lord Halverdene's invitation. He wanted to see what manner of life his cousin led in her own home, with such a husband as the man he had seen tonight. He had not asked for Beatrice's approval of her husband's invitation, for he divined that she would shrink from admitting even a kinsman to the secrets of her domestic life. His blood burned within him at the thought that such men as those battered *roués,* those second-rate racing men he had seen tonight, were free to enter the house where a refined and beautiful woman was mistress.

Captain Donelly travelled further north, spent a fortnight at a friend's shooting lodge in Argyllshire, shot a good many head of game, tramped over a good many miles of heather, ate a good many bannocks, drank his share of the famous Lochiel whisky, and bored himself stupendously. His heart was not in the business, and his friends found it out.

"You are a deuced good shot," said one of them, "but a d—d dull companion;" and Donelly owned that he was out of spirits and unhappy about someone whom he—whom he cared for.

He could not get Beatrice Halverdene's face out of his mind, with its wan smile and frequent look of pain. He could not forget Halverdene's brutal manner, the drunken laughter, the thickened utterance, and, worst of all, the raffish dissipated companions, the reprobates who were allowed to sit at meat and drink with this drunken sinner's wife.

To think that she had married this man for love, and that the first year of her wedded life had been an idyll! His home letters had told him, in a young sister's enthusiastic language, of Lady Halverdene's happy marriage, adoring, and adored by, her husband. It was not his coronet that had won her. She had married for love.

That yearning to see more of the woman he had loved in his boyhood grew upon Oscar Donelly in the lonely Scottish hills. His companions of the shooting lodge were sportsmen and nothing more. Their everlasting talk of sport wearied him. He was among them, but not of them; and one morning he pretended that his letters brought him an urgent summons southward, on family business, and a post-chaise took him to Glasgow the following afternoon in time for the coach which left that city at eight in the evening.

It was evening again when he left York in another post-chaise on his way to Halverdene, and it was past ten o'clock when he alighted from the chaise in front of the Queen Anne doorway, with its stone shell-shaped pediment, and tall narrow window on either side; windows within which the light showed dimly, as if the hall of the mansion were but sparely lighted.

"I hope everyone has not gone to bed," thought Oscar.

He felt that this night attack was rather a desperate style of acting upon a general invitation; but Lord Halverdene was not a man with whom he need be over-ceremonious, and the captain wanted to take his lordship's household by surprise, in order to arrive at the better knowledge of his cousin's domestic life. And yet, alas! What good could come of that knowledge to the lady or to himself? If her husband were unkind, what could he do to help her? If her life were unhappy, what could he do to make it happier?

A sleepy-looking servant opened the door and admitted him into a large and lofty hall, paved with black and white marble, and adorned with the most conventional and uninteresting of family portraits. The weather had been wet and gusty from early morning, when Captain Donelly left Newcastle outside the mail coach, preferring to be wet in the open air than to be dry in a stuffy vehicle with its full complement of passengers. He was chilled to the bone, and he looked almost resentfully at the wide fireplace with its sculptured marble chimney-piece surmounted by a bust of Minerva, forgetting that it was only the first week of September, and that people were still pretending to think it summer.

"Be good enough to bring in my portmanteau, and pay the postilion for me," said Oscar, counting some money into the sleepy footman's palm.

"Yes, I'll see to that," the footman answered in rather an off-hand tone. "You're the person that was sent for, I suppose?"

"The person that was sent for? What do you mean? I am Captain Donelly; her ladyship's cousin."

"I beg your pardon, sir," stammered the man, much humbled; "there was a person expected—from York—and I thought, seeing the portmanteau—and—I beg your pardon, sir." "His lordship is at home, I conclude?"

"Yes, sir, but he is not very well, and he went to bed two hours ago. Her ladyship and Miss Wilmot are in the morning-room. If you'll step this way, sir, I'll look to your portmanteau afterwards."

He led the way to a room at the other end of a long narrow corridor, which looked of older date than the entrance hall, flung open the door with the true London air, and announced—"Captain Donelly."

The sisters were seated far apart, Lucilla at the piano, but not playing, Lady Halverdene half hidden in a large armchair by the fireplace, where there was a cheery little fire, which revived Oscar's sinking spirits almost as much as the sight of his cousins.

"Oscar!" they cried simultaneously, and in neither face was there any pleasure mingled with the look of surprise.

It was not a cheering welcome. Captain Donelly could hardly misread the face of his cousin Beatrice, which expressed something akin to fear.

"You didn't expect me," he said, "but I hope you are not vexed with me for taking his lordship at his word so completely, and bursting in upon you without notice. You remember he said I might come at any time, there would always be room for me, even if it were only the ghost's room," he concluded, trying to be jocose.

"Yes, I remember," answered Beatrice, looking from her visitor to her sister with such obvious embarrassment that Oscar felt he ought not to remain, even although she was his kinswoman, and he had travelled a night and a day for the sole purpose of finding out what her home life was like.

"I see that my unexpected arrival embarrasses you," he said. "I have been very inconsiderate. A man's invitation counts for nothing when there is a lady in the case. I ought to have waited for you to ask me here. And I am so atrociously late, too. I thought I should have been here by eight o'clock at the latest, but the Newcastle Lightning is about the slowest coach I ever travelled by. If there is an inn within a walk I'll go there for to-night. I can come back to breakfast with you tomorrow morning; and then you can decide at your leisure whether you would like to have me for a few days or not. If Halverdene is ill you may prefer to be without visitors."

"Nonsense!" cried Lucilla. "Of course you must stay; even if we do put you in the ghost-room," she added, as if answering a look of her sister's.

"Would you mind? It is really one of the best rooms in the house—and as the ghost is so very shifty and intangible nobody need be afraid of him, need they?"

"I would not be afraid if he were the most palpable and clearly defined apparition in England," said Donelly, trying to infuse some cheerfulness into the situation.

Lucilla rang and ordered the cedar-room to be got ready for Captain Donelly.

"Be sure there is a good fire, and that everything is thoroughly aired," she said peremptorily; "and see that Captain Donelly's portmanteau is unpacked for him. And you must have supper," she said to Oscar, taking the matter into her own hands, while Lady Halverdene sat inert, and apparently uninterested, looking at the fire. I dare say you dined early, and perhaps badly into the bargain."

"Both," admitted Oscar; and Lucilla gave her orders for a snug little supper to be served in the room where they were sitting.

Her cousin could but admire her grace and brightness, her prompt decided way of settling things. All of energy and vivacity that Beatrice had once possessed—and he recalled the light-hearted shuttlecock player in the Devonshire orchard—seemed to have left her. Tonight she was dull and silent, and it wounded him to think that she was bored and annoyed by his uninvited presence.

"Come and sit by the fire," said Lucilla. "Beatrice is out of spirits because of his lordship's illness. You mustn't mind her."

"But I do mind. I feel very sorry to have intruded at such a time. Is Lord Halverdene really very ill?"

"Yes, he is very bad."

"What is it?"

"The doctors hardly give it a name. You know how mysterious doctors are. It is some kind of nervous complaint. They say it has been coming on for a long while, and that is about all they say. We have sent to York for a skilled attendant; and in the meantime Halverdene's valet is a very good nurse. There is no use in Beatrice moping. She can do nothing."

"That is the saddest part of it all," said Lady Halverdene, and then relapsed into silence.

"What a delightful room!" said Oscar, looking about, and admiring the panelled walls and low ceiling with its carved oak cross-beams.

"Yes, it is one of the old rooms. This wing was built in Charles II' s time, when the place was only a hunting-lodge; the Queen Anne front and wings were added fifty years later, so that the principal part of the mansion is only an afterthought! Your quarters are close by. I am very fond of this room, and Beatrice and his lordship are kind enough to let me call it my own, as it is in the unpopular end of the house, and nobody cares about it."

"I hope the ghost doesn't intrude here."

"Oh, no; he, she, or it is a conscientious ghost, and never breaks bounds."

And then Lucilla told him how she had spent one night in the haunted room for her own pleasure, and he questioned her as to what she had seen there.

"I don't believe I saw anything—really," she said. "Looking back at my experience in the sober light of common sense, I think the thing which scared me was only a bad dream—a very horrid dream—of the nightmare nature; the sense of some huge indescribable presence squatting on my chest, weighing me down into a bottomless pit of horror and suffocation. I went there prepared to be frightened, and the hideousness—the horrid feeling of the visitation—was quite equal to my darkest imaginings; but after all I believe it was only a dream, and that my own imagination was to blame for all I suffered."

Oscar moved about the room looking at the books and china, the pictures, which were few but good, and lastly at a row of miniatures mounted upon faded red velvet, which hung upon a panel near the fireplace.

"These are interesting," he said. "Family portraits, I conclude?"

"Yes, those two at the top are the boy and girl who used to sleep in the cedar nursery, and who both died. I believe that was what first gave the room its evil repute. And after, when another occupant of the room died young, people talked of it as an unlucky room, and it began to be considered fatal."

"It was not fatal to you, I am glad to think."

"No, and it is not going to be fatal to you, unless those servants are careless in the matter of airing things. Perhaps you would like to see the room before you sup?"

"Very much. I should like to make what our neighbours call *un brin de toilette* before I sit down to eat with my esteemed cousins."

"Then let it be only *un brin*" said Lucilla; "don't put yourself into dress clothes at this hour of the night, just because Beatrice and I are in evening gowns."

"I will do nothing that will deprive me of your society for more than ten minutes," said Oscar, gallantly; "but I am dying to see the ghost-room."

"You shall not be allowed to expire," Lucilla said gaily, as she rang the bell.

Her life and brightness charmed him. He began to wonder whether he had ever been in love with Beatrice—poor Beatrice, sitting by the fire, dull and despondent, weighed down by anxiety about a sick husband who was reported to have neglected and ill-used her when he was well.

Oscar pitied the downtrodden wife with all his heart; but he found it very difficult to associate her with the sparkling young beauty of the Devonian village. The sparkling beauty was here, but her name was no longer Beatrice. She was Lucilla, whose brilliant eyes, sunny curls, and white shoulders shone out in the sombre old panelled parlour, a revelation of unexpected beauty; Lucilla, of whom his earlier memories could only recall pigtails and a pinafore.

He was conducted to a room close by—*the* room, a spacious wainscoted chamber with three windows, one opening to the ground, a noble fire burning in a wide iron grate with old-fashioned hobs and an elaborately floriated back. The bedstead was a fine mahogany four-poster, with slim-fluted columns and handsome green silk curtains, nothing hearse-like or gloomy about it. Altogether, the room in the light of that glorious coal and wood fire, and with a pair of candles alight on the dressing-table, had a cheerful and comfortable aspect.

The footman had unpacked the portmanteau, had laid out brushes, and combs, and razors on the dressing-table, and placed all things ready for the guest. Oscar made a rapid toilet, and returned to the sitting-room, splendid in a dark brown coat, and a black velvet waistcoat worked with gold thread, and one of those all-conquering black satin stocks which are familiar to us in the early portraits of Dickens and D'Orsay. He felt that although he had been forbidden to put on evening dress he was not looking his worst.

A light impromptu supper was laid on a pembroke table near the fire, and the trio sat down together in the friendliest way. Lucilla carved a chicken with skill and *aplomb*—those were the days in which a lady was expected to be able to carve—while Oscar operated upon a ham. The footman opened a champagne bottle and filled the three tall narrow glasses. No butler had appeared on the scene, and Oscar concluded that functionary had gone to bed before his arrival.

Lucilla persuaded her sister to eat a little chicken and drink a little wine.

"You had positively nothing at dinner," she said; "you are killing yourself," at which Lady Halverdene looked at her reproachfully, and then with an evident effort put on an appearance of cheerfulness, and finally, beguiled into self-forgetfulness, joined in the light talk of the other two, and seemed almost happy.

They sat talking till the fire went out, and a loud clock in the distance struck twelve.

"Every stroke sounds a reproach," said Lucilla. "Upon my word, Oscar, you have tempted us into most unholy dissipation. Do you know that we usually light our chamber candlesticks and stalk solemnly up to bed at half-past ten?"

"I am ashamed of having made you so late."

"You have done us a kindness," said Lady Halverdene. "The nights are always too long when one is anxious."

"You ought not to be so anxious," Oscar said cheerfully; "with his lordship's fine physique he is sure to pull through, whatever the nature of his illness. He is the kind of man to make a good fight for life."

The candles were lighted. The footman reappeared, sleepier than ever, to put out the lights in the sitting-room. The little party dispersed, the two ladies to their distant apartments, the captain to his room close by, and silence and darkness came down upon the lonely country house.

Chapter 3
How Captain Donelly Met the Ghost

In spite of the fact that he was in a house whose master lay seriously ill—a fact which, no doubt, ought to have saddened him—Oscar Donelly was in excellent spirits as he paced slowly about the spacious cedar bedroom in the cheerful firelight. He had just made a discovery which had gladdened him, which opened up a bright vista of possible happiness. He had found out that his romantic passion for Beatrice Halverdene—the flame which had been fed by absence and fond imaginings-had burnt itself out, and that a newer and brighter flame had risen from the ashes of the old love.

He was in love with Lucilla—Lucilla, with whom he had an indisputable right to be in love if he pleased, and who was free to respond to his passion. Lucilla, who by the brightness of her smiles and the friendly accents of her voice, by all her pretty cares for his comfort, and the unqualified cordiality of her welcome, had shown him that he was by no means disagreeable in her eyes.

He walked up and down in the fire-glow, thinking of her looks, her words, her vivacious turns of speech, her arch smiles, her shrewd common sense; and anon meditating ways and means, and wondering whether he were financially worthy. He was neither rich nor poor. A dear old maiden aunt had left him an income which made him independent of his father, who had a small estate in County Limerick which must come to his only son by-and-by. The lookout was by no means desperate. He could afford to sell out and settle in Yorkshire, if Lucilla wanted to be near her sister. He had seen a good deal of hard fighting. He loved his profession, and would leave the army with regret; but Lucilla was worth a sacrifice. He was sure she would want to stay near her sister. She was the stronger spirit, the protector, the guardian angel. One brief hour of Halverdene's society had been enough to show him that some such sustaining influence was needful for Halverdene's wife.

He replenished his fire, heaping up the coals from a big copper scuttle, and looked about the room, admiring the play of light and shadow on the rich brown wainscote, the bright glints on the green silk curtains and pierced brass fender.

He had forgotten all ghostly traditions when he lay down to rest, full of happy fancies about the home that he was to create for Lucilla and himself within a few miles of Halverdene. A smallish house would do, if it were pretty, and picturesque as to situation. There must be a good stable, and some shooting; and no doubt he would have the run of the Halverdene covers.

The bed was of the old-fashioned luxurious order. A delightful bed for a good sleeper, a downy paradise for the first half-hour, but after that half-hour a couch of fever and unrest to the wakeful occupant. Happily, Oscar was tired with many hours of journeying on the top of stage coaches, and, while bodily weary, he had a mind at ease, no carking cares to pluck him from the verge of slumber's comfortable abyss. So for him the bed of downy feathers was the gate of paradise, and he was speedily threading dreamland's fairest labyrinth, albeit Lucilla had christened that very chamber the room of dreadful dreams.

He had laughed at the notion of supernatural manifestations. He had slept the long deep sleep of youth and health and hope.

A wan and sickly daylight was in the room when he woke suddenly to a revelation of horror, which in its spectral hideousness and its grim reality was worse than any vision of dread that Lucilla's stories had suggested to his imagination last night. A figure was kneeling upon the bed, crouching over him, with the strong grip of a burning hand upon his throat. A face, pallid and ghastly, was bending down close against his face, and two fiery eyes were glaring into his eyes.

If this were the ghost, verily it was a vision of fear to bring death or madness upon any young and sensitive creature that looked upon it. He who had never quailed before the Afghan guns, the savage Afghan faces, felt his blood run cold and his heart beat faster.

His first thought between sleeping and waking was, "No wonder the children died!" Then, as the shadows of sleep were shaken off, reason reasserted herself.

Could a ghost's hand hold him as this hand was holding him? Would a ghost's breath sound thick and laboured like the panting breath he felt upon his face; and was that hideous sound of grinding teeth a sound of any spiritual visitant? No: common sense told him that this was no inexplicable impalpable horror, but a very real and very human assailant—a madman, with one hand clawing him by the throat, and the other hand uplifted and flourishing an open razor.

It was not till he had torn himself free from the clutch of those burning fingers and had leapt to the other side of the wide bedstead, that he recognized his assailant as Lord Halverdene.

In the struggle to free himself he had thrown his enemy from the bed to the floor. He scrambled to his feet immediately, and the two men stood looking at each other with the width of the bed between them, one with a deadly weapon in his hand, the other totally unarmed.

Oscar looked despairingly towards the fireplace, which was on Halverdene's side of the bed. To reach it and get possessed of that useful weapon for emergencies, the poker, he must pass the madman, who stood at the corner of the bedstead ready with his razor, grinning and muttering, his body stooping forward, like an Indian trapper lying in wait for his quarry. He had wounded himself in the scuffle on the bed, and the blood was pouring from a gash on his cheek. He was in his night-shirt, with bare feet.

The bell-rope was on Oscar's side of the bed. He pulled it violently, and in that violence destroyed all chance of communicating his peril by means of the bell, for the hook and loop had both rusted with disuse, and that one sharp tug brought down the bell-rope. No hope there.

Should he try to parley with his foe—try to talk reasonably with a man who was evidently for the time being a homicidal maniac thirsting for his blood? That blood-bedabbled face mopping and mowing at him yonder by the bedpost, that threatening hand with the razor, did not promise much advantage from the force of persuasion.

The faint and sickly light that filtered through the close-drawn blinds told Oscar that it was, at latest, five o'clock. He and the maniac were perhaps the only mortals stirring in the rambling old house. He remembered the long narrow corridor, the isolated position of the room in which he had slept.

"God knows how far off the occupied rooms may be," he thought. "I shall be massacred here, and nobody the wiser, till the footman brings my shaving water at eight o'clock."

He had time to think this while he stood at bay, considering what was his best course. He would give the wretched man a chance, he thought, before encountering violence with violence.

"My dear Halverdene, this is too absurd!" he said, in a loud firm voice, looking fixedly at the gibbering face by the bedpost. "What have I done to offend you that you should break in upon me in the middle of the night? It's a curious kind of hospitality, after having invited me to take you unawares. By Jove! you have taken *me* unawares!" he added, trying to laugh off the situation, with that blood-stained faced staring at him.

"My wife's lover," muttered Halverdene—"my wife's lover! Kill him! kill him! kill him! That's what the devil said when he woke me out of my sleep just now—kill him! But Turner had hidden my pistols, and had locked my dressing-case with the razors for every day in the week—Monday, Tuesday, Wednesday. Today's Wednesday, ain't it? I wanted Wednesday's razor, to cut your throat; but the box was locked—curse that man of mine!"

All this was uttered rapidly, and sounded more like a monkey's chattering than human speech. Donelly was looking about him for a weapon, and as Halverdene came towards him with a wild leap, razor uplifted, he snatched up a heavy Chippendale chair, flung it straight at his assailant, knocking him down, and made a rush for the door.

The door was locked, the key gone. The madman had struggled up on to his knees, and was laughing at him, pointing at the door.

"Turner hid the pistols, and I hid the key," he said. "We'll have it out! We'll have it out! I can cut your throat with your own razor as well as with mine for Wednesday. We'll have it out!"

He was upon his feet by this time, and bounding across the room like a stag. Donelly remembered that his pistol-case was in a saddlebag that had been left in the hall. Before he could reach the hearth to snatch the poker the madman's clutch was upon him, and the razor would have been at his throat had not the assailant interrupted the business in hand by a violent peal of laughter at the facetiousness of the situation. That laughter gave Oscar time to grapple his foe; and then came a fight tor life, reason against unreason, the well-knit limbs and hardened sinews of athletic youth, matched against the hypernatural strength of lunacy in a frame impaired by habitual intemperance.

The razor seemed everywhere. It wounded both men, again and again. They were blinded with each other's blood. Again and again Oscar threw off his foe, and made his despairing rush for door or window, but that foe was always too quick for him. Before he could tear open the casement or batter down the door, the madman had him in his clutch again, and the fight had to be fought again.

The noise, the fury of it, the crashing of chairs, the thud of footsteps, should have waked the seven sleepers, Oscar thought in his despair. Now and again he made a monstrous effort and called aloud for help; but breathless and choking as he was, the cry was not loud enough to reach the end of the corridor, and the grey light was only just beginning to brighten into broader day.

He fought for his life, as a man to whom life was newly and wonderfully dear—and fell at last, aching in every bone, bruised and battered, as if he had been broken on the wheel: fell with Lucilla's name upon his lips, in the last moment of consciousness, which he believed the last moment of life.

"Lucilla!" echoed the savage, glaring down at him. "That's his hypocrisy."

His foe lying at his feet senseless, and to all appearances dead,

Lord Halverdene looked stupidly at the razor, dripping blood, and then let it fall.

He had forgotten to cut his victim's throat. He had also forgotten where he had hidden the key of the door, which was lying in the ashes under the grate; so he opened a window, and clambered out of it into the dewy garden, in his night raiment and with bare feet.

Before that deadly struggle in the cedar-room was finished, the butler who had been told off to take charge of Lord Halverdene, turn and turn with his lordship's body-servant, had awakened from a nap in his easy-chair, and had missed his patient from the bed where he had lain tossing, and muttering, and groaning, and whimpering all night, a victim to delirium *tremens* in its worst form.

When the watcher dropped asleep the door was locked, the key artfully hidden behind the candlestick on the mantelpiece; but not so artfully as to prevent Halverdene's finding it and opening the door of his prison. He had seen the man put the key there, with an elaborate pretence of looking for a box of matches; and he had waited his opportunity of getting out of the room.

He had a fixed idea in his mind, engendered of a conversation he had heard overnight from the adjoining dressing-room. The door of communication between the two rooms had been left ajar while the watcher ate his supper, brought to him by a housemaid, who explained that the reason she was so late in bringing the "tray" was the unexpected arrival of her ladyship's cousin, Captain Donelly, from the north.

"I've had to get his room ready," said the housemaid; "they've put him in the cedar-room—because it's furthest from this end of the house. He won't hear his lordship's goings on."

"Ah," said the butler, "he makes a pretty hullabaloo sometimes, I can tell you. I shall be very glad when the nurse comes from York."

That name of Donelly had been the red rag to the mad bull. In the first year of his marriage, someone had said something about Oscar Donelly which had sown a germ of jealousy in Halverdene's mind.

Civil as he had been to Donelly at York—ostentatiously civil—the embers of angry feeling had been smouldering, and with the drink-madness, they burst into sudden blaze, and the madman had but one thought—how to be revenged on his wife's first sweetheart.

The rest followed in natural sequence. Through the weary night of fever and unrest the patient watched his watcher as he sat in the easy-chair, now attentive to every movement of the restless form upon the bed, now trying to beguile his own weariness by spelling through a county paper. Halverdene had watched his custodian till the man fell asleep, and had seized the opportunity of escape.

They found him in the gardens, exhausted, and shivering in every limb, blood-stained from head to foot. He had not been in a good plight before, but this morning's work hastened the inevitable end. The wild excitement, the chill of that quarter of an hour in the garden, in the sunless dawn, half naked, barefoot on the wet grass—these experiences were fatal; and within a month of that conflict in the haunted room Lord Halverdene was a dead man, and Lady Halverdene had descended to the minor position of a childless dowager.

She had her own fortune, and she had Lucilla, and the devoted friendship of Oscar Donelly, Lucilla's affianced husband.

The struggle with the madman had left its mark upon the captain in more than one scar, which, although not so deep as a sabre-cut, would be slow to disappear; while the loss of blood from the cuts and gashes inflicted at close quarters had resulted in a serious attack of low fever which detained him at the village inn, where he was removed on the morning of his adventure, until a month after his lordship's funeral.

During that long and wasting illness, and tedious convalescence, Lucilla was his guardian angel. She and her maid went every day to supervise his rustic attendants and his faithful soldier servant, who had followed his master from the north, and who proved himself an admirable nurse.

The captain was just able to accompany his cousins to London when they left Halverdene, which had now passed into the possession of the dead man's uncle, a dry-as-dust county magistrate and scientific farmer, with a stout, homely wife and a prodigious family of children, descending in an unbroken chain from the accomplished eldest daughter of nineteen, to the prattling infant of two and a half.

When this gentleman and his wife came to take possession of Halverdene House, there was a tremendous exploration of rooms, and a tremendous talk of where such and such members of the ruddy-cheeked and healthy band should be bestowed. If there was one point upon which the new Lord Halverdene valued his own intelligence more than another, it was his profound mastery of the laws of health. He was a perambulating book of extracts from Andrew Combe and Southwood Smith.

"Sleep in a ground-floor bedroom! My children!" exclaimed his lordship, contemplating the cedar-room, which the housekeeper informed him had been once a nursery, and which she suggested might again serve for the same purpose, so many of the upstairs bedrooms being wanted for young ladies and gentlemen, tutor, and governess. "Does the woman think I am mad? A ground-floor room, on a level with the garden, a north-east aspect, and on clay! A murderous room!"

The housekeeper shook her head, gave a deep sigh, and on being interrogated told how that room was a haunted room, and had on more than one occasion proved fatal to the race of Halverdene.

"And yet no one has ever put a name to the ghost, or said what it was like," concluded the housekeeper.

"Ghost—bosh! fatal—yes, no doubt. This room would be pernicious to infant health, and possibly fatal to infant life. I know what country houses are—cesspools under drawing-rooms, rotten brick drains. None of my family will be allowed to occupy this old wing. Ceilings low, floors too near the earth, windows with only one small casement made to open; picturesque—abominable!"

His lordship the seventh baron was a great improver—a man of energetic temper who could not have endured life without something to build, improve, or spoil. He improved Beatrice Halverdene's old Caroline garden off the face of the earth; he pulled up the floor of the cedar bedroom, and was amply rewarded for his pains by finding an ancient cesspool, and a comparatively modern brick drain, both in the loathsome condition in which neglect and ignorance left half the fine old houses in the land when Queen Victoria's reign was young.

"Shall I tell you the ghost's name?" asked the seventh Lord Halverdene, when people pestered him for the secret of the haunted room. "The stories of strange apparitions in that room are all nonsense; but there is no doubt the little children had bad dreams, and no doubt their little innocent lives were sacrificed to the criminal ignorance of their parents. The ghost's name was Typhoid Fever."

LEONAUR

ALSO FROM LEONAUR
AVAILABLE IN SOFTCOVER OR HARDCOVER WITH DUST JACKET

THE LONG PATROL *by George Berrie*—A Novel of Light Horsemen from Gallipoli to the Palestine campaign of the First World War.

NAPOLEONIC WAR STORIES *by Arthur Quiller-Couch*—Tales of soldiers, spies, battles & sieges from the Peninsular & Waterloo campaings.

THE FIRST DETECTIVE *by Edgar Allan Poe*—The Complete Auguste Dupin Stories—The Murders in the Rue Morgue, The Mystery of Marie Rogêt & The Purloined Letter.

THE COMPLETE DR NIKOLA—MAN OF MYSTERY: 1 *by Guy Boothby*—*A Bid for Fortune & Dr Nikola Returns*—Guy Boothby's Dr.Nikola adventures continue to fascinate readers and enthusiasts of crime and mystery fiction because—in the manner of Raffles, the gentleman cracksman—here is character far removed from the uncompromising goodness of Holmes and Watson or the uncompromising evil of Professor Moriarty.

THE COMPLETE DR NIKOLA—MAN OF MYSTERY: 2 *by Guy Boothby*—*The Lust of Hate, Dr Nikola's Experiment & Farewell, Nikola*—Guy Boothby's Dr.Nikola adventures continue to fascinate readers and enthusiasts of crime and mystery fiction because—in the manner of Raffles, the gentleman cracksman—here is character far removed from the uncompromising goodness of Holmes and Watson or the uncompromising evil of Professor Moriarty.

THE CASEBOOKS OF MR J. G. REEDER: BOOK 1 *by Edgar Wallace*—*Room 13, The Mind of Mr J. G. Reeder* and *Terror Keep*—Edgar Wallace's sleuth—whose territory is the London of the 1920s—is an unlikely figure, more bank clerk than detective in appearance, ever wearing his square topped bowler, frock coat, cravat and muffler, Mr Reeder is usually inseparable from his umbrella.

THE CASEBOOKS OF MR J. G. REEDER: BOOK 2 *by Edgar Wallace*—*Red Aces, Mr J. G. Reeder Returns, The Guv'nor* and *The Man Who Passed*—Edgar Wallace's sleuth—whose territory is the London of the 1920s—is an unlikely figure, more bank clerk than detective in appearance, ever wearing his square topped bowler, frock coat, cravat and muffler, Mr Reeder is usually inseparable from his umbrella.

THE COMPLETE FOUR JUST MEN: VOLUME 1 *by Edgar Wallace*—*The Four Just Men, The Council of Justice & The Just Men of Cordova*—disillusioned with a world where the wicked and the abusers of power perpetually go unpunished, the Just Men set about to rectify matters according to their own standards, and retribution is dispensed on swift and deadly wings.

LEONAUR

ALSO FROM LEONAUR

AVAILABLE IN SOFTCOVER OR HARDCOVER WITH DUST JACKET

THE COMPLETE FOUR JUST MEN: VOLUME 2 *by Edgar Wallace*—*The Law of the Four Just Men & The Three Just Men*—disillusioned with a world where the wicked and the abusers of power perpetually go unpunished, the Just Men set about to rectify matters according to their own standards, and retribution is dispensed on swift and deadly wings.

THE COMPLETE RAFFLES: 1 *by E. W. Hornung*—*The Amateur Cracksman & The Black Mask*—By turns urbane gentleman about town and accomplished cricketer, life is just too ordinary for Raffles and that sets him on a series of adventures that have long been treasured as a real antidote to the 'white knights' who are the usual heroes of the crime fiction of this period.

THE COMPLETE RAFFLES: 2 *by E. W. Hornung*—*A Thief in the Night & Mr Justice Raffles*—By turns urbane gentleman about town and accomplished cricketer, life is just too ordinary for Raffles and that sets him on a series of adventures that have long been treasured as a real antidote to the 'white knights' who are the usual heroes of the crime fiction of this period.

THE COLLECTED SUPERNATURAL AND WEIRD FICTION OF WILKIE COLLINS: VOLUME 1 *by Wilkie Collins*—Contains one novel 'The Haunted Hotel', one novella 'Mad Monkton', three novelettes 'Mr Percy and the Prophet', 'The Biter Bit' and 'The Dead Alive' and eight short stories to chill the blood.

THE COLLECTED SUPERNATURAL AND WEIRD FICTION OF WILKIE COLLINS: VOLUME 2 *by Wilkie Collins*—Contains one novel 'The Two Destinies', three novellas 'The Frozen deep', 'Sister Rose' and 'The Yellow Mask' and two short stories to chill the blood.

THE COLLECTED SUPERNATURAL AND WEIRD FICTION OF WILKIE COLLINS: VOLUME 3 *by Wilkie Collins*—Contains one novel 'Dead Secret,' two novelettes 'Mrs Zant and the Ghost' and 'The Nun's Story of Gabriel's Marriage' and five short stories to chill the blood.

FUNNY BONES *selected by Dorothy Scarborough*—An Anthology of Humorous Ghost Stories.

MONTEZUMA'S CASTLE AND OTHER WEIRD TALES *by Charles B. Cory*—Cory has written a superb collection of eighteen ghostly and weird stories to chill and thrill the avid enthusiast of supernatural fiction.

SUPERNATURAL BUCHAN *by John Buchan*—Stories of Ancient Spirits, Uncanny Places & Strange Creatures.

LEONAUR

ALSO FROM LEONAUR
AVAILABLE IN SOFTCOVER OR HARDCOVER WITH DUST JACKET

MR MUKERJI'S GHOSTS *by S. Mukerji*—Supernatural tales from the British Raj period by India's Ghost story collector.

KIPLINGS GHOSTS *by Rudyard Kipling*—Twelve stories of Ghosts, Hauntings, Curses, Werewolves & Magic.